NOWHERE TO HIDE

Lindsay McKenna

Blue Turtle Publishing

Praise for Lindsay McKenna

"A treasure of a book...highly recommended reading that everyone will enjoy and learn from."

—Chief Michael Jaco, US Navy SEAL, retired, on Breaking Point

"Readers will root for this complex heroine, scarred both inside and out, and hope she finds peace with her steadfast and loving hero. Rife with realistic conflict and spiced with danger, this is a worthy page-turner."

—BookPage.com on Taking Fire
March 2015 Top Pick in Romance

"RUNNING FIRE....McKenna's dazzling eight Shadow Warriors novel (after Taking Fire) is a rip-roaring contemporary military romance with heart and heat. McKenna elicits tears, laughter, fist-pumping triumph, and most of all, a desire for the next tale in this powerful series."

—(starred review) Publisher's Weekly, 3.23.2015 on Running Fire

"...is fast-paced romantic suspense that renders a beautiful love story, start to finish. McKenna's writing is flawless, and her story line fully absorbing. More, please."

—Annalisa Pesek, Library Journal on Taking Fire

"Ms. McKenna masterfully blends the two different paces to convey a beautiful saga about love, trust, patience and having faith in each other."

—Fresh Fiction on Never Surrender

"Genuine and moving, this romantic story set in the complex world of military ops grabs at the heart."

—RT Book Reviews on Risk Taker

"McKenna does a beautiful job of illustrating difficult topics through the development of well-formed, sympathetic characters."

—Publisher's Weekly (starred review) on Wolf Haven
One of the Best Books of 2014, Publisher's Weekly

"McKenna delivers a story that is raw and heartfelt. The relationship between Kell and Leah is both passionate and tender. Kell is the hero every woman wants, and McKenna employs skill and s empathy to craft a physically and emotionally abused character in Leah. Using tension and steady pacing, McKenna is adept at expressing growing, tender love in the midst of high stakes danger."

—RT Book Reviews on Taking Fire

"Her military background lends authenticity to this outstanding tale, and readers will fall in love with the upstanding hero and his fierce determination to save the woman he loves."

—Publishers Weekly (starred review) on Never Surrender
One of the Best Books of 2014, Publisher's Weekly

"Readers will find this addition to the Shadow Warriors series full of intensity and action-packed romance. There is great chemistry between the characters and tremendous realism, making Breaking Point a great read."

—RT Book Reviews

"This sequel to Risk Taker is an action-packed, compelling story, and the sizzling chemistry between Ethan and Sarah makes this a good read."

—RT Book Reviews on Degree of Risk

"McKenna's military experience shines through i this moving tail...McKenna (High Country Rebel) skillfully takes readers on an emotional journey into modern warfare and two people's hearts."

—Publisher's Weekly on Down Range

Also available from

Blue Turtle Publishing

DELOS

Nowhere To Hide

Coming soon…
Tangled Pursuit
Forged in Fire
Broken Dreams

Harlequin/HQN/Harlequin Romantic Suspense

SHADOW WARRIORS

Running Fire
On Fire—ebook
Taking Fire
Zone of Fire—ebook
Never Surrender
Breaking Point
Degree of Risk
Risk Taker
Down Range
Danger Close—eBook

Dear Reader,

Welcome to the Delos Series! I spent five years creating this saga-series. Readers who are familiar with Morgan's Mercenaries (45 books strong), know that I wrote about a military family. This started back in the 1990's. You and I fell in love with the Trayhern Family. It was the right tone for the tenor of the times.

Today, we're global. Those who have Internet can be halfway around the world in the blink of an eye. There are no longer the boundaries we've known before. We are a huge melting pot of humanity, warts and all. I wanted to create a global family this time that reflects the world we live in. With this in mind, I created three families from three different parts of the world who hold all life sacred and important.

The Culver family is from Alexandria, Virginia. The Kemel family is from Kusadasi, Turkey. The Mykonos family is from Athens, Greece. And like today, family members meet, fall in love and marry a partner from another country. There is a mixing of blood, experience, knowledge, philosophies and an emphasis on what is important to each of them.

The three families have grown children who are a combination of American, Turkish and Greek bloodlines. And although their lineage is far flung, all three families believe in giving back to those who have less. The Kemel family formed the Delos charities in 1950. In 1990, Dilara Kemel-Badem met and married U.S. Air Force Major Robert Culver. She moved to Alexandria, Virginia and became the president of Delos charities. They raised three children: Talia (Tal), the oldest daughter and twins, Matt and Alexa.

In today's world of terror, nothing is safe anywhere on our planet, to fight terrorism the three Culver children went into the military. It is when one of the Delos charities in La Fortuna, Costa Rica, is attacked, two teachers murdered, that Robert and Dilara Culver decided their 1,800 charities worldwide needed protection. Artemis Security was created and became their in-house firm. And as they created this protection for their vast number of volunteers worldwide, they asked their grown children to leave the military and come home to run it.

In Book 1, Nowhere to Hide, is the story of Lia Cassidy, a volunteer to the school in La Fortuna. You will be on the ground floor of seeing how Artemis came into being. And how ex-SEAL, Cav Jordan, assigned to protect Lia as they rebuild the burned down school, falls in love with this valiant, brave young woman.

Book 2, Tangled Pursuit, you will meet Captain Tal Culver, U.S. Marine Corps. She has nearly nine years in the Corps. A natural leader, she is the assistant commanding officer for one of two sniper units out of Bagram, Afghanistan. She will become CEO of Artemis. U.S. Navy SEAL Chief Wyatt Lockwood, a brazen Texan who has had his eye on Tal for three years, decides it's time to get this woman of his (even though Tal doesn't know it yet), to give him a chance to catch and keep her.

Book 3, Forged in Fire, you will meet Delta Force Army Sergeant Matt Culver. He's been in the Army since eighteen and is a kidnapping and ransom (KNR) specialist out of Bagram, Afghanistan. Matt's enlistment is up in four months. During a holiday program over Thanksgiving at the base, he meets Dr. Dara McKinley, a pediatrician who volunteers her time at a charity in Kabul. They are on a collision course with one another. Matt will later become the director of KNR at Artemis.

Book 4, Broken Dreams, you will meet U.S. Air Force Captain Alexa Culver. She's an A-10 combat jet pilot, risking her life over six tours in Afghanistan. Unexpectedly she meets Gage Hunter, a quiet Marine Corps sniper who is a good friend of her brother, Matt. She finds herself helplessly drawn to the West Virginian with a soft drawl. Little do they realize when they go out to an Afghan village to give medical help to children, their lives will change forever. Alexa was planning on giving up her commission to go home to help run Artemis.

After you meet the Culver family and get to know them, their stories, and the people they fall deeply in love with, I will then be writing about the missions. These ops will come out of Delos charities that have need of protection from some faction in their country. Tal, Matt and Alexa, with a team of two hundred of the best security people in the world, will take the info and create a mission plan. One security contractor might be needed. It could be a man or a woman. Or two might be needed. The stories are fresh, intensely romantic, and heart pounding. You won't be able to stop reading!

What I love also, is being an "Indie" (independent) writer. In 2016 you will find 40,000 word novellas on each of the above characters. You'll go deeper into their individual stories. I have always wanted to write beyond the main book, but in brick 'n mortar publishing, it was almost impossible. Now? I can do it. Please drop me a line and let me know if you enjoy the novellas.

Let me hear from you about the Culver Family and the Delos series. Happy reading!

Dedication

To all my readers who loved the Morgan's Mercenary saga-series! Now there is a new one—the Delos Series! May you enjoy this vibrant, exciting global family!

CHAPTER 1

THE THUNDERING HOOF beats sent a minor quake through Lia's slender, nine-year-old body. Her laughter bubbled up as her long, bare legs gripped the barrel of her gelding, Goldy. The horse raced down a pathway between two huge fields of sugar beets filling row after row across a hundred acres, each plant bearing wavy green leaves. The wind whipped past Lia's tipped-up face, her eyes now closed and her arms thrown upwards toward the dusky August sky.

With each powerful beat of Goldy's hooves striking the dry, sandy soil, Lia gripped her horse tighter with her long thighs. She had only ten days until school started, and before she left she wanted to ride like the wind each evening. This was the best time, when the temperatures climbed down from the hundred-degree mark on this eastern border town in Oregon.

Goldy's white mane was long, whipping against Lia's slim body. Today, she wore only a pink tank top and dark blue shorts, as well as the tennis shoes her mother insisted she wear when she rode. She preferred that her horse wear only a faded old nylon halter and a lead rope. She used no saddle, but rode his damp, sleek gold back as if born to it, laughing as she felt the powerful ripple of his muscles beneath her bouncing butt. The wind trailed between her open fingers, drying her perspiration.

The pathway between the two large beet fields was a mile in length. Even though this horse, her companion since he was rescued from a dog food factory in Ontario, was now eighteen years old, he still raced at full speed down the beet-laden corridor. Lia just loved the sensation of the two of them in full flight, probably as much as Goldy did!

The wind made her eyes water, so she kept them shut. The rope halter hung around Goldy's neck within easy reach of her hand, but Lia didn't want to pick it up. Her horse had carried her like this many times, and it was a special joy, as if he were Pegasus and she his rider, racing with him across the pink and orange sunset. They were more than horse and rider. Lia trusted her gelding with her life.

Although Goldy was considered an old horse, he had the innate wisdom and years of experience to know how to take care of her.

Lia lived for these moments, the wind tearing at her long, curly brown hair streaked with gold highlights. Suddenly, everything shifted.

A soft moan caught in Lia's throat, her brow wrinkling as if to fend off an unseen threat. The night sky held colorful ribbons stacked upon each other along the western horizon. At first the sky was a pale blue, Lia watched anxiously as the sky turned pink, then fuchsia and finally, a blood red. No longer simply a color, the red became liquid, dripping down in huge, long streams toward her face, striking her and staining Goldy as he continued to race forward.

"NO!" Lia screamed, her voice cracking.

Caught in the web of her nightmare. She saw the flash of a steel blade glittering for a split second before it came down, slicing through her flesh. She felt the hot release of blood. Lia turned, striking out with her fists. She cried out for help but she knew none would appear.

Her attackers, Jorge Dominguez and Bruce Schaefer, were men she'd known for two years. They were Army mechanics she'd worked with at Bagram Air Base, near Kabul, Afghanistan. Why were they attacking her? Her mind reeling, she screamed as one man's hand gripped her shirt, trying to hold her down on the cold, smooth concrete floor of the building. Twisting away, panting, scrambling, Lia saw a second blade swinging down and heard the man curse as he sliced open her left cheek.

Crying out in shock and pain, she jerked away, the point of the knife ripping into her again, opening up a trail of blood down her outer right arm. She realized she had to escape or die!

Air exploded from her mouth as she wrestled, kicked and shrieked, trying to get away from her assailants. Their knives flashed again and this time she heard her trousers ripping. Kicking out, she felt a hot, burning slicing sensation down one calf and then the other as she lashed out with her boots, trying to fend them off.

She wouldn't give up! They would have to kill her before she stopped fighting. No man was going to take her down and rape her! No man! Rage and survival instinct entwined into a lethal, invisible fist, roaring up through Lia as she kicked one assailant in the face with her Army boot. Why were they doing this? Why?

She heard the crunch of his nose breaking beneath the heel of her boot and felt a moment of satisfaction as she heard him yelp in surprise, the blade dropping from his hand.

One more! One more man to take down and she would be free to run like hell! Her breath came in shallow sobs as she felt another blade slice into her, aiming to gut her, but Lia twisted away in time, the blade made a horizontal slice across her belly.

Blinded by blood pouring into her left eye, animal-like sounds erupted from her. Swinging her fists, she went after the brown-eyed Latino who lunged at her, unable to move quickly enough, Lia fell.

She landed on her back, screaming as he pounced. As he did, she shot both her boots upward and connected with the man's chest. The collision jarred every joint in her body, making her cry out in pain.

Her assailant cursed as he was thrown off to one side, his knife falling from his hand.

Rolling, scrambling blindly to her hands and knees, she staggered to her feet. It was nearly dark in the motor pool garage and all she could see was the red exit door light a hundred feet away.

Lia's boots struck the concrete, echoing hollowly. Her heart was beating hard and loud, she couldn't hear anything else. Terror and adrenaline pushed her forward towards the door. She had to get help!

It had all begun when she was assigned to close up the motor pool for the night. Why would these men she'd spent years with suddenly, and unaccountably, threaten her with knives and attempt to rape her.

Why? Why? Lia sobbed as she hit the door at a full run, her hands out, striking the bar so that it opened. The door was flung back, banging loudly against the building.

In the cool night air, Lia felt her head clear. She knew where to run—there was a highway nearby, and she could see headlights from the many military vehicles leaving the Army base. Weak from blood loss, she swayed but adrenaline kept her running. She pushed herself forward to the highway.

Almost blinded by the blood coursing down the left side of her face, she threw up her hands and nearly fell onto the two-lane highway. She reached the yellow line and waved frantically at an approaching Humvee.

"STOP! For God's sakes, STOP! She screamed."

Lia felt all the blood leave her head as she began falling to the ground. Shocked over the unexpected assault by the men she thought were her friends, the world exploded around her as she fainted from loss of blood and shock.

Lia jack-knifed into a sitting position. She was in bed in her small, one story white stucco house near La Fortuna, Costa Rica. Lia pressed her hands to her perspiring face, sobbing, gasping for air. Her chest heaved and hurt. Heart pounding, she shook with terror. She heard desperate sounds coming from a wounded animal, and realized they were coming from her.

Her hair, once long and curly, was now short, but it still curled a little in the dampness. No matter what she did, that nightmare, the night she was attacked, stalked her relentlessly.

And no matter how often she dreamed, beautiful, colorful dreams from her idyllic rural childhood in Oregon, they always changed. First came the hint of pink in the sky, and then darker pink, changing and congealing into blood as it began to fall across her eyes until all she saw was dark, crimson blood. Her blood.

Lia could still feel every one of the knife slashes. Her only consolation was she had fought back and escaped her attackers. Her ferocity had stunned them.

She sat there her knees drawn up against her body as she pressed her back into the headboard. The past haunted her even though she desperately tried to forget the men who attacked her and the Army hospital where'd she recuperated.

They had known that the motor pool was shut down for the night and it would be hours before anyone else would show up. Lia could never figure out why they had chosen her to rape. There were other Army women who worked in motor pool, as well. In all the years she had been deployed at the base, nothing like this had ever happened to her. Sometimes, Taliban mortared the base outside the fence, but that was all. Why her? It ate at her, and she had no answer.

Later, as she lay recovering in a bed at Landstuhl Medical Center, she gave thanks that her father, a former Army instructor, had taught her Krav Maga an Israeli form of street fighting. He had taught her how to survive an attack. She had instinctively used what she knew when her life was on the line, and it had been enough to get her out alive.

Automatically, her damp, trembling fingertips brushed the left side of her neck. She felt the scar across her throat, the one that had partially nicked her carotid artery. She had been bleeding to death from that one cut, which was why she'd fainted in the middle of the highway. It was a miracle she'd gotten that far.

Luckily, the driver of the Humvee was a physician. She was just leaving the base hospital for the night and thanks to her speedy intervention, Lia's life had been saved.

Lia had little memory of being taken to the Bagram hospital on the base. She did wake once in a fabric-draped cubicle in the emergency room. A half-dozen doctors and nurses were feverishly working on her, and she remembered the oxygen mask over her face and how the bright overhead lights had hurt her eyes.

She was still reliving all the details of that horrific night, the pain in her elbows, the weakness from losing four pints of blood. Later, a nurse told her that a body only held eight to twelve pints of blood, depending upon one's height and size.

After she'd awakened from the surgery, the nurse had gently patted her blue-gowned shoulder and told her where she was and what had happened. But only later did Lia's surgeon, who had used 150 stitches to close all the knife wounds, tell her she had nearly died.

The medical staff was mostly women, and for that she was glad. During her recovery, Lia would cringe whenever she saw men and would automatically tense if a male orderly entered her room to bring her a tray of food.

Her parents had flown in to be with her at Landstuhl Medical Center in Germany. The defensive wounds on her hands were telling. Her dad had held her hands and cried, knowing how hard she'd had to fight to get away. Her mother had clung to her dad, heartbroken over her daughter's pain.

Lia kept asking herself why would someone do this to her? Why? She'd had a lot of time to lie in that hospital room, each movement causing her pain from her stitches being pulled, to ponder that unanswerable question.

NCIS investigators, both women, had come to take her statement. Just speaking to them had left Lia exhausted. Later, one of the investigators had returned to tell her that the two men she'd named had been apprehended and asked if she wanted to press charges? Hell, yes!

Lia remembered looking at the investigator as if she were insane. Why wouldn't she press charges? Wouldn't any woman? These animals had almost killed her. At age twenty, her life could have been erased.

The investigator told her it would be a long, drawn out affair and it would be brutal emotionally for her. Lia didn't care. She remembered the outrage she'd felt toward Schaefer and Dominguez as they'd cornered and attacked her.

Shakily, Lia drew in a breath. Her mind racing, she forced herself to think about the present. She realized that her mouth was dry and that she was terribly thirsty. Throwing off the twisted sheet from her damp, gowned body, she eased her legs over the mattress, holding it tightly.

Since the attack, she always kept a night-light on down the hall, and her bedroom door open so she could see who was coming. The house was small but it was her private abode, a place of peace and safety.

She loved this little house. It sat near the Delos charity school building that was a classroom for children of La Fortuna, a small town near Arenal, a major volcano in northern Costa Rica.

Slowly pushing damp strands of hair off her sweaty brow, Lia sat there, trying to slow down her heartbeat and wrench her mind out of the toxic nightmare that hit her several times a month. That attack had happened five years ago. God, wouldn't this nightmare *ever* go away?

Schaefer and Dominguez had gotten only four years in prison from the Army. Just four years! Lia thought they should have been put away for life and the key thrown away. But there were so many lies and innuendos the two men had used in their defense, saying that she was a flirt, that she had rubbed her breasts and hips up against them. Implying that she was asking to be raped.

All lies! God, all lies. Lia uttered a slight sound of anguish, remembering the ten-month trial at Bagram. The defense attorneys had blamed her for the men's actions. Insane! They had claimed that if she hadn't worn tight shirts that showed off her ample breasts, it wouldn't have happened.

Worse, the jury of her peers, all male officers, listened stoically. Lia had only her parents for support, and although they were not allowed into the military UCMJ, Uniform Code of Military Justice, proceedings, they were there to hold her tightly afterward.

Lia never cried during the proceedings. No way was she going to break down in front of the two bastards who had nearly taken her life. They had, in fact, murdered a part of her soul.

Their handiwork was indisputable. They had sliced her seven times and she would have permanent scars across her body to remind her of that night for the rest of her life.

AFTER GETTING OUT of the Army, she had joined Delos Charity, wanting a job where she could help the poor or under educated. She had landed the job and chosen the small village of La Fortuna in northern Costa Rica, to spend her life in quiet solitude. Delos had given her and the other two teachers small homes near the school and she loved what she did.

Pushing herself off the bed, her knees weak, she stood up, feeling the pull of every one of those scars, especially on her lower calves. She shuffled across the cool floor and headed for the kitchen at the other end of the short hall. There was another night-light beneath the cupboards. Glancing at the clock, Lia saw it was only 1 A.M.

She pulled a glass from the cupboard and turned on the faucet. As she drank the tepid water, the stench of her own fear swept over her and sickened her. How she hated that smell!

Needing a shower, the Venetian blinds drawn so no one could see into her home, she pulled the light, flowery cotton gown over her head. Dropping it into the washbasin, Lia turned on the shower, anxious to get beneath the spray to wash away the smell of terror.

She picked up a pink cloth and dampened it beneath the slight warm spray, allowing the water to sluice across her shoulders and breasts. She tried to avoid looking at her naked body, now glistening beneath the bathroom's overhead light. Seeing the scars brought back all the horror of that night.

She took the Plumeria scented soap, a favorite fragrance of hers sent by her mom every month, and lathered her body with it. Gradually, its scent overrode the odor of fear. She sighed and turned to the Pikake shampoo, also sent by her mother, to wash her hair. The fragrance was different from Plumeria, but Lia loved the tropical scents. She felt cleansed and refreshed by them, and inhaled them deeply into her lungs. No more stench of death.

Each time she wiped the cloth across those long, deep scars, she remembered exactly when the cut had happened. Her Army psychiatrist, a blonde woman of deep compassion, had told her it would happen, but assured her that over time, the association would stop.

When? It was now five years later, and Lia had gotten so she hated her body. Her cells, her bones, her organs, remembered the assault upon them. Why couldn't she block it out?

Every day for five days a week, she worked from dawn to dusk at the school. She was tireless in her activity with those twenty-five Costa Rican children. She loved each and every one of them just as much as the two women teachers that taught them.

Working as an assistant to Maria and Sophia, Lia was the chief cook and bottle washer. She was responsible for the children's snacks, their main meal at lunch, and another snack before the yellow school bus, owned by Delos Charity, took them home each afternoon.

But now she had to sleep. Tomorrow was a busy day like all the rest, but she was grateful for the activity. The children of this country were a priority, and getting them educated was a national concern. In some remote areas, charities such as Delos had put schools on the ground, backed by the government.

Shuffling out of the kitchen, she wandered down the hall and back to her large bed. Lia saw that she'd torn the sheet from where it had been tucked in, and leaned over to tuck it back. As she straightened, she felt a deep fatigue in her bones. Lying down on the bed, she shut her eyes, waiting for the fan in the room to move the sluggish, humid air. She draped her arm across her eyes and released a tremulous sigh. So much pain, the memories swirled around in her brain, she wanted to forget all of it. And yet, that one moment had defined her life from age twenty to today, five years later.

Now, as the breeze from the fan cooled her, she buried her head in her pillow. Her greatest loss had been her hopes for a loving relationship. Since the assault, no man had wanted her. Lia, a natural team player, missed having a relationship, but after she'd been cut and scarred, her traumatized boyfriend, a soldier named Jerry, had walked away. It had been too much for him, and she'd seen it in his eyes when he'd visited her in the hospital, trying to be supportive. Once he'd seen the extent of her injuries and the stitches, his mouth had tightened. She sensed that he just wanted to get the hell out of the room. She had loved him and she thought Jerry had loved her, but that event had shown her differently.

Would this ever end? Lia was tired of wasting "poor me" tears on herself. Fortunately, her parents were wonderful. Her mom and dad, talked to her weekly. She really looked forward to sharing that link with them. Often, they asked her to come home to live with them, but Lia didn't want to do that. It would be admitting that she'd given up on ever having a normal relationship, including marriage and children.

Unconsciously, she reached up with her fingertips, moving lightly down the two-inch jagged scar on her left cheek. The blade had gone through it, scoring her gums and ripping it open. The surgery on that one scar had been the worst and the most devastating to Lia. Plastic surgeons paid by her parents to repair the damage only took out the puckers and scars that had been created as it healed.

The knife had sliced through thin, delicate muscles that helped her smile, helped her face be normal to someone looking at her. Unfortunately, it hadn't quite worked out that way. Now she felt like the monster from Notre Dame in Paris, France. She was, as she saw herself, an unnatural-looking woman, a hunchback of sorts, without the hunchback. Her face implied there was a terrible story behind the scar, and she felt everyone's eyes upon it, when meeting her for the first time. Although she could cover up the other wounds beneath her clothing, her face was there for everyone to see.

She remembered what had happened with a man who had been interested in her two years ago. Lia wished she could blot out her memories of that night. She had been very apprehensive, worried about what Manuel would think as he undressed her to make love to her.

It had been so hard to talk about her assault, about what had been done to her physical body, and she'd tried, but as he peeled off her clothes and saw the devastation across her body, he had stepped back from her.

Manuel had stood gazing at the scars, and Lia had felt as if a chasm was now separating them. He slowly shook his head, said, "I'm sorry," and slowly walked out the door. She knew he would never return.

Lia had sat on the bed, fighting tears of humiliation, knowing her body had disgusted him. Luckily, she was unlikely to run into him again because he wasn't a local. In fact, she never did see him again.

At least, Lia thought, *I can be grateful for that.*

Since then, she'd given up thinking in terms of relationships, surrendering to the reality of a life alone, without love, and without a partnership.

She instead shifted her focus to Delos, a place that welcomed her hard work and her love of children. At least Lia could do some good for them by giving them her love, care and attention. And those little ones were like bright flowers, radiant under her care.

She smiled. The children were curious little things. The first time Lia had stepped into the Home School Foundation building in La Fortuna, she had tried to gird herself for the children's curiosity about her scars. But unlike men, the children were simply curious and wanted to touch them. Lia had seen their sympathy in their large, wide eyes as she crouched down, allowing them to touch her scar, to feel it, to see sadness come to their tiny faces that never lied about anything.

The children had long ago accepted her as she was, and adored her because she was there for them. Her scars were never an issue; in fact, these children had seen their own share of misfortune, and it bonded them more closely with this American angel who was here to teach, love, and support them.

Finally, Lia fell into a light, restless sleep. She never slept deeply after a nightmare, and knew she'd wake up early, feeling ragged, tired and stressed out. But just the act of getting a shower, clean clothes, washing her hair and getting ready to go to the school that sat five hundred feet away from her small home, made her heart sing.

Tomorrow, they were taking the children in three rented vans to the Venado Caves, not far away. Because Lia's dad was a spelunker, she had grown up crawling into and discovering caves and loving them.

She had the two young women, Maria and Sophia, on hand to help with the children on field trips. And tomorrow, with all the children's lunches packed and in the vans, they would go on a wonderful adventure.

Lia knew the children would be wide-eyed with wonder as she led them into the large, outer portion of the massive cave system buried beneath the jungle terrain. They would see so many wonderful, natural sights…just thinking about it gave her heart a lift.

Those happy thoughts were the last she had as she drifted off to sleep. The past three years of living here in Costa Rica had begun to heal her wounded body and spirit, and brought her good dreams, like the one she was having now. They were filled with vibrant colors and fragrances as she dreamed of walking into the mouth of the Venado caves. That simple act erased the horrifying past as she focused on the natural beauty of this incredible country. She might not have a close, wonderful relationship with a man, but spelunking fed something in her soul.

Still, her heart yearned for the right man to walk into her life. She had just about accepted that the odds of that happening were so low, there was no point thinking about it. After all, who would want a carved-up woman with a jagged scar on one side of her face? No one…

CHAPTER 2

"**H**EY, JORDAN! GET off your sorry ass!" Butch kicked his buddy's bunk, a broken down affair in a grungy room where they had their base of operation. "There's a call for you from a General Culver. ASAP!"

Cav Jordan groaned, his head pounding with a splitting headache. Sonofabitch, he'd drunk too many damn pisco sours last night at that club in Las Flores here in Lima, Peru. Covering his pounding head, he cursed at Butch, his ex-SEAL buddy. "Tell 'em to call back in an hour. I'm in no shape to talk to anybody." He glared up at a grinning Butch.

"May be a PSD, personal security detail, buddy…"

"Fuck it, I can't think straight. I gotta get a shower and some coffee in me…."

Butch shrugged his big shoulders and grinned. "General Culver's been good to us over the years, Cav. Are you sure you can't mumble 'yes' and take his assignment?"

"No," Cav snarled, slowly pushing up on his unmade bunk. The place was the size of a damn refrigerator, with just enough room for a Peruvian army bunk. The damn things always had squeaky springs. "I need an hour."

"Roger that."

Cav growled again, pushing his long black hair off his heavily unshaven face. When was the last time he'd shaved? Blearily, he scowled at the morning sunlight slanting into the small window. His straight brows flattened. His eyes were barely able to stay open, the light hurting the hell out of them. Shit, he was still drunk.

His stomach rolled with nausea. Why the hell had he drunk that ex-Special Forces dude under the table at El Diablo, last night?

Pride, he thought grumpily, pushing his fingers across his dark, hairy chest. He sat there in a pair of blue boxer shorts that hadn't been washed for almost a week. Curling his lip, he could smell his sour flesh, mixed with the alcohol on his fetid breath. His mouth tasted like something that had died a week ago, and the smell made him want to throw up.

At twenty-six, Cav felt more like he was eighty. Glaring at the light, he pushed his shoulder-length hair behind him and got to his bare feet. Dammit, he *was* going to throw up!

Butch pushed a mug of steaming coffee in his direction as he emerged from the tiny bathroom, a towel draped around his hips. "Here, take this. You look like shit warmed over."

Smirking at his best friend, Cav snapped, "Just give me the fuckin' cup of coffee" as he plopped down on the creaky wooden stool at the small round table.

Grinning, Butch nursed his own coffee, his blue eyes dancing with mischief. "You're so sweet the morning after…."

Snorting, Cav lifted the coffee, his hand none too steady. "Why the hell do you look so damned perky this morning?" He lifted the cup to his lips, the fragrant brew making his empty stomach growl. At least the coffee smelled and tasted good. That was progress.

"Because," Butch said lightly, "I didn't get stone-assed drunk on pisco sours with that asshole special ops dude like you did. Really, Cav, you're an ex-SEAL and you let the bastard provoke you into a dumb drinking match."

Cav's eyes were red-rimmed and watering as he offered a one-shouldered shrug. "Ain't gonna let some Spec Four dude drink me under the table. Us SEALs are tough."

"Yeah…right. Well, you certainly look like you could pull off a PSD right now. Five-day beard, your hair looks like shit, you look like shit and your skin is pasty lookin'. Oh, and your hands shake."

"Up yours," Cav returned.

"I guess the General will call back."

"Did he say anything about the PSD?" Cav demanded, wiping his sweaty brow with the back of his forearm. Now, because he'd drunk so damned much, he was going to start sweating it out. It would mean another shower in an hour. Cav hated smelling like a drunk.

"Yeah. One of their Home School Foundation charities in northern Costa Rica just got burned to the ground last night. Seems a drug lord with his soldiers attacked it and murdered two women teachers. A third woman managed to escape into the jungle."

Cav's mouth twisted. "Great. Drug lords. What the hell is new down here in Central and South America?" he grumped. "What's he want me to do?"

"The woman who survived, Lia Cassidy, called in the attack to Delos Charity Central in Alexandria, Virginia. She's asking for help."

Cav slid his friend a surprised look. "Usually, charities are off limits, even to those bastards."

Shrugging, Butch muttered, "Apparently not any more. General Culver, who's over in Istanbul, Turkey right now on a NATO exercise, got a call from his wife, Dilara, who runs the charity. He said he thought of you as a PSD for this survivor, Lia Cassidy."

"Shit!"

"Hey, the pay is good, my man." Butch looked around their third-story apartment, which was small but clean—if they cleaned it. A housekeeper came in once a week to clean, their focus was to provide personal security for rich people who could pay their high fees.

"What's he offering?" Cav mumbled, sucking down the hot coffee and feeling his stomach roll again.

"Well, right now he wants you to go in undercover as a replacement teacher for the facility they're going to rebuild. That entails a lot more than just carrying a rifle around looking mean and efficient. He's offering you ten grand for a month."

Perking up, Cav liked the sound of that. "Seriously, dude?"

"Yeah," Butch said, puckering his lips. "Wish to hell I had a sugar daddy like this General in my back pocket like you do. Ten grand has a nice ring to it."

Wiping his sweaty brow, Cav grumbled, "This woman, Lia Cassidy? She must be someone important for them to throw that kind of money out."

"Dunno. He didn't give details. But he wants you undercover, no guns showing. He's already in touch with the Costa Rican government to give you permission to come into their country armed."

Cav knew this particular Central American country had no military force, only a police force. Guns were strictly forbidden by anyone except their own efficient police force. To be caught there with weapons meant an automatic prison sentence, a long one, and Cav knew that for a security clearance, government permission was a must.

"Okay," he said, his voice low and gravelly, "so far that sounds good. What else did he tell you?"

"That the drug lord suspected of doing this was Dante Medina, otherwise known as La Araña."

"The Spider? Who's he? Some local asshole?"

"No, Medina runs the northern highlands area of that country, growing cocaine and marijuana all around the Monteverde Cloud Forest area. Apparently he's pretty powerful," Butch said. "And he's not nice."

"What drug lord is?" Cav demanded, rubbing his aching forehead. He'd already tossed down some serious ibuprofen to dull that drumbeat clanging in his head. He silently cursed the Spec Four dude. He'd barely won the drinking match, watching as the guy passed out at the bar before he did.

Luckily, Butch had picked him up, paid the bar tab and hauled his sorry ass out of the seedy bar and to their beat-up Jeep parked out in front. Cav came to as Butch flopped him onto his bed in their apartment. Then, he promptly passed out again.

"La Araña is lethal," Butch warned, "and I suspect that's why General Culver is offering you this nice, big fat check for however many months you have to protect this survivor. Apparently he's a mean player and runs his soldiers and the whole area with a steel fist."

"And it's probably not wrapped in velvet, either," Cav said, a lopsided grin pulling at his mouth.

"No, I don't think so. Anyway, the overview the General gave me was that he and his wife are gonna fly into San José in five days. I guess that's when his NATO gig is finished, and he can get freed up to go with his wife to assess the damage to the building and to the charity itself. He wants you to meet him at the San José airport, and he's already wired the money into your bank account here in Lima. All you have to do is get presentable, buddy, and show up at that airport."

"That sounds easy enough," Cav rumbled. It didn't seem to be much of a PSD in Cav's estimation. Normally, he took on freelance security assignments for the rich and powerful. The CIA wouldn't hire him, even though he was an ex-SEAL and offered them a special deal, thanks to a hot mess in his sordid past.

Cav felt old anger stirring in him and didn't go there. He had enough nightmares about that fucked up op. He didn't want to think about it or allow it out of his kill box during his waking hours. And when it did escape, he'd hit the bottle to drown all his grief, rage and need to kill the Taliban who had delivered a devastating attack to his team.

"You got five days to clean up your act," Butch said, gesturing toward his beard. "If you're going undercover as an American teacher who speaks Spanish, you got to clean up real good, Bro, starting with this shaggy hair of yours and getting rid of that beard."

Grunting, Cav rose and walked over to the tiny kitchen, pouring another cup of coffee. "I'll look presentable. I don't need you mother-henning me."

Chuckling, Butch leaned back in his chair, grinning as he passed by to sit down at the table. "Oh, buddy, you need a keeper right now. We've been doing PSD's here in Peru for the past year, and when you don't have a gig, you're fuckin' drowning your head in a bottle of pisco."

Cav drank the coffee, saying nothing. Butch was his best friend on SEAL team Three, Bravo Platoon, and had torn a ligament in his knee. That had saved his life, because he'd had to miss that last op where his team was killed, except for him. He was the lone survivor.

"An American teacher, huh?" he muttered, thinking about the new job.

Grimacing, Butch gave him a dark look. "Yeah, you're posing as an English teacher. In Costa Rica, all children are taught two languages: Spanish and English. It's a pretty progressive country compared to the rest of those sorry-assed nations, if you ask me."

"Si habla Espanol," Cav said. "I think I handle that, no problemo."

"I've got my PSD gig coming up in a week, so we'll leave our sweet little apartment to poor Esmeralda. That gal's gonna shit at how bad this place looks. More work for her…"

"She always does, so it's nothing new," Cav muttered. The two of them never cooked and always ate out. Their dirty clothes were strewn all over the place, and Esmeralda, their housekeeper, always picked up everything, muttering under her breath, and shooting them looks that would drop a jaguar at ten feet. She was an older woman, round, five foot two, and part Quechua Indian with long, black braids.

Esmeralda hated dirt and dust as much as the men didn't mind living in it. Hell, after being in the desert of Afghanistan for six years, Cav was used to filth. It rubbed like fiery sandpaper into every part of his exposed body. He'd learned early on to wear a protective tribal *shemagh* around his neck to prevent that fine, gritty gray sand from leaking down his neck and into his inner body parts.

So what was a little dirt? Hell, their place was clean compared with where they'd lived all those years in Afghanistan.

But the old Indian woman didn't know that. She just muttered in pidgin Spanish and part Quechua, reprimanding them, shaking her finger at them and then pointing to the messes they'd left everywhere. Cav grinned and Butch patently ignored her.

"I guess the General's not callin' back," Butch said finally. "He said to meet him five days from now at the Costa Rica airport. He'll have his assistant email the particulars, so all you gotta do is show up. He also said he's emailing a photo of Lia Cassidy to you, so you can ID her once you're on the ground in San José. They'll have drivers and a rental SUV's, and you'll all be taken north to La Fortuna, the village where the attack occurred. Right now, the police are crawling all over the place trying to find out who torched the joint and murdered those two women."

"Cowards," Cav muttered.

Butch grimaced. "They were pro's, Cav." He held up his thumb and forefinger, pretending it was a gun. "A clean shot in the head to each woman, and then they were left outside the building, unmolested and in their nightgowns. I guess there are three small buildings that serve as living quarters for the three women."

Frowning, Cav said, "I wonder how the third woman, this Cassidy woman, got away?"

"Maybe she heard the shots," Butch offered.

Shrugging, Cav said gruffly, "I'll find out more when I get boots on the ground."

By mid-afternoon, Cav was over the worst of his hangover. He'd shaved, which he didn't do often, and now, as he stared in the foggy mirror in the bathroom, he saw all the small scars and cuts his face had accumulated over the years, since working with the team. He didn't look too closely at his bloodshot hazel eyes. There were bags beneath them, too. And he'd nicked himself twice with the damned dull razor.

No, he wasn't a pretty picture, but he had five days to try to look like a normal human being. He grinned. He'd found out since childhood there was no such thing as "normal." "Normal" was a setting on a clothes dryer.

Tomorrow, he'd go to the barbershop over in Los Flores and spend some money to get a decent haircut. No bilingual American teacher would show up looking like a junkyard dog, and Cav knew he had to play the part, especially since he was going in undercover.

"Hey," Butch whistled, stopping at the opened door to the bathroom. He waved a piece of paper in his direction. "I think your sorry ass just got a gold star." He chuckled. "Not that you *deserve* this kind of luck. Take a look, pardner."

Frowning, Cav wiped his hands on a towel and took the proffered piece of paper. When he turned it over, he froze. There was a colored photo of a woman, a damn beautiful woman. The name beneath it read, Lia Cassidy.

"I wonder if she's single?" Butch said, his grin turning evil. He waggled his bushy red eyebrows in Cav's direction.

Cav's scowl deepened as he quickly perused the photo. It showed a young woman with short, curly brown hair, edged in red and gold highlights. Her gray eyes were large, intelligent looking, and spaced far apart. He felt his whole lower body flame to life. The woman was truly a looker, with her oval face and wide, soft mouth. Cav could almost taste her lips beneath his. She had delicate ears and was wearing a set of white pearl earrings, along with a conservative white blouse to bring out her English complexion.

"She looks pretty serious to me," Butch said, craning his neck, studying the photo.

"I wonder when this was taken," Cav asked absently. In fact, he had a whole lot of questions about this woman who worked for Delos Charity.

Butch said, "I wonder if she's unattached?"

Making a sound of displeasure, Cav shook his head. "Your balls are your brains, Bro."

"Like yours aren't?" Butch returned mildly, needling his scowling friend.

"Women are nothing but trouble." Cav declared as he shoved the paper back into Butch's hand. "She's probably single, but attached. How many women her age are out there doing full-time charity work?"

"Yeah, and who knows? She might have some guy that she's already hooked up with? Maybe married."

"Doubtful," Cav muttered, brushing his teeth.

"Well, this PSD is pretty sweet, if you ask me. A good-looking woman thrown into the deal doesn't hurt."

"I'm not interested," Cav growled, spitting out the toothpaste and then rinsing his mouth out. "As far as I'm concerned, it's ten grand a month on two legs, that's all."

"Yeah, you and women seem to be at odds with one another."

"They're good for one night, and that's it."

Butch studied the photo. "She looks kind of sad." He turned it so Cav could stare at it. "Doesn't she?"

"What? Is that your SEAL intuition at work?" Cav wiped his mouth with the towel and dropped it onto the counter. Esmeralda was always on his ass to hang it up where he'd originally found it.

"Yeah. She's got really beautiful eyes," Butch sighed. "A man could lose his soul in 'em, if you asked me."

"I didn't," Cav snapped, yanking the paper from him and walking out of the bathroom. He headed down the hall to the kitchen.

"So," Butch crowed, following him. "You *do* like her!"

Cav wasn't going to give his friend satisfaction one way or another. He dropped the photo on his unmade bed and hauled out a small suitcase from beneath it. Butch was a damned good-looking dude and never had trouble inviting the señoritas over to their table, no matter which bar they frequented.

Latin women like Americans because they considered them rich, especially compared to the Latino patrons in the bar. It was probably true, although neither of them ever flashed cash. That would be stupid. It could get them rolled in some cobblestone back-alley some night.

The buddies always dressed down, never wore watches or jewelry, and sported a three or four-day growth of beard. And there was Cav's shaggy hair. They could pass for working class bastards or Americans strung out on drugs looking for a fix.

That was fine with Cav. As a SEAL, he had been taught how to blend in, not stand out. But for some reason, that picture of Lia Cassidy was beginning to bother him. She was incredibly beautiful, but Butch was right, there was real sadness in those huge gray eyes of hers. It needled the hell out of him. How could someone so young, bright and innocent looking be *that* sad. Hell, he himself carried that kind of sadness deep inside himself. And honestly, it was ball-aching grief that he had still not worked through over the loss of his team.

Cav had been the only survivor, barely clinging to life, and for what? So he could remember his other seven-team members? Those guys had all been brothers to him—the only family that had ever loved him, cared for him, supported him, and was, yes, even kind to him. His sea daddy, Master Chief Gordon Parker, had molded him well, and he'd taken to the transformation, dropping his angry, rebellious attitude and forging it into becoming a damn good SEAL.

Later, after packing his meager belongings, Cav sat down and picked up the picture of Lia Cassidy. It was a professional photo, taken with the lights at the right angles to bring out the best features of her face: her eyes and those beautifully shaped lips of hers. Her brows were softly winged above her soulful gray eyes and, he had to admit it, they tugged at his heart.

The color of her eyes was arresting, not quite silver but not pewter, either. They were the kind of eyes a man could stare into and lose himself. Her face was heart-shaped, her chin sporting a small dimple. Her high, starched white collar was lost in the curls of her hair, bringing out the slender length of her neck.

Eyes narrowing, Cav wondered if the photo had been retouched. He thought he detected a thin scar curving around the left side of her throat toward the center. But maybe it was his imagination—or their lousy printer acting up again. Still, it disturbed him because it was a familiar place a bad guy would choose to slice into a person's neck to open up their carotid artery. Once opened, the person would bleed out in a matter of two to three minutes.

Rubbing his forehead, he studied the picture again, wondering. Just…wondering.

He dropped the paper on his bunk. Clasping his hands between his opened thighs, he stared down at the wooden floor that needed to be swept and mopped. Butch was going on a PSD for a Lima mine baron who always feared for his life when he had to visit his many mines in Chile. He'd be gone for two weeks and Cav was looking at a minimum of four weeks away from their apartment.

Esmeralda was probably going to be happy as hell that her "two messy boys," as she called them, were away. At least the apartment would be clean until they got back.

His heart warmed towards the old Indian woman. Cav and Butch paid her a lot more than most women earned doing the same job, but they knew that Esmeralda was a grandmother to a huge family and that the extra money would go to feeding and clothing the children.

God knew, he and Butch earned on average about a hundred thousand dollars a year as freelance security operators. The world was growing more dangerous, not safer. And his kind was in demand more than ever.

At least he'd done something right. Their housekeeper, despite her grumpiness over their slovenly ways, got paid very well. Smiling a little, he glanced to his right where Lia's picture sat on his pillow. What would she look like if she smiled? Would those velvety gray eyes of hers shine? Would her skin blossom, her cheeks pink up?

Cav found himself wanting to know what this woman looked like when she smiled. Butch had been right: He was looking forward to this assignment, for once. It never hurt to be a bodyguard to a beautiful woman about his own age. And yes, Cav was a hardcore realist. He knew she was more than likely married, engaged or had a boyfriend. Someone as pretty as she was, would not be available. So why the hell did his silly-assed heart hope that she was?

CHAPTER 3

A<small>FTER MEETING ROBERT</small> and Dilara Culver at the San José airport, Cav rode with them in their black SUV, the driver taking them to a five star hotel, The Empress, in the capitol.

General Culver's attache', Major Dahlgren, had already arrived days earlier with his small, but highly efficient staff. The group was taken to a special, rented room at the hotel. Cav knew both Robert and Dilara from earlier assignments through the General, and had spoken by phone or Skype with them. He was comfortable with these people, and admired them for running the largest charity in the world. He could tell that the shocking attack on the La Fortuna school had left them deeply troubled.

As they entered the boardroom with its long mahogany table and black leather-and-chrome chairs, Robert pointed to one and told Cav, "Please take a seat."

"Yes, sir." Cav sat down. He found a huge manual in front of him, flanked by a glass of ice water. Culver's attache', in his mid-forties, had everything in place. The group sat at one end of the table, while the lieutenant brought down a screen at the other end. Robert sat at the head of the table, the Major next to him with his ever-present laptop. Dilara, dressed in an emerald green pantsuit of silk, her red hair held up by two gold combs, always looked elegant to Cav. He knew that the entire family, which comprised two of the largest shipping fleets in the world, was rich beyond most people's imagination.

He also knew that Dilara, who had Turkish and Greek blood, believed in giving back. They'd established 1,800 Delos charities around the world on six continents. Robert had told him once, during a PSD, that a billion dollars was spent annually on these charities. The money kept the charities thriving so they could continue helping the under-privileged and the uneducated. It also increased farm yields for farmers around the world.

Cav quite liked Robert and Dilara. He could see they were kind, well meaning, and strongly focused. Dilara was actually a big mother hen, but not in a smothering way.

Cal sat there in his civilian clothes, a light blue short-sleeved shirt, bone-colored chinos and a pair of leather hiking boots. Like any security operator, he always carried a light jacket to keep his weapon out of sight.

Dilara sat next to him, and on the other side of the table next to the Major was another manual. That meant another person was coming to this meeting.

"Who's sitting there?" he asked Dilara as a staff woman poured him coffee.

"Lia Cassidy will be here soon. We asked her to join us. She was there when the attack happened, so no one knows more about it than she does. She was the sole survivor. At this meeting, we're going to ask her a lot of questions to get her take on what happened and why it happened to our charity. She's been working nonstop with the Costa Rican police the last five days, since our two teachers were murdered."

Dilara compressed her red lips, her eyes troubled. "I'm worried for Lia. Thank God, she survived. This is just so shocking. We've *never* had one of our charities hit like this."

Robert looked up from his seat. "It's going to happen again and we've got to change course and strategy to protect all of them. We're not going to let our good people be hurt or killed."

"Was Lia wounded?" Cav wondered aloud.

Dilara sighed, clasping her hands in front of her. "No, thank goodness, she wasn't, but the poor thing is obviously in shock, grieving and utterly traumatized by this horrible event."

Nodding, Cav could imagine that she was. Women weren't used to violence like this. Hell, no one was but a trained operator, who handled it a helluva lot better than any civilian could. His thoughts were cut short when the door opened, and his gaze went instantly to the woman standing uncertainly in the doorway. She wore a simple white, long sleeved linen blouse and jeans, with sandals on her feet. Cav couldn't tell which was whiter—her face or her blouse.

His incisive gaze missed nothing. Yes, this was Lia Cassidy, but something was terribly wrong. He spotted the long scar on her left cheek, which seemed to stand out, claiming his immediate attention. Her gray eyes were bloodshot, and her mouth was thinned with what he bet was a whole lot of suppressed emotion. To say she look exhausted was an understatement. There were shadows beneath her large, intelligent eyes. Her hair, naturally curly, was soft and feminine around her face, but cut almost too short for his taste. Worse, as he inspected her from head to toe, he saw the telltale scar that curved around the left side of her neck.

He'd been right: the photo had been retouched. And the photo sent to him had been angled towards the right side of her face, hiding the scar on the left side.

His heart lurched, and the sensation was so damned unexpected, Cav stirred uncomfortably. For an instant, her eyes met his. Again, he felt the impact of deep sadness surround him. Then, her gaze moved to Dilara, who was quickly getting up to greet her.

"Lia," she called huskily, hurrying around the table, her arms opened wide. "Oh, you poor thing. Come here!" and she rushed to Lia's side.

Cav sat back and watched Robert stop what he was doing, instantly getting to his feet and bringing his full attention to the gaunt woman who stood, ghostlike, in the opened doorway. Clearly, both of these people thought a great deal of Lia Cassidy. Dilara got to her first, gently enfolding her in her arms and hugging her tightly. Robert came and stood nearby, his hand laid gently on Lia's sagging shoulder.

Lia buried her face into Dilara's neck, clinging tightly to her. Yes, these people knew her well, and damned if his heart didn't stir as he watched this scene. Disturbed by the scars he saw on Lia's face and neck, Cav wondered what the hell had happened to her. Robert hadn't given him a dossier on Lia, so he was left with his own theories on how she had received those scars.

Cav really didn't want to be touched by this show of unexpected emotion. He'd never seen Dilara in person, but the woman exuded a profound maternal energy. He watched as Lia collapsed, almost literally, into her arms. Her face was hidden, but he believed she was silently battling back tears that wanted to fall.

Dilara was the same height as Lia, and Robert continued gently patting her shoulder, his mouth tight, obviously moved by the meeting.

This was the first time Cav had seen Culver get emotional. Usually, the Air Force general was all cut and dried, typical of officers of his rank.

Meanwhile, the Major stuck his head into his laptop, as if ignoring what was going on behind him. His other attache', the Lieutenant, ducked his head, too, pretending to deal with paperwork in front of him. There was something so fragile, and yet so appealing about Lia Cassidy, but damned if Cav could define it.

So why was his heart in this? His own emotions had definitely been stirred, which flummoxed Cav even more than the scene in front of him. Just the way Lia's long, slender hands gripped Dilara told him she was in deep pain. And Dilara's soft murmurs in Turkish as she held Lia made him uncomfortable. He wished he had a laptop to hide behind, too.

Finally, Lia broke free of Dilara's warm, comforting arms, gave her an apologetic glance, and took two quick swipes at her eyes. She had sworn to herself that she wouldn't cry in front of them.

"I'm okay," she whispered thickly, taking a step away from Dilara, whose eyes were luminous with tears. "It's all right," she said, forcing a partial smile that failed miserably.

"We're so sorry to put you through this so soon after everything happened," Dilara whispered, her fingers resting on Lia's shoulder. "But we're desperate for information." She opened her hands in apology. "You survived, thank God. And we know how tough it is come down here to this meeting. Is there anything we can get you? Have you eaten yet?"

Lia fought to push her grief and shock deep down into her. "I'm not hungry. Maybe a little coffee? And this meeting has to take place." Lia pasted on a brave smile for them, wanting them to stop worrying about her.

"This has never happened before," Robert told her, walking to the table, pulling out a chair and gesturing for her to sit down. "We are here to not only find out what happened, but how we can help you, Lia."

Pushing her damp fingers down her linen slacks, Lia's gaze came back to the man stoically watching her across the table from where she sat down. She saw the Major next to her lift his head from his laptop and give her a cursory nod of hello. The other officer did the same.

"There's a lot to be decided," Lia whispered.

Dilara walked around the table and sat down next to Cav. "Let me introduce everyone to you, Lia."

The Major poured her some coffee and pushed it in front of Lia. She gave him a look of thanks, her fingers curling around the warmth of the cup. But inside, she felt icy cold. The attack that had occurred right after she'd gone back to bed, right after her violent nightmare, had torn her world apart.

When Dilara placed Lia's hand on the yet-to-be-introduced man with the thoughtful hazel eyes, she felt her heart beat a little faster. She knew he was military, even though he wore civilian clothes. His training almost dripped off him; she could see it in his sharp glance and his effort to appear casual, but she wasn't fooled—she could feel the tension radiating from him.

"This is Cavanaugh Jordan," Dilara said, patting his broad shoulder. "Because Robert and I want you safe, we called in a security contractor who's already worked for Robert—several times, in fact, on different missions. We hired Cav to be your bodyguard for now, Lia. Neither of us feels you're safe at La Fortuna right now, and until we can figure out what's going on and know you'll be safe again, Cav will be at your side like a shadow."

Lia lifted her head and met Cal's flat, emotionless stare. "Oh," was all she managed. Then, turning to Dilara, "But I've never had a security detail before."

"You will now," Robert said. "We're not losing you, too."

Lia felt her heart speed up. The man sitting across from her gave nothing away, and yet she could sense his reaction to her. Automatically, she touched her scar on her cheek, then looked away from him and forced herself to focus on Robert, who was looking grim.

"The police said they sent you their investigation reports, sir?" Cav spoke up now.

"Yes," Robert said, pointing at the Major's laptop. "We have everything on their ongoing investigation. But we want boots on the ground Intel, which," looking now at Lia, "only you can provide us."

Lia knew she would be driving down to San José to give them an eyewitness report. But why five days after it happened? She still felt like ground meat exposed to air, and could barely check her own emotions.

"Where do you want me to start?" she asked the general.

"Most important is *why* did it happen," Robert said. "Do you have any ideas?"

"I think I do, sir, but I can't prove it. I've already told my suspicions to the Costa Rican police detectives." She opened her hands. "Dante Medina, La Araña, is the regional drug lord in the northern highlands. He has a villa near La Fortuna, up in the jungle. 'The Spider' is a regional drug lord. He and his men grow marijuana and cocaine in the jungle. He's married to a woman named Suelo, who's about twenty-eight. They have three sons—two, four, and eight, and he keeps two mistresses at a villa in La Fortuna, Pilar, seventeen, and Marta, fifteen. These girls are sex slaves, closely guarded by his soldiers at the La Fortuna villa." Lia's voice dropped into a painful whisper. "His third mistress, Lupe Zavala, eighteen, escaped and ran to us for help, which we gave her. She flew out of the country and back to her country, Guatemala."

Lia forced herself to look at the General. "Lupe came to us five days earlier than the attack. She begged Maria Gonzalez and Sophia Casales, the teachers, to take her in. I wasn't there at the time, but when I returned from my errands the teachers had taken Lupe in. She was a mess, terribly beaten up, and the teachers cared for her in their homes. I went and got the doctor from Tabacon Resort, who was kind enough to come and care for Lupe."

"Had this happened before?" Robert asked.

Lia shook her head, keeping her hand covering her left cheek. She could feel the security contractor's gaze, like heat, on her face and inwardly, she cringed, knowing that he must be disgusted, like every other stranger who first saw her face. "No. Oh, we'd run into Lupe and the other two mistresses at the grocery store in La Fortuna, but they always had a guard with them, so we never really stopped to talk to them." Grimacing, Lia added, "All three of us knew that these women were prisoners at Medina's villa. I mean, it was local common knowledge."

"Why weren't the police called long before this happened?" Dilara asked.

Lia looked up at her. "Because everyone is deathly afraid of Medina, Dilara. You don't know how dangerous he is. He's killed before, and he won't hesitate to get his revenge if someone crosses him. People live in absolute fear of him."

The Major at the laptop flashed a photo onscreen of the destroyed, charred remains of their school. Gesturing toward it, Lia said,

"Now you know why."

"But our school has been there for thirty years," protested Dilara, "and with the approval of the Costa Rican government." Her eyes showed confusion. What had changed?

Lia had known this was going to be a brutal session, but it couldn't be helped. Robert and Dilara couldn't make wise decisions without good Intel, and she was the only one alive who could provide it. For a split second, her gaze met Jordan's, and the protective feeling she received from him caught her completely off guard. She desperately needed to feel as if someone were keeping her safe right now.

Focusing on Dilara, she said, "It was common knowledge in the village that no one was to help his mistresses or to create any trouble for them."

"And because our teachers gave Lupe sanctuary," Robert growled, "Medina attacked our charity?"

"Yes," Lia said wearily. "Look, he considers those women his property. He's a monster, Robert. We've always known it. We were careful to keep everything the charity did away from him, his villa, and his mistresses."

"Until Lupe came to you for help," Dilara said softly.

"I saw her an hour after she asked for help," Lia said. "Her face was a mess. Medina had used his fists on her, possibly broken her nose. And he'd also whipped her. Medina didn't like something she did or said, so he strung her up, stripped her to the waist and whipped her ten times with something…I'm not sure what…but her shoulders and upper back were bloody. I immediately drove over to the Tabacon Resort and got their doctor."

"I wonder if Medina will go after the doctor, too?" Robert murmured.

"Oh, the doctor knows how vengeful Medina is," Lia said, "but the owners of that particular resort are very, very powerful, with strong political ties to the capitol. I seriously doubt Medina will attack the doctor or do his family any harm. You see, the reason Medina has free rein up at La Fortuna is because there are no Costa Rican police force up there. All the major resorts have their own security forces. And La Fortuna is only a mile or two from most of the other forty resorts in the area."

Grimly Robert looked to his wife. "This is a typical situation that can develop here. The resorts probably loan a security officer to the village whenever one is needed."

"Yes," Lia confirmed, "That's exactly what they do. All the children of the workers at these resorts come to our school in La Fortuna. Up until very recently, we had a great working relationship between the resorts, the village and our charity."

"Any indication that Medina has already targeted you?" Robert asked Lia.

Shrugging, Lia said, "I don't know. Probably. Even though I wasn't there when Maria and Sophia took Lupe in, I've worked at this school for years. And Medina and his soldiers know everyone in the area."

Robert swung his gaze to Cav. "You're to be with her at all times."

"Yes, sir," he murmured, registering the distress in Lia's eyes.

"But, sir?" broke in Lia, "If this man comes in with a gun and everyone in the village knows it, Medina will consider him a threat."

"Cav is going undercover as a replacement teacher," Robert told her. "He can play the part. He's going to be a bilingual educator, supposedly teaching English to the children."

Lia stared across the table at Cav, and again felt something comforting emanating from him.

"Do you speak Spanish?" She asked him directly. She had yet to hear him say much of anything. Clearly, he was a big, bad guard dog, and Lia admitted she felt relief flowing through her. She knew how much a security contractor cost and she was sorry that the Culvers had to spend large sums to keep her safe. That money should be going for books, pencils, notebooks, instead.

"I'm passable in Spanish," Cav assured her quietly, noting her concern. He wanted to reassure her, but under the present circumstances, with his two bosses present, he needed to stick to terse responses.

Lia felt a sliver of calm enter her, and realized that with this man she felt safe, in a way. She knew he had to be disgusted by her scars because men always were. Except for Robert, who treated her as whole and worthy.

Tearing her gaze from Cav's, she told the General, "I don't want you to be putting money out to protect me. It isn't right."

Robert shrugged. "Well, first we need to know if you're staying or if you would like to be transferred to another charity, Lia. We don't want to lose you, but we will certainly understand if you want to leave

La Fortuna under the circumstances."

Lia's mouth tightened, and she felt anger rise within her. "Look, I'm not leaving those children in a lurch, but I do need to know what you're going to do and when. Are you going to rebuild the school? If you do rebuild...I want to be a part of the process. I know I'm not a teacher, but I do all the other jobs necessary to keep the charity running smoothly there."

Dilara said, "We've already discussed this, Lia. We're rebuilding the school. We're not going to let a drug lord dictate to us, but it does mean we change what we do there so that no attack like this ever happens to us or our volunteers again."

"Then," Lia said to her, "you're going to need security guards."

"We've also come to that conclusion," Robert told her. "And that's why we've hired Cav to be there with you for the duration."

"Are you sure you want to stay?" Dilara asked Lia gently.

Lia rasped, "Medina is *not* chasing me off, Dilara. Those children deserve an education. The only way I won't stay is if you're not going to rebuild the school."

"We're rebuilding," Robert promised her. "We have plans in the works with a San José construction company to get the school rebuilt in two months."

Lia clasped her hands, feeling nervous as she now turned to the General. "I know this is none of my business, but what are you going to do about Maria's and Sophia's families? They were depending on their salaries to take care of their families' needs."

"No worries," Dilara said. "Robert and I are setting up a fund for each family. They'll receive a stipend each month. We're not going to allow their families to fall into abject poverty. Furthermore, our Home Education team is already hard at work to find capable teachers to replace Maria and Sophia."

"And this time, Lia, we're hiring three teachers instead of two." Robert smiled faintly. "We know from Maria's transmissions to Dilara's staff that you were pinch-hitting a lot, so we're going to relieve you fully of those duties so you can focus on what you do best, which is to manage the entire charity here at La Fortuna."

"That's fantastic. Then, are you expanding the school?"

The Major took a small manual and slid it over to Lia. "This is the full blueprint for the new school."

As she read, Lia caressed the manual, giving Robert a grateful look. "This…this is wonderful, Robert. I was so afraid that, after what happened, you'd walk away from the area and these precious children."

Robert gave her an understanding look. "We might have, Lia, if Dilara and I weren't so bull-headed about children in the world deserving a good education, whether or not they're poor." He sighed. "The world has changed, unfortunately. Some of our charities in third world countries have experienced theft, some of our volunteers were robbed at gunpoint, and now…this."

Robert looked up at the slide of the charred remains, and then turned to Lia. "This is top secret, but we want you to know that our entire family had a meeting a few days ago. We're going to create Artemis Security, an internal security company that Tal, our oldest daughter, has agreed to run. She's still a captain in the Marine Corps in Afghanistan with her sniper unit, but once we get the place built, she's handing in her commission to come home and take the helm."

"And," Dilara said, "Do you know our fraternal twins, Matt and Alexa? Matt is in Delta Force and over in Afghanistan right now. His enlistment runs out next March. He's agreed to come home and run the KNR (kidnap and ransom), division at Artemis."

Her eyes shone. "And Alexa, who is an Air Force captain and flies the A-10 Warthog over in Afghanistan, has agreed to take over the Women's Division at Artemis for us." Her voice rose with pride. "We'll have all three of our children home, out of a war zone, and working behind the scenes to give all of our charities worldwide the best security we can provide."

"Why," Lia said, clearly impressed, "that's a wonderful idea, Dilara!"

"Yes," Robert said gravely. "And you're the tip of the spear here, Lia. The charity was attacked and we lost good people. Artemis Security is going to be our reaction and answer to this kind of terrorism. We're invested completely in protecting all our people who work for Delos."

Robert gave Cav a nod. "Jordan here is the first security contractor we've hired, even though Artemis is a year from coming online. We're going to be assessing each charity to see if any of the other divisions need immediate security, like this one did. It's a big job, but we've already hired a staff of ex-military experts who were under my command in the Air Force, and they're getting contractors to help some of our more beleaguered or threatened charities."

"Wow," said Lia, smiling for the first time. "That's awesome!"

Dilara said, "It's just sad that we have to do this, Lia. You know, my mother created Delos Charities when I was eighteen years old. When I was thirty, I took over the helm. I'm forty-eight now. In all of those years, our charities were always welcomed with open arms by local people they served, no matter what country we placed one in." She frowned. "Robert keeps telling me that the world changed when 9/11 happened, and I've been resisting it, but no longer. I just wish," and her voice filled with anguish, "that we'd had reports on the threat level to you at La Fortuna."

"That's something else that will change," Robert told her. "Because, Lia, you were in the Army, I'm putting you in charge of a weekly threat assessment report that will go directly to Dilara's new security company. We want to know, from now on, what's going on locally around the charity you serve. And if there are threats, we're dividing them into three different levels. Level Three means we call the government of that country and get police there to assist you. If it's a Level Two threat, we will be activating our own internal security response to whatever the threat is. We'll either send down a single security contractor or a team, depending upon the situation."

"And," Dilara told Lia, "if you send in a Level One threat, we'll have a jet with a response team of experts who can keep you and the charity safe within twenty-four hours of the call to Artemis Security."

Lia sat back, eyes wide, stunned by this information. "That's an incredible concept!"

Thoughtfully, Robert said, "Yes, and if we'd had that in place here we might have been able to avoid the murder of two fine young women. I could care less about a building burning—we can always rebuild. But we can never replace those two women, and that's the hardest part of this situation. However, we will take care of Maria and Sophia's survivors."

Lia's heart filled with love for these two people. As bad as the world was, she realized, there were people like Robert and Dilara, as well as their Turkish, Greek and American families out there, making a difference for the poor of the world. "I'm so glad you let me come to work for you," she told them, her voice choking a bit as she fought back sudden tears. "I'm so proud to work for you."

Dilara whispered, "You work *with* us, Lia, you don't work *for* us.

We're just a larger family—a sort of cosmic family, if you will. We consider all our wonderful volunteers our children, too," and she gave Lia a wobbly smile, tears glimmering in her eyes.

Lia swallowed twice. "I just don't ever want to do anything else besides this work, Dilara, I really don't. These children at La Fortuna are truly worth fighting for, and worth protecting," she told them in a fierce whisper. "And that's why I'm not quitting. I want to go back there and get a new building on the ground. I'll help the new teachers who come in to assist. I just don't want those children missing a year of school or more."

"Do you have some ideas on how we can support your efforts while we rebuild?" Robert asked her, getting down to details.

"I do," she replied, and began to lie out an impressive concept. It took forty-five minutes to describe, and the two Air Force officers who were part of Robert's huge staff busily typed away on their laptops, getting down every word of her plan.

Lia fully expected that Robert or Dilara would have other great ideas to add to it, or would want to tweak hers in some way. When she finished, she drank her coffee, now cold.

Robert nodded, a pleased look on his face. "Your military training is showing, Lia, and I'm extremely impressed with your plan and your ideas. It's solid as a rock. I have nothing to add to it." He looked at Dilara. "What do you think?"

Smiling warmly, Dilara said, "I *love* the whole plan, Lia! I see no reason not to implement it as is. We'll do it the moment you get back to La Fortuna with us. I'll have our accounting department wire transfer adequate funds to do what you envision. I've brought down an entire new office supply system, including a new laptop and satellite phone for your use. My assistant, Sandy, will come with us to the village and help you get it all set up. You'll have 24/7 contact with me directly, as well as others on my staff. You aren't going to be left out here to fend for yourself with the threat of Medina hanging over you. That, I promise!"

Lia sat back, stunned. She hadn't thought her plan was actually going to be accepted, but she knew Dilara moved mountains when she wanted to. After all, her family had the clout, the power and the money to do whatever she wished.

She happened to look across the table for a moment and saw a faint smile on Cav's face. She'd tried to pretend he wasn't there, because every time she caught his gaze, she felt something warm and clean move through her, it was probably nothing more than a pipe dream.

"Let's get through the rest of this," Robert told them. He looked over at Cav and then at his watch. "We're going to be wrapping up here in thirty minutes. Cav, and from now on, I want you to be Lia's driver. You will take her in the company van back to La Fortuna."

Lia began to protest, giving Cav an apologetic look. "There's no need for that. I can drive myself."

"No," Cav told her quietly, "If this drug lord wants to attack you while you're in the van, do you know what evasion tactics to take?"

Nonplussed, she muttered, "Of course not" Just because she'd been in the Army, she was a mechanic, not a black ops person who would have such skills.

Shrugging, Cav said, "I'm happy to drive the van, Ms. Cassidy. Maybe you can get a little sleep on the way home."

Lia had a lot of retorts on her lips, but she swallowed all of them. And honestly, she had no quarrel with him. His eyes told her she had nothing to worry about. In fact, he actually seemed concerned about her, though he'd said nothing to betray it. She just felt it.

However, she knew enough about professional operators to know that Cav had his game face on. He was on the job, and when they were in that mode, no one could know what they were thinking or feeling.

But his eyes...his eyes spoke directly to her. Why did her silly heart start galloping when their glances met? Why did hope slowly wind its way through her? Just that faint smile playing on his mouth made her yearn, once again, for a relationship...a real one...with the right man.

CHAPTER 4

C AV SAW THE wariness in Lia's eyes as he opened the door to the white van on the passenger side. He was looking around the busy entrance of the hotel, watching all the parties on their way out. The Delos logo of a rising sun on the side of the white van was bright red and yellow, easy to spot—especially by the bad guys.

"Thanks," Lia murmured gratefully. But when he cupped his hand beneath her elbow to help her into the high van, she froze momentarily.

"Hey, I don't bite," he assured her. Cav supposed in Lia's present state of mind, she might be startled by his unexpected touch. But dammit, he needed to protect this woman. She looked fragile, as if she might break. Now that he knew she'd been in the military, he'd assumed she had a strong backbone. But after having survived that murderous attack, anyone in their right mind would be shaken and shocked, so her skittish behavior was pretty understandable.

He felt Lia relax as he kept his hand on her elbow, seeming to accept his courtly gesture. They stood there looking at one another, and this time, this close, he clearly saw that deep welt of a scar on her left cheek. It made his gut clench. Lia had such a flawless complexion, but not around the scar….

Her cheeks instantly became red. She was blushing. He felt her waver, but smiled to reassure her.

"Thanks," she murmured, quickly getting into the van.

Cav got the impression that she didn't want any man close to her, and right now, she wasn't up for him touching her, even if it was well meant.

He had a lot of questions for this enigmatic woman. In the boardroom, he'd been visibly touched by her impassioned plea to stay and help the children. There weren't many women he knew who would stay after surviving a brutal attack, one she'd miraculously survived. It made him want to know a lot more about her.

As Cav shut the door, he remained alert as he walked around the front of the van. Despite the scar, he found her very attractive. Sure, the scar on her face was unfortunate, but it didn't take anything away from her beauty. Hell, he had so many scars on his body he'd lost count.

Climbing in, he saw the lead black SUV move ahead. That one had three other security men inside. Robert Culver had come down here with a small armada of ex-military contractors because he hadn't known what to expect at La Fortuna. He wasn't going to put his wife, himself or the rest of his team at risk.

Glancing to his left, Cav said, "Ready?"

Lia nodded, quickly putting on her seat belt.

Cav drove the van as the second vehicle in the group. Behind them would be Dilara and Robert, with two contractors on board. Behind them was the staff in two other SUV's, with an operator in each one. The last vehicle was a huge truck loaded down with supplies for Lia's village.

Cav admired her guts. Out of the corner of his eye, he looked at Lia's profile, thinking that her face could be found on a Greek vase. "You have to be tired," he said, sliding a glance at her in the rear view mirror.

"I am. Exhausted, if you want the truth."

He drove out of the airport, following four car lengths behind the first van. "Understandable. You've been through a lot."

Rubbing her brow, she muttered, "Yes. But I'm far better off than Maria or Sophia. I'm just grateful I'm alive."

"It helps to be an optimist in situations like this."

Lia stared at Cav's profile for a moment. She heard the grittiness in his voice. He was so tall, over six feet, and his shoulders were thrown back with pride, typical of a military person.

"I don't like the other choice. Do you?" she replied, her hands folded stiffly in her lap. Just being this close to Cav was doing odd things to her. It had been so long since she'd had a relationship with a man, she'd nearly forgotten what it was like to be attracted to one.

"No, the other choice sucks, that's for sure," Cav agreed.

Cav had an interesting face that spoke of a lot of life experience. The feathery lines at the corners of his eyes revealed that he squinted a lot. Or maybe laughed a lot. Lia had little experience with black ops people, so she wasn't even sure they did laugh—at least, not on the job.

She took a quick peek at his profile. One corner of his mouth had turned upward in a half-grin, and he had both hands on the wheel. She imagined his eyes were constantly moving, looking for potential trouble. While she didn't think there was any trouble here in the busy, prosperous city of San José, Cav was getting paid to be alert and ever watchful.

It felt nice, actually, to have a guard dog, but Cav was a truly handsome species, in her eyes.

Noticing the white scars and nicks over his large, long fingered hands, and the deep tan, she figured he had been outdoors a lot, probably in the Middle East. She noted his well muscled back. He probably worked out daily, but he wasn't excessively muscular.

As she took glances at him from time to time as he drove, she realized how many scars he had on the arm nearest her. Hah! She'd thought she had scars? This guy had her beat!

"I've never had a guard before. Is there a protocol to it?" she asked, clearly wanting some guidance from him.

"Some," he murmured, checking his rear view mirror. The whole armada, and it was certainly that, was now on a freeway heading north toward the Monte Verde Cloud Forest Reserve. "General Culver wants me in close proximity to you at all times."

"What does that mean?" she asked, frowning. She was still jumpy as hell from the attack on the school, which spilled over to extreme nervousness around men. It wasn't that she was afraid of Cav. She just hadn't expected him to be so…polite. What man nowadays helped a woman into a car? Or shut her door for her?

While unexpected, Lia was enjoying that little bit of pampering. It was actually very nice.

"I go everywhere with you. If you have to go to the grocery store, I'm with you. If you need to go anywhere, I drive you to and from your destination."

"I hope you don't go into the women's restroom with me!" She laughed, joking.

"I've been known to do that, too."

She stared open-mouthed at him. "You're kidding—aren't you?" She saw amusement gleaming in his hazel eyes.

"Not at all."

"But," she sputtered, "That's awful!" This man had been very close to her earlier, and Lia had felt the coiled power in Cav's body as he stood waiting for her at the open van door.

"What's awful," he said, raising his dark brows. "Is taking a bullet while you're in a stall." Then, he turned his head, pinning her with a dark look. "And General Culver wants you tailed. That's what a tail does...they're your shadow."

Snorting, she muttered, "Well, we'll see about that. I don't want a strange man with me in a woman's restroom, bullets or no bullets." Lia could swear he was smiling, but damned if his face wasn't absolutely expressionless. And whether she wanted to or not, she *enjoyed* looking at him. He'd stirred her lower body into a new awakening, just like that!

She suddenly realized that she wasn't focusing on the report she'd submitted in the boardroom. Should she feel guilty?

No, she had to admit, she was more interested in Cav at the moment. What had this man suffered? He had far more scars than she did, but they weren't on his face. Unconsciously, she touched her scar on her cheek.

"Is that hurting you?"

Startled, her hand dropped away. For a moment, she caught him not wearing his game face. Instead, she saw concern in his eyes. For her.

"No, I'm fine," she said with embarrassment, feeling her face heat up. She stared straight ahead, tensing, afraid of what he might say. She couldn't link his compassionate nature with his being a man. Nearly every other man who'd seen that scar had shown disgust, or gave her a look that that spoke volumes about how it messed up her face.

Truth be known, Lia had never given much thought to her looks, even though her mother, Susan, had always said she was beautiful. Didn't every mother think her child was beautiful?

Cav held out his arm toward her. "I've got you beat by a mile on that score," he said, giving her an amused look.

Lia stared at his hard, muscled arm, so close to hers. Her fingers itched to slide along his darkly bronzed flesh and feel that black hair sprinkled across his forearm. It was tempting. She curved her fingers into her palms, keeping them on her lap.

"Yes, you do," she whispered.

Cav put his hand on the wheel once more. He'd recognized the fear in her gray eyes when he mentioned her scar, and she'd actually yanked her fingers away from it, as if she'd been burned. Now, he knew how sensitive she was about it, and he wanted to calm her down. He actually felt a need to hold this woman in his arms, a reaction he'd never had before on the job.

In truth, his heart had been engaged from the moment he'd seen her standing so uncertainly in the doorway of the boardroom. She looked like a deer ready to run pursued by a nearby predator.

Would he want to have great sex with her? Absolutely. But this other feeling of *personally* wanting to protect her was very uncommon in his experience. It actually reminded him of the feeling he often had around children. For him, children always needed to be protected. Hell, he knew that better than most.

This wasn't the first time he'd worked to protect a female, but it was always all business. He'd never wanted to ask them personal questions or get to know them on a one-to-one basis. On the other hand, with Lia, he wanted to bombard her with hundreds of questions.

He was sorry he'd upset her about her scar. He could see it in her sudden stiffness, the way she sat up in the seat, her hands fisted in her lap when he'd asked her if that scar was hurting her. The woman had suffered enough trauma without him stirring up whatever had created that scar on her face.

"Aren't you going to ask me how I got all my scars?" He kept his voice light and teasing, adding a slight curve to his mouth. Instantly, Cav saw Lia relax. She leaned back in the seat, her fists uncurling.

"Did you get them as an operator?"

"Yes, I did. I joined the SEALs at eighteen and stayed until I was twenty-five. You get a lot of nicks and scratches doing that kind of boots-on-the-ground work." He glanced at her profile through the rear view mirror. Those sweet lips of hers had softened, and he sensed she was heaving a huge sigh of relief. Obviously, if he talked about himself, she was comfortable with that.

"I've heard about you guys, but I never met one while I was in the military," she admitted.

"What branch were you in?" Cav asked, and saw her tighten up a little. As an operator, he knew body language. It was the nonverbal language of a human being—and was used sixty percent, versus the forty percent verbal language. He'd been trained to observe even the most minute body changes and could read them with great accuracy. He had her file, read it and memorized it. Cav knew the answer to the question, but he needed to establish some connection and trust with Lia. Her military file had a large, redacted section, so he had no way of knowing what that was about. And it was important he knew why that part was hidden from the world.

"I was in the Army. Motor pool."

"Officer or enlisted?" She went rigid again. Why? He wondered if she'd been in combat, maybe a PTSD survivor. The questions he had for her were on a long, long list.

"Enlisted. I was a sergeant, an E-5."

Now, even her voice was going tense. Lia usually had a mellow voice, a soothing alto, and it relaxed him when she spoke.

"I was an E-5 when I got out, Petty Officer, second class," he offered.

Her mouth relaxed, giving him another clue. Cav wasn't the greatest communicator, but hell, in his business, being the quiet type was a decided asset. But with Lia, he was just the opposite. He could see that she didn't want to talk about herself just yet. If he opened up about himself, she became at ease once more. What the hell was she hiding?

"Did you like being a SEAL?" she wondered aloud, turning to him.

"Yeah, as a kid I'd always wanted to be one. They were kind of my comic book heroes."

Not that his childhood was a fairy tale. It was an ongoing nightmare, but he definitely wasn't going there.

"I loved comic books," she said in a new, delighted voice. "I devoured them as a child."

"Who was your favorite?" Cav leapt on that like a bee discovering a flower. Lia, he was learning, was not only mysterious—she was hiding from the world.

"I love the X-Men. Especially Wolverine," and she smiled a little. "He was so scarred and been so badly wounded by brutal men."

Another puzzle piece. Clearly, some man or men had hurt her. Was that what the scar on her face and throat were all about? Cav ached to ask the question, but it was way too soon. He desperately needed to establish a platform of trust with this skittish woman with the beautiful diamond gray eyes.

"Do you have a soft heart toward wounded animals," Cav kept his voice light, with a little teasing, hoping to draw her out a bit more.

Lia turned, studying him for a long moment. "Are all operators like you?"

"Like what?"

"Always asking sensitive, insightful questions?"

Shrugging, Cav gave her a lopsided grin. "I don't know. Is that what I do?"

"Yes. You're very good at it." *Almost too good.* She swore she could feel Cav probing her, and the caring that burned in his hazel eyes told her he was sincerely interested in her.

But why? Was he coming on to her? It didn't feel like it. She'd had enough relationships and God knew, had been hit on enough in the military, to know when a man wanted one thing from her.

But Cav's inspection of her, that gentle prying, didn't feel at all like that. This was a watershed moment for her, because ninety-nine percent of the men who had hit on her weren't coming from the direction Cav clearly was. She had so little experience with a man like him, she felt inept and vulnerable.

"When I was in Afghanistan, because I spoke Pashto, one of the main languages for that country, I was often called in on interrogations at Bagram. From a lot of early experience, I learned you got more with honey than vinegar."

Cav was definitely honey, Lia decided. "I was at Bagram," she blurted out, then snapped her mouth shut. Damn! Her attack had happened there. Her fists curled on her thighs and she stared straight ahead, trying to will Cav into not pursuing her statement.

"Really?" Cav saw her face drain of color after she'd said it. The vibe coming off her right now was stark terror. Okay, then, step around it. He opened his hands on the wheel and said, "It was a big base. At its peak, there were twenty-two thousand people there."

Out of the corner of his eye, he saw her draw in a deep breath, close her eyes for a moment and then reopen them. He was headed the right direction now.

"Let's talk about Wolverine? You up for that?" he teased. Even more relief showed in her face after that last comment.

"I loved Wolverine as a teen," she admitted. "As badly scarred and hurt as he was, he never took it out on others. All he did was protect the innocent and save others' lives."

Cav absorbed her words, her voice suddenly filled with emotion. And he felt his own body react powerfully as she revealed herself at that one moment. Her eyes had gone from dull to shining. Her pale cheeks had flooded with pink. She was animated and engaged with him, a heady experience.

His question had drawn her out of that hole she'd dug for herself. What was she hiding from? Cav wanted to ask her, but instead asked, "Did you have pets when you were growing up?"

She smiled softly. "I had a horse, Goldy. He was a palomino. My dog, Champ, was a beautiful German Shepherd. And my cat, which was black as night, was called Inky."

"Sounds like you had a lot of furry, four-footed friends," Cav said, watching the incredible change in her face. If he'd thought Lia was attractive before, she was positively glowing now, her eyes, a radiant silver, and her pursed mouth, soft and so kissable. Her skin glowed, and she was alive again, her hands open, gesturing.

"I loved them so much. We rescued Champ from the dog pound. Inky was starving and I found him in a back-alley, so weak he couldn't move. Goldy was going to be sold to a dog food factory. They were going to kill him and grind him up. Ugh, it was awful," and she placed her hands against her lips in memory of that time.

"Sounds like they got a good home with you, though," Cav said, wanting to accent the positive of her animal rescues. "How old were you when you got Goldy?"

"I was eleven. My Dad is a farmer. He grows sugar beets in Oregon. I went with him one day because he wanted to buy some chicks from the feed and seed store. I saw Goldy and seven other poor horses being off-loaded at the dog food factory. I hated that place because I knew they killed horses there and I loved horses. Goldy escaped and ran out of the corral. I got my Dad involved and a couple of the other guys who worked there. They were able to keep Goldy in a blind alley. I watched my Dad, who is so good with animals walk up to him, talking to him a real quiet voice, and Goldy stood stock-still. Dad was able to put the halter and lead rope on him."

Cav heard the wistfulness in her tone, that faraway look in her eyes. "What happened next?"

"I started to cry as my dad led Goldy out of the alley. I begged him to bring Goldy home, that I couldn't stand to see him being killed for dog food."

"And your dad? What did he do?"

"He couldn't stand to see me cry," Lia said wryly, shaking her head. "He told me to dry my tears, that he'd buy Goldy and we'd get him sent by trailer to our farm. I was the happiest kid in the world at that moment."

Grinning, Cav said, "I can see it now. Your Dad is like lots of us guys, we hate to see a woman or child cry. We feel helpless because we can't fix it."

"Funny, Dad always said that, too."

"Was he in the military?"

"No."

Cav wanted to ask her how she got into the Army, but restrained himself. "Not only do you rescue animals, you also rescue kids that need help. Is that why you joined Delos?"

Instantly, her face became soft and maternal. This woman could not keep a game face if she tried! Cav was secretly thrilled, because if he couldn't pry Lia open verbally, he had his non-verbal skills in place to get to her.

What threw him was that she trusted him enough to answer his questions without wondering why he was asking them. Cav felt their connection strongly. There was no doubt about it.

She was going to be more than just an assignment, as someone to be protected at all cost. As a contractor, he was not to allow any emotional ties between himself and a client. But damn it, this woman invited those feelings without even realizing she was doing it. Cav didn't think for a moment that she was like this with everyone, but who knew?

"I'm a sucker for kids and animals, that's true." She smiled and gave a slight shrug. "I mean they're innocent. Vulnerable. They need to be protected by the adults and the community around them. That's the way I was raised, and that's who I am today."

Images of his own childhood brought up anger and regret in Cav, if she only knew about his sordid childhood. Hell, going through BUD/s, the six-month SEAL school for recruits was easy compared to surviving daily with his cocaine-addicted father. Cav never knew, from the time he woke up in the morning, if he would see nightfall.

"That's a good way to be raised," he agreed, trying to keep the feelings out of his voice. "Do you have brothers? Sisters?"

"No, I'm an only child."

"And your Dad is a beet farmer in Oregon. What does your mother do?"

"She's a CPA for a bank in Ontario, Oregon. She's actually the head of the department."

"You have a set of brainy parents, then. You said you were in motor pool? Did your dad teach you about mechanics at a young age?"

She smiled a little. "I think you're inside my head, reading my mind, Mr. Jordan."

"Call me Cav." He shot a glance toward her. "How would you like to be addressed?"

"Call me Lia."

"So, Lia? Did you help your dad in the barn, fixing the tractor and that sort of thing?"

"Yes. I've always been fascinated with machinery. I think I got my Dad's gene for that stuff. At the Delo's school, I took care of the electric, plumbing and air conditioning. If it broke, I tried to fix it first before calling in an expert. It saved our charity money, and I got to use my skills."

"What else did you do there?"

"I wasn't a teacher, although I love to teach. I didn't have the certificates for it. I made the kids' lunches and two snacks in our small kitchen. I was also the manager of the facilities, for lack of a better description."

"A jack of all trades and master of all of them, I bet." Cav met her gaze and felt as if a hand had gripped his heart in that moment. Right now, at this minute, Lia looked so much younger, fresh and alive. And then he realized as the armada sped out of San José, on a four-lane freeway heading north toward the forest and jungle, that she had finally—finally—relaxed. Not only that, she was beginning to trust him. That meant a lot to him, because in Cav's business trust was the last thing you ever gave another person.

Every human was a potential threat, a potential killer. Cav trusted no one, but it was natural for him, having grown up in a family where he knew his father couldn't be trusted not go after him or his helpless mother. At first, his mother had tried to protect Cav, but after his father gave her a broken nose, arm and jaw one year, her spirit was broken.

So Cav's legacy was to trust no one. Maybe that was why he never got into any serious relationship with a woman. He didn't trust women, either.

However, it was imperative that his PSD, in this case, Lia, trust him a hundred percent. Cav told himself this was what he was doing, but the truth was, he was eager for personal information about her. Why? Because she excited him in ways he'd never felt in his life. And while it was far more than about sex, that was in the mix, too.

"Well, I don't know about being an expert in everything mechanical," Lia countered, shaking her head. "You know, we all have our strengths and weaknesses."

Cav liked her humility. He would bet she was amazing at fixing cars, trucks, tractors or anything else with an engine in it. "Can you give me an idea of a day in your life at the charity? Before it was burnt to the ground?"

She sighed, rubbing her face. "I get up at 0600. Get my coffee, take a shower and get over to the school at 0700. We start classes at 0900. We had five classrooms for the different grades that Maria and Sophia taught. Different groups of kids would come in at different times. I was responsible for knowing the teacher's lesson plan, having the books and anything else needed in that classroom for the teacher and the children to use." She gave him a wry look. "This is really boring stuff."

"Take my word for it, Lia, there's nothing boring about you." As soon as Cav spoke them, he wished he could retract them. But he couldn't. Even his voice had changed, thickened with emotion. When he glanced at her, he saw Lia's winged brows lift in surprise.

Lia didn't know how to take Cav's comment, but there was something in his eyes and voice that sent excitement and hope through her.

"Then," she continued, "I would then take the time to clean up the place, clean the bathrooms and wash windows or clear cobwebs. At 1000, I had a snack prepared for all the children. At 1100, I made all the children's lunches, and they'd eat in the dining room together. I'd wash all the dishes afterward and clean things up. At 1400, I had another little snack for the kids and then we'd put them down for a nap in our sleeping room for an hour. At 1500, the bus came by and all the kids got on it. They were delivered back to their homes in La Fortuna and the surrounding area."

"And you still weren't done?"

She offered him a smile. "No. We had a washer and dryer on the premises and I washed all the bedding the children slept on, along with the light blankets over them, towels, washcloths and dried them in our dryer. By the time 1700 rolled around, I was done for the day and went home."

"Tell me about your home?" Cav kept tabs on the armada as it sped along at sixty miles per hour. Up ahead, the gradient changed and he could see the low jungle mountains painted like pale green watercolor ghosts, rising out of the horizon in the distance. That was the beginning of what was known as the northern highlands of Costa Rica.

"Home is a little one bedroom white stucco house that's still standing after the attack." She frowned. "Medina's soldiers ransacked Maria and Sophia's home on the other side of the school. They're still standing, but they tore them apart and they're going to need a lot of work, paint and effort to get them livable once more."

"And what about the normal places you go on a weekly basis?"

"Oh, gosh," Lia mumbled, "Can I take a rain check on this, Cav? I suddenly need to sleep. If I don't, I'll keel over. I didn't get much in the past five days."

"Sure," he said, "No problem. Go to sleep. I'll wake you up when we get there."

Lia gave him a grateful look and laid the seat down so she could stretch out. "Thanks…" she whispered, closing her eyes. Almost immediately, she spun into a deep, healing sleep. Cav made her feel safe. She liked him. He seemed genuinely concerned about her safety. And there was more. The look in his hazel eyes when he'd said, *Take my word for it? There's nothing boring about you,* her heart leapt. She recognized that steady, burning gaze. It was that of a man wanting a woman.

CHAPTER 5

D RIVING THE VAN, Cav tried to resist the emotions that were bubbling just beneath the surface. Lia had instantly fallen asleep, exhausted from the events of the past five days. As he followed the lead SUV all the way to the edge of the massive Monte Verde Cloud Forest Reserve, Cav occasionally slid a glance over at her. He knew that his priority was to stay alert to all activity around them, including the cars and trucks passing them in the faster lane. He was wearing an earpiece and could hear everything the lead security contractor, an ex-SEAL named Tanner, was saying.

Cav knew of him—Tanner had been with Seal Team One, while Cav had been with Seal Team Three. He knew that Tanner was a highly competent ex-SEAL and he was glad the operator was at the helm of this mission.

Now, Lia had moved to her side and was facing him, one hand beneath her cheek, her legs drawn up. Cav was surprised she hadn't gone into a full fetal position—he'd seen it often in Afghanistan with young Afghan children who slept like that. It was a defensive position adopted when people didn't feel safe, aware that they could die. And hell, over there? Yeah, every village he'd frequented as a SEAL had been a potential gateway to death.

His brow furrowed as he kept his eyes on the road. Although he didn't want to go there, he flashed back to the eighteen years he'd been living at home. He'd slept in a fetal position every night. He might have started out lying on his back or side, but when he woke up in the morning, he was always curled up on his side like a frightened animal with knees to his chest.

Had he been frightened? Hell, yes. Every day. Once, when his mother had tried to step between his father and Cav, his father had jerked a butcher knife from the kitchen counter, holding it in such a position that eight-year-old Cav thought it would slice his mother's throat open. Even today, he could feel the same icy fear grip his throat and gut when he remembered that scene.

Luckily, his father still had some control and hadn't followed through. Today, Cav often read of men who killed their spouses and children. What a piss-poor state this world was coming to! Hell, he'd personally gone through that potential scenario so many times he'd lost count.

His damp fingers moved around the steering wheel, even though the air conditioning in the van kept it comfortable. Every time Cav relived those years, which he hated to do, he would experience a physical reaction. His hatred for his father had made him grow up fast. When he was fifteen, his father had pulled out his belt to use on him once again. Finally, Cav was ready to fight back.

Unconsciously, he rubbed the bridge of his nose. It still had a bump to remind him how his father, high on coke, had gone ballistic when Cav had yelled he was never going to get belt-whipped again. Cav didn't remember a whole lot about that event. He knew what it was like to "lose it." Once he'd picked himself up off the floor, his nose running blood, he'd attacked his father.

Although his father had broken his nose and bloodied him, Cav had gotten in some serious punches, blackening his father's eye.

Only when his mother rushed into the house after work and found them on the kitchen floor pummeling each other did she scream. That scream finally broke up the fight.

But Cav was ecstatic. He'd given his father the worst of it, the culmination of fifteen years of rage from the abuse he'd received. And while his mind had blanked out some of the details, his scars were there to remind him of the day he'd physically resisted his father.

Afterward, the house had quieted. It was almost like a morgue. His mother was shaken and tried to help him, but he walked unaided to the bathroom and took care of himself. That wasn't new. Cav had always taken care of himself since he was essentially on his own as a kid.

Normally, the highlight of Cav's day was going to school. It was a peaceful place compared with his crazy household. Because he hated coming home in the evening, he tried to arrive there as late as he could. But he knew that if he wasn't there for dinner, his father would beat him, so he always managed to get home on time.

He loved school because it was a place of protection for him. His teachers liked him, supported him and most important, cared for and praised him. He wasn't the most brilliant student in the school, but he wasn't stupid, either. And Cav was great at sports, math and science.

He was useless in English and composition, for sure, and even now, he was a man of action, not letters. Cav had learned to accept who he was, and he rarely had regrets about the man he'd become.

Glancing momentarily down at a sleeping Lia, he again wondered what it was about her that turned him inside out and made him yearn so badly for time alone with her. He actually felt as if his soul was urging him to learn what lay in Lia's heart, her mind. What events and people had shaped her? Clearly, she was a rural woman, raised on hard farm work. That tended to breed discipline, common sense and responsibility in a person, in Cav's experience.

Just seeing the soft slope of her cheek, slightly pink, looking like velvet, made him want to feel it beneath his fingertips. He also noticed that Lia was definitely underweight. Didn't they feed her enough up there at La Fortuna? Or was she working so hard, she skipped her own meals in favor of the teachers' or students' needs?

Lia had a big heart, just like Dilara. She had to—what other kind of woman would want to do this kind of work daily, nonstop. He'd seen the fire in Lia's gray eyes, the determined set of her jaw during the meeting, her commitment to ensure that her children would not be left in the lurch from the catastrophic events of the past few days.

One of the biggest surprises for Cav was that Lia had come with a solid plan for rebuilding the school's program, keeping classes ongoing while new teachers were located and hired. They would know that they would be protected so they didn't have to worry about giving their lives in order to teach.

There was such fight and so much heart in Lia—maybe that's what appealed to him so strongly. Cav suspected that the scars on her face and neck had come from violence done to her, probably while in the Army. It was actually rare that a mechanic from a motor pool would be outside the wire, the fence that protected Bagram from attack, but while there were drivers for such trucks, she had hinted that she was working in the garage, not as a driver.

Being a mechanic suited her, he thought. She had the smarts, for sure, and her keen eyes seemed to miss nothing. He wondered what she saw behind his own façade. Did she also feel that palpable connection he felt with her, or was it just one way?

He watched the armada behind him move steadily along, keeping the required distance between vehicles. Up ahead, the taller jungle trees were becoming visible, and the rounded, undulating mountains clothed in various textures and shades of green closed in on them. Cav looked at his watch. In another two hours, they'd be well into the northern highlands and near La Fortuna and Lia's home.

Lia was clearly enjoying her nap. The corners of her mouth were soft, no longer tight and drawn inward. The stress on her face was gone, showing just how beautiful she really was when not feeling under threat. Cav fantasized briefly, wondering what her curly hair would feel like if he ran his fingers through that short, shining mass.

He wondered why she had cut her hair so short. Even some men's hair was longer than hers! Yet, there was nothing mannish about Lia.

Cav remembered being in Afghanistan, his hair nearly to his shoulders. He'd worn a thick, unkempt beard for the duration of his deployment there because every SEAL wanted to blend in like an Islamic male, with long hair and bearded faces.

Lia didn't seem to care if she fit in or not. Clearly, her passions were for those children of La Fortuna. She was like a mother bear, growling and standing her ground, pleading for help for them. And her cries hadn't fallen on deaf ears. Robert and Dilara Culver were just as passionate about backing Lia's ideas and her plan for building a new school.

But Cav had a feeling that if Lia needed to fight her way through something, she had the guts to do just that. She might be slender and underweight, but Cav would never dismiss her inner strength and her sense of purpose.

Cav had always liked fighters. He also liked survivors because he'd been one himself. Maybe that was what had drawn him so powerfully to Lia.

The road went from a four lane down to a two lane, and the armada slowed accordingly. The trees were over a hundred feet tall, standing like proud soldiers on either side of the highway. They blotted out the sun as the vehicles climbed slowly but surely into the mountainous jungle area.

Lia slowly awoke as the van left the asphalt and slowed down, the tires crunching on the dry dirt road that led to La Fortuna. Her mind felt spongy and she groaned and slowly sat up, realizing she'd slept on her left side. The van rattled and trembled over the rutted dirt road, and she glanced over at Cav.

He turned, noting her half-closed eyes. "Sleep well?"

Lia muttered, "It felt like I'd died." Rubbing her eyes, she looked around, seeing that the sun had changed and gone to the west, slanting across the tops of the jungle trees that surrounded them in every direction. The small town of La Fortuna sat a mile away, its colorful stucco homes looking to Lia like Easter eggs.

"We're almost home," she whispered expectantly, sitting up and adjusting the seat.

Cav said, "Home. That has a nice ring to it."

Lia's mind still wasn't functioning. She felt as if she had cotton jammed between her ears. "It does, doesn't it?" And damn it! She couldn't help but think what it would be like be drawn to a man like Cav.

Whoa! She stopped herself suddenly. *What craziness was this?* Lia felt a headache coming on. Damn. She got these when she was under severe stress, and she was definitely there, about as stressed as she could be.

"Does The Spider or his guards frequent La Fortuna?" Cav asked her.

"Rarely. We're more apt to run into them at the local grocery store. Why?"

"Just wondering." Cav's eyes swept the dirt hillside that sloped gently into a bowl. La Fortuna sat down in a depression so he could see everything around the small village. It was nothing but bare dirt slopes. Why wouldn't plants grow around it, or had someone cleared the area of jungle vegetation?

That was more than likely. Cav knew it was the dry season in Costa Rica, but in the rainy season La Fortuna must turn into a mud pit. There was no greenery on these slopes to stop the erosion of the soil from filtering into the town. He saw cars and dust eddies on certain streets of the town as they approached it.

Tanner called in on Cav's earpiece, directing everyone to follow his lead to the location of the burned-out school. They made a turn, heading down the center of town, which surprisingly featured an asphalt road.

"We're going to the school," Lia told him, clearing her throat, her voice still thick and drowsy.

Cav glanced over at her. "Are you awake enough to talk a bit?"

"Sure."

"Part of a PSD is getting the client to trust the contractor." He gave her a warm look. "That's me and you. When we stop, you don't just automatically get out of the vehicle. I'll look around first and make sure things are okay. Then, I'll get out, walk around the van and check things out further. Only then will I come over and open the door for you. Agreed, Lia?"

"Okay," she said.

"If I ever tell you, 'Down,' I need you to hit the deck instantly. Don't question me. And when you do, I'll be stepping in front of you and aiming myself at whatever the threat is. Don't get up or do anything unless I instruct you. Okay?" Cav drilled her with an intense look.

Swallowing hard, Lia nodded. "You're putting yourself between me and a potential knife or bullet?" She didn't want to hurt Cav for any reason. Yet, she knew he'd been hurt. It was there in his strong, lined face, with that harsh presence reflected behind his penetrating hazel eyes.

He shrugged. "That's why we get paid the big bucks. Don't worry, okay? I'm not intending to sacrifice you or me if it comes to a threat. What I need to know is that you'll follow my orders instantly and not question me. I can't have you hesitate. You move as fast as you can, all right?"

In response, she began, "The night Medina's men hit here…" and gestured toward a huge, burned out building standing in deep black and gray rubble.

"Yes?" he waited expectantly.

"I heard the gunfire and I ran. My house has two exits and I took the back door and ran as hard and fast as I could for the jungle."

Cav slowed the van as Tanner's SUV came to a halt in front of them. He saw the jungle about a hundred yards away from the school. "Did you ever see their faces?"

She shook her head, feeling that old fear rise up within her. "No, I just heard the roar of the fire and men's voice yelling at one another. I saw some shadows but that's all…"

"It's a long sprint to that wall of jungle," Cav said, calculating the distance from the house.

"And I never thought I'd make it," she acknowledged. "I was expecting to take slugs in my back every minute." Her voice quavered a bit as the painful memories resurfaced.

He heard her terror, but his eyes were on Tanner and his men, who were dismounting from the SUV. They would first do a walk-around while everyone remained in their vehicles. Lia's gray eyes had grown dark as she stared at the destroyed school, and he wanted to slide his arms around her hunched shoulders. If only he could.

"But you made it to the jungle," he said firmly. "What did you do then?"

Lia didn't answer. She wiped her brow, trying to will away the headache behind her eyes as she watched the four men armed with M4 rifles move with silent precision around the area, looking for a threat. She saw none.

The school and their three small homes sat on a dirt plain close to the jungle wall. One could see someone approach from a half mile away in three directions, and she wondered if Medina's men had come out of the jungle instead.

Cav watched Tanner and his men while he listened to their short, abrupt conversations. The group thoroughly scouted the area, with Tanner standing a head taller than the others.

"This place is so open that I think Medina and his men came out of the jungle," Cav told her. "That way, they could do the damage, fade away, and never be seen."

"That's what I think, too," Lia said hollowly, watching Tanner order his men to the three small stucco homes surrounding the burned-out school. She was impressed with the way they approached each house, opened the door and then disappeared inside. She didn't like them inside her home, but she understood they were clearing it, just in case.

Still, her small home was her womb, her safe place. But five nights ago, it hadn't been safe at all. She lifted her chin and met Cav's warm gaze on her. "I'm glad you're here," Lia said, her statement taking him by surprise.

Rubbing her hands over her upper arms, Lia felt suddenly cold and clammy as the sounds, the odors, the roar of flames and the yells of the soldiers came back to her in a rush.

"I am, too," Cav confessed, holding her gaze. He could almost bet she was remembering that attack, and he fought anew his urge to sweep her into his arms. Cav could almost feel her body against his, feel her instinctive trust of him. He liked that she was scared and didn't try to hide it from him.

"Here's my little house," she said proudly, gesturing toward the white stucco building with its two small windows and a red painted door between them. "This has been a place of safety for me." She chewed nervously at her lower lip, staring at her home as Tanner's men left it, closing the door behind them.

"Was it the only place you felt safe?" Cav wondered.

"Yes," she whispered.

"Well, we'll just have to make it safe for you again," Cav said firmly. He knew he could make her feel safe in this unsafe world of hers.

"Medina is a constant threat, Cav. It never goes away. The three of us knew about him." She sighed and whispered, "The only way he won't be a threat is if he's dead."

Cav already wanted to take the bastard out, but said nothing, just nodded his head. When Tanner gave them the "all clear" over the mike, Cav said, "I'm going to get out now." He unstrapped his seat belt. "Wait for me to open the door for you."

Lia pulled off her safety belt and nodded. She watched Cav move with an animal-like grace. Unable to keep her eyes off his large, square hands, she saw real strength in them but there was a soft underside to this man that she sensed he rarely showed to anyone. Why? What ghosts from his past was he carrying around like unwanted friends? She certainly had her ghosts and they were with her ever day whether she wanted them to be or not.

Cav pulled on his dark glasses and shut the door, leaving her alone in the cab. She was intrigued by the security detail, having never been a part of one before. Now, she watched as the security contractors emerged from each vehicle, armed and deadly as they went about the business of keeping their clients safe.

Lia was very glad that Cav had been assigned to her. The other men looked hard and unforgiving, while Cav seemed, well, more approachable. She liked that he talked with her, asked her questions, and had avoided more serious questions he could have asked, and didn't.

Cav opened her door, acting like a human shield as she slid off the seat, her feet touching the dusty, hard pack ground. His hand wrapped around her upper arm and he gently placed her in front of him so he had her back. Right now, that felt damn comforting to Lia as she walked over towards Robert and Dilara. Lia felt her heart break as she saw the devastation in their faces, looking at the rubble that had once been a school. Dilara was wiping her eyes.

As she approached the group, she saw the other contractors fanning out in a circle around them, alert, guns in harnesses across their chests, fingers near the trigger. They all wore shooting gloves, dark glasses and civilian clothes like jeans, t-shirts and baseball caps on their head. Cav didn't wear anything on his head, and she saw the sun glinting against his black hair. She liked the way he looked, the way he walked, and the way he conducted himself like the warrior he obviously was.

"This is awful…" Dilara said softly, tears streaming down her cheeks.

Robert placed his arm around his wife, awkwardly patting her arm, his face grim.

Lia felt warm tears coming to her eyes. She swore she would not cry, and choked them back. "We'll rebuild," she told Dilara in a surprisingly strong voice. "We're not going to let a drug lord chase us out of here."

She saw the deep pain on Dilara's face, and knew that the deaths of Maria and Sophia were haunting her. They haunted Lia, too, but she'd learned five years ago that tears only provided momentary relief. And Lia was tired of crying.

She swore to herself that she wasn't going to let Medina and his murdering soldiers take away what was left of her soul. Not this time.

Cav watched the scene from afar, wanting to walk up to Lia and place an arm around her hunched shoulders, just as Robert was consoling his weeping wife. But he knew he couldn't. That wasn't part of his assignment.

"This place is safe enough," Tanner said, coming up to him.

"The jungle is my only worry," Cav confided.

Tanner nodded. "Those bastards hid in that jungle, came out in the dark and did their dirty work, and then faded back into it. Far as I know, there's been no identification of Medina or his soldiers by anyone."

"My detail doesn't remember seeing any of them," he said, making damn sure that Tanner didn't know his growing emotional attachment to Lia.

Snorting, Tanner kicked up the red clay with the toe of his combat boot, disgust written in his hard face. A puff of dust followed his effort. "You know you're in a shitload of trouble here by yourself, don't you?"

Cav's mouth quirked. "Nothing I'm not used to."

"I think the General needs to give you more help." Tanner looked toward Robert Culver. "Don't you?"

"No."

Tanner gave him a close look and then lifted his chin, studying the woman. "She's a looker, scar or no scar on her face," he muttered more to himself than to Cav. "You lucked out, Jordan."

Holding on to his mounting desire to protect Lia, he shot a look at Tanner. "She's hurting, bad."

"Yeah, it's obvious." And then Tanner asked, "How close does the General want you to tail her?"

"Shadow." Cav glared at Tanner, just daring him to say something.

Tanner's looked at Cav, then said wryly, "Twice the luck, Jordan."

Bristling inwardly, Cav knew Tanner was envious, and every protective cell in him rose. He wanted to deck the ex-SEAL for his interested look at Lia. "Go to hell, brother."

Chuckling, Tanner clapped him on the shoulder, turned and walked away.

Cav resumed his casual walk, his gaze seeking anything that seemed out of place. Tanner was insinuating that because he had to stay in that small house with Lia at night, he might be able to sleep with her. Anger burned through him at the suggestion that he'd take advantage of his client.

Cav wasn't sure what Lia would say about it, feeling that she'd be highly uncomfortable with a strange male in that tiny house with her. Hoping against hope he was wrong, Cav strolled around the edges of the burned school. He saw bullet marks on the walls of all three small stucco houses that the teachers and Lia lived in. Medina was leaving a clear message, no question about that.

Vaguely, he heard Dilara sobbing, and turned to see her, with Lia beside her. There was such heart in Lia as she reached out, sliding her arm around Dilara's waist and witnessing the woman's grief and tears.

Turning away, his gut tightening, Cav swallowed twice to tamp down his rising emotions. There was no place for feelings here, not for contractors. Emotions were a distraction of the worst kind.

As he wandered around, he saw Tanner call two of his operators over and watched as they headed for the line of jungle trees. It was a wise move, Cav thought, to check out the tree line. Who knew what lurked in there?

Continuing his walk around, he saw a group of children coming their way across the dirt field. They were all ages, dressed in colorful clothes, their black hair in braids, pony tails for the girls, or bowl-shaped cuts for the boy's hair. It was a ragtag group of children from six-years old on up to the late teens, Cav guessed, checking them out.

CHAPTER 6

WHEN LIA HEARD the cries of her children, she released Dilara. The poor woman was trying to blot away all her tears, and Lia understood better than anyone how devastating it was to stand here in the carnage. She excused herself, murmuring that she was going to meet some of their students. Robert nodded, and Dilara struggled to stop crying.

Cav immediately moved to her side. "Where are you going?"

Gesturing, Lia said, "To the kids…" They filled her heart with joy despite the terrible events that surrounded them. "They're going to need someone to hold them," she told him, quickening her stride across the hard-packed dirt.

Cav grunted in agreement and said nothing, remaining alert. He kept his stride steady, glad for the .45 pistol in the back of his belt, beneath his jacket. He was glad it was hidden from the children racing toward them, their faces mirroring joy.

To his relief, he could see no threat nearby. Further in the distance, he saw a number of adults now filtering out from between their homes, walking the half-mile to where the school had once rested. They were probably the parents of the children now racing like the wind to reach Lia.

He watched, captivated, as she knelt down on one knee, her arms wide open as the children flew to her side like a flock of frightened young birds. In just seconds, ten children of all ages surrounded Lia, holding on to her and hugging her, some crying, some not. They all huddled around her, clinging to her, their tiny heads buried into her slender frame until Cav couldn't see her any more.

How could Lia give so much of herself when she was suffering and grief-stricken herself? It was beyond Cav's understanding, but it touched him deeply as he stood awkwardly, watching the tears on the little faces of the children, their small bodies squirming around Lia, their branch-thin arms eager to hold onto her in any way they could.

Cav could hear her murmuring words in Spanish, picking up a word or two in the process. Their sobs tore at him because he remembered when he'd gone in hiding in the garage, burying himself among some old, smelly tarps tossed in a corner. He'd held his hand over his mouth and cried just as these children cried.

Yet, despite their fears, Lia's soothing voice filtered through it all, calming, touching and holding them. How Cav wished he'd had his mother come to find him and hold him, just as Lia was holding the squirming mass of frightened children, loving them, caring for them.

But his mother had never done this. It had left a hollowness within Cav so deep that this wound had never healed. God! Just watching the children with Lia as she dried their cheeks, smiled at them and reassured them, he wished she would hold him like that. Something whispered to him that Lia could heal him, too. It was an insane thought, because Cav had gotten used to the feeling that a part of his heart was hollow, a deep hole that could never be filled.

The children were quieting now, calming down because Lia was giving them love and protection. How badly Cav wanted to give Lia that same sense of protection. He might not be whole, but he could at least do that for her because that's all he knew: how to protect. And he was damned good at it.

He saw one little girl in a pair of blue coveralls and a pink tee gently touch the scar on the left side of Lia's face, gently moving her small hand down its length. And Lia had not flinched, instead turning her head and kissing the little girl's forehead, pulling her tightly to her.

Children were so honest and guileless, Cav thought as he remained on high alert, turning and looking around him. He liked hearing Lia's low voice as she spoke to the children in their native Spanish. She was soothing them because they, too, were grieving, shaken by what had happened. He heard Lia explain that God called Maria and Sophia to heaven, and that they were happy to be there with Him. She told them that new teachers were coming, but that the children could go to the local Catholic Church and if they wanted, light a candle at the altar and pray for their teachers who were now in heaven.

Cav cursed softly and turned away, feeling vulnerable. He was struck by the simple displays of Lia's courage as she cared for those ten shaken children, ignoring her own pain, focused only on helping them cope.

Cav saw Robert and Dilara move toward them, devastation written across Dilara's face. Clearly the couple cared for their charities as if they were their own children.

When Dilara and Robert approached, Lia slowly stood, the children clinging to her legs, hips and waist, wherever they could hold on to her. They'd never seen the couple before, and Dilara put on a gentle smile for their benefit. Dilara and Robert halted a few feet away, giving Lia time to lean down and tell the children in Spanish that this was her family, and that they had built the school.

She repeated that it would be built again and that new teachers were going to come and teach them in two month's time. The children stared at them with big eyes, their arms around Lia, unwilling to move.

Dilara smiled warmly and knelt down in the dirt, as did Robert. They spoke softly to the children in their native language, telling them how sorry they were that their school had burned to the ground. With smiles, they reinforced that there was good news: a new one would be built shortly.

Lia crouched down, the children still attached to her. But they were now curious about these two new people. Fear had been replaced by keen curiosity. They wiped their wet cheeks with their tiny hands, shyly staring at Robert and Dilara. Robert was a mountain of a man, tall and heavily muscled—a far cry from the small, lean build of typical Costa Rican men.

Then, one little girl slowly stepped toward Dilara, sucking her thumb. Lia whispered approval, urging her forward with her hand on her back. She told them that Dilara was like the mother of all of them. That did it. The girl took several steps toward her, taking her thumb out of her mouth, smiling.

Dilara melted. She was an incredibly compassionate person and had hoped the children would feel the sunlight of her smile. Now, she opened her arms to the little girl and when the child stepped into her embrace, several other girls left Lia's embrace, heading for Dilara. Pretty soon, five little girls were in Dilara's embrace, pressing themselves willingly against her, burying their heads in her breast.

Tears burned in Lia's eyes and she looked up and saw Cav staring down at her, raw pain in his eyes. Lia gave him a gentle smile and then returned her attention to the five little boys still huddled in her arms.

The girls were bolder, and Lia's smile widened as Dilara's face turned to utter joy. No one loved children more than these two devoted people, and Lia saw Robert's hard face open and become vulnerable. The instant he lost that general's mask he wore so well, all the little boys flocked up to him, climbing in and around him, chattering in Spanish, wanting to be held by him, too.

Lia remained crouched, her smile deepening as Robert grinned and spoke to the boys in Spanish, taking them into his long, bear-like arms. She saw the boys snuggling deeply into his embrace as his eyes glittered with tears.

Kids did that to a person, Lia had discovered long ago. Their little hearts were so innocent, so full of life and love that no one could be around them long and not have it affect them deeply, as it was doing right now.

Standing, Lia caught Cav's glance. "I'm going to meet the parents," she said. There were at least twenty adults now walking across the low lands. They would have questions, worries and concerns, and Lia knew she was the one who had to take the helm and be there for them, as well.

Cav walked by her side as she strode quickly toward the group.

"Are you up for this?" he asked, concerned.

"I have to be," she assured him. "So yes, I am."

Cav heard the grit in her voice and saw the set of her jaw. "Isn't' there anyone who can help you?"

"No. Maria and Sophia were the only others who could." She glanced up at him. "It's up to me to hold the families together now, Cav. There's no one else. I'll be fine."

Cav nodded, resisting the urge to protect her from the pain she would be dealing with from the children's parents. He intuitively knew how much this would take out of her. "Who's going to help you?" he asked again.

"No one, Cav. And that's just the way it is."

He slowed when the group of parents began to surround Lia. He knew he needed to be outside the group to watch and protect her, so he faded into the background as the worried parents quickly fired a barrage of questions at her.

Lia took it with grace and calm, and Cav could see that her confident demeanor was already helping the parents cope, just as it has soothed their frightened children.

He glanced over his shoulder, watching Dilara and Robert with the ten children. When they stood up, the little girls trailed around Dilara, the boys around Robert as they all walked toward where Cav stood with Lia.

Meanwhile, the other contractors were doing their job. He saw Tanner and his two men return from the jungle tree line. Nothing. Well, that was good.

The warmth of the mid-afternoon sun was making Cav sweat. He didn't like wearing the lightweight jacket, but it was a necessity. A number of other contractors had formed a loose circle around the huddled group of parents with Lia. Cav wondered if they were equally touched by Lia's magical touch with children as well as adults. Probably not.

For the next thirty minutes, Lia became the air control tower operator, introducing Dilara and Robert to the parents. When Robert told them in Spanish that they were not only rebuilding the school, but hiring three new teachers, a shout of joy went up among them. Cav found himself grinning and knew it was Lia's serenity that kept everyone on calm. He marveled at her power and influence over people.

At first, Cav thought it was just with him, but now, as Lia interacted with the parents, he realized she was a natural leader. She could effectively influence her troops, whoever and wherever they might be.

The children had released Dilara and Robert, seeking their particular set of parents and everyone was asking Lia questions. He had a sudden feeling of gratitude that Tanner and the others were responsible for the entire group, allowing him to focus solely on Lia.

The breeze was humid, and Cav picked up the scent of the nearby jungle. The humidity had curled Lia's short hair even more, and Cav noticed the blush of pink in her cheeks as she spoke animatedly to the parents. Sometimes, to help Lia with an answer, Dilara would answer a question, or Robert would. Neither of them wanted to be the center of attention. They, like Cav, had realized quickly that these parents relied heavily on Lia's calm leadership.

Lia began to organize the parents, asking some of the women to contact the other children's parents. She gave them the name of a nearby resort, La Orquídea, "The Orchid," hired by Robert's team to "loan" them five separate rooms where children from various grade levels could go to school five days a week. The resort was being paid handsomely for their help.

She then asked the mothers to tell the other mothers that she needed help in the classrooms daily. If they could organize help for her, Lia would teach the material for each class. Although she wasn't a certified teacher, Lia remembered the lesson plans. Further, Robert's team had already obtained books, new desks and chairs for each of those five rooms. Everything would be taught from the books the children had been using, but now, everything would be new.

Dilara had made sure that new coloring books, crayons, paints, sketching pads and other creative tools were also included in the huge van that had driven up with the armada. A woman at the resort had been hired to fix two snacks and lunch for the children, taking that responsibility off Lia's shoulders.

And speaking of snacks, Lia's stomach was growling! In two days, she told the parents, the bus would show up at the same time to pick up their children and drive them to Orquídea Resort for a day's worth of schooling and activities.

The parents came forward and hugged Lia and Dilara, crying and thanking both of them for their loyalty to their precious children.

Turning away, Lia caught a tender look from Cav's, but just as quickly, it was gone. She was finding that when they were alone, he didn't wear that professional, game face. Walking over to him, she said, "Robert just said that we're all going to the Tabacon Resort for an early dinner."

"Fine," he said, placing his hand beneath her elbow, guiding her toward him.

As tired as she was, Lia felt heat where his hand briefly rested. She wanted his touch, looked forward to those unexpected times. Why had she not seen disgust in his eyes over her scars? Never once had she seen Cav look repulsed over them as all other men had.

Even Tanner and his men looked long and hard at her face, and she believed they had a harsh reaction to what they saw. But Cav had never looked at her like they did.

She walked in front of him and he opened the van door. Climbing in, she felt exhaustion winnow through her, and she leaned back against the headrest, closing her eyes. Then, the driver's side door opened and she instantly felt Cav's quiet, powerful presence. She sighed.

"Did you put your seat belt on?" he asked solicitously.

"Oh…" and she sat up, frowning. "I forgot…"

"You're whipped," he said, putting the van in gear as Tanner's SUV slowly moved out. "The resort isn't far from here. Too bad you can't get a quick nap."

Touched by his concern, she glanced over at Cav. He still had his dark glasses on, so she couldn't see his beautiful eyes in their shades of green, gold and umber. "Me, too. I'll get it tonight."

"What else do you have to do after dinner?"

"Robert and Dilara want me to join them for a last meeting at the resort to iron out all the details."

Scowling, Cav muttered, "Don't they realize how beat you are? They didn't go through a life-and-death situation five days ago." He was feeling damned protective of her. "Can't they schedule this meeting for tomorrow morning or something? Give you some time to rest?" He felt irritable, acting more like a mother hen toward Lia than a bodyguard. His was not to question. And he was and dammit, he couldn't help but become protective of her under the circumstances.

"I agree," she said, smiling faintly. "But Robert is leaving after the meeting for San José, and Dilara will stay here with me for the next few days, helping me sort out everything. She'll make sure I have enough people to help me pull this schooling off."

"Robert's a busy man."

"So is Dilara. But she wants to meet the new teachers who are coming up two days from now."

"And it all falls on your shoulders," he said, turning onto the major asphalt road that led in a north-westerly direction away from La Fortuna. Very soon, the armada was entering thick jungle that hugged both sides of the road. Traffic was dense and Cav knew there were almost forty resorts in this area.

"Hey," she said, patting her shoulders. "I was born with a strong set of these."

"So was I, but it's damned nice sometimes to shuck the load and just rest for a while," he told her.

Lia felt his warm energy surrounding her, infusing her with his strength. Cav really cared. "Do all contractors care like you do?"

Cav cocked his head, slanting a glance her way for a second. "What?"

Opening her hands, she said, "Your concern is really evident. It feels real. I was just wondering if part of your job is to do this, to make me feel good even though I'm exhausted."

His hands gripped the wheel a little tighter as he crafted his answer. "Every contractor is different, Lia. Yes, there are security procedures we all follow, but I guess the personality of the individual contractor plays a big part."

In his case, it was a lot more. Cav knew he didn't dare reveal his personal interest in Lia. That would be the end of his PSD and General Culver would haul his ass out of here so fast it would make him dizzy.

Worse, Lia had so much on her plate, dealing with the shock of the attack, the loss of two good friends, that he needed to keep her stable, not add to her stress.

Hell, he didn't even know if she had a special someone in her life. Cav had to think she did, and he needed to find out sooner or later. Preferably, sooner.

"Well, I like your style of PSD," she murmured, giving him a shy look. "You must have been the oldest in your family, taking care of your other siblings."

"I was an only kid, like you," he murmured, not wanting to go there. "Sorry, but I can't talk personally right now," he apologized, lessening the harshness of his tone.

"Sure, I understand." And she did.

Two miles away, the resort of La Orquídea sat on a small hill, the jungle cut away from its white, gleaming walls in the low western sun's rays. It was a huge resort, and soon the convoy was inside the black, wrought iron fence that surrounded it. He saw a lot of tourists, children and a number of two and three-story buildings. Tanner pulled up in front of a set of buildings near the edge of the huge, bustling complex.

As he parked and got out, Lia dutifully remained in the van, waiting while Cav walked around to her door. Little did she know he had only one wish: To get her safely home for some well-earned rest.

CHAPTER 7

L IA FELT LIKE as if she were going to fall over from exhaustion as Cav opened the door to her house. It was nearly dark, and they could hear the hooting of the monkeys nearby. The last of the tropical birds were sending out a final song as she stumbled into the living room.

Cav closed the door and waited there, girding himself for whatever reaction Lia would have to him staying in this house with her. He'd been trying to broach the topic off and on all day, but there was never time for him to pull her aside and tell her about it. She looked fragile, with dark shadows beneath her gray eyes. Lia plopped down on the couch opposite the door, pulled off her sandals and lifted her left foot, rubbing her toes gently.

"Listen," he said, remaining near the door, "you need to know that I'll be staying with you in this house every night from now on, Lia."

Frowning, Lia stopped rubbing her aching toes. "What?"

Cav gestured around. "Just tell me where I can sleep. I'll try to stay out of your way. My job is to ensure no one comes in either door to get to you."

Her eyes widened, her heart slamming downward as she digested his words. "You're staying HERE?" For whatever reason, Lia thought he'd be staying somewhere else. Then, her pulse ratcheted up as she studied him. "Are you serious, Cav?" While a part of her was actually thrilled with the idea, a bigger part was in panic mode.

What about her weekly nightmares? She had them at least twice a week, and her terrified screams would scare him to death. Worse, she'd be humiliated.

Lia felt him tense, anticipating her resistance.

"I'm dead serious," Cav assured her. "I was given this detail to shadow you, Lia, remember? I told you all about it on the drive up here earlier."

"But," she said, collapsing back into the couch, "I thought…well I didn't know it meant you were staying here, in my house…" and her voice trailed off.

Cav shrugged and looked around. "It means exactly that. General Culver wants me close to you at all times, since Medina probably has a hit out on you."

And he'd make sure she'd stay safe, no matter what happened. Lia considered her situation, and said haltingly, "But this house is very small for two people."

"Hey, the couch looks good to me." Cav pulled off his jacket, removed the pistol out from behind his back and set it on a small desk near the door.

Lia's weary face betrayed her inability to deal with her situation right now. The truth was, a killer was hunting her, and Cav didn't want to emphasize that point tonight. Both of them needed rest.

"Look," he said, keeping his voice low, "this can work. You just go about your normal routine and I'll make a point of staying out of the way. I'll take this couch if that's okay with you. How many bathrooms do you have?"

"One," she muttered unhappily.

"Okay, no problem." Cav looked to the left towards the kitchen, with its small, round table flanked by two chairs. "I need to case this place and check for bugs."

Too tired to argue, Lia nodded wearily. "Will it take long?"

"No," he promised. "I'm quick."

Lia watched him walk toward the kitchen, checking the window, opening and then closing and locking it. He disappeared into her bedroom, and she grimaced. Her bed was a mess and she hadn't made it in days. He probably thought she was a slob. That wasn't like her, but the last five days had been chaotic.

Cav walked soundlessly, despite his height and bulk, through the kitchen and down the hall, testing the rear door. Within five minutes, he'd cased the place and returned to the living room. He took the gray, overstuffed chair opposite the couch.

"No bugs," he reported. "Do you have air conditioning?"

"Yes," she pointed to the wall. "There."

"You don't run it unless you're home, do you?"

"Right. Electricity is expensive here."

"What do you want it set at?"

"65 degrees. Does that work for you?"

He nodded. "That works," he said, rising and setting the thermostat and turning it on.

"I'm so tired my words are slurring," Lia admitted, slowly rising. "I'm going to turn in."

"Go ahead," Cav urged. "I'll stay out here until you're in bed."

Lia hesitated at the entrance to the kitchen. "I have to keep my bedroom door open or I won't get any cool air in there."

"That's fine," Cav said. Lia looked haunted, the skin across her cheeks taut, eyes closing from exhaustion.

"There's an extra pillow and sheets in the linen closet near the back door. Help yourself." Because she was so tired, she felt emotionally numb. She'd felt this way since the attack, and for a split second, she almost blurted, *Stay with me. Hold me. Make my nightmares go away.*

How stupid. Cav might be a brave warrior, but he couldn't take on her personal battles, especially with her toxic past. No one could do it but her.

Lia couldn't shake her sense that she needed him. It was almost physical and she turned, afraid she'd say something. Damn, she resented her weakness! So she padded barefoot down the hall, the tiles soothing to her, and coolly called over her shoulder, "Good night, Cav. Thanks."

Cav lay in the darkness, a sliver of moon shining through the gauzy white curtains drawn across the two windows in the living room. The couch, thank God, wasn't soft. It was hard and nicely supported his long back.

He couldn't sleep for a lot of reasons, even though he, too, was exhausted. In fact, he'd snapped wide-awake after Lia had left the bathroom and showered, the scent of her still haunting him.

The fragrance of the soap reminded him of the sweet smell of plumeria from Hawaii. It lingered in the large bathroom, which had a tub and shower in it. Cav had an acute sense of smell. His SEAL team often accused him of being able to smell Taliban half a mile away if the wind was right.

Now, closing his eyes, Lia's scent in the room drove him crazy, made him want what he couldn't have. Her fragrance stirred him at his deepest levels, not just the physical one.

Groaning to himself, he knew he needed to find a woman—and soon. Lia was off limits because she was his detail. His job was to provide her safety and protection, not take her to bed. What the hell was going on with him?

Cav knew plenty of willing women at Coronado when he was a SEAL. All he had to do was walk into a SEAL bar and there they were, ripe, willing and eager. In contrast, Lia was anything but ready. Her reserve cautioned him that something terrible had occurred to her, even before the school was burned down five days ago.

WHAT had happened to her? And how did she get those scars?

Sitting up, he wiped his smarting eyes and glared at the dark, shadowy front door. The clock on the small table read 0200. Getting up, he pulled on his chinos and his Nikes, and then went to the weapon's bag he'd stored down at the end of the couch. Now was as good a time as any to scout outside the house, listen to the normal night sounds, and see if anything dangerous was moving around.

Pulling a set of night goggles over his head, he let them rest against his chest. Then, he picked up his M4 and quietly moved to the rear door. He wanted to check in on Lia in her bedroom, but resisted.

Outside, the cooling breeze moved past him as he quietly closed the door behind him. The house stood on a flat plain. In the distance, he saw glimmering sulfur lights along the main. Remaining in the shadows, his M4 in a chest harness, he stood still and listened to the familiar jungle sounds. A few birds squawked, thunder rumbled in the distance, and he saw the flash of lightning many miles west. The breeze felt good against his skin and he carefully perused the jungle tree line. If anyone were going to attack, they would come from that direction, no question. It would be foolish for the drug soldiers to walk up to Lia's house out in the open.

Pulling up his NVA's, night vision goggles, he settled them across his eyes and flicked them on. Everything became two-dimensional and a grainy green at that point. But he could see everything. If a shadow moved along that tree line, he'd spot it in a heartbeat. Liking his location at the corner of the house far from Lia's bedroom, he stood and communed with the night and its silent denizens.

At one point, he saw a jaguar poke his head out of the cover of the tree line, but the cat quickly reversed his course when a dog in the village began howling. Like the shadow he was, the jaguar melted back into the darkness.

Bats were everywhere, flitting across the low-hanging sky. The milky opalescence of the moon filtered through the thinner spots here and there. It was easy to squat back on his haunches, the M4 across his knees, arms on top of it, to watch and listen.

For the next hour, at different points around the house, Cav slowly moved into another position, crouched, waited and watched.

By the time 3 A.M. arrived, he'd made a full circuit, convinced that the only thing moving were the insects, the bats and predators deep in the jungle.

The dog that had been barking had stopped. The rustle of the leaves against one another as a thunderstorm moved in their direction convinced him to go back inside.

Inside, Cav closed the door, locking it. Frowning, he remained tense as a faraway sound drifted toward him. What was he hearing? Cocking his head, he realized it was coming from Lia's bedroom, or close to it.

He moved silently down the hall and halted abruptly as he saw Lia. She was in a light blue cotton gown that fell to her knees, and she was walking back and forth between the bedroom and the kitchen. Her eyes were wide open.

What the hell?

Cav watched her. Although her eyes were open, she wasn't blinking. Confused, he wondered if she saw him. She was breathing hard, her hand against her chest, just walking back and forth.

Sleepwalking? Was that it? Cav's gut tightened over that possibility. Lia's hair was mussed, making her look very young, and the open neck of her gown revealed her slender collarbones and long neck. Then, he saw long scars on her calves and her arms, which she kept hidden by day.

She was walking to the sink, washing her hands, drying them on a towel, turning and then walking to her bedroom.

He heard her whimper from time to time, saying nothing he could make sense of. Cav watched her wash her hand five times in fifteen minutes. Now, he was convinced Lia was sleepwalking, because if she were really awake, she'd have seen him standing here in the doorway of the kitchen.

Cav felt Lia's pain. How many times had his mother told him that she'd found him sleepwalking as a child? *Far too many.* Cav never remembered any of those times, but his mother had smiled sweetly at him, fluffed his hair and said that she'd had a conversation with him while he was sleepwalking. Cav never recalled any of those conversations.

He just wished he knew what Lia was whimpering about. Her sounds were like those of an animal caught with its paw in a painful trap. He saw her brow scrunch and heard her breathe fast and hard. Then, she was washing her hands, again and again. What had happened to her?

His mind moved back to those times when his mother would gently tease him at breakfast the next morning. "You were sleepwalking again," she'd tease, and then asked," Don't you remember talking to me?"

Apparently, she'd always ask him where he was going, and he'd reply that he was running away from his father. Where would he go? Anywhere to get away from him.

Cav always felt humiliated and stupid for not remembering, because above all, he believed his mother. She had always been good to him, loving and trying her best to protect him from his druggie dad.

Now, Lia walked back into the bedroom. Should he stand in the kitchen so she would be fully aware of him? Should he talk to her? What would it do? Would it scare the hell out of her? Make her scream? Awaken her?

Cav had researched online the causes of sleepwalking. What he read, he didn't like. Certain foods, sleep deprivation, traumatic incidents, or Post Traumatic Stress Disorder, otherwise known as PTSD, could cause it.

Grimly, he wondered how often this occurred in Lia, and how long it had been going on. And of course, she wouldn't know because sleepwalkers never did.

Cav had learned that when he had a sleepwalking episode, it was hell waking up the next morning. His head felt as if it was caked with mud, and he didn't even have the strength to pull himself awake. All his senses were distorted, slow to come online, and he felt tired.

As he grew older, he began to see his episodes were directly linked to fights with his father when he would be beaten, yelled at, or hit with that damned thick belt he always wore around his waist.

Was Lia's sleepwalking due to the trauma of the school burning down? Could it be the loss of her good friends, Maria and Sophia? Cav thought it was entirely possible, based upon his own experiences. A SEAL shrink who had talked to Cav after a harrowing mission had asked him if he ever had such episodes. He didn't want to tell her, but finally, he admitted to it "once or twice."

She smiled sympathetically and somehow got inside his head, won his trust and listened to him spill his guts out. He'd been afraid he'd be kicked out of the SEALs, but nothing happened. The shrink had held their conversation private and sacred; she was the first woman he'd ever trusted after his mother.

He owed that SEAL shrink, Dr. Amanda Hunter, a debt of thanks. She told him it was a normal response to being under threat. Some people, she'd told him, acted out what had happened. Some people dreamed about an event time and again until the shock of the incident wore off. Sleepwalking was just another way of doing the same thing if it occurred because of a trauma or shock. It was a way of healing the wound that scarred one's soul. And by doing that, it was a good thing.

Eventually, most people stopped sleepwalking once they removed themselves from the source of the threat.

Cav had found that true for himself, and to his knowledge, he'd never sleepwalked again after leaving his father's house.

Now, Cav hoped that Lia had finally gone back to bed. But she hadn't. Again, she came out of her room in that same trance-like state. It was actually the deepest sleep a human being could know, which is why people never remembered the incident.

He slowly walked into the kitchen, watching her closely for a reaction. Her eyes were glazed, unseeing as she headed to the sink.

"Lia?" he asked softly, "What are you doing?"

She hesitated at the sink, lifting her hands, opening them and slowly turning them in front of herself. "My hands…they're bloody. The cuts…they hurt so much. I'm bleeding. I need to stop it. I need to wash the blood off…"

"Okay," he rasped, "go ahead and clean yourself up."

She opened the faucets, placing her hands beneath them.

Cav watched, distressed, as she washed each finger separately, making whimpering sounds as she did so. The soap dish was there, but she didn't see it, intent only on washing her hands again and again.

Finally, she stopped, pulled the towel of a nearby hook, and slowly patted them dry.

"Lia? Why are your hands bloody?" He saw her brow draw down, her hands stilling in the towel as she considered his question.

"The men…they attacked me. I thought they were going to kill me. I-I fought back. My hands…my hands are so cut up——," and she sobbed, gripping them within the damp towel.

"Lia, it's all right. They've stopped bleeding. You're safe now. The men are gone." It took everything Cav had to stop from walking that half step forward and pulling her into his arms. But he knew not to touch her. To do so could cause major shock. Talking to the person was okay, but not touching them or trying to awaken them from that deep, unconscious state.

"R-really?" she whispered, pulling the towel away, lifting her long slender hand, studying her fingers as she opened and closed them.

"Yes, they're fine. You've washed the blood off. You need to go to bed now and sleep. Your hands are fine, okay?"

She sighed and placed the towel on the hook. "Okay…." and she turned and shuffled off towards her bedroom.

Cav followed to be sure she indeed got into bed. She sat down on the edge of the mattress, staring off into her own private world.

"I need you to sleep, Lia. Come and lie down, okay? I'll cover you up."

"Oh," she murmured, pushing her palms against her nightgown. "I-I'm cold…I'm always cold now…so cold…."

Cav stepped over to her, knowing she didn't see him but could only hear him. "Come on, you'll be warm soon."

Nodding, Lia lifted her legs and pushed them beneath the sheet and thin blanket. She lay protectively on her side, drawing her knees up toward her chest. Even in the shadowy gray light, Cav could see a long, savage scar that scored her right calf from top to bottom.

He lightly placed the blanket across her shoulders. "There," he said comfortingly, forcing himself not to touch her as she closed her eyes, burrowing her head into the pillow, gripping it with her hands. "You'll be fine now, Lia. Go to sleep. Your hands are clean. You're safe."

CHAPTER 8

THE STRONG AROMA of freshly made coffee made Lia's nose twitch. She moaned, pressing her head deeper into her pillow, not wanting to wake up. Slowly, she moved her legs outward, giving a luxurious stretch beneath the covers. Her fingers moved against the pillow and she heard other sounds drifting into the opened door of her bedroom. She thought she heard soft classical music drifting from somewhere, but she wasn't sure.

It felt so good to languish between sleep and wakefulness, and for some reason, she felt safe...really safe. It was an alien feeling to her, and it actually pulled her toward the surface of wakefulness, abandoning the warm cocoon of further sleep.

When she forced open her eyes, she saw sunlight peeking here and there around the drawn blind on her window. Huh! She never slept this long, what was going on? Lia hadn't slept so deeply in so long that it simply felt luxurious to stay in bed dozing.

She heard a soft knock on her open door and turned her head in that direction. Cav stood in the doorway, holding a cup of coffee invitingly towards her. Instantly, she felt that strong wave of protection emanating from him, encircling her, shielding her from the dangers that swirled around her.

"Interested in some coffee?" he asked, holding it out to her.

Lia groaned and sat up, suddenly realizing that he could see the scars on her arms. Her first reaction was to grab the sheet and haul it up and over her, but she felt silly even considering it. Her nightgown was sleeveless.

She drew up her knees and whispered, "Yes, but later. I need to wake up. What time is it?" and she twisted toward the bed stand. Her eyes widened when she saw it was eight A.M.

Oh, my God! She was late!

Before she could leap out of bed, Cav gave her an intense look, walked into her bedroom, and placed the cup of coffee on her night table.

"Relax," he growled. "Dilara said that she'd meet you at noon over at Tabacon."

"What?" she murmured, rubbing her eyes confused.

"I talked earlier with Dilara," he said, halting briefly at the doorway, his hand resting on the jamb. "She said for you to sleep in and take it easy this morning. I'll drive you over to Tabacon at eleven-thirty." Cav quietly closed the door, leaving her to get up when she was ready.

Stunned by the turn of events and relieved Cav had closed the door, Lia scooted out of bed. She hung her legs over the edge, her soles connecting with the cooler wooden floor. Reaching gratefully for the fragrant coffee, she slid it between her hands, taking small sips. It tasted so good!

Outside, she heard the jungle sounds of morning. Her mind bucked and resisted, urging her to return to sleep.

Glancing at the clock, Lia realized she had slept nearly twelve hours and she'd had no nightmare. Thank God for that! She lived in abject fear that she'd start screaming, scare the hell out of Cav and embarrass herself. She needed to warn him about that, but she'd been too tired last night.

Humming with pleasure, she closed her eyes, sipped the coffee, and realized that for once she didn't have to rush off to work. Then, she was struck with the memory of her loss of Maria and Sophia. Her two friends had been brutally murdered.

Her mind jolted awake and she realized that Cav had been sleeping out on that couch in the living room. He was her "guard dog." Lia, while appreciating his adherence to his responsibilities, still wasn't comfortable with him being in her home. Could she convince Robert Culver to change the PSD orders? But then, how could he keep her safe? She'd met Medina twice, and a cold shudder worked through her.

Cav was definitely the lesser of two evils. In fact, in her heart she knew Cav was the opposite of evil. Not only was he being paid to shield her and put his life on the line for her, he had also looked at her this morning with real caring and tenderness. It had surprised her, and his mouth, usually thinned, was more relaxed.

Cav was just too good-looking, Lia decided with a sigh, feeling the coffee working its magic on her drowsy brain. He had changed into a dark green polo shirt that stretched across his powerful shoulders and chest. Today, he wore jeans instead of chinos, and they hugged his lower body in the most delicious way.

Lia shook her head and reminded herself again that men were turned off by how she looked. Just because she pined for a genuine relationship didn't mean she'd ever get one, so she had to stop fantasizing about it.

Now, she was sure he'd seen the scars on both her arms. *What a mess.* She was afraid that Cav had found her pitiful to look at, thus the softness in his look was probably pity.

For Lia, it was one more load to carry. And she didn't want Cav asking her how she'd gotten those scars, either. Would he? A chill came over her as she considered it, never wanting to go there.

She'd tried it once and gotten rebuffed. There wouldn't be a second time. Right now, she felt too fragile emotionally to handle Cav if he rejected her, too. What must he think having to guard her now that he'd seen more of her scars?

Finishing the coffee, Lia felt as if she'd been given a momentary reprieve from the hard fourteen-hour days she knew were ahead of her. Warmth flowed through her as she stood up and pulled on her seersucker robe. It fell to the tops of her ankles and would hide her body, should Cav still be out there. She had to get to the bathroom to get a shower and hoped he wasn't in the kitchen. Slowly, she opened the door.

She was greeted by the scent of bacon frying, and she tightened the sash around her waist, her curiosity piqued. She'd had no bacon in her fridge, so where had it come from? As she walked down the short hall, she stood uncertainly at the edge of the kitchen. Cav was standing over the stove, working two skillets. One had bacon frying in it, and the other held cut-up potatoes.

Cav twisted a look in her direction. "Interested in breakfast?"

"It sure smells good," Lia admitted, drawing closer. She made sure the collar of her robe was up to hide her throat. "I didn't know you could cook."

He gave her a modest smile, flipping some of the frying potatoes with a spatula. "I learned to either cook, or starve. I'm no chef, but I do think I make a pretty mean breakfast." He gestured to a small bag of potatoes sitting on the counter. "I figured since Dilara was letting you rest up this morning, the least I could do was spoil you with my limited skills and make you breakfast."

All her fear dissolved when she saw him drop the game face he usually wore. Her heart flew open and she was left without words, because that same flame of tenderness was in his glance towards her. Gripping the collar of her robe, she whispered, "That's really nice of you…"

"Why don't you have a shower?" He pointed to the coffee pot. "Grab yourself a second cup, and take your time because you actually have some this morning. How do you like your eggs?"

She came and stood near the counter, watching him cook. "Where on earth did you get the bacon?"

"I had one of the security guys bring it to me earlier."

"Oh…" She licked her lips and said, "I like hard scrambled eggs. Can you make them that way?"

"I'll try." He cut her a boyish grin. "Like I said, I'm pretty limited when it comes to cooking, but I'll do my best."

Cav looked clean-shaven, his hair still damp from an early shower. He looked good in her small kitchen, the breadth of his shoulders reminding her of his underlying power as a security contractor. Although she saw no weapons around, and he wasn't wearing his jacket, she knew they must be nearby.

It was nice not to see them out; it only reminded Lia of the fragile peace that hovered over the area. She was perfectly aware that Medina had a hit out on her and that it was only a matter of time before…

Managing to give Cav a warm look, she murmured, "I'll be out in a little bit. Thanks…"

Cav said nothing as she hurried for the bathroom down the hall. He was sorry that she felt she had to grip that collar around her throat to hide her scar. As he took the potatoes off the burner, he heard the door to the bathroom quietly close.

Every cell in his body was in protection mode where Lia was concerned. After her sleepwalking incident, he'd barely slept; shocked at the number of scars he'd seen on her body. She didn't seem to realize she'd had a sleepwalking episode, which didn't surprise Cav. The shadows beneath her eyes last night were gone this morning. If anything, Lia looked well rested, and for that, he was grateful.

He was damned glad he'd called Dilara Culver at six A.M., woke her up out of her sleep and told her that Lia needed some time off. Now, he put the bacon onto a plate and turned off the stove. If Dilara was annoyed that he'd awakened her early at the Tabacon Resort, she didn't show it. Instead, when Cav had told her Lia needed some downtime because she was stressed out, Dilara had quickly agreed and moved the nine A.M. meeting to noon.

Cav thanked her and wanted to ask Dilara if she knew what had happened to Lia, but nixed the question. Right now, he wanted everyone focused on the school, moving the children to the other resort, and getting the new teachers on board. His personal need-to-know could wait.

Dammit, he ached to hold Lia. She looked like a lost waif in that robe of hers this morning. It was a thin blue cotton robe that hid her, that's true. But in another way, showed him her slender, womanly curves, too. The scars bothered him a lot. Who had done this to her? What had happened to her? He'd seen her hands before last night, aware of white scars, puckered flesh in the webbing and hadn't put it together until their conversation. Someone had violently attacked her. She had defensive wounds of fighting back, which explained the amount of scars and scar tissue on her beautiful, slender hands. Cav grieved for her. He wondered if Lia had anyone to help or support her after it had happened. She talked warmly about her parents. After it happened, had they been there for her? He hoped so.

He read the shame in her eyes as she clutched the material to her slender neck.

Cav went back to the scene the night before. It was clear that Lia did not want him to see her scars, but while she was sleepwalking, he'd seen them on her arms, legs and hands. Where else had she been cut? With the number of cuts on her, it was lucky she'd survived at all!

Cav knew how to use a knife to do lethal damage to an enemy, and he knew that one cut across her neck was enough to sever a carotid artery and bleed someone out in a matter of minutes.

Bothered deeply, he frowned as he brought down two plates. He heard the shower running, glad that Lia had extra time to relax. He'd set the table for her, put some bread in the toaster on the counter, found some butter and jam in her fridge to give her a nice, low stress breakfast. The woman deserved that much, given what she'd already gone through.

As he set the table, Cav knew a previous life-and-death experience had occurred with Lia. Now, she'd had another one six days ago. Personally, as an operator, he knew a lethal confrontation with the Taliban had played out in his nightly dreams for years. And he also knew that if a new event occurred, it would stir up past events.

They would converge like the perfect storm in his unconscious, and then he'd have nightmares.

Maybe Lia sleepwalked instead. Cav knew that unless Lia broached it, as a contractor, he couldn't get personal. He was there to protect, not interrogate or become a father confessor.

Dammit, he cared about this woman whether he wanted to honestly admit it or not. She was a kind person who was passionate working for Delos charity and helping children and destitute families. There was NOTHING not to like about Lia. Not one damned thing. The scars didn't bother him. Hell, he had so many that as far as Cav was concerned, they told a story, that was all.

He heard the door open. Looking up from setting the small table, he saw Lia had washed her hair, the curls dark around her oval face. She still wore that robe, and still held the collar closed at her neck.

Straightening, he said, "Do you feel like you're among the living now?"

"Much more so," she admitted with a half smile. "I'll get dressed and be right out."

Cav could smell the soap she'd used on her skin, and he'd also picked up her womanly scent as she passed through the kitchen. "Okay, see you in a bit. You want one or two pieces of toast?" he asked casually, masking his other thoughts.

Hesitating at the door to her bedroom, Lia turned. "Oh…I'm not really that hungry, Cav."

He straightened. "You're underweight, Lia. You need to try and eat more. How about one piece of toast?" and he held her gaze. Her eyes were clear now and she was awake and functioning fully. Those dark curls only made her look more like a girl, not the mature woman Cav knew she was. He also saw that the scar on her face was raised, and needed some lotion on it.

"I'll try to have some toast," she agreed.

"I'll make your hard scrambled eggs now."

"That would be great. Thanks…"

Cav watched the door close. It was obvious to him that Lia was completely uncomfortable with him underfoot. She was going to hide not only her scars from him, but herself as well. He could see it in her eyes. Only when she was truly tired did he see the real Lia. Then, she didn't have the energy to pull up the wall she was hiding behind right now.

Cav told himself to relax, to give her time to adjust to his presence, but it was tough. He realized Lia had no other emotional support right now, and he wanted to give her what she needed. Last night had been a special hell for him because his first reaction was to hold Lia and replace the terror on her face with trust. Of course, that was impossible, so he had to stand there and helplessly witness her repeated hand washing.

Just as he put the bowl of potatoes on the table along with the bacon, Lia came out of the bedroom. Glancing up, he saw she was wearing a set of loose jeans and a bright yellow tee that brought out the red and gold highlights in her damp hair. He was pleased to see that she looked more relaxed than he'd seen her so far.

"What can I do to help?" she offered with a smile.

"Nothing," he said, pulling out a chair for her. "Sit down and enjoy a cup of coffee." He met her gaze and saw the warmth in it, and privately swore he saw something else too, but couldn't define it. "I'll get those eggs going," he said briskly.

He poured her a fresh cup of coffee, setting it down in front of her. The toast popped up and he brought it over on a plate. "Butter and jam there," he said, pointing toward it.

"Why do I feel you're like a grumpy old mother hen?" she turned, meeting his gaze. Indeed, Lia felt his care and she was lapping it up like a starved animal. It had been so long since anyone had cared for her like this. Oh, when she was home, her parents did, but she hadn't seen them in over a year. She was long overdue for a visit.

"You're my detail. It's my job to take care of you," he said firmly.

"I didn't know it extended to you becoming my cook."

Cav chuckled and turned to the stove, grabbing four eggs and cracking them. "You need a little TLC, Lia. Let me at least do that for you every now and again." Cav was taking a helluva chance by saying that. It wasn't proper. He was supposed to be a shadow in her life, pretty much unseen, not a companion who traded teasing remarks with her.

The flush of pink across her cheeks endeared her to him even more. Cav noticed the pucker on her scar was less pronounced, figuring that she'd applied some kind of special lotion to it. Turning away, he devoted his attention solely to scrambling the eggs because if he didn't, he was going to get way too familiar with her, and that wasn't a good thing.

His heart, however, yearned for just that kind of connection with this woman. He couldn't look at her long, graceful fingers now without seeing blood on them, hearing the terror in her voice, seeing it in her eyes.

And through it all, she was behaving normally. Cav found that amazing. It spoke of her inner strength and resolve. More than anything, that impressed him. It took real courage to keep on going, to try to live after nearly dying. He knew that he hadn't done as well as Lia had. At least she was out in the world, being sociable and doing something important.

Him? Hell, he hid in a tiny apartment in Lima between assignments, drowning his pain in pisco sours at least once a week and numbing himself so he didn't have to confront his painful history as a SEAL.

CHAPTER 9

LIA TRIED TO tamp down her impatience with Cav's attempts to mother her. At the same time, she appreciated that he cared so much. They sat at her small table for breakfast, and it was lovely and intimate. She had put a spoonful of the eggs and potatoes on her plate, along with one piece of bacon. Cav, on the other hand, had piled his plate with food.

"Is that all you're going to eat?" he asked, pointing his fork at her bright green plate.

Joy bubbled up within her, and she smiled at the concern on his face. "What? I don't eat like the lumberjack you are." He'd put shredded cheese on top of the eggs and from the way he was wolfing them down, they tasted incredible. She saw his eyes light with amusement as he dug into the fare.

"You're skinny, Lia. You need to put more meat on your bones."

"Oh, I see. And you're my mother, now?" She saw his grin deepen, but he said nothing, shoveling in his food like a starving man. Actually, today Lia did have an appetite. Over the past week, food hadn't sat well in her stomach, and most mornings, she ended up vomiting.

Lia was no stranger to that reaction. She'd always had a sensitive stomach when emotionally upset. But this morning Cav's quiet, strong presence made her feel really safe, and her stomach was growling, telling her she needed to eat. The first few bites were tentative because Lia would know instantly if she were going to deal with an upset stomach or not.

"Have you always eaten like a bird?" Cav goaded.

Lia saw the care in his eyes, despite his playful teasing. It was like a warm blanket surrounding her. She could get used to this, she thought. But then, someday, Cav would leave and she'd be alone again, as always.

"Just…sometimes," she admitted between bites.

"Is there a reason for it?"

She watched him slather strawberry jam across two pieces of his toast on the edge of his plate. "I was born with a sensitive stomach."

"What does that mean?"

She shrugged. "My Mom has one, too. I guess I inherited it."

He studied her. "What does a sensitive stomach do?"

Lia grimaced. "It's not polite table talk, Cav." She saw him scowl, but he returned to his food. Feeling guilty because she knew he was genuinely concerned, she whispered, "When I get emotionally upset about something, I get nauseous."

Cav nodded. He knew what a sensitive stomach was, but pretended ignorance. Somehow, he had to draw Lia out, get her to talk and to trust him. His first task was to find out where and how he could goad her into talking. He'd seen the guilt in her eyes when she'd tried to deflect his question.

"I'm sorry," he said. "That can't be a very pleasant symptom of stress."

Her mouth quirked. "It's not, believe me."

"Does it happen all the time?"

"No, thank God, it doesn't."

"Just on big things? Like this attack by Medina?" He saw her gray eyes grow dark and he cursed himself. Not wanting to cause Lia pain was a major objective for Cav, but how else was he to plumb her depths and find out who she was and what made her that way?

"Yes…" and she felt the grief coming up. She turned her attention on the food Cav had prepared for her, forcing herself to eat more. Miraculously, her stomach didn't roil this time around when Medina's name was mentioned. Lia found that amazing!

"What are some of your happiest memories when you were younger?"

She smiled a little. "Riding Goldy bareback with just a halter. Racing along the edge of one of my Dad's sugar beet fields, the wind whipping through my hair, my hands outstretched. I loved the feeling of the wind tearing between my fingers. The way Goldy galloped, that wonderful rocking motion."

"That's a nice image you just created," Cav said, touched by the wistful quality of her voice, the dreamy look that came into her gray eyes. It just made him want to kiss those soft, full lips of hers even more. "Do you get to ride around here at all?"

"No, I'm way too busy."

"But some of the resorts offer horseback rides?"

"Yes, some do."

"Have you ever gone over there to ride?"

"No, I'm way too busy with the kids and the school."

"I see. So if you had time, would you?"

"I'd love to."

Cav finished off all his breakfast and noticed that Lia was continuing to eat. He'd purposely left some scrambled eggs in a bowl, and he saw her put some more on her plate.

"Finish them off, Lia. I'm done," he told her.

Lia nodded and scraped them onto her plate. "Do you like horses, Cav?"

Heartened that she was opening up a little, he pushed the empty plate aside and pulled over his cup of coffee. "Well, unlike you, I didn't live in farm country."

"Do you like horses, though?"

"I like all animals." He added wryly, "It's just the two-legged variety that I don't trust." He saw her eyes deepen with sympathy.

"All two-leggeds?"

"Well," he hedged, "maybe not ALL."

"Do you trust me?"

The question hit him hard. Cav didn't want to destroy the small amount of trust he'd worked so hard to build with her. "Yes, I do. I did from the moment I met you."

He saw her tilt her chin, her eyes narrowing slightly as she studied. The silence between them grew. Cav would have given anything to know what she was thinking.

"Seriously?"

A wry smile edged his lips. "Yeah, seriously."

"But how could you *know* you could trust me?"

"SEAL intuition." He watched Lia digest that blunt statement. Cav rarely spoke about this part of being an operator. She looked confused, so he went a bit further.

"When you deal in life-and-death situations all the time," he told her quietly, "you develop this knowing, Lia. For example, I can feel when an enemy is near me, even if I can't see him yet. I just *know* he's there."

"Will you know *where* he is?"

"Sometimes I'll get a hit, and I'll look in a particular area first, but if it yields nothing, I'll look elsewhere until I can locate him."

"Wow!" she murmured, impressed, diving into her eggs.

Cav pushed the toast toward her and Lia glanced at him. "Are you like this with the people you actually trust? Do you always push their toast toward them?"

Chuckling, he said, "The people close to me know I'll do stuff like that. Yes."

"Have you always been a mother hen in disguise?"

He liked the radiance that he now saw in her eyes, and was delighted to see her opening up even more to him. He smiled back at her. "Pretty much. I guess you found me out."

"Is this part of what being my guard demands of you?"

"No. Like I said, operators are all different. I tend to want to natter around my detail."

"Natter?" she laughed, meeting his eyes.

Cav felt heat move through him like a warm sunbeam. For a moment he felt euphoric. He rarely felt happiness, but right now, hell, he was celebrating! Lia had finally come out from behind that massive wall, and her laugh was low and husky.

He had a sudden thought: Would she look that way when they made love? Cav found himself veering away from using the word "sex" with this woman because he wanted more—an emotional and mental connection with her. Sex was a physical release. But with Lia? He wanted her on every level. He wanted to absorb her, soak up that dreamy look in her eyes right now, hear her sighs, her cries of pleasure, knowing he could please her.

"I love the word, 'natter,'" Lia said. "What does it mean to you, Cav?"

Now it was his turn to blush. Dammit, he could feel the heat sweep up from his neck and into his face. "It was a term my mother always used," he admitted, his voice lowering. "I was a pretty quiet kid, and she'd draw me out by nattering."

"Talking?"

"Being chatty." He shrugged. "Sometimes I was pretty down on myself, and she'd see it and come and sit with me and just talk."

"What would she talk about?"

Cav felt that, suddenly, Lia had turned the tables on him. He was the one who was supposed to ask the insightful questions to gently draw her out. Now, it was his turn, and he realized that Lia needed this kind of feedback. He'd seen her blossom before when he'd openly talk to her about himself or his background.

"Oh, anything. She'd tell me about someone at work, their trials and troubles. Or she'd describe how a cardinal landed on the window of her office and pecked on it…stuff like that."

Cav did not want to go into his sordid adolescent years, nor did he want to lie to her. She had perked up and devoted her full attention to him, forgetting about the eggs momentarily.

"You need to finish your breakfast," he noted, pointing at the eggs still on her fork.

"Are you nattering at me again?" she grinned, and dutifully turned her attention to her food.

He chuckled. "I guess I am."

"You are your mother's son."

"Yeah, and it's a good feeling." And it was. He'd loved his mother fiercely until the day she'd died of a heart attack. He had been eighteen, a month away from joining the Navy, when it had happened.

Lia was eating well now. When she finished the eggs, she brought over the toast, pulling it apart and slathering butter over it.

"She used to tell me everyone needed a little nattering every now and then," Cav added with a slow smile.

"She obviously loved and cared about you very much," Lia said softly.

"You're the same way with children," he said, turning the tables back on her. "Yesterday, you were a mother hen with those kids who came running to see you."

Color warmed her cheeks. "You know, I've known these kids and their parents for four years. They're like family," she explained.

"I could tell."

She chewed on the toast and kept her gaze on him. "They deserve protection and help. Medina doesn't come up here often, but when he does, I see the whole village contract."

"What do you mean?"

"Medina drives fear into people and now you can see why. He

comes up here maybe four times a year, spends a week and then leaves. The adults are deathly afraid of him and their fears play out to their children. We saw kids with more upset stomachs, loss of appetite, and clingier behavior as a result."

"It makes sense," Cav said, remembering his own reaction to leaving school and having to go home to his abusive father. He'd always been a skinny kid growing up. Only when he left for the SEALs had he started to bloom. He gained fifty pounds in weight and muscle, and was happy living with his fellow SEALs.

But he understood as few others could what Lia was observing in her charges, who lived in a state of insecurity.

"I wish he would go away and never come back," Lia muttered, shaking her head. "He's pure evil…"

Cav decided to change the subject. "I'm impressed by how much those kids love you."

She rallied. "I feel like a spiritual aunt to them. They're my heart."

"And their parents seemed to know you very well, too."

"I'm a known quantity to this village and its people. I love being here. It makes me feel good to do something positive for so many."

Cav took a chance. "I imagine the man in your life doesn't mind sharing you with so many others."

Lia frowned. "I have no man in my life. The kids are my life, Cav. It's better that way."

"What about you? Are you married?" she asked, surprising him.

His brows lifted. "Me? No. I'm single and unattached. In my business, I'm gone way too much to sustain a relationship. Women want to settle down, have a home, have children. I'd never be there that much, and it wouldn't be fair to her or the kids."

"That's kind of a lonely existence," Lia said, finishing her toast. She placed the plate aside and picked up her coffee, studying him.

"Yeah," he admitted heavily, "sometimes, it is." *Like right now.* But the words remained unspoken as he calmly watched her.

"Why do you do this kind of work, Cav?"

"Because it makes me feel good."

Her lips curved. "What? Nattering with your clients?"

Heat stirred in him as her gray eyes sparkled with happiness. "The nattering is free. I don't charge for it."

She released a delighted, full-throated laugh.

Just being with Lia invited all kinds of dreams and fantasies, he was discovering. And dreams had never come true for Cav, except for once: when he'd achieved his dream of becoming a SEAL. Lightning never struck twice in the same place, so Lia was an unexpected gift that had slammed into his life. A lonely, gut-wrenching sadness moved through him, leaving him craving Lia as never before.

Sipping her coffee, Lia relaxed into the quiet that surrounded them in the room. The morning sunlight filtered in, giving her quaint home a warm glow. Suddenly, she put down her cup and became serious.

"Listen," she began in a low voice, "You need to know something about me, since you're staying here at night."

Cav said nothing, but gave her a nod, wondering if she was going to tell him about her sleepwalking. He felt her armoring up, as if to protect herself from his reaction.

"I—well, I get nightmares sometimes," and she risked a quick glance over at Cav. She saw no change in his expression except for a slight darkening of his eyes. "I get them maybe twice a week." She sighed and looked away." And since this attack by Medina, I've gotten them three times in the last six days. It's not something I'm very proud of."

"If it makes you feel any better, I get them, too." Cav stunned her with his admission. He found himself opening up to her as she was doing to him.

Lia's mouth dropped open. "I didn't think black ops people got them!"

"It's bad P.R. to admit it, but we do." And he gave her a wry smile. "I know very few guys from my team who don't get them every now and again."

Her ashamed expression now turned to relief. "Well! That makes me feel a lot better than I did before." She moved the cup between her hands, staring down at it. "Sometimes, I wake myself up with my own screams, Cav. You need to know that."

Instead of shrinking away from her, Lia saw the same caring, helpful expression on his face—the one she was having trouble getting used to. Was this man for real?

"Is there any way I can help you when it happens?" was all he said.

That was all it took. Tears burned in her eyes at his words, but even more, from that tender look in his eyes.

Men had run *from* her, not toward her. "Well…I…uh, no…there's nothing you can do…" She gave him a helpless look. "I wish there was, but there isn't."

"If it happens again, would you like me to come in and sit with you? Would that help?" He was going to give her a choice, not push himself on her. Cav knew in his soul that Lia would feel safe if he embraced her.

Lia chewed on her lower lip. "I don't know. I never had anyone around when it happened."

Cav wanted to ask questions—so damned many. If he did, he knew she'd close up. "If it happens again, how do you want me to respond?"

"I don't know…" she whispered, clearly in pain. "I live alone. I've lived alone for so long…"

Cav saw that she was resisting his suggestions, and quickly reverted to a simple, "No worries. How about if it happens, we'll just take it one step at a time. You can tell me then what you want or don't want? Okay? No pressure here, Lia. If you want me to stay away, I will."

That was a complete lie and Cav knew it.

The instant relief he saw in her eyes told him he'd been right about not putting undue stress on her right now. It was the last thing he wanted to do. He stood, giving her a slight smile as he gathered up the dishes. "We need to leave in about forty-five minutes. I'm going to do dishes."

"I can help."

"No way. You just go about doing something that you enjoy doing. I think I can handle washing a few dishes." He said it teasingly and left for the kitchen.

Lia sat at the table, chewing on her lower lip. Every moment she was with him was pushing her closer to falling into Cav's arms. But if she awoke from one of her nightmares, how might he react to seeing her scars?

And should she tell Cav what happened? One man had seen them and he'd run away from her, unable to deal with her trauma. Could Cav? He was so different from the men she'd drawn into her life before the assault. Cav was quiet, keenly alert, missed nothing and said little. A small stream of warmth curled around her lower body, reminding her that she was physically drawn to this man, as well. And he was single! No attachments! Lia found that hard to believe.

She sat at the table, her mind moving ahead to today's business lunch with her boss. Lia was sure Dilara, a woman dynamo, who never sat still long, had created a long list for them to go over after lunch. There was so much to be done. Lia knew the five rooms at the new location were probably already set up for the classrooms. Tomorrow, three new teachers would arrive. Lia was glad that some of her responsibilities were removed because she didn't feel as strong as before.

In fact, she felt weaker, which wasn't like her at all. But she had felt that way after her assault, too. The doctors had called it "shock." Of course it was, and Cav seemed sensitive to that. He certainly knew she didn't want him close by if she had a nightmare.

She felt a bit of relief now because at least she'd warned Cav that she might wake up screaming. As he was there to protect her, she didn't want him thinking she was screaming because someone had broken into her bedroom. Now, he would know it was only a nightmare.

The sound of dishes clinking, the smell of soapsuds, made her relax. In a way, it was nice having Cav here. He'd gone out of his way to make her breakfast and had offered to help her during times of stress. Lia knew she was tired, but the long night's sleep made her feel far better than she had all week.

Wandering through the kitchen after pouring herself another cup of coffee, Lia felt decidedly decadent. She had never had such an enjoyable time-out, thanks to Cav and Dilara. She deeply appreciated not having to rush through her morning, as usual. She loved the fact that she could actually dawdle. She could actually make her bed and smooth out the cover and fluff the pillows. These were little things, but Lia was used to being neat as a pin. Even this morning, she'd noticed that the place looked neater than ever. Cav had definitely been at work.

She closed the door to her bedroom, treasuring the quiet time alone. Her life had been filled with children and their demands and needs. Now, Cav was giving her time that she hadn't realized she needed. And she did.

At her desk, she opened her laptop and downloaded five days' worth of emails. Lia would take some of her newfound time to email her worried parents and reassure them. She knew both of them would be relieved to hear from her. Even more, they'd be happy to hear she had someone to protect her.

It took forty-five minutes for her to get the bulk of her emails sent. There were several from Dilara, who had penned them regarding the names, backgrounds, and arrival times of the new teachers.

As fast as the assault had been, Robert and Dilara and the Delos team were responding with equal swiftness. For a moment, Lia felt as if her world had taken a major change in direction.

Maria and Sophia had been murdered, and their families must be grieving deeply for them. And yet, the children of La Fortuna would continue being taught from the same books, just by different teachers.

It all felt surreal to Lia as she shut off her laptop and closed the lid. She stood and went to her small closet, pulling out a long-sleeved white cotton shirt to hide the bulk of her scars on her arms. She didn't want people staring at her.

Why wasn't she as sensitive about Cav seeing them? Normally, Lia never left the house without wearing a long-sleeved blouse and jeans. He had to have seen her arm scars, but if he did, he wasn't saying anything. Even more hopeful, he hadn't stared at her arms like so many others did.

She pulled a comb through her curly brown hair, touched the silky strands, looking at herself in the dresser mirror. It was such a mannish cut. Lia decided she wanted her hair to grow longer and look more feminine.

Suddenly, Lia was facing the fact that before and since the slaughter of her friends, she had lived her life for others. Now, she was standing on the brink of living a life that would bring her happiness, too. What an incredible turn of events that would be!

CHAPTER 10

D ILARA BEAMED AT Lia as they finished up four hours' work in
the rented office space at the resort. "Tomorrow, the teachers
arrive," she announced. "They will be driven up here in a van by
Tanner and his men."

"Where are you going to put them? We only have two houses
available near the new school," Lia asked, closing the large notebook.

"For now, we'll use Maria's home, which has two bedrooms. We
can bunk two of them there." Dilara reached out and touched Lia's
hand. "You stay where you are. You are happy in your place, aren't
you?"

"I love my little house," Lia said, her voice rising with emotion.
She was well aware that Cav was standing outside the room on guard.
There was only one way in and out of the room, and it had no
windows that posed a potential threat.

Dilara nodded and removed her hand. "And are you getting along
with Cav?" she asked innocently.

"Yes, he's very nice."

"Robert handpicked him for you. Did you know that?"

"No, but Cav was definitely the right choice," Lia agreed. Curious,
she wondered where this was going.

"My husband has formed many alliances in the black ops community over the last twenty years," she said. "He's used Cav on other
jobs, and felt he was a good fit for you."

Lia loved Dilara's honesty and warmth. She certainly knew how to
dress! Today, Dilara wore a cream-colored silk pantsuit that brought
out her Turkish skin tones. With her red hair bound up by two gold
combs, she was beautiful and perfect. *Unlike me*, Lia thought with a

touch of envy.

"Dilara, can I ask you something? Did Robert give Cav a file on me?"

"Just your personnel file. Not the other file that gives in-depth on each employee. Usually he does, but this attack threw all of us into fast-forward. Why?"

"I was just wondering."

Lia knew that Dilara was a well-known matchmaker. She had hired Maria and Sophia four years ago when both were single, and had later hired two young men from San José to come up to the Home School Charity and live in La Fortuna. A year later, Maria and Sophia had each married one of them!

"You aren't thinking what I'm thinking, are you?" Lia demanded, giving Dilara a wary look.

Giggling, Dilara rose and smoothed down her pantsuit trousers with her slender hands. "Robert did the picking, Lia. Not me."

"Hmmph." Lia stood up, preparing to head out.

"I know Cav," Dilara said, now serious.

Lia sat down again.

"I've worked with him before on details," she said. "He's a lot less hard-nosed than a lot of operators, and Robert felt that, under the circumstances, you needed someone like him. Some of these black ops guys are like icebergs. They never communicate with their charges."

"Cav certainly talks," Lia admitted, smiling to herself. She scooped up the notebook.

"Even more important," continued Dilara, "He's trustworthy, Lia, in every way. I hope he's making you feel safe."

"Yes, he is. Very." *No doubt about that*, Lia agreed.

Dilara smiled. "Do I sense you like him just a little bit? You do know he's single?"

Squirming, Lia admitted, "Yes, I like him. And yes, I know he's single."

Reaching out, Dilara brushed Lia's cheek. "You're so beautiful, Lia. I wish you'd see that in yourself. I know what happened to you, but darling girl, you are such a catch for the right man."

Instantly, Lia froze. "I don't think I have the energy or heart to try again," she whispered.

Dilara's gaze softened and she slid her arm around Lia's shoulders. "Now, you listen to me," she whispered, squeezing Lia gently. "I feel strongly that you and Cav share a lot in common, and he has many more scars than you do. And frankly, human beings were not meant to live their lives alone, which you've been doing since that assault five years ago."

Her eyes glimmered with tears. "You're a beautiful young woman with such heart and soul. Both Robert and I would love to see you happily married. To the right guy, of course."

"I wanted all of that once, Dilara," Lia agreed, pulling away from the woman's embrace, then giving her an apologetic look. "I'm not whole anymore. I never will be. Who wants a broken woman with scars inside and out, when there are so many more women who are whole?"

Dilara gave her a cool look as she put the papers in her eel skin brief case. "No one is perfect, Lia. They may look like they are, but they aren't. We're all imperfect and we carry a number of scars. Some are just more obvious than others. Cav has his share of scars believe me. You need to realize that your scars don't make you who you are, and they never will."

Lia had heard this speech from Dilara before. She knew her boss believed in what she was saying, but it simply didn't affect Lia the same way.

"Maybe I just need more time."

Closing her briefcase, Dilara smiled a little. "Cav is good for you. Let him be there for you, Lia. He might be able to show you a way to consider your scars secondary, not primary, in your life."

"I wish," Lia said, giving Dilara a quick hug. She could smell the spicy scent of the perfume Dilara always wore. It wasn't strong, but Lia had always loved that faint fragrance. "Thanks," Lia murmured, kissing her friend's cheek. "I know you care…."

"We always will," Dilara told her, giving her a stern look. "Robert and I consider you part of our global family. You're like our daughter, did you know that?"

Indeed she did. "I love that you're like a cosmic mother to all of us," Lia said, grateful for her friend's love and caring.

Dilara opened the door. "I'm leaving now for San José. I'll be there the rest of the week. You have my hotel and my satellite phone number if you need anything." She touched Lia's shoulder. "Don't try to do it all. Let these new teachers and the mothers from the village help you as we start up the classes at the other resort, promise?"

"I promise," Lia said, catching sight of Cav down the hall. He was standing near the wall, his hands in front of him in a "parade rest" position. Her heart soared when his eyes met hers, and his warm smile sent waves of happiness through her. She could get used to the tender looks he gave her sometimes. It was the closest thing to feeling whole she'd had in a long time.

Lia walked with Dilara to where Cav stood.

"We're done, Cav," Dilara told him. "Can you ask one of the operators to bring the SUV around to the front of the hotel for me?"

Nodding, Cav spoke into his mouthpiece and then said, "Done. Come on, I'll escort you out to the car."

Lia luxuriated in the safety shield Cav surrounded her with, and wondered if Dilara felt it, too. By the time they arrived at the glass doors, a driver had pulled up in a black SUV. Lia saw another operator dismount from the passenger side seat and open the door of the car for Dilara.

Dilara turned, threw her arm around Cav's broad shoulders and drew him against her, whispering something in his ear as she did so. Lia thought it unusual that she'd treat one of her contractors that way, but now she knew there was a deeper connection between them.

Lia was interested in Cav's reaction to Dilara's warm gesture. He didn't seem surprised by it, but curved an arm gently around her waist and hugged her back. Whatever she whispered in his ear made Cav flush, a loose grin tugging at his mouth as he released her.

"I'll see what I can do," he told Dilara in a low, deep voice.

She beamed and pinched his cheek. "You do that, Cav. I'll be watching."

Cav was blushing furiously, and Lia thought it made him look very young and very approachable. Now, she wished she had the courage to do what Dilara had just done: throw her arms around his capable, solid shoulders.

Lia wasn't jealous. She just wished she had the courage to show how she really felt about Cav and his personal style of protecting her.

The gold highlights in his eyes told her he was happy. Dilara had the ability to lift everyone and make them feel good about themselves, know that they were important, and reinforce that they were a part of her and Robert's huge global family.

The sunlight was hot and in the west, the breeze erratic. Cav stood at Lia's shoulder, allowing the team to get Dilara into the SUV. He slid his hand beneath Lia's elbow, guiding her to one side of the entrance, out of the way of people checking in or leaving. Groups of children stood by their parents at this resort all ages.

He saw that Lia's face was still relaxed, as she stood so close that their arms almost grazed one another. Did she know how much he wanted her in his arms, with her body against his? Every day.

At odd moments when he could relax, he'd dream of them together in bed, loving one another. He wasn't going to let go of that dream, no matter how impossible it appeared to be. There was just something, like a seed within his soul that knew they were made for one another. All he had to do was prove it to Lia.

Lia lifted her hand, smiling, as Dilara waved good-bye to them. She loved this woman. She loved Robert, too. They cared. And Lia knew not everyone did. Right now, she could feel Cav caring for her, and she melted into his nearness. As Dilara's SUV drove around the circle and out toward the main road, she turned to Cav.

"What did Dilara whisper to you?"

He eyed her. "It's top secret. Can't tell."

"You were blushing."

Cav grinned down at her. "I guess I was. Dilara has a way of getting to everyone. But you know that already, don't you?" He cupped her elbow. "Come on, we'll go through the parking lot, get the SUV and I'll take you home."

Lia didn't want to be influenced by his gritty words, but she was. *Home. With Cav.* Already she was comfortable with his presence, wanting him nearby, but not just as a guard dog. Rather, she needed the emotional support he effortlessly gave her.

As he drove them out of the massive asphalt parking lot, she saw Arenal, one of the most active volcanoes in the world, not far away. The Spanish name meant 'sandy areas,' and during the day she would often hear what sounded like a low-level jet roaring over the area. In truth, it was a glop of lava being thrown out of the throat of the active volcano. Luckily, the volcano's footprint and direction was southwest and all the resorts were northeast of the volcano and out of harm's way.

"How are you doing?" Cav asked her as he drove down the winding asphalt road.

"Tired, but good. Dilara is such a strategist and planner," and she gave him an overview of their four hours of work and decision-making. By the time she was done, they were back at the original school. Cav parked the SUV and she remained in the car, looking around. Already, she could see several loads of lumber, and large gray bricks had been off loaded in nearby pallets.

Tomorrow was Saturday, the day the new teachers were due to arrive. On Monday, the people who were going to rebuild the school would gather there. Lia knew she was going to be super busy.

When they arrived at her house, Cav opened the door for Lia and then stepped inside, clearing the place before he allowed her inside. So far, it seemed that no one wanted to attack her home.

Every morning, Cav searched the ground for any suspicious foot-prints and found none. His gut told him that this wasn't over, but he didn't want to heighten Lia's already super-charged wariness over the situation.

"How about I throw something together for dinner?" he called from the hallway.

Lia smiled a little as she finished drinking water at the sink. "What? Now you're going to become my full time chef, too?" She watched Cav as he sauntered into the kitchen and leaned against the frame, his arms wrapped around his chest as he studied her with half-closed eyes.

"I don't know," he said teasingly. "Depends on whether you like what I make. My buddy and roommate, Butch, burned everything, so I ended up making dinner a lot so I wouldn't have to worry about food poisoning."

"Do you work with him?"

Nodding, Cav said, "Yes, he's a security contractor like me and an ex-SEAL. A good person."

Lia set the glass down on the counter. "How about this? If I'm dragging myself in when I get home at night, you can cook. But if I'm feeling pretty good, I'll take a turn at it. Fair enough?"

"I can go for that." He liked the sound of this idea.

"I'm going to get a quick shower. It's so hot, my blouse is damp with sweat."

Nodding, Cav pushed off from the jamb and walked into the kitchen. "You know, you hide in that long-sleeved blouse, Lia, and you don't need to."

She frowned. His encouraging tone told her it wasn't a judgment, but a suggestion. "I—can't."

"Because of your scars?" Cav asked gently. He reached out, his fingertips grazing her upper sleeve. "Don't hide, Lia. You don't need to. They're just scars. No big deal." He held her gaze and watched the pain rise up again. "I've already seen them. They'll never define who you are to me."

Stunned, she looked away, riveted by the touch of his fingers trailing lightly down her upper arm.

"People…men…always stare at them…at me," she choked out. "I hate it, Cav." Instinctively, she curved her hand across her arm, keeping the sleeve in place.

"Hey," he murmured, placing his finger beneath her chin, gently urging her to look at him, "Never be ashamed of who you are or what you've gone through and survived." His voice lowered. "In my eyes, you're incredibly beautiful. You don't need to hide who you are. When I first saw you, I saw your gray eyes and then your mouth and the color of your hair. I wasn't even aware of the scars until later."

He removed his finger, but remained standing so close to her, feeling her reaction to his impassioned words. Cav could never take her scars away, but he could get her to see that they were a *part* of her life journey, not the journey itself. "I'll never ask you what happened," he said, "but if you ever want to tell me, I'll listen. That's a promise."

If he didn't take a step back, Cav knew he would kiss her. He saw her black pupils grow larger and knew she had read his intent. For a second, he felt her yearning for him, and then, her confusion.

He forced himself to step away and gruffly ordered, "Go get your shower. I'll make us a meal."

Shaken, Lia gave him a brief nod. How badly she wanted to fall into Cav's arms! The look in his eyes told her he couldn't care less about her scars. He wanted HER! But how could that be? She walked down the hall, wrapped in shock combined with euphoria. Did she read his look correctly or was it her vivid, hungry imagination? His words rang in her ears, in her heart over and over again as she got her cooling shower.

Afterward, she dried and pulled on her long blue cotton bathrobe. Draping her damp blouse over her arm, she padded barefoot to the laundry room and put them in the washer.

She smelled the aroma of chicken frying in the kitchen and heard Cav moving around. Standing in the laundry room, Lia felt fear, and then hope. She knew that Cav was going to kiss her soon. She just knew it. The look in his hazel eyes, the gold flecks deepening in them, told her.

Slowly, she released the grip of the collar around her neck, allowing it to lie flat, exposing the entire slash across her neck. Cav had been right: he'd already seen those scars.

And no man had spoken to her as boldly as he'd just done. How badly she wanted to believe that the damn scars meant nothing to him, that he really did see her, not them, first. She felt a surge of courage thread through her, and her skin still tingled where he'd brushed beneath her chin with his calloused finger.

If Cav was that gutsy to call her out on the scars, then she had to be strong enough—brave enough—to stop hiding from him.

Lia realized he'd been privy to her scars since he'd met her down in San José and had never stared at them. Instead, he always caught and held her gaze. He was an intense, focused man, and Lia always felt the full weight of his attention when he spoke to her.

Still not ready to face him, Lia tried to make sense of it all. She realized some of her confusion was from her terror of being humiliated once more. And once he undressed her and saw her lower body, he might draw back.

On the other hand, Cav had told her he wouldn't ask what had happened to her. That was such a huge relief, she'd nearly sobbed in relief in front of him. She knew she had to start releasing herself from her shame and humiliation. Could she believe Cav? This man saw only her gray eyes, her mouth, her hair. And the low vibration in his voice told her he liked what he saw.

Cav had not said a word about a relationship, but she'd seen evidence of his feelings in his eyes, heard it in his voice. Lia knew she was very poor at reading men accurately, and it was her fault. She'd had years of loneliness and isolation without someone in her life. Oh, her children helped because she imagined them as her own. Instead of focusing on her loneliness, she focused on them. In return, they loved her and never embarrassed her about her scars. If adults could be like her children, Lia knew she could eventually get over her wounds. Finally, she forced herself out of the laundry room, refusing to draw the collar up to hide her neck. As she passed through the kitchen, she saw Cav glance up from his work over a salad he was putting together.

"Feel cleaner?"

"Yes," she mumbled, hurrying toward her bedroom. Her heart

was pounding, as she recognized that same tenderness in his expression, though she barely met his gaze. Lia shut the door to her bedroom and leaned against it, closing her eyes, shaky with relief. Placing her hand over her heart, she took in a deep, ragged breath, opened her eyes and forced herself to snap out of it.

She pulled pale green linen trousers from her closet and chose a short-sleeved, dark green tee to go with it. The trousers would hide her legs. Cav had seen her arms. It was time to stop hiding completely.

As she dressed and combed her hair, Lia tried to gird herself. Would Cav continue to talk about it? She hoped not. There was enough in what he had said to mull his words over for a long time.

Cav placed the fried chicken, baked beans and a salad on the table for them. When Lia quietly entered the kitchen, he saw the wariness in her eyes, and then he noticed that she'd stopped wearing that damned long-sleeved white blouse. Now, the scars on her upper arms were plainly visible. He felt a sense of pride in this beautiful, frightened woman, and silently applauded her courage to stop hiding. He wanted badly to say much more, but knew better.

"Can you grab the butter out of the fridge?" he asked. He saw the tension in her body begin to melt.

"Sure. Anything else?" she asked, opening the door.

"Any salad dressings in there? I haven't had time to look."

"Yes, I'll get them," she said, crouching down.

Cav almost felt like part of a married couple. He got the plates and flatware from the drawer, placing them on the table while she brought out the butter on a narrow plate, plus two types of salad dressing.

"You're pretty good at scrounging things up from the fridge," she said, gesturing to the salads. "I didn't even know I had a mango in there."

He grinned from across the table. "It was hidden deep in the veggie drawer."

"Leave it to a black ops guy to find the hidden mango."

Chuckling despite himself, Cav saw a slight tinge of pink come to her cheeks, that full mouth of hers pulling shyly into a smile as she teased him back.

"Hey, it would be pretty embarrassing if I couldn't even find a mango in the vegetable drawer," Cal pointed out with a slight grin.

Laughing softly, Lia was now enjoying herself. She saw the gleam in his eyes and heard the mellow warmth in his voice as he walked into the kitchen. "I'm sure they didn't give you any tests for finding mangos in a fridge, did they?" she shot back.

Cav brought out a saucer with four slices of whole wheat bread on it, setting it down on the table between them. "You're right about that," he said, coming around the table and pulling out her chair for her.

"Thanks," she said, enjoying his nearness. There was such power and strength around Cav, yet she felt completely comfortable with it. With other men, she shrank inward because of the power men had once used against her.

"Welcome." Cav moved to the other side of the table. "Eat up."

Lia took the smallest piece of chicken, a thigh, and put it on her plate along with two scoops of beans. Of course, Cav took two huge chicken breasts, leaving a thigh for her, and nearly all the beans. His salad was twice as large as hers.

"That's a lot of food for just two people," she said, picking up her knife and fork. "But it looks wonderful. Thanks for making all of this."

"Sounds as if you never have sit-down meals."

"Sometimes, I do, but other times, I'm whipped. Then, all I want to do is go to sleep. When I wake up, I nosh on whatever's in the fridge."

He raised a brow as he cut into the succulent chicken dusted with Caribbean spices. "Which is why you're way too skinny for your height."

"Oh," she grumbled, "don't start, Cav."

"Okay, I won't pick on you tonight," he said lightly. He saw the glint of rebellion in her eyes, the set of her luscious mouth. He'd like to kiss that soft mouth and then open it beneath his. The scorching thought singed his lower body, as always. "But I do expect you to clean up your plate." He stabbed his fork toward her salad. "And I went to a lot of trouble to make that into a salad you'd love to eat. I even found some slivered almonds near the mango."

A grudging smile pulled at her lips. "You're really adept at using guilt, aren't you, Mr. Jordan."

He gave her a proud look. "If it will make you eat, yeah, I'll use it, Ms. Cassidy. Whatever it takes to put about twenty more pounds on you."

Lia bowed her head, not wanting Cav to see her reaction. "You're like my Dad," she muttered defiantly, cutting into her chicken. "I was a picky eater as a kid, so he'd start needling me, pushing me and daring me at the table."

"I think I'd like to meet him. Sounds like my kind of dude."

Lia said nothing, paying attention to the food on her plate, which tasted delicious. She found the baked beans had some brown sugar in them, and she gulped them down with gusto, then went back for seconds. And then thirds! By the time she got to her salad, which had been very artfully arranged, she started to laugh.

"What is this?" and she turned the bowl around toward Cav. Amongst the greens, he'd cut two eyes, a nose, and a smiling mouth out of the mango. With the slivered almonds, he'd made what look like hair across the top of the salad face.

She couldn't stop from giggling because she hadn't noticed it until just now.

Cav gave her a very pleased look. "Just a bit of arts and crafts. Hey, my mother always did that for me. On the pancakes, she'd cut up pieces of bananas and strawberries and make faces on them for me. When I was young, I was a really picky eater. She knew I loved fruit, so she put faces on everything to get me to eat it." He smiled broadly. "It worked. Today, I'll eat anything, even if it's still moving."

"Ugh!" Lia said, turning the salad around, loving the idea of a face made of mango and almonds. "I can't handle raw meat. Makes me sick."

"Well," he continued, his voice droll, "as a SEAL, if you run out of MRE's on a patrol or mission, you eat what you can find. And usually, because making a fire would give away our position, we'd eat sushi. Even if it was a sacrificial goat."

Wrinkling her nose, she put the balsamic vinaigrette on her salad. "I'd never made it as a SEAL."

"I like you just the way you are," Cav said lightly. "You're a very brave, resourceful woman, Lia. I like being around people like you."

CHAPTER 11

"WHY THE HELL isn't that Cassidy woman dead yet?" Medina demanded of the two men who stood uncertainly before him. His dark brown eyes narrowed on Bruce Schaefer, an ex-Army soldier. "You were given orders. What the hell have you been doing?"

Schaefer pushed his finger through his short blond hair and gave his boss a helpless look. "Sir, Jorge and I have been *trying*. The problem is that Delos Charity has hired security contractors. A bunch of them."

Jorge Dominguez added, "We've been doing our best, Patron. We know you want her killed like the other two women. But she's got a contractor with her every second of every day and night."

Snorting, Medina gestured sharply for his mistress to leave them. She was seventeen years old, a Russian sex slave he'd bought two weeks ago, and had been raised in her trade since a child. She knew how to please a man. Her red hair and green eyes were alluring, but she had no conversation to offer Medina. Instead, she pouted playfully and used her seductive wiles to keep him interested. Now, at his order, she rose gracefully and left the room. After she left, Medina eyed his two nervous soldiers. "I want that woman dead. She's the bitch who drove Lupe to the airport here in San José."

Bruce wrung his hands, feeling the sweat staining his tropical shirt and shorts. He and his men had to dress like tourists so they wouldn't stand out in the crowds around Arenal and the nearby resorts. "We can't do much, Patron. There are always a bunch of operators in town, everywhere, not just by the woman. We saw an important-looking man and a woman from somewhere else who went to visit where the school was. And someone is dropping off truckloads of construction material there. I think they're going to rebuild the school, Patron. I would bet on it."

Snorting, Medina pushed his sandaled feet off the burgundy leather couch and stood up. Glaring, he yelled, "I don't care if they show up with an army! You haven't completed the job I gave you. I told you all three women were to be killed and that school burned down."

His voice became a sinister hiss. "And if you don't get this done in the next week, I'll send someone else to do it. And if I have to do that, he'll be killing both of you first. Now, vamoose!"

He dismissed them with a wave of his manicured hand, and the men jumped back, then hurried out the room. Medina cursed softly, his hands behind his back as he paced angrily back and forth across the white tiled floor. Ordinarily, his two ex-Army soldiers were good at what they did, but this time, they'd screwed up badly.

It didn't matter that the Cassidy woman had run into the jungle and hidden from them. It just made his men look more stupid, since she was obviously smarter than he'd given her credit for.

He scooped up several printed photos his men had taken of the school area and studied the men's faces with intensity. He knew none of them personally, but one thing he did know: they were black ops, no question.

Delos Charity had hired the best. Schaefer and Dominguez were hardly of that caliber—they had no black ops training or background. Just the look on those men's faces told him they meant business.

Medina knew they cost a fortune, each getting a minimum of a hundred thousand dollars a year for jobs like this. Rubbing his neatly trimmed black beard, he halted at the crystal clear blue oval pool, ignoring the white tiles with hand-painted dolphins around the inner edge of the pool. His dead mistress had loved dolphins.

Unfortunately for her, Medina didn't care for her whining and had drowned her two days after the pool had been refilled. The last thing she'd seen was the dolphin tiles.

He was thinking about one thing now, how to get to the Cassidy woman. He held up a photo that showed her with a tall, powerful looking hombre standing next to her. The guy was wearing the telltale light jacket and Medina knew he had a pistol in the back of his belt. There was probably a smaller one in a sheath on one of his ankles, hidden by his bone-colored chinos. The deadly look in the man's eyes told Medina this operator knew his business. He was literally bristling with protectiveness for that bitch.

The more he studied her scarred face, the more he began to change his mind about killing her. Lia Cassidy wasn't bad looking except for the scars. He was a man who liked uniqueness among the women who sexually served him.

Among his "harem," as he referred to it, he had one woman who had been tortured by the Taliban. She was an Afghan village woman who had fought back, and they'd scarred her body quite well. And then, they'd sold her to a Pakistani sex trade dealer. She'd eventually showed up at a private party in Russia, and he'd bid on her.

A slight smile came to his thin mouth as he studied Cassidy's face and neck. He knew how she'd gotten those scars and the others she hid beneath her clothing. Bruce and Jorge had grudgingly admitted they'd tried to knife her to death when she'd fought them trying to rape her.

One thing he liked about his Afghan bitch was that to this day, she fought. She fought him every time he took her, and that only excited Medina more. She had fire and spirit. Well, so did this Cassidy woman.

Deciding to change the order, Medina gestured to a nearby servant.

"Get Schaefer and Dominguez back here," he snapped to his butler.

Medina was sitting in his wingback chair when they arrived, breathing hard. Their room was in the small barracks behind his palatial villa in San José, a good ten-minute walk from here. The entire two acres were shielded from view by ten-foot-high bougainvillea that surrounded the place. No one went through that brush because the murderous thorns would easily tear a person's flesh wide open. It was far more effective than stringing concertina wire.

"Yes, Patron?" Schaefer huffed, standing at attention in front of Medina.

"I'm changing my order," he told them lazily. "You are to capture Cassidy, not kill her. I want her taken alive, brought here to the villa." He saw Schaefer's blue eyes widen. It was none of their business why he'd changed his mind. "Do whatever you need to do in order to capture her." He waved a finger at the men. "Under no circumstances do you harm her. I want her handled with great care. If I see one bruise on her flesh, I'll make sure you're beaten within an inch of your mongrel life."

"But," Bruce stumbled, "she fought like a wildcat the last time we tried to take her, Patron."

Shrugging, Medina said, "No one bruises my merchandise. Do as I ordered. And since this is a little tougher to pull off, I'll give you two weeks." His voice flattened. "After that? If you haven't brought me Cassidy alive and well, I'll send out someone who will, but you'll both be dead men walking."

Where had the week gone? Lia was grateful that the five classrooms at The Orchid Resort were working well with the children. Everything was going smoothly because of the time, care and money that Robert and Dilara had poured into reviving the charity school.

As she stood with Cav watching the workers crawl all over the new structure, she smiled. No expense had been spared for this new school. It was to be made of brick, fireproofed, with state-of-the-art materials and construction. Dilara had bought twenty-five computers to be set up for the children in the new section of the larger school. Everyone was optimistic and excited and the parents were doing more than their share to help the building get quickly resurrected.

Many of the fathers would come over during the last few hours of daylight, after working all day at their jobs, and lend a hand with the San José construction workers who'd been hired to build it.

It was nearly five P.M., the sun in the west and the sky cloudy and threatening in the east. There would be thunderstorms later in the evening. She heard a low sound like a jet passing overhead. It was Arenal coughing out another huge stone from its throat and spitting it into the air. The monkeys were screaming and hooting now, as they usually did the last few hours before dusk. A squadron of bright colored green parrots flew overhead, going to their nightly roosting place.

In the past week, thanks to Cav's influence, she had shed her white cotton long-sleeved shirt. Every day, she chose a colorful capped tee, trying to get used to allowing people to see her scars. To her surprise, most would look once but not stare or gawk. And once they saw them, they ignored them. That was amazing to Lia.

What had changed? Maybe it was her attitude change, due to Cav's influence. She admitted that having him with her was a boon, and he wasn't smothering her or irritating her with his nearness. Everyone was treating her as if she was whole and had no scars.

Cav was making her stronger by the day, whether he knew it or not. She glanced up at his rugged profile, smiling warmly. The man was always on guard, never resting and focusing on her every need. How could she dislike anything about him? In fact, Lia wanted to know him much more personally now that she'd had a taste of what he could bring to her life.

"I can't believe how far along the workers are on the school," she confided to Cav.

He glanced over at her. "I think the men from the village are making up the difference," he ventured.

Nodding, she watched the twenty plus men hard at work. "I'm amazed that the rebuilding is coming along so well. Paca, Juanita and Tomasa are doing a wonderful job of teaching, too. It really makes my day a lot easier."

"Things are moving nicely, thanks to you," Cav quickly pointed out. "You're the go-to-person when anyone needs guidance or direction."

"They're catching on fast, though," Lia said.

"They sure are." Cav looked across the dry, dusty plain and then down at Lia. He wanted to praise her courage for no longer wearing that long-sleeved blouse. She seemed less tense and he sensed it was because of him, and how he was treating her daily.

Lia worked harder than anyone at the resort to maintain that seamless comfort level for the children, and she did it so well. All three teachers appreciated her and the children adored her like a second mother who lovingly spoiled them.

He found himself smiling a little. "Tomorrow is Saturday," he said, holding her upturned gaze. "I'd like to take you on a picnic of sorts."

She tilted her head, drowning in his green and gold gaze. "A picnic?"

"Yeah, for the two of us. I found out from Dilara when I turned in my weekly report that you like to go caving. Is that true?"

"Yes, my dad is a spelunker. He began teaching me the ropes, literally, when I was ten years old. I loved going with him. Caves are magical."

Hearing the excitement in her voice, Cav said, "Tomorrow morning after breakfast, I'd like to drive us over to the Venado Caves. As a SEAL, I was taught ropes, climbing and caving. I'm probably not as good as you, but I thought we might bring a lunch along and spend the day exploring. What do you think?"

Never had Cav wanted Lia to say "yes" more than right now. He'd been wracking his brain to find a way to relieve her of her brutal daily schedule. And now that everything was working well, he knew she could afford a day off—with him.

Lia's heart bounded. "Oh, Cav, I'd LOVE to do that with you! In fact, before the school was burned down and Maria and Sophia were killed, we were planning an all day visit with the kids at the caves. I've been in them many times, and I'd chosen a beautiful spot that was easy for them to access."

Her cheeks became pinker, that mouth of hers so soft and tantalizing that his whole lower body ached. This was the first time he'd seen such radiance in her gray eyes, as if someone had offered her the world. Being able to share that kind of joy with her raced through him, and hope for more intimacy warmed his heart.

Lia was always so serious, a hard, responsible worker. Oh, she would smile and even laugh and tease the children, but then, she'd return to wearing her serious mask.

A grin tugged at his mouth. "Okay, you're on. You have climbing gear?"

"Oh," she bubbled, "I do!"

"I'd asked one of Tanner's operators when he was down in San José to pick up some equipment. He's bringing it back later today. We should have enough carabiners, ropes and other stuff to do some serious spelunking tomorrow."

"Indeed we do! I've got all my nylon ropes coiled and under my bed in a box," she laughed. "Gosh, I haven't gone caving in…well…a long time."

He wanted to reach out and slide his fingers through her hair, but resisted. "Okay, you're on. I'll make us some peanut butter sandwiches."

"Yes, that's good fuel," she agreed happily.

"I bought some protein bars, too. They're always good in a pinch."

"Excellent," Lia said, rubbing her hands together. "Have you ever been in this cave system, Cav?"

"No."

"It's a glorious place for beginners up to professionals, just depending on which cave area you want to explore."

"Well," he murmured, "how about some training wheels caves? I haven't done it in a long time and I'm pretty rusty. I'm sure you can show me the ropes."

He was enjoying this so much, especially seeing Lia's face light up like a child's at Christmas. Her mantle of serious responsibility had suddenly disappeared, and she was showing him a part of himself he'd never seen before.

Confidence radiated from her, and a spirit of competition was emerging, one he loved to see.

"You're on!"

LIA COULD BARELY sit still at dinner that night. Cav had fried up some steaks he'd bought at the grocery store earlier. He tended to like diced up potatoes fried with onions and green peppers, and so did Lia. She enjoyed it all.

When he made dinner at night, he always put a funny face on her salad bowl, telling her she had to eat *all* of it. Lia figured she'd gained five pounds in the last week, now that Cav insisted on cooking for them every night. He told her she was too tired do make dinner after her long days at the resort.

While he cooked, she had pulled out her box of spelunking gear and dragged it into the living room. He'd zip back and forth from the kitchen, look through her gear, make comments, ask questions and then trade caving stories and experiences.

It was after dinner when a knock came at the door. Instantly, Cav went into operator mode. He gestured for her to move away from the door and behind him. Looking through the peephole in the door, he said, "Relax. It's Steve. He's brought us our climbing gear."

A six-foot-tall man with red hair and green eyes, hauled in a huge cardboard box. Then, he went out to the Jeep and retrieved a second box. Both were put in the living room. After he left, Lia was itching to see what was in the boxes, and Cav sat down next to her. He pulled one box over. "I wasn't sure you'd have gear, so I bought you some…go ahead. Open it."

Touched by his thoughtfulness, she opened it up and gasped. "Oh, my God!" and her hands flew to her mouth, he eyes widening.

Cav opened up the other box that held his gear. "What? Is it all right?"

She stared over at him. "This must have cost a fortune, Cav!"

"You're worth it." He gestured toward the box. "Just take a look at the contents, okay? I know Venado is a wet, living cave system, so I guessed at some of the sizes of your footgear."

Stunned, she said, "This cost so much money…"

"Don't worry about it, okay? It looks like your gear is pretty complete, but if you find something in there that you could use and don't have, just pull it out and put it with your box of stuff. I'll have Steve take the rest back for a refund."

Lia was impressed with the equipment. "So, you've been studying up on Venado?"

He grinned a little. "Yeah. When Dilara told me you caved, that got me excited. I like caving, too."

"Is that what she whispered to you that day before she left the hotel?"

Cav had the good grace to blush a little. "Yeah, she said you knew caving. She knew I liked caving, so we put it together."

"She's such a matchmaker!" Lia said, laughing. "Who knew?"

He laughed with her and it felt damn good to be sharing something that brought her utter happiness. Since finding out they were going to go caving, her eyes were radiant with joy. Lia was like sunlight to his dark heart. "Yeah, I've watched her pull a few fast ones on friends of mine in the security area."

"What happened to them?" Lia asked, curious.

"They're all married now."

Chuckling, Lia said, "That's Dilara. She has an amazing gift for pairing people up. They might not see it, but she does," and she picked up a shiny new red helmet, lusting after it. Hers was a blue one, scraped, scratched and bearing many marks of rocks that she'd had to wriggle beneath to make it through narrow openings.

"She's dangerous," Cav muttered, scowling.

Hooting, Lia put the helmet aside, running her fingers over the ropes. They were strong and new, unlike hers. But hers were still sturdy and durable. "Well, you don't have to worry. Robert said *he'd* chosen you. So, we're safe."

Giving her a sly look, Cav muttered, "Be careful. I've seen plenty of married people and it's a foregone conclusion the woman runs the roost. Robert might have chosen me for this detail, but what makes you think Dilara didn't put that idea into his ear, hmmm?" and he gloated as he grinned, watching her eyes widen beautifully, her lips parting.

"Oh," she said, "I hadn't thought of that…" Dilara had told her Robert had specially chosen Cav for her. "She did say that he chose you because you were…well, less hard, I guess. Whatever that means," and she held his amused gaze.

"Hard?"

"Well, you know? Not so withdrawn, maybe? Dilara said you were a natterer."

He tipped his head back and laughed heartily. Suddenly, he felt a deep rush of happiness, then teased, "I'm sure Dilara did *not* use that word. What did she really say?"

"Caught red-handed," Lia admitted, holding up her hands, smiling. "She said you were pretty decent at communication."

Grunting, Cav pulled the ropes aside, studying the flashlight, picking it up in his hands. "Some guys are pretty stoic," he agreed.

"Don't they ever talk to the person they're protecting?"

"Only when necessary. They feel that being chatty is a distraction. And it can be at times."

"You never make me feel like that."

"I don't want to," Cav said, holding her curious gaze. "I run my detail differently than most. Educating my client is top of my list. If I can get him or her to fully trust me, that's as good as it gets— especially if it's a woman. She just naturally wants to know more than a male does."

"Then why not put women on details with women?"

He liked the way she thought. "There are very few women operators out there. I'm sure, over time, there will be. I've met a few of them and they're good at what they do."

"Do you like being put on a detail with a woman?" she wondered.

"Makes no difference to me, Lia. I tend to get along with both sexes without any problems. Some of my operator friends won't take on a female detail, though."

"Why not?"

"Because women like to communicate and they don't."

"It goes back to being distracted?"

"Exactly."

"Then you must be special, Cav because you can focus and not be distracted and still talk to me."

"Dilara has accused me of being whole-brained," he deadpanned, fighting a smile as he pulled up his rubber caving shoes.

"Oh, she has a theory, Lia said, smiling, "that men are left-brain hemisphere dominant and women are right-brain dominant."

"Right, and her theory is that there's a small percentage of humans of both sexes that are whole-brained, using both hemispheres instead of preferring one."

"Then she gave you a real compliment!"

"Well," he said lightly, "the proof is in the pudding, isn't it? It's how you feel about it, about our relationship, that counts."

Lia sighed and rubbed her hands on her jeans. "I thought," she admitted hesitantly, giving him a guilty look, "that it would be awful to have you underfoot. Especially here in my little house."

"And?"

"And, I actually like it. I'm happy that you're here. I know this is a job for you, but for me…" she held his narrowing gaze, "…it makes me feel safe for the first time in a long time."

It took every ounce of his control for Cav to sit there looking relaxed, as if he were unaffected by her soft words. The look in her eyes, the gratitude, the relief, brought a lump to his throat. He tore his gaze from hers, afraid to say too much. "Well," he said gruffly, "get used to it."

"You know," Lia confided, "As a kid, I learned to be really self-reliant." She swallowed hard. "And I was until…well…things happened. And since then, I've never been the same. I lack the confidence I used to have, and I really miss it. I want it back, but I don't know how to retrieve it."

"Well," Cav said, his voice rough with emotion, "maybe getting back into caving will help you find what you want."

"I guess I never lost my confidence there," she laughed wryly. "I feel strong and good about that, no problem. Besides, it's a passion of mine, Cav."

"Like riding your horse, Goldy?" he wondered.

She gave him a sweet smile. "Especially riding Goldy full speed down the edge of my Dad's beet fields, yes. I truly, truly miss that."

Maybe the idea of caving was the smartest thing he'd ever done. Thanks to Dilara, who had suggested it. He wondered what she had seen in the future for himself and Lia?

Something told him that Dilara had urged the General to pair him up with Lia. And he was damned pleased she had. The woman was *such* a wily matchmaker!

CHAPTER 12

LIA TRIED TO contain her delight as Cav drove the black SUV toward El Tanque. She knew the way well, and as the asphalt two-lane road threaded through the jungle, she told him to turn north to Monterrey. From there, it would be a short hop to the town of Jicarito. That morning, Cav had made them a full breakfast of bacon and pancakes, and she'd stuffed herself, knowing that she'd need food for energy this morning.

Always thinking ahead, he'd also made an extra pot of coffee and poured it into a large thermos so they could drink some on the way to the Venado Cave complex. Above them, the sky was cottony with clouds drifting across the Monte Verde forest. Slivers of pale blue sky were above them, and it was a typical beautiful morning in the dry season.

There were few cars on the road at 7 A.M., which was exactly what they wanted. Lia was eager to be first to arrive at the caves.

"You think there'll be many early birds at the caves?" Cav asked.

"No. Generally, the tourists are brought up around 10 A.M. in buses from the resorts near La Fortuna." She smiled in anticipation. "We should have three hours of caving without a lot of chatter from tourists."

"Suits me," Cav agreed. He looked in his rearview mirror out of habit and saw a white Toyota pick-up following them at a distance. It had been with them since they'd left the village. Of course, there were a lot of white pick-ups all around La Fortuna and most of the workers at the resorts drove them. He didn't think it was unusual, but he'd still keep an eye on it.

He looked over at Lia. She had surprised him this morning. Normally she wore pants to cover her legs and the scars on her calves. Today, when she'd emerged from her shower, she had on black, body-hugging caving pants that revealed her lower legs to just below her knees. The scars were clearly visible, but he made no mention of them.

Silently applauding Lia's courage to stop hiding, he found himself wanting to pick her up, twirl her around, and celebrate her courage.

Deep in thought, he came back to the present and made a turn at the sign that said "Jicarito."

"It takes about forty-five minutes to make this trip one way," Lia said.

"Have you come up here often?" Cav wanted to know.

"About every five or six weeks," she admitted. "The silence, the beauty and the awe I feel in caves keeps calling me back to them."

"Is it kind of like a place of healing?" he surprised her by asking.

"Yes, for me, it is," Lia admitted. "I always feel better after caving for a few hours. Renewed, even." Her heart expanded she felt his eyes on her—it was the look of a man wanting his woman. They'd never spoken about it, but it was clear to both of them that the feeling was mutual.

She could taste the yearning within herself to kiss this man—really kiss him. And this morning, when she'd boldly swapped out her jeans for her nylon caving trousers that clearly showed the long scars on her calves, he'd never flinched. Nor had he stared at her legs. Instead, Cav treated her as he always did—as if she were a normal, whole woman, not a damaged one.

And again, she'd breathed a sigh of relief. She was glad her idealistic nature, long buried, was still alive and well. Now, Lia sat in the car, completely happy to be in Cav's company and on her way to one of her favorite places.

"Your trousers," he said, "look like a combo of good, heavy canvas and spandex."

She touched her black pants. "Well, the cave is wet, and I'd rather risk some scrapes on my lower legs than have them encased in material. I usually cave with these pants, my rubber boots and my black tee."

"They look good on you, Lia. Nice fit."

Lia said nothing, but secretly she was thrilled. "Thanks," she said, trying to sound casual.

Cav wore a set of coveralls, and Lia knew that experienced cavers often wore them with waterproof nylon clothing. The coveralls were made of heavy tough cotton that could stand up to the abrasions from crawling through caves. Cav also wore a bright red t-shirt beneath the coveralls. He looked absolutely perfect.

Slowing as they entered the sleepy town of Jicarito, Lia pointed to a dirt road on the left. "We'll go about three kilometers down this dirt road," she told him. "And the place is located on a farmer's land. It's not protected by the national park. The farmer will charge us for our caving, but he's a very nice man."

"You said this was a live cave system?" Cav asked as he glanced into his rear-view mirror. Again, he saw the white Toyota pickup drift by where they turned. His suspicions rose, but it hadn't turned off to follow them, so he kept it on his checklist to remain alert.

"In the world of caving, there are dry caves, which means the evolutionary bacteria and other plant material are gone. In a living cave, it's still there and allows the cave to grow. It also means the cave is wet, which creates the right conditions for beautiful limestone sculptures," Lia explained.

The gravel road crunched beneath the wide tires of the SUV, a thin strip of rock in a jungle that rose on both sides of them. The cloud forest was beautiful this time of morning, and Cav sped up a bit so the humid cool air could enter the vehicle.

They arrived shortly afterward, and Cav noted that there was one other truck in the parking lot. He and Lia climbed out of the SUV. Cav walked to the rear of the vehicle and opened up it to get their gear.

The cave entrance was a huge triangular opening surrounded by jungle foliage on all sides. There were signs guiding those who wanted to enter Venado, but right now, they were alone and he liked it.

"Okay," he murmured, pulling the box of equipment to the rear bumper, "Guess it's time to suit up."

Lia wore thick-soled rubber boots that hugged her ankles. She knew that cavers often received sprained ankles. That wasn't something she wanted to happen when she was a kilometer inside a cave system. She pulled on her kneepads for protection from the rocks, and then her elbow pads. Her fanny pack, actually a small, waterproofed Pelican box, held a small first aid kit, a space blanket, a candle and matches, an Ace bandage for sprains and Ziploc bags.

Lia placed the fanny pack around her waist and pushed it to her the small of her back. Then, she made sure she had enough protein bars in a heavy Ziploc pouch. A plastic water bottle was next. In another pouch, she carried spare batteries for the light attached to her helmet, knowing that a pitch, black cave was no place to find yourself without a light.

She saw Cav pack an extra shirt in case one of them got cold. Although the temperature in the caves was around seventy-five degrees, this was a wet cave. They'd be swimming or crawling through a lot of water to reach the area she wanted to show him.

Lia tucked her garden gloves into her belt. Once she entered the cave, she'd pull them on to protect the cave from bacteria she might carry on her hands, as well as protect her hands from the sharp, jagged limestone rocks.

She noticed that Cav wore heavy hiking boots with thick treads. They were made of waterproof nylon, which enclosed and protected his ankles. "You've done this a time or two before, haven't you?" she guessed aloud.

He grinned as he belted up with his own pack around his waist. "A time or two." Picking up his red helmet, he settled it on his head and strapped it beneath his chin. "You ready?"

"Yep, I've got everything." She looked at the plastic wristwatch. "It's going to take us two hours to reach Boca de la Culebra, 'The Mouth of the Snake.' There are no lights strung through the cave, so it'll be completely dark. The reason I want to take you to this particular cave is because there's a natural opening above it and lots of light to see the chamber. It's really beautiful."

Cav took his GoPro waterproof camera and tucked it in his pack. "I'm ready. Where do we pay?"

Lia settled the helmet on her head, but didn't strap it on. "Follow me," she waved, walking down a muddy, gravel path toward a small house near the cave entrance.

Cav enjoyed walking behind Lia; the woman had the sweetest hips, and he liked watching them move. Today, he wanted her to relax and enjoy herself. Looking around, he saw they were the only people there except for the man who would welcome them to the caves.

Although Cav wanted to relax, he couldn't. He was still on the job, and the likelihood of Medina's men jumping them in Venado was low, but there was a good chance they'd try when they left. Sure, they could hide well enough in the jungle surrounding this place. And of course, Cav had tucked his Sig Sauer pistol into a side pocket, wrapped in a

Ziploc in case he needed it.

After paying their admission fees, they found themselves walking on a boardwalk into the adit entrance to the cave. Lia led the way, familiar with it. Cav liked the yellow ochre limestone that gleamed with the sheen of humidity. As they moved deeper, he saw Lia strap her helmet on and turn on the light. He did the same.

The gravelly entrance turned slippery and Cav heard water running somewhere ahead of them as darkness closed in, surrounding them. Only their lights on their helmets lit up the area enough to see where they were placing their feet.

Looking up, Cal saw large gray bats hanging upside down above them on the tunnel's wide ceiling. He actually found caves comforting, and Cav was happy that he and Lia were alone, sharing these special moments.

He saw Lia stop and pull out her waterproof map of the system and walked over to her, his light focused on her map. "We're at Emgrada principal. Our next juncture should be Tunnel Humedo, right?"

"Right," Lia agreed, smiling up at him. She held up the map, using her index finger. "We're here. In about a thousand feet, we are going to move to the right. We'll pass another tunnel on the right first, but we don't want to take that one. We want the second tunnel."

"Roger," he said, touching her upturned face. Lia's skin already glistened with perspiration. The cave was very humid, and Cav's clothes were sticking to him. "Feels like it could rain in here," he said wryly, his eyes following the light.

She laughed softly, folding up the map and tucking it into the pocket of her pants. Her skin prickled with pleasure as he'd brushed her cheek with his fingertips. It felt like the most right thing in the world to Lia. "Oh, yeah, and you're going to be soaked by it. Hey, are you doing okay?"

He heard concern in her low voice. Reaching out, he moved some curls away from her left eye. Cav couldn't help it; he wanted to touch this woman so badly. Her hair was damp and silky beneath his fingertips. "I'm doing fine. You?" his voice growing thick with yearning.

Her lips parted beneath his second unexpected touch. Cav saw her gray eyes change with arousal. This was the first time he'd openly reached out to touch her.

Lia felt her skin prickle with pleasure as he moved strands of hair away from her eyes. Her voice was oddly off key. "Um…fine…just fine…" His green and gold eyes were deeply shadowed, but she easily read Cav's intent. He wanted to kiss her.

She wasn't sure what to do next. Lia simply didn't trust herself to read any man, especially Cav. His unexpected touches were welcome and she loved the sudden intimacy that had leapt between them. And she wanted more. Did she have the courage to kiss him back? Or first? And what would it mean if she did? Where was this possibly leading?

Cav wasn't supposed to be a permanent fixture in her life. He was transient, and she needed someone permanent, something she could build on over time.

Lia gave herself an inward shake. Cav invited her to fantasize and dream. But she wouldn't fool herself after the debacle with Jerry. She had been shattered once and Lia couldn't find the heart or courage to try again.

Turning, Lia continued slowly forward, her boots slopping from the ever-present water that was sometimes nearly ankle deep. The limestone gravel that littered the floor was hidden from view, so she had to pay attention to where she was placing her boots. Although Lia had been in this cave at least forty times in the last four years, she never took her experience for granted. Caves were living beings, constantly shape-shifting and changing. Earthquakes in this region added to the changeability of the rocks and gravel beneath her feet.

They came to the second tunnel. She turned. "We go about five hundred feet and then we get into a pretty narrow tunnel. Off and on, we'll be down on our hands and knees, squeezing through some tight places."

"Okay, good to know." In the flash of the light on his helmet, several bats flew past them, disturbed by the human invaders in their territory.

He studied her. "You still doing okay?" Caving was difficult and strenuous activity, and where they were going, it was going get tougher according to the map.

"I feel like I'm walking on air," she said smiling as she tucked the map away. "You?"

"Feeling good," he agreed, meeting her smile, wanting to lean down a few inches and kiss the hell out of her. This time, Cav saw that she wanted to kiss him, too. It was there, clear in her large gray eyes that softened by the second as he held her gaze. Straightening up, he resisted. Barely. "I'm ready."

So was she, but not for what he thought. Lia licked her lower lip, turning around, heading down the tunnel. Her heart was yearning for Cav's touch once more. He'd *almost* kissed her—she'd seen it in his eyes.

What would she do? Her emotions seesawed as she took the tunnel, her hands out on the walls as they got narrower the farther they walked.

Lia halted at another tunnel to their right. She pulled out the map and Cav leaned close, looking over her shoulder. Inhaling his male scent, her lower body contracted with real need. Cav was reminding her how long she'd gone without sex.

She saw him as more than that, however. He'd touched her heart and by the way he treated her on a daily basis, he was helping her unveil herself to the world once more. Cav was healing her, whether he realized it or not.

They began to hunch over as the tunnel ceiling began to slowly lower. Finally, after another half hour, they came to a pool of blue water. Lia crouched down near it and Cav came and joined her. Their lights flashed around, showing the ocher walls gleaming with water trickling from upper, unknown sources. That water fed the pool in front of them. It was oblong and disappeared into the gloom beyond their headlamps.

"Time for a break," Lia told him. She leaned against the damp wall in her crouch, pulling a protein bar from her pack.

Cav took the other wall, facing her. The tunnel was about four to six feet wide. He sat down and stretched his legs as much as he could near her. Lia's face gleamed with perspiration and humidity. Her naturally curly hair was curled even more tightly around her face. As he peeled the paper from his bar, he said, "What do you like most about caving?"

She munched and gave his question some thought. "The silence." She gestured toward the pool. "I love the sound of the drips into water, the rush of wind around me as I walk in a dark adit. I always feel like I'm in the womb of the earth. In my imagination, I think of caves as being Mother Earth's natural womb. And I find it protective. You're going to laugh, but sometimes, I feel as if she's invisibly surrounding me with her love. Here, I feel so free and natural."

"How long have you been spelunking? You said age ten, right?"

"Yes, with my dad."

"Did you always feel this way about caves?" Cav wondered, trapped by the serene look on her face now. The change in Lia was amazing to him. Out in the world, she had such a serious demeanor. Here, her face was free of all tension, her gray eyes glistening with excitement, her mouth no longer tight or stretched, but soft and so very kissable.

She squirmed a little. "Well, maybe the last five years I've found a refuge of sorts in caving. Before, it was about exploration, discovery and seeing so many beautiful things revealed in the light of my headlamp." She gave the transparent blue pool a warm look. "Now, I find peace down here..."

Cav studied her profile and heard the pain, but he also understood the need for a place like this. She had been attacked and nearly killed by the knife attack. He could imagine a place like this where she felt as safe as a baby in a womb, where she could relax and just be herself.

"Down here," he offered pensively, "you don't have to worry about people staring at you. Right?"

She turned her head, meeting his shadowed gaze. "Yes."

There was such weight and tiredness behind her answer. Cav reached out, allowing his fingers to graze her lower leg. "You don't have to go through this alone, you know."

Lia felt like a dry sponge soaking up his tender male touch. Her heart beat harder and she felt his hand rest around her damp ankle. She could have pulled it away from him, but she didn't want to.

"Some days," she quavered, her voice fading into the breeze that ebbed and flowed around them, "it's very hard for me to face the world. Here," and she lifted her hand, fingers moving gracefully outward, "I don't have to worry about what people think of me when they see me and my scars..."

"But here you get nurtured, sustained, right?"

She had trouble responding, since her skin was tingling beneath his calloused hand, now lying comfortably against her ankle. The bottom of the scar was beneath his fingertips. And yet, oddly, Lia felt comforted by his contact. "How..." she choked, "How could you know this?" Was he a mind reader? Sometimes, Lia swore Cav was exactly that.

Now, he'd framed something for her, his words a nice, tidy portrait of what she was thinking or feeling.

"As a SEAL, you're taught a lot of body language, both verbal and nonverbal. We always need to read the enemy, so I guess I've applied that skill to everyone I meet, more or less."

With Lia, he applied all of his experience to read her accurately, but Cav wasn't about to say that, though. The fact that she was allowing him to place his hand across her ankle sent a powerful need through him. She was entrusting herself to him on an intimate level by allowing him to touch her like this. He hadn't consciously thought about it, but her words made him want to soothe her, help her.

"You're pretty good," she said, finishing off her protein bar. "You've sure pinned me."

"Does it bother you?" and he held her gaze.

"No. It did at first, but over the past week, I guess you've grown on me—or vice versa," and she gave him a quick grin.

Cav lifted his hand away from her ankle, not wanting to overstay his welcome. He'd seen Lia's expression change, grow languid, and saw the yearning in her eyes. Cav was very astute when it came to knowing whether there was something between him and a woman he wanted to take to bed. And he'd never wanted to take a woman more than he did her.

Lia had no idea how much of his heart she already owned. And if she knew that, what would she do?

Cav returned, "We're a good team," and tucked the paper into his pocket. He pulled on his gloves once more. "You ready to swim this pool?"

Rousing herself, she nodded. "Yes. The depth is between ankle deep to up to your waist," she told him, slowly standing, dodging some rocks that hung down from the overhead. "Half way through, we can swim to the other end. It remains about waist deep to the other end of it."

She chuckled. "As a SEAL, I'm sure you'll find this a lot of fun."

"I will. Want me to lead?"

"No, let me. About once or twice a year during the rainy season, this tunnel is inaccessible because the water is nearly to the top of the adit here," and she pointed upward. "But during flood time, it digs new pockets and holes beneath the pool. I want to carefully explore it. No sense in falling into a six-foot-deep hole we can't see."

She was right about that, and Cav nodded. "Lead the way. I have your back."

For the next fifteen minutes, Lia found new potholes in the pool and called over her shoulder to Cav to alert him. The water was a tepid, mirroring the cave's year-round warmth. Climbing out the other end, dripping wet, Lia made her way to a nearby white limestone alcove. She watched Cav make the journey without any problem. His hair was plastered against his skull, flesh gleaming beneath the lamplight as he left the pool. He grinned over at her.

"Refreshing. At least it took the sweat off us."

She laughed and nodded, standing. Arranging her gear around her waist, she said, "The adit gets wider and we won't have to hunch over." She thought that at this moment, Cav looked about seventeen, now that he wasn't wearing his usual rugged, stern look. Caving had a way of stripping off the layers, the masks, that people wore, Lia had discovered a long time ago. Turning, she said, "The stalactites get bigger and you're going to have to be careful or you'll get punctured by one of them from here on until about five hundred feet up the adit."

Cav liked the overhead limestone structure formed from the calcium salts found in the sedimentary rock. They always reminded him of an icicle hanging from the roof downward.

Lia was right, some were very sharply pointed at the ends, and could damn well puncture a distracted caver's body before they knew what had happened.

Fortunately, the limestone floor was nubby and rough, but over the years stalagmites had broken off by tourists muddling along in the adit. It was a shame. True cavers left everything untouched and unbroken. They left no footprints in the caves they explored. Tourists were different. No one had taught them cave ethics, as witnessed by the destroyed stalagmites crunching beneath his boots as he walked along the dark entryway.

For the next hour, Cav followed Lia through chest-high water. In other areas, they squeezed through holes in the limestone that most people wouldn't believe an adult could get through. But they did. They crawled on their hands and knees in some parts of the lowered adit as their helmets scraped the ceiling. A river was flowing through the bottom of the adit now as they continued on in silence. Only the drip, drip, drip of water could be heard, along with the squish of their boots against the floor.

Cav's admiration for Lia mounted as they struggled through another hole in the cave wall, landing in a pit of mud. By the time they'd crawled through it, they were covered head to toe with it.

As Lia came out of the mud pit, they were met by another pool of water, which Cav gladly swam into. He washed the mud off his body along the way and by the time they reached the other side of it, they were in a huge cavern. Slowly standing, the water dripping off him, Cav came and stood next to Lia. The hours to get here to Boca del la Culebra had been worth it.

Sunlight flooded through a huge opening halfway up a landslide area of rock and debris with soil at the bottom. Shafts of powerful sunlight made his eyes water; he held up his hand to shade his eyes while they adjusted. The hole was huge. Tons of limestone rocks had broken up and created a path that could be climbed out of it.

The sun's rays within the cave created an amazing sight as Cav turned slowly around, absorbing the natural beauty surrounding them. There were caramel, cream, sienna and stark white limestone in the rounded cave. He could hear the water running nearby, above the blue sky, filmy white clouds and the sun made him want to go one step further.

"Well?" Lia asked, turning, smiling, "was this worth it or what?"

He grinned and held her shining eyes. "Oh yeah, every second of it." Without thinking, he took his thumb and gently removed a smudge of mud from across her cheek where the scar lay. He briefly felt the scar itself and too late, realized what he'd done. Instead of moving away, Cav made a smooth movement of his thumb and removed the remainder of the mud. For a moment, he saw a flicker of fear in Lia's eyes, but she hadn't jerked away from him, nor had she gasped or acted shocked by his touch.

"Mud," he said, keeping his smile in place, holding her gaze, watching her reaction over his gesture. "Do I have any on me?" he teased.

Lia made a wry movement with her lips, trying not to be overwhelmed by this seductive dance between them. He'd touched her scar and hadn't winced like Jerry had. His smile never changed, nor did the tender look in his eyes that burned with need for her. It took her a moment to absorb what had just taken place between them. Then he leaned down so she could inspect his face.

"Oh, you're muddy all right," she laughed, and removed her red neckerchief from around her neck. "Just can't take you anywhere," she teased, dipping the already damp cloth into a nearby pool. Straightening, she placed her hand on his recently shaven cheek and said, "Hold still."

CHAPTER 13

THE MOMENT LIA slid her hand along the hard line of Cav's jaw, her heart and her need thundered simultaneously. Cav stood very still while she worked to get the mud off his broad brow, down his other temple and jaw. She knew that Cav wanted her and she wanted him.

Her hand trembled slightly as she cleaned off his face. His pure male scent entered her as she inhaled it deeply into herself, feeling her entire body go on red alert.

She could feel the tension radiating off his body, but he stood stock still, unmoving, except that his gaze was upon her face and she could feel it as she concentrated on removing the mud from him.

"There!" she breathed, releasing him as if he were a hot stove and her fingers were being burned. It had been so long since she'd really touched a man, and it sent a hunger through her that she could no longer ignore.

Before she'd had her kids to take care of, and with so much to do, she didn't have time to dwell on herself, or the fact she was a twenty-six year old woman with a sex drive. All of that got sublimated and ignored.

"Thanks," Cav said gruffly, rubbing his jaw. "Now I think I'm being treated like one of those children you take care of," he teased, a crooked grin tugging at his mouth.

Crouching down over a small pool, she quickly cleaned her neckerchief. "I do a lot of runny noses," she answered, looking up briefly, meeting his warm gaze. Heat sheeted through her from the burning look Cav gave her. Lia wished she could call him on what was going on between them. He was obviously drawn to her, for whatever his reasons. And her reasons? Why was she drawn so powerfully to Cav? She had never been treated so well by any man. Cav was like a fevered dream that Lia was sure was pure fantasy. But he really did exist. And he wanted her.

"Thanks for cleaning me off," he said gruffly.

"No problem." She pulled the damp neckerchief around her neck, tying it loosely. "I have a special surprise for you," she said. Taking a huge chance, she reached out, curling her fingers around his, tugging him forward. "Follow me?" Lia felt his strong hand curve warmly around hers, and Cav gave it a squeeze, and then released her. Her heart was in her throat—Lia was shaky after being so bold. Before the assault, she'd been a bold and confident woman. Afterward? A mere shadow of her real self and she hated it. But Cav was helping her regain her old self, and for that, she was grateful. Looking up, she saw that hunger banked in his eyes. It felt so good to be wanted but she felt trepidation mingling with her hopes.

"Lead on," Cav urged, following her across the debris-strewn floor toward the slope that led up to the hole in the cave wall.

Lia led Cav up the rocky slope and took him outside of the cave. There was a narrow V-like precipice outside it, covered with thick green grass and a few trees. "This is what I wanted to show you," she said smiling, pointing toward the West.

Cav turned and saw the volcano, Arenal, the canopy of the cloud forest and a plain beyond it, plus a lake. "Beautiful," he murmured, catching her gaze. Lia stood near enough to him that their hands almost brushed against one another. He belatedly realized that when he'd touched her ankle, something had changed subtly between them. At the time, he didn't catch it. Maybe when he'd wiped the mud off her scarred cheek? Whatever it was, it was good, and he could feel something magical throbbing between them. It was something he wanted to act upon.

"Isn't it remarkable that inside the cave system, we're always climbing up and down, but we're not that aware of the elevation differences unless our ears pop?" Lia turned, gesturing around the panorama. "We're roughly two thousand feet above the jungle and plain. Did it feel like we were climbing that much?"

"At times, yes," Cav said, enjoying her excitement. Outside, the sunlight cascaded down upon them between the transparent wafts of clouds below them, just above the jungle canopy. The breeze was humid and it felt good to be outside breathing in fresh, clean air. Inside, the cave had an odor. Not a bad one, but a musty one. All caves smelled. It was just a question of how good or bad the odor was. There were a lot of bats living in Venado, so bat guano was pretty acrid and present, especially if they moved past a colony area. At a few spots, Cav's eyes had burned and watered with tears from the intense smell.

"You did bring along those peanut butter sandwiches, I hope?" Lia unbuckled her pack around her waist, dropping it into the grass. She slid her fingers through her damp hair, trying to tame some of the curls from sticking to her face and temples. Looking around, she found some flatter rocks to sit on.

"I did," Cav said. He brought out two hard plastic cases from his pack and sat down beside her. Handing her one, he said, "This is an incredible sight." She was, too, but he swallowed the rest of his words. Their fingers briefly touched as he gave her the sandwich.

"Thanks," Lia said. "I love coming up here," she admitted. "It's a place where I can think. Where I can't be disturbed. I guess I'm one of those people who are deep thinkers at times, and I hate being jolted out of my line of thought."

Cav watched her sink her teeth into the thick sandwich he'd made earlier. He was hungry, salivating to taste that protein rich peanut butter. Between bites, he said, "This is a good place to do just that."

Lia seemed happier than he'd ever seen her. Her hair was drying beneath the sunlight, the red and gold highlights dancing in her curled strands. Her cheeks were pink, and she looked luminous to him even though they were bedraggled-looking in their damp, soiled clothes. Mud was still here and there on the fabric they wore.

Lia stretched her legs out before her. Funny, she was no longer hesitant about Cav seeing her scarred legs. "I have so many questions for you," she said, catching his sideward glance.

"Oh?" Cav chewed on the sandwich, seeing a wicked look come to her eyes. In the past week he'd revealed more of himself to her than he ever done with anyone. By doing so, it had opened a door between them.

He'd trusted her first with information. Cav wasn't sure Lia had always been this closed up, or whether it had been more recent because of that assault upon her?

"Like what?"

"Well," she said, "I'd like to know more about you. I mean, I know you were a SEAL, but that's a job you did. And I know it speaks to you, who you are, but there's far more to you than that."

Shrugging, Cav said, "I think we're all who we are because of many things coming into play." Discomfort moved through Cav because he saw the focus of her gray eyes darken upon him. He could feel Lia reaching out to him. This was the first time she'd openly asked him questions about himself. If he wanted their trust to grow, he knew he was going to have to remain open to her.

He worried what she'd ask him. "If you're going to ask me about my time as a SEAL, everything I did was top secret, and I can't answer your questions."

Wrinkling her nose, she said, "Oh, I know that. I was in the Army and a mechanic, but I was aware all black ops were top secret. No," and she tilted her head, really studying him, "we've talked about some of my growing up years. You talked about your Mom. I know you're an only child like me. But I was wondering where you lived, what your father is like, and if you have other family nearby?"

His gut clenched and Cav stopped eating his sandwich, staring out over the bucolic scene of the jungle and the volcano. What was he going to do? Say? He heard the sincerity in Lia's husky voice, saw she clearly cared about him and wanted to know more.

Dammit. He frowned. "Honestly? My childhood was nothing to write home about, Lia. It wasn't anything like yours."

"I'm so sorry to hear that," she murmured, reaching over, fingers brushing his shoulder. "I just wondered what has made you who you are, Cav."

Gritting his teeth, he forced himself to eat. Maybe it would buy him some time. His skin warmed beneath her unexpected touch. Lia was reaching out, her confidence growing enough that she made physical contact with him. Cav wanted so much more than that from her, and he knew damn well if he didn't remain vulnerable with her, that growing intimacy between them would stop.

Cav didn't want that, and desperation made him swallow a lot of bitterness her question had dug up.

Lia was one of those people who wore her heart on her sleeve. She couldn't help being who she was, and God knew, Cav was constantly reacting to this woman's maternal care she shared so lovingly with others. She fed his darkened soul in ways he couldn't express in words. And Cav did NOT want to lose the ground he'd opened up with Lia.

He reminded himself that she was deeply wounded and he wasn't, so he was the one who needed to step up to the plate. Not her.

He finished off his sandwich and rubbed his hands down the thighs of his damp coveralls. "Okay, I hope you're ready for this," he warned her grimly. "If you think I had a happy childhood? I didn't, Lia. My old man was a drug addict. From the time I could remember, he took cocaine. It was his drug of choice."

He searched her wide eyes and saw instant sympathy come to them. Clasping his hands between his open thighs, staring out at the jungle, unable to hold her gaze, he said in a low tone, "He beat the shit out of my mother and me when he was high on drugs. Even as a young kid, I tried to stop him from beating up on my Mom. But then, he'd turn on me."

"I'm so sorry," Lia whispered, reaching out again to rest her hand on his shoulder.

Something broke open in him then, and Cav relaxed a little. "My mother was a victim of constant abuse. I hated and feared my father, and tried so many times when I was a kid to get her to leave him, but she'd never finished high school and had married my father after she got pregnant. All she could do was work at a fast food restaurant, with no way of climbing out of the poverty we were in."

Lia sighed and slid her arm around his shoulders, leaning against his right arm. "How did you survive?"

Cav was aware of her arm around him, as if to protect him. He had a broad set of shoulders and she was much smaller than he was. Now, her fingers were curling gently against his damp shirt.

"Sometimes…" he cut her a quick look, "I wasn't sure I'd wake up to see the next morning. It was that bad."

"Couldn't your Mom do anything? Couldn't she get him put in jail?"

He snorted and looked down at his tightly clasped hands. "My Mom put out a restraining order on him once. He came back to the house, busted her nose and blackened her eyes. When the cops came, she wouldn't charge him and there was nothing they could do." His mouth flattened. "I was ten at the time. And I knew it was going to be hell from then on."

"My God," she whispered. "It must have been awful for both of you."

"School was my escape," Cav admitted, clearing his throat. If he looked into Lia's eyes, he was going to haul her into his arms and hold her so tightly he'd probably squeeze her to death. So he kept his gaze anywhere but on her.

Just the movement of her hand against his back, her caring, dissolved the shield he'd hidden behind all his life. Lia had a way of sliding quietly into his heart and holding it gently in her hands. In that blinding moment, Cav realized that Lia was healing to him. This wasn't a one-way relationship, either. He was helping her get back on her feet as much as she was helping him. A lump formed in his throat.

"I imagine you were glad to escape at age eighteen and go into the SEALs?"

"Better believe it." His words were loaded with relief.

"What about your Mom? Is she still with him?"

Shaking his head, he said, "She died of a sudden heart attack a month before I left to go into the Navy."

A low gasp came from Lia. "Oh, no!"

Cav made the mistake of looking in her eyes. They were filled with tears—for him. For his abused mother. "Hey," he growled, turning, using his thumbs to push away the tears trailing down her cheeks. "Don't waste your tears on us."

His gruffly spoken words only made more tears come. His fingers sent tingles across her cheeks and she drowned in his pleading expression. She saw so much in his eyes, now alive with agony, with need for her, with frustration.

His palms were warm and dry against her face and she tried to stop from crying, but she'd always been easily touched by the plight of others. She had never cried for herself, but she had cried for people or animals in pain.

Now, Cav was in pain. She saw it in his eyes and felt her heart break over the horror of eighteen years at the hands of a crazed drug addict and then, to lose his mother like that.

Lia did something that her heart whispered she must do. She leaned forward, her hands tentative on Cav's shoulders, lifting her chin, seeking…finding…the tortured line of his mouth.

Her world exploded around her. She had closed her eyes, leaning into Cav, wanting to absorb his pain, try to make him feel better. The overwhelming desire to kiss him drove her to boldly step out of her own fear and hesitancy. For a split second, Cav froze. And then, his hands tightened around her face, guiding her, drawing her against his mouth, angling her, nudging her lips open. Lost in a haze of light, joy, and need, she eagerly accepted his hunger. He moved his mouth powerfully against hers, a sense of starvation, of need for her. An avalanche of heat and fire roared to life within her lower, dormant body.

She felt him tremble as he hauled her against his chest, felt him control himself for her sake, his mouth gentling against hers.

A moan caught in her throat as he opened his fingers, sliding them through her hair, cherishing her, caught up in the heat and molten moment that glowed wildly between them. Her heart beat in triple-time as he moved her around for deeper access to her, bringing her closer in his arms, cradling her, his mouth locked with hers, not allowing her to escape.

But Lia didn't want to go anywhere. She was relaxing into his embrace, feeling his hand trailing down her jaw, slipping around her neck, following the curved line of her spine. His mouth was cajoling. Breathing shallowly, she eagerly returned his kiss, a deep ache grew between her legs, and wetness coated the insides of her thighs.

Shyly, she moved her hand up from his shoulder to his thick neck, feeling the pulse of his jugular against her fingertips. His breathing was short and hard as he suddenly realized he might be hurting her. He softened his mouth against hers, silently demanding she fully reciprocate by exploring him.

That was all Lia needed. Her fingers curved against his jaw and she deepened their kiss, her body molding urgently to his. The moment her breasts touched Cav's chest, a whimper lodged within her throat. Now, Lia knew just how sexually starved she really was.

Cav held her as if she were fragile glass that could break. His gentleness brought more tears into her now closed eyes. He was so excruciatingly tender after controlling his initial reaction to kissing her. His fingers moved lightly across her scalp, tiny sparks of heat rippled across her. Never had she been so wonderfully held, kissed and touched.

Their mouths gradually left one another. Lia was breathing erratically, gripping Cav's arms, she slowly opened her eyes, drowning in his dark, hungry gaze. The gold in his eyes was primary, the green and sienna combining to tell her how very much more he wanted to do than just kiss her.

His mouth moved and he shook his head, easing her out of the curve of his arm. "I wasn't expecting that," he said, his voice low and unsteady as he searched her eyes. "Lia? Are you okay?"

She felt suddenly unsteady as she sat up and regained her original posture, fingertips on her lips that radiated with the power of his mouth upon hers. "I-I was so tired of being scared, Cav."

"What do you mean? Did I scare you?"

She saw the disbelief in his expression. Allowing her hands to open, she whispered, "I've wanted to kiss you since I first met you." She felt heat rush to her face but pressed on. "I wanted to kiss you and I was so tired of always running scared, always worried about a man being disgusted with me...not wanting to kiss me back." Lia saw his eyes flare first, with relief, and then concern.

"How could I be disgusted with you?" he demanded, his voice a rasp.

Lia fought back more tears. Valiantly, she resisted. "My scars..." and she touched her cheek. "I'm ugly."

Cav shook his head, his mouth twisting. "Baby, you are so far away from ugly the word doesn't even exist in my world when I look at you. Okay?" and he reached out, capturing her fingers against her facial scar, tucking her hand between his as he leaned forward.

"Listen to me, will you? The first time I saw your picture, I saw *you*. And you were beautiful to me. I didn't see your scars, Lia. Do you believe me?" Urgency thrummed through him. Never had Cav wanted her to believe him more than right now.

"Y-you never looked at my scars. You seemed to always see ME, not them," she offered, her voice choked with emotion. The line of his mouth softened.

"I always see you, Lia, not your scars." He frowned and released her hand, cupping her left cheek, stroking the area of the scar. "This does not define you, baby. It never has and it never will. It's a medal of valor for what you survived—" Cav instantly halted, realizing by her reaction he'd said too much. Allowing his hand to drop away, he saw her fine, thin brows move down, confusion in her eyes as she stared at him.

"H-how did you know what I survived?"

Oh, hell! Cav had allowed his emotions, his need to help her, blow his cover. Looking away, he turned, calmly picking up her hands and holding them, speaking in a quiet voice. "I found out the night I came to guard you at your home."

"Really? How?" Her voice was shaking now.

"I got up around 0200 and did a walk around the outside of the house. I was getting acquainted with the night sounds and what went on around the house." His hands tightened a little around hers. "I came back into the house and hour later and heard a noise in the kitchen, like water running. I didn't know what it was, so I walked quietly to the entrance. You were standing at the sink, scrubbing your hands for all they were worth."

He saw her face crumple. "Oh, God…I was sleepwalking…"

"Yeah," he muttered, "I figured it out as I stood there." Releasing her hands, Cav straightened, moving his shoulders as if to remove a load he was carrying. "The reason I realized it, Lia, was because as a kid I used to sleepwalk. My Mom would hear me and get up. She'd find me in some part of the house packing a small suitcase. She'd ask me where I was going. I'd tell her I was running away because I hated my father. Then, at breakfast the next morning, my Mom would tell me she found me sleepwalking. I never remembered any of the episodes, but I was doing it two or three times a week."

Cav drew in a ragged breath, holding her gaze. "That's how I figured out you were sleepwalking. Your eyes were glazed, and you could clearly see me standing in the doorway of the kitchen, but you didn't see me."

"What happened next?" she asked hollowly.

"I asked you what you were doing. You said you were trying to wash your cuts and blood off between and around your fingers and hands." Cav winced inwardly, seeing terror come to Lia's face. "I asked you what happened," he began, his voice gruff. "You said two men had jumped you and you fought and ran away from them."

Lia gave a little cry, her hands flying to her mouth, staring at Cav. It felt as if her world had fallen out from beneath her. Cav sat there, stoic, his gaze gentle as he held hers, his hands clasped between his thighs.

He shook his head and reached out, easing her hands from her mouth, holding one of them between his. "These are defensive wounds," he told her, tracing some of the worst with his index finger across her fingers and into her palm. "I knew whatever had happened to you, baby, it had to be a life-and-death fight."

He folded her hand between his, holding it, holding her wavering gaze. "That's all I know, Lia. I didn't want to burden you any more than you already are." He snorted softly and hitched one shoulder, giving her a wry look. "But you have that effect on me. When I get around you, my emotions start unraveling just naturally and it takes everything I have to control myself and think about what I will tell you and what I won't speak about. And I guess I blew it just now."

Lia sat there staring at Cav. He looked deeply sorry, his mouth pulled down, the corners drawn in, his brows dipping. Slowly, he released her hand and she gripped them in her lap. "Did Dilara tell you about what happened?"

"No. I knew nothing until the night you sleepwalked. I more or less put it together. I don't know the details." He took a deep breath. "And you don't have to tell me if you don't want to. I'll understand."

Her fingers tingled where he'd traced her puckered scars in the webbing between her fingers. All she could do was sit there and allow the emotions to roll through her like waves from a tsunami. Slowly, Lia rubbed her face, feeling cold inside, dreading what she was about to say to Cav.

She whispered painfully, "You've been so nice to me. You treated me like I was whole, Cav. Do you know how nice that felt? Five years of being stared at like I was a freak or a side show," and she touched her neck scar. "I was so tired of it all. I tried to hide my scars. I just wanted peace. I didn't want constant reminders of my attackers by people staring at the scars instead of meeting my eyes…"

Five years' worth of exhaustion flowed through her, erasing the beauty of the kiss Cav had shared with her.

"You deserve to hear it from me." She lifted her lashes, meeting his weary gaze. Just talking about this was exhausting her and Cav. There was such anguish in his eyes for her. Not disgust. But caring.

Lia struggled with her fear and pain. Cav deserved to know the truth and it hurt so much to speak about the assault, that it made her mouth dry. Pulling out her plastic bottle, she drank water, capped it and launched into the attack, leaving nothing out.

Cav felt the weight of the terror that Lia felt as the two men took their military knives to her. He boiled with rage as he listened, his white-knuckled hands clasped tightly between his legs. What Lia had done, her bravery in fighting the two men off, was nothing short of mind-blowing. She wasn't a very strongly built woman, and she wasn't that tall. Thank God her father had taught her Krav Maga! Knowing that street-fighting tactic had helped save her life.

The sun had shifted by the time she finished, her voice little more than a hoarse whisper, her hands fluttering nervously from time to time. Lia tried to still her raw emotions, waiting for Cav's eyes to mirror disgust.

"So, that's the whole story. I know I'm not whole. I lost so much during that fight. Before it happened, I was such a risk taker and I was fearless." She looked over at him, finally, and saw nothing but sympathy in his eyes.

"I'm a shadow of my former self, Cav. I hide. I don't want people staring at me. The children...well, they're curious about the scars, they ask me about them and I tell them a fib. I tell them I fell and cut myself. They believe me, and they love me anyway. They think nothing more about it. And," her lower lip trembled, "they treat me as if I'm normal."

Cav had thought he knew what pain was. But he didn't. Not until he'd heard how Lia had nearly died and bled out. He saw tears in her eyes. "Have you cried since you were attacked?"

"I *refuse* to cry any more tears, Cav. It's not helping me. I have to get stronger. I can't keep hiding like this..."

He roused, reached out, his large hand covering her clasped hands in her lap. "Then let me hold you when you're ready."

CHAPTER 14

LIA SAID NOTHING, holding herself so tightly she seemed to be shielding herself.

"There are so many people who treat you as whole," Cav went on quietly, watching her as she listened. "Dilara and Robert. Myself. Your kids. Those three new teachers thought nothing of your scars, either."

"You're right," she agreed, moving her fingers nervously. "When people get to know me, they don't see the scars as much."

Struggling to understand, he said, "Then who...or what...made you feel like hiding, Lia?"

Weakly, she shrugged. "The first three years after being cut up, I was an emotional basket case. If it hadn't been for Dilara and my parents helping to put me back together again, I don't think I'd be where I am today. I felt carved up, Cav."

Looking away, she whispered, "I had a boyfriend at the time the attack happened. Jerry came and saw me after the attack and he couldn't look me in the eyes. He saw all the wounds and he shook his head and left me. He never returned. I saw the disgust, the revulsion, in his eye for me. He looked at me as if I were a monster. And then, two years ago, I got into a relationship with Manuel. I was desperate for a mature, ongoing relationship...I went too fast. I know it was partly my fault because I'm such an idealist. I was just so lonely," and she met his hooded gaze, feeling old pain renewed. "He showed interest in me and I thought...well, because he made little of the scars he saw, it would be okay as we got more..."

She pushed her fingers through her hair, her voice shaky. "Anyway, how stupid and short-sighted I was. When he saw the others," and she gestured to her arms and legs, "I guess he began to see me as one big, ugly scar walking around. There was such horror in his face, his eyes. Manuel didn't want to touch me. He…couldn't…"

Cav cursed softly. "Then he was the second man to show interest in you?"

"Yes." Lia fought against the burn of tears in the back of her eyes, giving him a sad, broken smile. "I thought wrongly that he liked me, my personality, that the scars didn't bother him." Her lips tightened. "In all fairness to Manuel, I never prepared him for the extent of my wounds, or where they were at. I'm sure it was a shock to him…"

"What did he do?" Cav demanded.

"He reared back. He wouldn't touch me. All he could do was stare at them…"

Cav sat unmoving. He could see how fragile Lia really was in that moment. "Then," he said, his voice harsh and low, "he wanted you for only one thing…sex. He never cared about you as a person, Lia. You realize that now, don't you?"

Cav was desperate for her to see that. It could mean she could finally see both of those men in a different light. He knew very few women could have a night of sex for sex's sake and then walk away without any emotional attachment. And Lia wasn't one of those women. Jerry had cut her to her soul with the way he'd handled the situation. Manuel had burned it into her soul that she was some kind of freak of nature and therefore, undesirable.

"I try to tell myself that," she said wryly. "On some days it actually works. On others, it doesn't."

"You can't carry their immaturity and his selfishness around with you and make it your own, Lia. How they reacted to you, is on them, not you."

The psychic damage he'd done to Lia was major, and Cav began to understand her shyness, her need to hide her scars beneath her clothing. Jerry had, for all intents and purpose, carved her up with the invisible blade of rejection. The second man had destroyed her confidence in herself as a woman. He watched her feelings play out across her desolate looking expression.

Nodding, Lia whispered, "I know that, logically. I've had therapy off and on over the years, trying to deal with their rejection and disgust. It's one thing to know something mentally, Cav. It's another to know it here," and she pressed her hand to her heart. "I've just felt so shattered and unsure of myself since then. I came to realize I would never have someone who wanted me for the person I am, not the scars I wear."

Cav had to be careful. He could feel her frailness. "Have you ever talked to anyone else about this other than your therapist?"

"No... I-I just didn't have the strength to do it."

He reached over, grazing her hair. "You've told me. That's an important step, Lia. You're a lot stronger than you think you are." He searched her mournful eyes, feeling her yearning for intimacy, and her resistance to scaling the wall she'd built to keep it away.

Lia slowly stood up and moved her palms down the sides of her pants. "Since you've walked into my life, Cav, I feel stronger. I guess my confessing all this to you proves that, doesn't it?"

Calmly, he said, "Not every man is like those two, Lia. I have my issues, but your scars don't turn me off. I see you. I see your heart, your smile and your laughter. I watch you build those kids esteem. You value them and they know that."

"I guess you see me differently, then."

Cav nodded, watching her walk out toward the edge of the cliff. He drank in the shape of her lean, graceful body, understanding why she was underweight. Don't eat and you'll disappear. Just another way to hide, isn't it?

"Well," he told her proudly, "you've made a very brave step forward in sharing it all with me."

Turning, she looked down at him. "And you're not disgusted by it?"

"No. I'm pissed off as hell at the two men scarred you up. If I ever find them, they're dead men walking."

"Well, they're out of prison now. I don't know where they are, and I don't care."

"They didn't get long enough sentences," he ground out. "They should be put away for life because they altered your life forever."

She nodded. "Isn't that the truth? I feel like I live in a prison within my own body. That the scars define me not who I am or what I can do. It's a special prison all of its own."

"I wonder if you'd never met Jerry or Manuel, and hadn't lived through that kind of humiliation, whether you'd be seeing yourself differently now, Lia. What do you think?" Cav wasn't going to allow her to use them as a reason to stay in hiding from life and love. He knew he had to get her to think outside the shaming experiences and see herself in a more positive light.

She turned, giving him a thoughtful look. "I'm sure I would."

"Then," Cav said lightly, slowly unwinding and standing, "why do you give them so much power over you and how you see yourself? They are only a couple of men, Lia, and an immature jerks at best. Why hurt yourself because they couldn't appreciate you on so many other levels?"

He saw her eyes grow wide as she realized the truth in his words. Cav knew he'd just opened a special door into her vulnerable heart, and he was going to tread lightly. Lia needed to stand outside herself and see herself as he saw her. *He saw her as whole and beautiful.*

"You're right," she murmured. "Why am I doing it to myself?"

"After Manuel? Did you ever try again to have a relationship?" he probed.

"I never felt confident enough to put myself out there to find out," she admitted, stubbing the toe of her boot into the grass, frowning. "I didn't feel ready."

"Had you hidden in your clothing before Jerry?"

"No," she admitted, "I hadn't."

"So why give them so much of your power over you as a woman?"

Lia nodded and studied him through her lashes. "You should have been a shrink, Cav."

Giving her a careless grin, he picked up her waist belt, walked over and handed it to her. "SEAL stuff, that's all. We were taught a lot of psychology because in our business, if we go undercover we need to be able to accurately read others."

"Well," she said, taking the belt and giving him grateful look, it has helped me."

Cav wanted to kiss her again, but decided to tug playfully at her hair near her nape. "Come on, it'll take us a couple of hours to get back to the entrance."

Rallying, Lia smiled a little as he brushed her nape, feeling a delightful skittering of pleasure throughout her neck and shoulders. Gazing up into his eyes, she whispered, "Your mother must have been an incredibly sensitive person, Cav."

"Why do you say that?"

"Because she raised her son to be that way, too."

Cav liked that Lia saw him in that light. They swam through a pool, crawled through a tunnel of mud, the bats flying around them from time to time, giving Cav time to replay what had happened between them this morning. As they came out to the last adit leading them to the opening, he wanted Lia even more.

Her courage in telling him about the attack had stunned him, and he was even more impressed when she told him about Jerry and Manuel. The jerks had done a lot of damage to her self-esteem.

The late afternoon sunlight was trickling through the canopy as they emerged from the tunnel. There were a lot of tourists, children through adults, coming and going from the entrance. As they approached the more touristy areas of the system, the noise doubled and tripled. Cav missed the silence, hearing the cave breathing, and the soft whir of a bat's wings inches from his head. As Lia joined him, he saw the stress on her face from the noise surrounding them.

It had hit him earlier that his mother and Lia were emotionally quite similar.

Both were sensitive. His mother had been beaten down over time, while Lia had experienced one devastating act and then two more with men who only wanted sex from her. These had beaten her down, too.

Cav desperately hoped that Lia could work herself out from beneath her fears and trauma, unlike his mother, who'd refused to leave his father. He would never understand why she hadn't left him. She had been brainwashed for years into believing she was unworthy of respect, from the age of fifteen, when she'd had him, until she'd died at age thirty-three of a heart attack.

Now, walking to the SUV, Cav grew alert. The place now had at least ten buses in the lot, with many more tourists milling around. He opened the rear door and handed Lia the small canvas bag that had clean, dry clothes in them. They would take showers at a brick building near the office and get cleaned up before driving back to La Fortuna. He put all her gear and his into a box in the back of the SUV, shutting and locking it.

"Let's go get cleaned up," he said, smiling at her.

She laughed, opening her muddy hands. "I'm ready!"

Cav saw new light in her eyes. It was hope. If he'd been able to give her that with one kiss, listening to her story and then supporting her with his words, he was more than grateful. So much could have gone wrong today on that cliff as they shared and talked. But it hadn't.

He'd been able to thread the needle with Lia and their trust in one another was even more solid as a result. Lia's sway of her hips did nothing but incite lust in Cav. Some day, he hoped that he could take her to bed and love her, truly love her, as she deserved. Then, and only then, would she honestly know how much he had fallen in love with her.

As Cav took his shower in the men's side of the building, scrubbing his hair with shampoo, he admitted to himself that he loved Lia. The idea of love, of loving a woman, had never extended beyond the bedroom before, but with Lia, he enjoyed listening to her thoughts and watching how her mind worked. He instinctively absorbed the rainbow of emotions she wore on her face.

She was one of the most guileless women he'd ever met yet she had lured him in sweetly and quietly captured his heart. He saw her as a deep, quiet well of water that he wanted to jump into so he could discover what was at its depths.

Cav had just finished tying his dry hiking boots and was standing when he heard a scream from the direction of the women's shower room. It was on the other side of the men's, with only a brick wall separating them.

Instantly, he drew the Sig from his belt, racing out of the shower area. Tourists were screaming and running everywhere, and there were shouts as Cav skidded around the corner of the building. He spotted two men dragging Lia between them. She was fighting like a wildcat, kicking, screaming and trying to escape.

His mind instantly went into SEAL mode. Both men were taller than Lia. Their destination was apparently a white van parked near the wall of the jungle.

He held up his Sig, racing toward them. They appeared to be carrying no weapons, save for a knife in each of their belts. His focus centered on the knives as he checked out Lia's body. Good, there was no blood and no marks on her from the rear view.

Visitors to the caves were scattering, frightened, screaming. Women were gathering up their children. Men looked shocked. Cav knew he was alone in this kidnapping. No one had weapons and everyone feared for their own lives. They weren't running toward trying to help Lia. They were running the opposite direction. Sonofabitch!

All the noise went away as Cav halted fifty feet away from the van. He shouted at the men, and the tall, blond, white man wearing a red baseball cap jerked a look back across his shoulder. His blue eyes widened as he saw Cav lift the pistol in both hands, aiming it at him.

"Let her go!" Cav roared, "Or I shoot!"

The second man, a Latino, shorter with black hair and brown eyes, released Lia, turning and pulling a pistol out of his belt.

Cav fired, the Sig bucking in his hands. The man flew back four feet; his arms pumping like windmills until he slammed into the ground.

The blond man cursed, bared his teeth, and yanked a .45 from his belt.

No way.

Cav fired again, shooting to kill.

Lia screamed and fell backward as the man, now being hurled to her left, released his hold around her wrist.

People were racing around, screaming, and cars were taking off, spurting mud and dirt beneath their tires.

Cav's heart came back to a slow pound. Now, his only focus was on Lia as she got unsteadily to her hands and knees. He heard her sobbing, saw that her pale apricot tee was ripped at her shoulder. He snapped his head around, looking for other threats and listening for sounds of danger.

He saw no one else at the white van they had been heading for.

"Stay down," Cav yelled to her, keeping his pistol up, now pointed at the vehicle. He was taking no chances.

Lia instantly flattened against the ground, covering her head with her hands. Racing to the van, Cav moved his pistol from the front open window toward the back. He saw ropes in the rear and a sleeping bag. That was all. The two men had come alone.

Allowing his pistol to drop to one hand, Cav quickly rounded the van and knelt down near Lia.

"Are you hurt?" he rasped, his hand on her arm, helping her sit up. Lia's face was smudged with dirt, the entire front of her tee dusty along with her jeans. She'd lost a sandal in the battle with the two men. Tears streaked down her dusty face.

"Oh, God," she cried, gripping Cav's arm, "Those are the two who tried to rape me at Bagram! They're the ones that sliced me up!" she sobbed.

Stunned, Cav looked around. He saw the owner hurrying toward them, a cell phone in hand. He was probably calling the *policia* and an ambulance.

Glancing to his right, he saw the Latino he'd shot begin to move. The blond man was dead. "Stay here," he ordered Lia harshly, rising. Pulling out the flex cuffs he always carried, he walked over to the Latino, who was now groaning in pain. Cav saw blood on the man's chest and jerked him over on his back.

"You sonofabitch," he snarled, keeping the pistol in his face. "Move and you're dead."

The man gasped, clearly terrified. Cav knew he'd punctured his right lung. Looking up, he called in Spanish to the owner, "Get me some aluminum foil or some plastic wrap. Pronto!"

The man halted, nodding. He spun around and ran for the small ticket house.

Cav knelt down, yanking him up by his shirt, snarling in Spanish, "Who the hell are you?"

"D-don't kill me!" the man gasped, throwing up his left hand.

"Tell me who you're working for or I will," he hissed, tightening his grip on the collar, choking the Latino. Cav figured it was the drug lord, Medina and these two were hit men, but he wanted to be sure, to know fully what he was up against.

"M-medina! Dante Medina," he screamed. "I'm dying! I'm dying! Help me!"

Cursing him, Cav released him, allowing him to drop to the ground. "Move and you die."

He stood, watching the owner come running back with foil waving in his hand.

Cav jerked the Latino into a sitting position, flex-cuffing his hands behind him. He shoved the Sig into his belt and grabbed the foil. In a matter of moments, he had the foil flush with the bullet wound in the Latino's chest. Almost instantly, the man started to breathe better, his eyes round with terror.

"I called the *policia*," the owner panted. "What else can I do, Senor?"

"Watch him," Cav growled, straightening. "You called an ambulance?"

"Si, si, they are on their way…"

"If he moves, tell me," Cav told him, walking to Lia.

Leaning down, Cav placed his hands on Lia's upper arms. "You're okay now," he told her quietly, holding her tearful gaze. "It's over. You're safe, baby. Safe. Do you hear me? No one's going to hurt you any more."

His voice thickened as he fought to keep his emotions at bay. It was easy with the two kidnappers. But with Lia? She was shaking her arms wrapped around herself, sitting on the ground, whimpers tearing out between her contorted lips.

"T-they grabbed me as I was coming out of the showers," she babbled. "I-I didn't expect—Oh, God, Cav, they were trying to kidnap me!"

Whispering her name, he hauled Lia into his arms, holding her tightly against him, trying to give her a sense of safety. The sobs ripping out of her sounded like those of a wounded animal caught in a trap.

Turning his head, he watched the Latino on the ground. The owner was watching him, his hand on his hips, anger on his face. The whole parking area was now devoid of vans and cars. Everyone had rushed to their vehicles, getting out of the line of fire. Cav couldn't blame them. Tourists were hurriedly running to the busses awaiting them, wanting to get away as well.

He returned his focus to Lia, gently massaging her shoulders, wanting her to cry until her terror had been fully released. He kept whispering words of solace to her. She clung to him, her fingers digging into the fabric across his chest, her face pressed hard against him, the front of his t-shirt damp with her tears.

This time, Cav knew she was crying for herself. He kissed her hair, her damp temples, letting her know that she was safe.

Angry with himself, Cav knew he'd let down his guard. He should have stood outside Lia's shower stall area and waited for her. Dammit, anyway! But Lia had insisted she'd be fine and insisted he go get his shower.

And she'd almost been kidnapped. *Sonofabitch!* He stilled the anger and stuffed it into his "kill box" deep down inside him. He'd be writing a report to Robert Culver later on this incident, and he knew his boss would chew him a new ass, for sure. He'd allowed Lia to dissuade him and he shouldn't have.

Now, he took stock of Lia. Except for some bruises around her wrists where they'd grabbed her, Cav couldn't see any other marks. Had they threatened her with those knives again? Were the knives they wore now the same ones that they'd used to cut her five years earlier?

His eyes narrowed as he inspected the blond kidnapper who laid dead, a long combat knife in the sheath on his right side. Despite his mistakes, he felt deeply satisfied that he'd been there to kill the bastard and sorry he hadn't killed his partner. But one of them needed to be alive to talk. And talk he would—or else, Cav grimly thought.

"Can you stand?" he asked Lia gently.

Sniffing, Lia gave a jerky nod. "I-I'm so dirty…"

He smiled a little as he lifted her easily to her feet, keeping his arm around her waist, holding her against him.

"Want to take another shower?"

Lia looked at the men to the right and left of her, and Cav felt her shrinking into his embrace. Wanting to get her away from the scene, he said, "Come on, let's get you to the shower. I'll stand guard while you get clean. And I'll shake out your clothes and try to get rid of some of the dirt on them."

"O-okay," Lia said, looking around for the first time. Her knees felt wobbly and she was still shaking from the assault. Cav patiently led her across the parking lot and back to the showers. He guided her into one and helped her sit down on the stone bench.

"The *policia* will be here soon," he told her, his hand on the curtain above. "Take your time, okay? I'll be right outside this curtain."

CHAPTER 15

EVERYTHING WAS A blur for Lia. She sat in the office with two *policia* who took her statement. Cav never left her side. The desire to run still tunneled through her, but Cav's calm presence helped her focus as she related exactly what had happened. Sometimes, she broke into English instead of Spanish, and then Cav would interpret for her, noting that Lia's hands wouldn't stop shaking.

Everything was in chaos. The *policia* were trying to put together the pieces of three criminal acts. There was Lia's aborted kidnapping, Cav's fatal shooting of Schaefer, and his serious wounding of Dominguez, who was now in the hospital. The word was that he would live.

Lia would never forget the murderous look in Cav's eyes as they took the injured Dominguez into the ambulance. In that split second, she'd seen Cav, the SEAL, on full alert, protecting her with his life. He wanted to move his fingers across her tight, drawn up shoulders as the *policia* questioned her. But he couldn't. Not as a professional security contractor. Besides it would confuse the policia. He did give her bottled water, urging her to drink and remain hydrated during the long interview session.

Finally, Cav called a halt to it, telling the two officers that he needed to get Lia to a doctor because she was injured, too. The men immediately agreed. They told Cav he needed to visit the La Fortuna police headquarters to issue his report on the situation. Cav knew that because he had permission to carry a pistol here, he wouldn't get jail time. He promised he would go to the police precinct office and talk to the detectives about his role in the shootings after he dropped Lia off at her home.

Cav came and pulled over a stool in front of Lia's chair after the policia left the interrogation room. There were no cameras in it, the blinds drawn. It was private for the moment and he took advantage of it for her sake. "Tell me what you need," he asked gently, holding her hands in his.

So powerful were her feelings for Cal at that moment that she was at a loss for words. Finally, she said, "I just want to go home."

"Okay, then, let's do it." He leaned forward and kissed her brow. "Come on, let's go," he said, standing up and drawing her into his arms.

Lia crumpled against him, her arms going around his waist, pressing her cheek into his chest, feeling safe at last.

Cav had saved her life today. Saved her! She didn't even want to think what those two were going to do to her this time. Cav's hand moved comfortingly against her back, skating across her hips and then coming back to her shoulders, she felt as if he were magically removing all the terror and tension still inhabiting her.

Lia pulled away, looking up into his green and gold eyes. He looked like the operator he was, his mask still in place. "My clothes smell dusty and I need to go home and change into something clean."

Cav held her gaze. "So let's make it happen."

The day had started out so beautifully for Lia. The talk she'd had with Cav up on the cliff near the cave had made her heart sing, and their kiss…their kiss had melted her soul and removed that armor she'd hidden behind for so long.

She'd stepped out of the shower, dressed and was leaving when her whole world upended. Lia had frozen, shocked at suddenly seeing not one, but two of her previous assailants from the motor pool. What on earth were Schaefer and Dominguez doing here? Only when they'd dragged her out had she screamed and started to fight back.

On the way back to La Fortuna, Lia's mind began to revive, but Cav was quiet as he drove the SUV. He'd already had several conversations over his mic with Tanner, who was still in the area. Most important to Lia was that when Cav had to give his statement at the police department, Tanner would remain as her guard in her home while he was absent.

Next, Cav had picked up the satellite phone and called Dilara in Alexandria, Virginia at the Delos Charity Headquarters. He filled her in, as well, and Lia felt badly as she sat there, her clammy hands in her lap, hearing Cav tell Dilara that he had messed up. He knew he should have remained at the women's shower entrance while she got cleaned up. Guilt ate at Lia because she'd persuaded Cav that it was all right. Yet, he'd accepted all the blame, never mentioning their conversation.

She prayed that Dilara wouldn't fire him. When Cav finished with the conversation and turned off the phone, she asked, "Will you get fired?"

Cav smiled reassuringly. "No. It just goes on my record. That's all."

"Why didn't you tell her I had a part in that? I'm the one who pleaded with you to let me be and to go take your shower."

Cav said somberly, "Because it was my job, Lia. I shouldn't have left you open to attack."

Rubbing her arm, feeling chilled, she whispered, "Is this over?"

"I don't know. We'll know more when the police detectives interrogate Dominguez from his hospital bed."

"He said Dante Medina sent them to get me." She saw Cav's mouth draw downward. "Why were they kidnapping me? Did he order it? What was he going to do with me?"

"Those are all good questions," he said gently, reaching out, squeezing her hand in her lap for a moment. Returning his hand to the steering wheel, he said, "Right now, you're safe. Focus on that. And Tanner will take good care of you while I talk to the police."

She nodded and closed her eyes, leaning back against the seat, her mind swirling with so many questions, but no answers. Had Medina been involved with her rape five years ago? She didn't think so. At least, it hadn't come out at the trial that put Schaefer and Dominguez away for four years in prison.

She opened her eyes and again was struck by Cav's strong, hard profile. He was still in operator mode; she could feel it and see it.

"Medina is a new player in this," she offered. "His name was never brought up in the original trial against Schaefer and Dominguez. I wonder how long they've been down here? Did they know I was here? Did they find and follow me down here to get revenge?"

"I know," Cav admitted. "I'm asking myself the same questions. The fact it wasn't brought up at their trial tells me this is new, but hopefully Dominguez is going to sing like a canary and spill everything he knows."

"I wish I could be there for that interrogation," she muttered.

"No, you don't." Cav didn't know how the Costa Rican police operated, but he knew what he'd do to squeeze the truth out of that bastard, Dominguez. "I won't be present, either. We'll find out after they talk to him after surgery."

Looking out the window at the jungle on either side of the road, she muttered, "Why Medina? Do you think he knows about me putting those two soldiers in prison for attacking me?" She sent Cav a terrified look.

"It's possible," Cav said, "that those two told Medina about you. More likely, though, Medina knew you drove Lupe to the San José airport so she could escape to her own country, free of Medina once and for all. He could be in this because he wants revenge on you for helping her escape."

"Yes," she said wearily, rubbing her brow, "I thought of that angle, too."

"I think Schaefer and Dominguez were already working for Medina," he said grimly. "And they may have told their boss you threw their asses in prison for attacking you earlier. Medina wants revenge against anyone who helped Lupe to freedom. I think that's his whole *modus operandi.*"

Opening his hands on the wheel for a moment, he added gently, "And I don't think Medina cares if his two soldiers had crossed paths with you before. I think he's focused on kidnapping you because of your role in Lupe's escape. What he was going to do with you, I have no idea."

Cav had his own ideas about that, however. He knew Medina worked in the sex slave trade. And Cav would be damned if he thought he was going there with Lia.

His own theory was that Medina would either keep her as his unwilling mistress, or would sell Lia to the highest bidder. Either way, it was a very troubling scenario. His mouth tightened. No way was he going to elaborate on those possibilities with Lia.

"Cav, I feel like there's a noose around my neck and it's tightening around me," she admitted heavily, giving him a worried look.

"Look, we need to take this a step at a time. You have good protection from Tanner and me. I'm not letting you out of my sight, Lia, until Dominguez spills what he knows to the police. And even then, you can't get rid of me. First, we need to understand the bigger picture of what's going on here."

Giving a short nod, Lia tried to tamp down her out-of-control emotions. "You know, I thought…I thought…I was safe down here, Cav. I never dreamed that Schaefer and Dominguez would find me again. My God, it's my worst nightmare…"

"They're all dirt bags," Cav growled. "People like Medina hire idiots like these two and send them out into the field. In the final analysis, he could care less about those two clowns. They were beyond stupid to try and kidnap you in a tourist area where there would be so many eyewitnesses. These guys were rank amateurs."

"I guess you're right. I never thought about it from that angle."

Cav wanted to add that a real operator would have waited until she was alone, shot her up with a drug to dope her, then carried her limp body to the trunk of a car. But there was no way Cav would tell her any of this, either. Lia had a very active imagination to begin with, and many of her fears were based on reality, and he had no desire to stoke any of them right now.

"Do what you normally do," he told her quietly. "And let me and Tanner do what we're good at. We'll get the whole story in the next day or so. We know Medina has his sights on you and until we can figure out why and what, you're going to be protected."

"Okay," she said, her voice strained. "I feel like I'm still a target. It's just a feeling…"

"Feelings count, but let me get this sorted out and then we'll make plans according to what we know." Cav didn't blame her for feeling that way.

He wasn't sure whether Medina knew that his men had botched Lia's kidnapping, but more troubling was the possibility that Medina would send out another man or team to come after her. Once he got Lia home and met with Tanner, he'd take his colleague aside and share his concerns.

When Cav drove up to Lia's house, Tanner met them at the door. He had two other operators with him, and they all looked grim. Cav introduced Lia to them and took her directly into the house, asking Tanner to wait outside. He nodded, his eyes dark, but said nothing more.

Once inside, Cav went to the kitchen cabinet, where he'd spotted a small bottle of brandy earlier that week. Pouring a shot, he took it to her in her bedroom. She was sitting on the edge of the bed, pulling off her boots.

"Here," he told her, "drink this down fast. It will help settle your nerves."

She took it, saying, "I use this brandy in some of my recipes."

He smiled crookedly. "Well, right now it's going to help you relax a little."

Lia tipped it into her mouth and slugged it down. Then she gasped, her hand swiping across her mouth as if it were on fire.

Cav took the empty shot glass and set it on the bed stand, watching her cheeks turn red. He knew she wasn't much for alcohol and it must have been burning all the way down. "I'm going out to talk with Tanner now," he told her, placing his hand on her shoulder. "I'll be back in a few minutes."

She nodded, her hand against her throat, her voice raspy. "Okay…thanks…"

He leaned down, pressing a kiss to her hair. Her eyes changed from fear to gratitude.

Tanner listened to Cav's report on what happened at the Venado Caves. His men, both former SEALs, listened closely too, saying nothing. When he finished, Cav asked, "What do you think?"

"I think Medina's the reason those two were sent after Lia," Tanner said, resting his hands on his hips, his gaze skimming the area for potential threat. "I think he wants to get revenge. We'd been talking to the *policía*, anyway, because Dilara and Robert were coming in. We needed to get the lay of the land. The detectives at La Fortuna precinct said Medina was a mean sonofabitch who believed in an 'eye for an eye' when it came to messing with his interests. And he considered the women at his villa his property," he added grimly.

"If Dominguez supports that theory," Cav said, scowling, "then it means Medina will probably send someone else after Lia. He's not going to stop just because two of his soldiers got caught trying to kidnap her."

"Right on," Tanner agreed. "I'm hoping if Dominguez spills his guts and implicates Medina, the Costa Rican police will go after him and take him down."

Cav rubbed his jaw and grimaced. "Medina's been operating here for a long time and they haven't touched him yet."

"Well," Tanner said, "Maybe this time they will. You know General Culver has global reach because he works with NATO. He could put pressure on the Costa Rican government to move in and take out

Medina."

"If they don't arrest Medina," Cav added, "then he'll be free to come after Lia again."

"Maybe," Tanner said, lifting his chin and looking up at the wispy, fog-like clouds starting to form over the jungle again. "Lia needs to return to the States and work with Dilara at the main office in Alexandria. She'll be safe there." His unwavering gaze held Cav's own. "Here, she's a target."

"My thoughts were the same," Cav admitted. "But I don't know if she'll go. She has attachments here."

"First things first," Tanner said. "Get over to the precinct and give your statement. I'll coordinate everything from my end. Just have the *policia* send me an email document of their interview with you. We need to keep Robert and Dilara updated as things develop."

"Right," Cav agreed. "I already told Lia you'd be on watch while I go talk to the *policia.*"

"Yeah," Tanner said, "I'll remain in the house while my guys stay nearby." His eyes grew thoughtful. "We'll take good care of her. Don't worry."

Cav nodded. "Thanks," he said, shaking Tanner's hand. He knew full well that Tanner realized Cav was emotionally involved with Lia, and he didn't care. What was true—was true.

Lia slowly woke up when she heard two men talking in low tones in the living room. The door to her room was open and she slowly wiped the sleep out of her eyes. She noticed it was almost dark out and slowly sat up. Having taken off her dirty clothes, she'd pulled on a clean white tee and a pair of dark blue linen trousers. Her feet were bare. She heard a door open and close. Pushing to her feet, she met Cav in the kitchen as he was walking toward her bedroom door. His face was unreadable and she felt that guardian-like energy around him.

"What's going on?" she mumbled, halting in front of him. "Is everything okay?"

Cav reached out to touch her cheek, observing the worry in her drowsy, half-opened eyes. "How about a cup of coffee to wake you up? Are you hungry?" He knew that when Lia was upset, she wouldn't eat.

"Coffee sounds good," she muttered, sitting at the kitchen table. "Did you just get back from the police station?"

"Yes, I got here about twenty minutes ago," he said, puttering in the kitchen to make them coffee. "The *policía* took my statement. I'm cleared and still carrying a weapon on me. I went over to the hospital and talked to the detectives over there." He flipped the switch on the coffee maker and then opened the cabinet door, pulling down two mugs. Bringing them to the table, he saw anxiety growing in her eyes. Cav sat down at her elbow. "Dominguez just got out of surgery and he's going to make it."

"Thank God," Lia muttered, rubbing her face, trying to wake up. "What did he say?"

"He spilled a lot. First, he confirmed that Medina was out for revenge after you drove Lupe to the San José airport."

Lia eyed him, her lips thinning. "Did Medina know that he and Schaefer had already served prison time for assaulting me?"

"Yes," Cav admitted, moving the cup slowly around between his long fingers. "Originally, Dominguez said Medina was going to kill you, but later he decided to kidnap you."

Eyes widening, Lia sat up. "But…why?"

Cav wasn't going to lie to her about this. "Medina was going to keep you at the La Fortuna villa as a replacement for Lupe." He saw her eyes widen. She paled as the implications of his words hit home.

He reached out and growled, "Don't worry. It's not going to happen."

Shaken, Lia stared back at Cav. "What's stopping him?"

"The Costa Rican government for starters. I talked to the *policía* chief here at La Fortuna. Because Dominguez has implicated Medina directly, they're finally going after him. They've been wanting to get him for a long time, but now they have a witness, Dominguez. Plus you." Cav looked at her closely, gauging her strength to do what might come later.

"You know what this means, right? They'll take Medina down and put him in jail. Then, there will be a court case and you'll have to testify."

"As will Dominguez, right?" she countered.

"Yes." He reached out, moving his fingers slowly up and down her lower arm. "But it could be hard on you, Lia."

"*If* they catch Medina…it could take them *years* to come to trial," Lia muttered. "And then I'll be a target of whoever takes over his operation. He could even run it from his jail cell."

"All true," Cav agreed, unable to deny the points she made. "And that's if they can catch him. I'm not sure how well the Costa Rican police will get the job done. They seem efficient enough and knowledgeable, but…"

She turned her hand over, sliding her fingers between Cav's, seeking his warmth and support. "This is such a hot mess," she uttered, exhaustion edging her words.

"The whole thing puts you at risk," he agreed. "Even if Medina is caught, he can still come after you with what's left of his empire."

"I know," she said wearily, absorbing his touch, his fingers wrapping around hers. Right now, Lia desperately needed Cav. He represented protection, but even more, her heart was involved with Cav, the man, not Cav, the operator. She knew she was putting him at risk, too.

"All I wanted to do is work for Delos Charities and help the kids here at La Fortuna, Cav. It all seemed so simple until we helped Lupe escape. God!" She shook her head, looking away for a moment. "Now, everything's changed. Even if Medina is caught and jailed, he still holds power here in the northern highlands. It won't matter if he's in prison or not; he'll still go after what he wants."

"Look, Lia," Cav began gently, "We need to get you out of here. I know how much you love your kids and I know you've made a life for yourself down here." He saw anguish enter her gray eyes. "Dilara and Robert are worried about you. They realize now that Medina isn't going to stop trying to take out his revenge on you. If you were home, in the States, you'd be safer."

Lia felt her world crashing down upon her. Thank goodness for Cav's quiet, solid presence. He was helping her steady her emotions. She whispered, "I know I'm putting everyone at risk down here. I realize that now that Medina has targeted me. As long as I stay here, the school they're rebuilding is at risk too, as are the new teachers. And the children…"

She took a deep breath, and then lifted her gaze to his. "As are you and Tanner's men. Medina is well known for seeking revenge, Cav. He doesn't stop. I've seen it before."

"Yeah," he muttered, "that's about the bottom line on all of this, Lia." He gave her another minute then asked, "How do you feel about leaving? You might work with Dilara at headquarters instead."

She looked down at their joined hands. "I don't want to," she said, her voice wobbly. "But I know I have to. I won't put others at risk for me, Cav. I won't do it."

He squeezed her hand. "I think it's the best option for now." He lifted her hand and kissed it, proud of her commitment to those she loved. "Even if you leave and the police capture Medina, he could still take revenge on the Delos school they're rebuilding. Nothing is assured, Lia. But getting you out of here will go a long way by removing you from his gun sights." His voice thickened. "I really like what we've discovered with one another, and I'm not willing to give it up, either. But I want you out of here because you are his target." He searched her face for her compliance. She was silent, so he went on.

"Lia, I want the right to get to know you under less stressful circumstances. I want you to have a life again. I strongly feel you need to leave here as soon as you can. Medina doesn't know that the police are going to arrest him in San José at his villa. And as soon as they do, he's going to put the word out to take you out."

He caressed her cheek. "I want you safe, Lia, and back home in the States. It will be good for both you and Dilara if you work with Delos in Virginia. And selfishly, I admit that I'll sleep a helluva lot better knowing you're stateside."

"You're right," she agreed. "Of course I hate the idea of leaving, but you're right, Cav. I won't put others at risk here."

At that, Cav told Lia the final reason she should return to the States. "I took the liberty of speaking to Dilara about this after I found out what the Costa Rican government is going to do. She wants you home so much, she's setting up a condo near headquarters, just for you. You'll have a home to go to, and Dilara will take good care of you during this transition."

"Okay," she agreed, grateful, yet feeling her heart breaking into a thousand pieces. She was going to leave four years of her life behind, a life that she had loved. She would miss everyone, especially the children and their parents. Blotting her tears, Lia stole a look into Cav's face.

Now, she saw so much he couldn't hide from her because they were connected. "And what about us?" she asked, forcing herself to speak the scariest words. "I don't want to lose what we have. But I know you'll be off this PSD as soon as I fly out of here. What then, Cav?"

He took a deep breath and put his other hand on top of hers. "Nothing changes, Lia. Just because you leave the country we're in now, doesn't mean you're leaving me behind."

"But," she stumbled, "your job of guarding me will be done once I get on a plane for the States."

"Yes," he admitted heavily, "it will."

"And you'll go back to working with Robert, accepting new missions from him." She saw the rawness in his expression, glad that he wasn't hiding from her any longer. Cav had always been open and vulnerable with her and she could feel him struggling to answer her questions.

"I need to talk to the General," Cav admitted. He stroked her fingers, watching her, weighing how she felt. Cav could feel how torn up she was, how much she was losing when she thought of leaving La Fortuna. "We'll work something out," he promised her. "You just walked into my life, Lia and I don't want to lose what we have. I want the time, the space, the freedom from danger so we can explore a future together, don't you?"

He drilled her with an intense look, trying to see into her heart—one that had already been shredded by the last twenty-four hours. Did she have the internal strength, literally, the heart, to include him in her life once she got to Virginia? Or not? Lia had been through so much that Cav honestly didn't know the answer. And that scared him more than facing a bullet or dying.

CHAPTER 16

LIA THOUGHT SHE'D known what it felt like to have her heart ripped open, but she hadn't. Not until now. She felt Cav's suffering, his need for her. That kiss out on the precipice had sealed something beautiful between them, but right now, it couldn't be acted upon.

"Yes," she whispered, her voice shaky, "I want the chance to get to know you, Cav."

Instantly, she saw relief sweep over him, his mouth softening at the corners. Suddenly, his radio came to life, and he murmured, "Sorry…" as he turned to answer the call. Then, she saw his face tighten, and terror moved through her. She tensed, waiting to hear what had happened.

Cav ended the call and turned to her. "Tanner just picked up info on Medina," he told her, his voice low. "He knows what happened to his men, and that his plan to kidnap you failed. The police apparently have a bug in his villa. They've called to tell us that Medina is putting out a hit on you. Right now."

Stunned, Lia could only stare at Cav.

"We're leaving here in about ten minutes," Cav told her. "Let's get your suitcase. Put in whatever you'll need, okay? Tanner says that Dilara has been informed, and she's already bought you a first-class ticket on the next jet leaving Costa Rica for Washington, D.C." He looked at his watch. "That's four hours from now. We'll get you to the airport, keep you guarded and get you on that flight home."

Everything was moving at lightning speed as Lia hurried into her bedroom. Cav had pulled her one suitcase from beneath her bed and opened it atop her mattress. Her hands shook, her mind whirling as to what to take with her and what to leave behind. She felt herself beginning to panic. Medina wanted her dead or kidnapped—and Medina usually got what he wanted.

Cav moved quietly around, now fully on guard, in warrior mode. Soon, she heard a van pull up outside the door.

"Stay here," Cav ordered, squeezing her shoulder. In a few moments, Tanner and two other operators were in the house, waiting for her to finish packing. When Lia came into the living room, she felt as if she'd entered a war zone. The men carried M4 rifles in harnesses, their faces hard, their eyes alert. The only time she'd been more frightened was when Schaefer and Dominguez had attacked her five years ago.

"I'll take the suitcase," Cav said, gently placing his hand on the small of her back. He looked over at Tanner and gave a nod.

Instantly, two of the operators opened the door and checked, then cleared the immediate area outside the door. They stood on either side, motioning Lia to leave the house. Cav helped her into the van and sat next to the window. She sat beside him, her mind in shock, her body needing his closeness.

The driver was ready to roar away, waiting for Tanner, who was the last in. He sat in the passenger side seat and spoke in low tones into his mic as the van lurched forward.

Cav curled his arm around Lia's shoulders. Even though she was buckled into her safety belt, Lia desperately needed his touch. She could tell by the stern look on the men's faces that they were prepared for an attack on the van.

She wasn't surprised, knowing Medina, and that he was hell-bent on revenge against her. This was how he operated. Now, he had zeroed in on her.

She slid her hand across Cav's thigh, feeling the hard, curved muscles beneath his jeans. He wrapped his hand around her upper arm and slowly moved it up and down in a soothing motion.

Soon they were far south of La Fortuna. Lia's one regret was that she hadn't had a chance to say good-bye to the children she loved and their parents. They had all become so close over the years. Shakily wiping tears away, she felt Cav hug her and hold her for a moment. He was always tuned into her, and she knew he felt her pain almost as deeply as she did.

He smiled down at her encouragingly. "You'll see. Things will calm down for you once we get you on that plane for the States."

She whispered, "Cav, I hate to leave like this, but I know it's best. Do you think Medina will try to kill the three teachers, or take out his anger by hurting the people of La Fortuna?"

Cav shrugged. "I don't know. But Robert Culver just released ten new security operators for this mission. They're already on their way down here to San José to join up with our team." His mouth tightened. "If Medina thinks he's going to harm anyone at La Fortuna, he and his men will run into a black ops army that's a helluva lot more professional than his ragtag group. And the Costa Rican government has approved this maneuver. They're sending fifteen police in five vans north to La Fortuna, right now."

Lia looked somewhat reassured, at least for now, and he leaned over to press a kiss on her forehead. "So don't worry about them, okay? Robert is working directly with the government here, and the police are already devising a plan to get Medina at his villa in the capitol."

"I'm so glad," she whispered, true relief in her voice. "I've caused everyone so much trouble, so much grief."

"Hey, this isn't your fault," Cav returned sharply. "You were a pawn in a bigger game Medina was playing. If I'd been in your shoes, I'd have driven Lupe to the airport to escape, too." He squeezed her shoulder. "You, Maria and Sophia all did the right thing for Lupe, for the right reasons."

"And now," Tanner broke in to address Lia, "We're taking that dirt-bag down, with or without Costa Rican help. The team, General Culver just unleashed, is entirely composed of Delta Force operators from the Army." His mouth curved into a ruthless smile. "They're on top secret orders to come here. Those operators are going to be looking forward to this mission, believe me."

Her eyes widened. "But…that's military! You're civilians."

Tanner gave her a grim smile, his eyes glittering. "This government has an agreement in place where the U.S. can bring in military if the government asks for it. And they've asked."

New relief moved through Lia, and she actually sagged against Cav, closing her eyes. "Thank God…"

Tanner said, "Look, stop worrying about everyone else, Lia. Let's just take care of you. Everyone on this Op agrees that you need to leave the country. Until the Costa Rican government can clean up

Medina's mess, get him in custody—and I hope like hell kill a whole bunch of his soldiers—you are his target."

Opening her eyes, she nodded. "I got it, Tanner. That's why I'm here."

"Good."

"It's best this way," Cav agreed softly. "Robert and Dilara have moved heaven and hell to keep you safe. They aren't going to have people like you hunted down like this."

"It must have taken a lot of resources and time for them to do that," Lia said thoughtfully.

"It did, but because of Robert is respected by military communities worldwide, he can ask for and receive things most officers could never get. He's the right man in the right place for this kind of thing."

Lia rubbed at her tired eyes. "Everything is moving so fast..."

"Yeah, but that's the mark of an effective military operation." Cav didn't add that the billions of dollars generated from the Artemis and Delos shipping lines didn't hurt, either. He was sure that Robert and Dilara were throwing a lot of cash into this operation, but they'd never admit it, especially to Lia, who was feeling guilty enough that all this was her fault.

Damn, thought Cav, he was falling so deeply in love with this woman, and he was so proud that she was a fighter. He could see she didn't want to leave La Fortuna and would have stayed if he hadn't made it clear that she was directly in Medina's gun sights. And she was, right now.

Cav, like the rest of the operators, was on constant guard, alert for anything that looked remotely out of place as the van sped down the freeway toward San José.

At the airport, police commander Miguel Chavez met them. He escorted her, brandishing his power and security clearance, down into the bowels of the airport. They finally entered a small room with no windows, where Cav waited with Lia while two more operators stood at armed guard outside the room.

Cav had gotten Lia a bottle of cold water, which she had gripped between her hands as she sat on the metal chair in the small room.

"How are you doing?" he asked, crouching in front of her, his hands resting on her thighs.

Lia was numb, and could only say, "Okay."

"You're such a beautiful fibber," he murmured tenderly, moving his hands slowly up and down her thighs. He saw that his touch settled her down, her shoulders dropping the tension she was holding in them. "In another forty minutes, you'll be boarded first. There will be two air marshals on that flight, Lia, to protect you. You'll be fine."

She turned and faced him. "I worry about you, Cav, and about all these guys. You're going to get into the fight to get Medina as soon as you get me on board that plane, aren't you?" She saw him give her a rueful smile, like a little boy caught with his hand in the cookie jar.

"Busted."

"I wish you wouldn't go, Cav," she blurted out, unable to hide her emotions now. "I know I don't have a right to ask you that."

"Yes," he growled, "You have *every* right, Lia."

It was painful for her to look at him, so she looked away. "I know we barely know one another, but there's something good between us, Cav. I can feel it. When you kissed me, I felt as if I'd never been kissed before. And you did it so well…" She saw his eyes turn dark with emotion, and his hands stilled on her thighs as she absorbed their strength and warmth. She had never wanted him more.

"Listen," he growled, then softened his tone as he cupped her face. "This is one of the few times I *want* to be on an operation, Lia. I want Medina so damn bad I can taste it. That bastard is as good as dead. He just doesn't know it yet. And I hope like hell I'm the man who puts the bullet into that sick bastard's brain. I want to know that he'll never, ever bother you or any other woman again. This man needs to be taken out."

She felt a chill from his icy declaration. Here was Cav, her warrior, fully unveiled. Shaken, Lia whispered, "Then please be very, very careful, Cav. I can't lose you," and she reached out to him, touching his face and feeling a day's worth of beard beneath her fingertips.

Just as quickly, Cav's feral look was replaced by the gentle, strong man she was falling in love with. She knew he wanted to kiss her as he moved his thumb lightly across her lips.

"When this is over, I'm coming home to you, Lia. I'm sure Robert has another assignment for me, but I'm going to reject it. I want time with you…"

Nothing had ever sounded so good to her. She leaned forward, seeking and finding his lips, releasing a low moan of need as his mouth took hers with unbelievable gentleness. Lia wanted so much more from this man!

She, too, wanted a chance to for them to know each other without being under threat. His mouth slid against her lips now, and she hungrily pressed hers against his, wanting so much more from him, wanting to give equally back to him.

Cav held her, savoring her natural sweetness, her taste, her fragrance. Her fingers open and closed against his shoulders as she eagerly kissed him in return.

His heart was pounding in his chest, his erection painful with need. Time was what they both needed. Time for her to heal, and time for them to explore what they would do next.

"HOW ARE YOU feeling, Lia?" Dilara came into Lia's condo. It was on the fifth floor overlooking the beautiful city of Alexandria, Virginia.

Lia laid out tuna sandwiches, sweet pickles and Fritos on the small kitchen table for them. "I'm okay," she said, giving her boss her best smile. That wasn't entirely true. She had been home for two days and hadn't heard a word from Cav. She was going crazy inside with worry about him. "Have you heard anything from Tanner and his group? Do they have Medina in custody?" she asked Dilara.

Closing the door to the small, homey condo, Dilara said, "That's why I came over here. It's not something I wanted to discuss with you over the telephone."

Lia froze. "Is Cav all right?" The words tore with such intensity from her lips that Dilara's calm expression turned to one of sympathy.

Dilara came over and placed her hands on Lia's shoulders. "Medina is dead. Cav is fine. One of Tanner's men got wounded, but nothing critical, thank God. Cav's fine, Lia. Sit down a minute, okay?"

Relieved, Lia sat before her knees collapsed beneath her. Dilara sat down and held Lia's hand.

"Tanner just called me, and I had my driver bring me over here to see you in person," she said, patting Lia's hand. "Cav had a flesh wound on his arm, but he's fine. The doctor patched him up."

Lia sat very still. She kept searching Dilara's face, still anxious. "He's really all right?"

"Yes, darling, he's fine. Tanner is taking the team north and they're going to be working with the Delta Force group. Next, they're going after Medina's jungle locations where they're growing marijuana and cocaine. The team is going to take out the drug soldiers who are enslaving the local farmers and forcing them to grow coca plants for cocaine. The Costa Rican police are there, too. They found all the places in the Cloud Forest where Medina was holding farmers and their families as slaves and hostages."

There was grim satisfaction in her husky voice. "They're dismantling his entire northern highlands operation. Once they get done, those farmers and their families will be free. All of Medina's soldiers who kept them hostage, working like slaves on their own land, will be rounded up and captured."

Pressing her hand to her heart, Lia whispered, "That's wonderful. Does that mean that La Fortuna will be safe now? My kids? Their parents? The new school teachers?"

Smiling, Dilara nodded. "Yes, indeed! All will be safe and sound once they finish with this massive operation. But it's going to take a few months before the area is actually back in the hands of the local farmers. Tanner was telling my husband that it's going to take at least two months, maybe a little longer. Medina had his spidery hands into everything. It's unbelievable."

"Oh," Lia muttered, "La Araña, The Spider, was very well known in La Fortuna. We also knew how extensive his control was over local people and farmers."

Dilara shook her head. "I only wish, Lia, you had told me."

"I didn't think," she admitted. "I mean, Medina left us alone. Well…until Lupe escaped and we helped her leave the country."

Dilara released her hand. "I understand. We're a charity. We're there to help, not to be law enforcers."

"We had learned to co-exist with Medina's operation," Lia explained haltingly. "I've been giving this whole situation a lot of thought, Dilara. If I, or someone connected with the local charity, had given you an insider's view of the politics, the good, bad and ugly of the area, you would have been more aware of the total situation. But we just accepted it."

"Because of what we've learned from this experience, Robert and I are going to change how we work with all our charities," Dilara picked up her eel-skin briefcase, opening it on her lap and handing over a small manual to Lia. "I know we talked to you about it when we first flew into San Jose, at the hotel. It was an idea we had, but it was just that. Now, we've moved on it and it's real. While you're here with us, I would like to use not only your military background, but your four years at our Home School at La Fortuna. Robert has put this together with some of the best military strategists in the U.S. He's also worked with high officials from the CIA." She patted the manual. "This is top secret, for your eyes only, Lia. I want you to go through it, page by page, and make comments as you see fit. This manual is an amalgam of the best military minds in the world, but now, we need people in the trenches, like you, to look at it. Think outside the box, and once you're done, let me know. We'll then convene in our boardroom with Robert, and discuss any changes or ideas you might have to improve on what's already there. Okay?"

Stunned, Lia nodded, placing her hands over the bright red cover of the manual. "What is this, anyway? A game plan? A working concept?"

Dilara sat back, her mouth pursed. "We as a family have concluded that in today's environment, threats are escalating on every continent where we have a charity. Therefore, they'll need us to provide security so they can survive and thrive. In response to today's growing threat environment, Robert created Artemis as an internal Delos Charity security company we can call on at a moment's notice." She pointed at the manual. "You know that Tal, Matt and Alexa, our children, are all in the military."

Lia nodded. "Yes, I was aware that Tal is a Marine Corps captain who heads up a sniper group at Bagram presently. Alexa is a captain in the U.S. Air Force and flies an A-10 in Afghanistan, and Matt is a Delta Force operator out of Bagram. Is that correct?"

"Correct. We are asking our children to come home, to leave the military so they can run Artemis Security. I want Tal, the oldest, to become CEO. Matt has a lot of experience in KNR, kidnapping and ransom. We want him to head up that department. Alexa wants to head up the Women's Division. Each of them has a world of experience in the military, and has a wide network of people they can work with. Robert's brothers, John and Pete Culver, are working with us, too. John is an admiral in the U.S. Navy, so that gives us access to that force if necessary. Pete is a Marine Corps general, and can bring Marines into a situation, if approved by the State Department."

Lia's eyes widened. "Wow," she murmured, "you're setting up a clandestine security operation under the umbrella of Delos. And while you're creating a security corporation within Delos, you'll still have the

U.S. military available, too?"

Holding up her hands, Dilara said, "In a word, yes, but Robert is working with John and Pete, plus many other Pentagon high level contacts, to bring this together and make it work. The State Department recognizes that all non-government charitable organizations are under attack globally. They understand the need for what we're creating and are willing to underwrite what we're doing for political reasons. This country cannot be seen sending in troops to a charity under siege. But we can use black ops, paid civilian security operators and stealth, quietly moving behind-the-scenes to get to that charity and give its people and buildings protection. There are many other countries who are looking to what we're doing, wanting to use it as a template if it works. We're going to have a lot of eyes watching what we do and whether we're successful at it or not."

"That makes a lot of sense," Lia said. "You've more or less done that with Medina down in Costa Rica."

She grimaced. "Yes, but let me tell you, we learned a lot from that experience. Robert had to scramble to get Army help, and if he hadn't had the respect, clout and power he does within the military, he couldn't have done it. I told him that if we'd had our own security teams of men and women who were once military, we could have inserted our own team into that situation faster and more efficiently. Robert agreed with me, which is what got us both thinking about creating Artemis Security."

"And your children would be perfect fit for it," Lia said, her excitement rising. "They all have at least six or seven years of combat experience, don't they?"

"Correct." Dilara sighed. "I must tell you, Lia, as a mother I'm so happy that our children are on board with this. Tal and Alexa can hand in their commission and quit at any time. Matt can't get free until next March when his present enlistment runs out. But it's going to take us nine months to a year to put this concept on the ground. There's so much to it, and that's why I wanted your eyes on it. You know what it's like to be in a charity overseas. Costa Rica is usually very safe, the best in South or Central America, but they still have issues that could jeopardize people at our charities down there. If that's the case there is no country where we have a Delos charity that can be considered completely is safe. We must do something about this now." Her eyes glistened with unshed tears. "And to have to lose Maria and Sophia to

Medina just breaks my heart."

Lia reached out and touched her arm as Dilara wiped her eyes. "If we'd had Artemis Security online, if we'd been receiving weekly reports on the political environment surrounding each charity location, we would have known where there might be issues."

"And what would you have done if I had written such a report on Medina?" Lia wondered.

"Artemis Security would have looked at the situation, talked to you, talked to the government involved, and then assessed the threat level. They could have sent down a security contractor or more than one to protect all of you. We could have alerted the government. If they wanted to get involved, we would have coordinated something with them. If not, then we'd go in with a handpicked individual or team to keep our charity and our people safe. We recognize that not every government has a military or the money, manpower or guts to respond to a threat situation to one of our charities. By creating Artemis Security, we can."

"This is quite a paradigm shift for a charity," Lia said, holding Dilara's gaze. She saw the concern in her boss' eyes, knew that her love for people was always at the forefront of everything she did. Her heart swelled with pride knowing that she worked with Delos Charities.

"Unfortunately," Dilara sighed, "yes, it is. But our world has changed, I'm sorry to say. It's not the world you and I grew up in. Especially me, since I'm in my forties," and she smiled a little. "I grew up in a safe world, Lia. There were no school shootings, no mass murders of innocent people, no beheadings, and no terrorism. If we are to continue to help those who need us, we must protect our property, our volunteers and paid staff. We can't leave them open the way you, Maria and Sophia were left vulnerable so that Medina could kill. I will go to my grave with their deaths on my conscience, and I never want this to happen again. Delos is about hope for a brighter future for the people who come through our doors. That's why our charity logo is a rising sun. It's about hope, giving people who are in the dark, a way out, a way to a better life. We're here to provide them medical help, education and give them help in agriculture so they can grow better, bigger crops for their people."

"I understand," Lia whispered, deeply affected by Dilara's passionate words. She was one of the wealthiest women in the world, but to Lia, Dilara was not the socialite the entertainment magazines touted. They didn't really know this Turkish-Greek woman with a heart as big as the world. Lia had often heard her say during charity meetings, "money isn't something we can't take with us once we die." Their money, billions, would be placed into Delos Charities. Dilara was a fierce advocate that education was the only tool that would lift people out of poverty and give them a chance for a decent life, free from starvation.

Lia loved working in home schools and had, in her four years, seen the children of La Fortuna blossom with the education Delos provided them. The world was a better place because these children were being educated. Education bred understanding, not fear or kept people imprisoned in darkness. And Dilara, in Lia's mind, was a torch of hope in this broken world. She was a rising sun of hope for those who had so little.

"I'll read this and make notes," Lia promised, eager to dig in and help.

"Good. I'm really relying on you, Lia, because you've spent time in our Home School program. I want to find someone in our Farm Foundation area and our Safe House charities to read the manual, too." She gave Lia a proud look. "You were my choice for the Home School portion."

Blushing, Lia said, "I'm sure there are other teachers who are certified, who can do better than I can."

"No, that's not true," Dilara said. "For four years, you have run the Home School charity in La Fortuna in every way but classroom teaching. You know about the building, the plumbing, electrical, the water, as well as coordinating the lesson plans, getting supplies ordered and to the classrooms. You do all the logistics, Lia. A teacher teaches. What you do? You're like a manager who oversees the entire operation from beginning to end.

You really are the right person to be reading this manual. And you are especially valuable to us because of the managerial position you held at La Fortuna. No, you can give us a full overview on this operation, whereas a teacher could not. Does that make sense to you now?" Dilara gave her a reassuring smile.

Lia felt tears threaten to overtake her. "Y-yes, it does. I guess I never saw myself in that capacity. All I wanted to do was help serve, and make those kids' lives better."

"Well, you have and you do," Dilara patted her hand. "But I have one more thing I must speak to you about."

"What?" Lia hoped it wasn't anything bad. She'd seen enough of that to last a lifetime.

"Robert and I are already starting to hire key staff for Artemis Security. Among them, we're reaching out to key individuals from our charities, and hiring them to come and work here, with us. Robert has had a real estate company buy a huge farm just outside Alexandria that we're going to convert into Artemis Security. It's going to take nine months to convert the three-story farmhouse into a major security operation. We've created three key departments based on the charities' outreach programs: Safe House, Home School and Farm Foundation."

She halted, and then gripped Lia's hand. "I very much want to hire you to run the Home School Department, Lia. You're perfect for the position. You not only have experience and management knowledge, but you also have a military background. We're trying to hire managers with military experience because Artemis is ultimately about security and protecting our people out in the field. That needs key people with a military background so they can make good decisions based upon their knowledge. You make sound decisions with such a multi-career background already.

I can promise that you'll have your own office, as many assistants as you need, and you'll run that department. You'll answer to Tal, Matt, Alexa, as well as, Robert and me. The department managers are the top tier in Artemis and you will be one of them. You will help create policy to be carried out in the field. This is a job for someone who loves educating children, who's fierce about it. And you are, Lia. I can promise you a very handsome salary. You will be helping Delos move into the twenty-first century with Artemis. We are going to transform our global charity to keep our people safe. What do you say?"

CHAPTER 17

L IA HAD DISCOVERED that late June in Alexandria, Virginia was absolutely beautiful. She was at the old farmhouse outside the bustling, busy town, ensconced in her new office on the fifth floor. It was Monday and she was working on a manual to be sent to all Home School Delos charities in South and Central America.

Outside her bulletproof window was a huge green pasture surrounded by a freshly painted white fence. The farmhouse had been converted into Artemis Security, but from the outside, if someone drove along the narrow, two-lane asphalt road, looked like a farmhouse from the mid-1850s.

Inside, however, it was a very different story. Lia could hear the carpenters, the drywall people, the electricians and the construction workers humming throughout the three-story above ground structure. They were also adding two floors beneath the building. They'd prepared her office first because she was the only employee on site so far. Tomorrow, three women would be in the newly painted HR, Human Resources, office on the first floor. Lia was on the top floor, where all the managers would eventually be located.

Even though she was excited about her new job, Lia's heart and mind were never far from Cav. Since being shuttled out of Costa Rica a week ago, he'd contacted her once. They had chatted via webcam so he could let her know he was okay. He'd been back in San José after taking down Medina, and reported that he and the team of Delta Force operators were going back into the northern highlands to begin dismantling the huge cocaine network Medina had put together.

Lia had tried to keep their conversation light, feeling the pressure on Cav. It wasn't that he tried to hide anything from her, but the camera showed the tension at the corners of his mouth and eyes. She knew how dangerous his mission was going to be.

Medina's soldiers were stationed at every farm with the latest weapons, with orders to protect the farms and keep the cocaine flowing for distribution. All she could hope was that Cav's years of experience would keep him safe.

On her desk were a landline phone, satellite phone, desktop computer, and a radio connected to the men and women directing the building of Artemis. When her sat phone buzzed, she frowned, then looked at the number. It was Cav! She picked it up eagerly. "Cav? Are you all right?" Lia tried to keep the worry out of her voice.

"I'm fine. I just wanted to let you know that Dilara is ordering me up to see her. She's going to offer me a job and I'll potentially be working at Artemis Security. I don't know the details yet, and I've got an appointment to speak to her about next Monday. We're just about finished mopping up Medina's operation here, and she wants me to put in for a job with their new security company. Could you use some company at your condo Friday evening?"

Hearing the amusement in his teasing tone lifted all her worries. "I'd love that! When are you coming in? Which airport? I just bought a car and I can pick you up."

"Sounds great." Cav gave her his flight information, and Lia's hand shook as she wrote it down. She didn't have an office assistant yet, but Dilara had promised she'd have one as soon as the HR department was up and running. Then, she'd have all the people she needed to work on the global manual.

"I can hardly wait to see you," Cav growled. "Get ready, because we're picking up where we left off."

Heat flowed through Lia's body. "I'd love nothing more than that, Cav. You're coming in on a Friday evening, so I'll have the entire weekend to spend with you."

"Good. Because I've got plans…"

She laughed, feeling freer than she had in the last five years. "Okay, I wonder if they're the same as mine?"

"Let's compare notes when I get home to you."

"Stay safe and I'll see you soon."

"Always," he promised her.

Lia sighed as she set the phone down on her desk, her heart thumping wildly. Cav was coming home! That was wonderful news, but she was curious as to what Dilara was up to.

Why was she hiring Cav for Artemis? Since he already worked for the charity, maybe she was creating a new job for him?

"Hi, there," Dilara called, poking her head into her office, "How do you like your new digs, Lia?"

Turning, Lia smiled broadly as the older woman walked in. Dilara always looked like a fashion plate as well she should coming from a family of wealth. She wore only the finest clothes, but they were always understated and elegant. This morning, she wore a light pink linen pantsuit with a gold collar around her throat and dangling, Turkish earrings.

"Hey, come on in. I just heard from Cav!"

Dilara smiled and closed the door, sauntering over to the burgundy leather chair next to Lia's tiger maple desk. "Did you, now?" she said innocently, her ever-present eel skin briefcase next to the chair.

Lia leaned back in her leather chair. "Okay, what's going on?" she baited. "Why are you asking him back here?"

Dilara smiled wickedly. "You need an assistant, don't you?"

"What?" Eyes widening, Lia was at a loss for words. "Cav…he's the one you chose as my assistant?"

"I bet you didn't know that he has a Bachelor of Arts from Cal Poly in Comparative Ethnic Studies. He also has a minor in African and Asian studies, which I feel strongly, will help you when you guide your teachers to create specific teaching manuals for our charities in those countries. What do you think?"

"No, he never told me about his academic background. I mean he never talked about having a degree."

"We have his resume on file at the main office," Dilara confided. "I've known for sometime about his background and have been looking for a way to use it." Her eyes danced with mischief. "You're our Central and South American specialist. You won't have issues guiding our teaching staff to create teaching manuals and updating them for these Latin countries. But you need specialists in other parts of the world who can help you."

"No question," Lia admitted. "So you're looking to Cav to help me with manuals for your Asian and African charities?"

"Yes, and I've got my eye on another operator who has a similar degree for our European operations. We'll see if he wants to trade in his M4 for a spot here in your department," she smiled.

Shaking her head, Lia said, "This is such a huge project, Dilara."

"Tell me about it," Dilara laughed. "But getting our HR department online soon will take a big load off me, which I'll transfer to the three women we've hired. I think you'll like them. Two of the three have a military background, so you should get along well. There's a lot of work to do to get your Home School Department fully functioning, with lots of school manuals that need updating as well as bringing in the correct teaching staff to write them."

"Sometimes," Lia admitted, "I see the bigger picture and wonder how I can do it all, and do it well."

"Well, you can't, Lia. See, that's why you're the manager. You'll direct people who know the specific areas. But you'll be their visionary, their guiding hand, to bring it all together. I have an appointment to talk with Cav next Monday about the job offer we have for him."

"He doesn't know he'll be working with me?"

"No, not yet." Her lips twitched. "He knows I'll be giving him a job if he wants it, just not WHERE in Artemis. Yet. I've a feeling once he knows he'll leap at the opportunity. Besides, I think you two are sweet on one another, and this is something you'd both want. Am I right?"

The answer seemed obvious, but Lia was still cautious. "We haven't talked about any of that," she admitted. "Everything blew up on us in La Fortuna, so we're still getting to know one another."

"I've known Cav for awhile. He's a wonderful person, Lia, but I think you already know that."

Lia sobered. "I tried to not get entangled with him, Dilara. I was worried that he'd be like every other man, and think I was ugly because of my knife wounds."

"He's not like that," Dilara protested.

"I've found that out," Lia admitted softly. "He sees *me*, not the scars."

"And that's the kind of person I want working with Artemis and with you." She pulled a few manuals from her briefcase and set them on the desk. "Now, these are the manuals we're presently using for our African, European and Asian Home School charities. Take your time going through them. If Cav takes the job, you can hand him two of them and he can work with our education specialists, whom we'll be hiring in about a week. Because Cav knows the political environment of a given continent, he can add his knowledge into the updating of our school manual. Then, all you have to do is read it, pass it on to our Education Department and let them make the final changes. Then, we'll have new manuals for the start of the school season next year."

"Sounds easy enough," Lia said. "I'm picking Cav up at Reagan International Friday evening."

Dilara stood up, smoothing her linen trousers. "We have a condo rented for him."

"He's staying with me for the weekend, but I'll pass along the information on his condo when I see him."

"I thought that might be the case." Dilara grinned and pulled out a packet from the side of her briefcase, handing it to Lia. "If and when he makes it over to his condo, which by the way is a floor above yours, he can make himself at home. He knows to be at my office at 9 A.M. Monday morning."

"Yes," Lia promised, taking the manila packet. She could feel a set of keys in it.

Waving to her, Dilara opened the door. "See you later. Have a good weekend…"

EXHAUSTION PULLED AT Cav as he deplaned and joined hundreds of other people moving toward the security exit. He carried a dark green duffle bag in his left hand. Friday night, in Washington, D.C., was a far cry from the humid jungle of the Monte Verde Cloud Forest in Costa Rica.

Most exciting for him was that he was finally going to see Lia, with no threats to spending time together. His lower body stirred, and he had to remind himself that all they'd shared were some touches and kisses. Not his bed. *Yet.*

Cav spotted Lia before she even saw him. She was standing off to one side near the wall. He smiled, seeing that she was wearing a tasteful pale cream-colored pantsuit with a bright red blouse that brought out her hair's rich highlights.

The fact that she was allowing it to grow pleased him, and she looked terrific, the longer hair enhancing her oval face and her sensual lips. God, he'd missed her, especially since he'd gotten used to having her in his life. His heart pulsed with need for her, and he watched her moving nervously from one sandaled foot to another, his grin broadening. She never could stand still for long.

As he emerged from behind a group of businessmen walking quickly out of security, Cav saw Lia catch sight of him. Her gray eyes widened and he saw the joy shining on her face. Quickly, he lengthened his considerable stride, leaving most of the passengers behind. As he neared Lia, he dropped his canvas bag to the floor and opened his arms wide.

"Cav!" she cried, throwing her arms around his neck, hugging him.

Groaning with pleasure, Cav accepted her frontal assault with a laugh, bringing her tightly up against his entire body, feeling how soft she was. Catching a scent that reminded him of cloves, her hair silky against his face, he heard her choke out his name, holding him as hard as she could.

"Oh, Cav!" she muffled against his neck. "I've missed you so much!"

He let her feet touch the floor, then held her, kissed her hair, kissed her temple. "Come here," he growled, tilting her face upward, his mouth descending upon hers. Every cell in his body glowed as she eagerly kissed him, reminding him of a happy, wriggling puppy. There was nothing but joy as he kissed her again, then backed off slightly, trying to control his hunger for her.

Cav was aware that they were in public, and that others were watching them. Always protective of Lia, he moved so that he placed her near the wall, his back toward the crowd, shielding her from curious, prying eyes.

After another kiss, they came up for air. Timing was everything, and Cav knew it. Allowing her to ease from him, keeping his hands on her shoulders, he smiled down at her. "You have no idea how much I've been looking forward to this...to you," and he caressed her face, hoping Lia wouldn't wince or pull away as his fingers grazed the scar on her beautiful flesh.

This time, she didn't react. That was a good sign. Grateful, Cav leaned down, kissing her cheek, her lips, not able to get enough of her.

"Same here," she whispered, sliding her hand up his arm. "I missed you so much!"

He smiled. "Then why don't you take me home with you?" and he leaned over, picking up his duffle bag. He liked the blush that graced her cheeks, making her eyes look even larger.

"In a heartbeat!" she laughed. "I'm parked in short term. Do you have luggage?"

"No, just this." He held it up. "I always travel light in my business."

She grinned and slid her hand into his. Instead, Cav lifted his right arm, sliding it around her shoulders, tucking her next to him. That was unexpected, but Lia loved it. Loved him. Sliding her arm around his waist, she said, "This way," and led him down the busy hall toward an exit.

Just getting out into the evening air was a relief, and Cav breathed deeply. He hated airplane air. On Friday nights, Reagan International was a beehive of activity. Cav remained alert from habit, keeping Lia against him as they walked to the parking lot. Above them, the summer sky was clear and cloudless. On the horizon was a faint strip of yellow and orange, the last of the sunset.

"How have you really been?" he asked, gazing down at her. He could hardly believe they were together again.

"Busy. And I love what I'm doing." Then, she admitted, "But I've been missing you terribly."

He squeezed her gently as they slowed. "We're going to build on what we started in Costa Rica. Sound good?"

"Does it ever!" she agreed. Halting in front of a silver Kia Sorrento SUV, Lia pulled out the keys from her small purse. "Come on, I'm taking you to my new condo."

Cav opened the door for her and then threw his duffle into the back seat. "Let's go." As they drove down the freeway toward Alexandria, he asked, "Do you have the keys to my condo? Dilara said I've got one a floor above where you're staying."

"They're in my purse." She glanced over at him, overjoyed to see him in her front seat. "You'll be home in civilization again. That has to feel good."

"It always does. The more you travel, the more you know how good we have it here in the U.S." He gazed at her profile, noticing how relaxed she'd become. "How's your new job as department head suiting you?"

"Well," she admitted, chewing on her lower lip, "I've never been a manager before. Dilara is hiring a lot of people to support our Home School Department."

"Don't worry, you've already been a manager at La Fortuna. What you do comes natural to you, Lia, and you're good at it. You kept the entire charity moving forward without missing a beat."

She gratefully accepted his compliment. "I guess I never saw myself in that capacity. I was just trying to keep things on an even keel so the teachers could teach the kids."

"You did an outstanding job," he praised.

She risked a quick glance. Cav seemed at peace. She loved his long, lanky body and the way he lounged like a cougar resting on an overhanging rock ledge. There was a dangerous quality to him, which thrilled her.

The danger for her was giving her heart to this man. They'd had so little time together, and Lia worried about how Cav would react to her belly scar. It was the worst one, and had disgusted Jerry. Would it him? It made wanting to love Cav a hot-and-cold temptation to Lia. Her heart and mind wanted him. But could he accept her?

She desperately wanted to broach the topic with him, but until he brought it up, she would wait. It would be foolish to discuss it right now. She knew he was tired. Somehow, they would ease into that conversation later. Still, Lia dreaded talking to him about it.

"I didn't know you had a BA in Comparative Ethnic Studies. I'm impressed," she added with a quick smile.

"Dilara must have told you. I know. We had no time down there to discuss such things. Trying to get personal info about each other was pretty tough under the circumstances, wasn't it?"

"I couldn't agree more. But we have time now."

"You know, people have always fascinated me," he told her. "And with my SEAL background in Asia, getting a BA in Ethnic Studies was a natural decision. I've spent a lot of top secret time in Africa, as well."

"Your experiences are going to be so helpful to us if you take the job" she said, new appreciation for this man rising in her.

"I'd like a job where I can be near you, Lia. I'm tired of being a contractor. I'd like to have a job where I don't have to travel and be away from you." Cav liked the way the lights along the freeway danced on the gold and red highlights in her hair. "I like your longer hair. Do you?"

Touching a strand, she smiled. "Yes, I do."

"Did you always wear it short?"

Her heart hitched for a moment. "Well," she answered in a low tone, "until the assault five years ago, I had long hair. In the Army, I always wore it up or in a ponytail. When I wasn't on duty, I wore it down. I loved it long."

He reached out, sliding his fingers across her shoulder. "I'm glad you're letting it grow again." It showed him that she was working through the trauma and it no longer had such a tight hold on her. He saw her eyes change, saw hope in them. Hope for them, maybe? Cav didn't know, but he intended to find out pretty soon.

"Me, too," she murmured.

Cav didn't want to start talking about her assault. Not yet. He saw fear skitter in her eyes for a split second, and then it was gone. But he could sense that Lia was nervous about their burgeoning relationship.

"You'll be happy to know that the Delta Force team dismantled all of Medina's network of soldiers," he reported. "There were forty-two farms in a hundred mile area in the highlands where he'd forced farmers and their families to grow coca."

"Was anyone hurt?" Lia asked.

"Steve, one of Tanner's operators, got wounded but nothing serious. The rest were a lot of stupid-assed soldiers. I got a bullet crease and it was nothing to write home about. They didn't realize who they were up against," and he smiled a little with satisfaction. "The families who were hostages and forced to work for Medina and the soldiers were liberated. They're a pretty happy group right now."

"I would imagine they are. I had no idea what Medina was doing in that region."

"No one did until Dominguez spilled everything."

"Is the government going to help those poor farmers get back on their feet?"

"Yes, it's already in play. The soldiers we rounded up are already in jail and awaiting their trials. They'll all get twenty-five years or more in prison." His voice lowered. "Serve the bastards right."

"A lot of good came out of this," she whispered.

"Maybe so, but it will never make up for the loss of Maria and Sophia," Cav said gently, moving his hand on her shoulder. "But we did get the best possible outcome."

"Thanks to Dilara and Robert," Lia added.

"They are two amazing people," Cal agreed, then watched as Lia turned in to a twelve-story building that housed the condos.

She pulled into the parking garage beneath the building and got out. Cav brought his canvas bag and she walked him to the elevator. "What would you like to do now, Cav? You look really tired."

He stepped into the elevator. "Come with me and see what my condo looks like. Then, I'd like to take a quick shower, put some clean clothes on and then come down and see what your digs look like. Sound like a plan?"

Did it ever! She stepped into the elevator with him, pressing the tenth floor button. "I made you some dinner if you want it."

"You didn't have to do that, Lia, but I'm glad you did."

"It's nothing special," she warned. "But it's edible."

Chuckling, Cav said, "Thanks for being so thoughtful! Sure, I'll take you up on it."

Cav's apartment was much like her own. It was fifteen hundred square feet, with two bedrooms, a large kitchen and living room, plus a bathroom and a half. It was a corner apartment like hers, the thin, transparent white curtains were pulled back so that they could look toward the capitol and the monuments. For Lia, it was always a beautiful sight.

"Nice digs," he murmured, turning and tossing his bag on a flowery fabric sofa. Turning, Cav pulled Lia close to him. She placed her hands against his chest, looking up at him. "What I'm looking at right now" he whispered, leaning down while placing small kisses along her hairline, "is so much more beautiful…"

Lia closed her eyes, absorbing his cherishing kisses, butterfly light against her. "I like you spoiling me," she admitted, smiling softly.

Cav eased back, watching her eyes go soft with arousal. He knew she wanted him, but needed to hear it from her. "Tell me what you want, Lia. Give me some boundaries so I know how to behave myself."

When he saw relief in her eyes, he knew he'd struck the right chord with her. "Above all, I don't want to pressure or crowd you. That's why I'm asking." He caressed her cheek, drowning in her sparkling gray eyes radiating love for him.

Cav knew it was love. And he'd bet a year's worth of paychecks from Delos that Lia was worried about him crowding or pushing her too soon.

"I want to get to know you, Cav. When we were together before, it was always under dangerous circumstances. I couldn't really talk with you because it would have been a distraction. And frankly, I was an emotional mess. I still am, but now that I've been stateside, I'm feeling lighter and less worried."

"Being in a safe place always does that," he agreed, trailing his fingers through her curly hair. He saw that his touch made her eyes grow luminous with yearning. Lia wasn't a woman who played games, which he appreciated. What you saw was what you were getting.

When she was happy, it was obvious. If she was hurting, he saw it in her demeanor. She never tried to hide things from him.

For his part, Cav felt so damned lucky to have walked into her life. It was rare to find someone emotionally honest these days. And dating was its own version of a minefield.

"I want to really know who you are, Cav," Lia said, as if reading his mind.

"Tell me more," he encouraged her as he eased her against him. She sank against him like it was the most natural thing in the world.

"What does that mean?"

"That if you take the job Dilara will offer you? I'd like to plan time outside of the office for just us."

"What if I make you dinner some nights? Invite you up to eat here in my condo?" He suspected he was in for a long courtship, but the prospect didn't deter him. He wanted Lia coming to him whole, not worried about her scars. Cav knew the only way he could make that happen was by putting her in comfortable circumstances and not crowding her.

"That would be nice," she whispered, nuzzling beneath his jaw as she absorbed his warm embrace. Lia could feel his erection and her own body responded in kind. How badly she wanted to say, *"I want to go to bed with you right now."* Because she did.

"If I take the job Dilara will be offering me next Monday? I've been thinking," he tipped her chin upward, holding her lustrous gaze. "Next weekend we might want to explore some of those nice caves nearby. We had a great time spelunking at Venado, didn't we? And I'd like to share that with you. What do you think?"

Instantly, he saw her perk up and grin.

The way into Lia's heart was clearly through things she loved to do in her spare time. And Cav had more than a few ideas in that direction to lure her into his arms. Some day, she would want to love him fully, without worrying about her scars, and he was going to make it happen.

"I'd love to go caving with you again, Cav," she whispered, touched by his consideration.

CHAPTER 18

A FTER DINNER AT Lia's condo, Cav rose and walked into the living room. The open concept gave her modern looking condo an openness he appreciated. She had slid the cream-colored curtains aside so the corner windows would give them a full view of the capitol gleaming in the darkness. Turning, he held out his hand in her direction.

"Come sit with me for a minute. I'll help you clean up in a bit." Because they'd worked well as a domestic team back in La Fortuna, Cav thought this was a nice habit he wanted to encourage.

When they'd arrived at her condo, Lia had gone into her bedroom, climbed out of the business suit she'd worn at Artemis and put on a pair of loose jade green trousers. She remained barefoot and topped the pants with a soft, sleeveless, pale orange tee. It had felt wonderful to be able to no longer hide herself from Cav. She'd seen the hunger in his eyes when she'd come out of the hallway in her comfy clothes. It made her feel good. Feminine. Wanted. And now, her lower body was quivering, wanting Cav to touch her. At last, there was an opportunity for him to do that.

He stood by the pale blue leather sofa, watching Lia move, that sway of her hips that made his erection grow thicker. Cav had traded in his clothes for a pair of worn jeans and a black t-shirt, along with a pair of black Nike sneakers.

Lia came to him, sliding her hand into his. He saw the yearning in her eyes, even though they'd kept their conversation light and social.

Cav was hungry for personal time with Lia, and he sat down in the corner, releasing her hand so she could decide how close or far from him she wanted to sit. He couldn't believe it when she came and nestled beneath his arm, turning her body toward him, her head coming to rest on his shoulder, her hand on his upper chest. Yes! This was what they wanted, what he'd been waiting for all his life.

Lia was teaching him about a new approach to intimacy—creating trust between them. Now, he curved his hand around her shoulder, feeling her nuzzle his neck, hearing her sigh and relax against him. He pressed a light kiss to her hair. More than anything, Lia was helping him heal from the many old, open wounds created when he was so young. One day, he would tell her just how much she had dressed those open, seeping wounds so deep within him.

"This is even better than that chocolate cake you made for dessert," Cav teased, and she laughed softly.

"Much better," she agreed.

Moving his fingers lightly across her bare upper arm, he leaned his head against hers, closing his eyes as she melted into him. "This is nice. Very nice," he admitted in a gruff tone. Cav wanted to do so much more. He wanted to touch her, kiss her, move her across his lap, embrace her, open her up to all the pleasures he knew he could give her.

There was a special hell for men like him, he decided sourly, as he felt her press her breasts against his chest, snuggling like a cuddling bunny into his arms. If Lia didn't make a move, a signal to indicate she wanted something further from him, he was going to stand down as much as it killed him physically.

"I never thought," she whispered, sliding her fingers across his t-shirt, "that I'd see you this soon." And then she added, "I even wondered if I'd ever see you again."

"No chance of that," he growled. "Just because we crashed into each other's life doesn't mean we don't have something serious to build on, Lia."

She eased back a bit, her head resting on his shoulder, eyes half closed, studying him in the silence. "I feel the same, Cav. It's just that I have a lot of issues to work through. But you know that, and I appreciate you giving me the space to deal with them—actually, within myself."

"It's been a long, tough five years for you," he agreed quietly, seeing the concern in Lia's gaze. "You're not a woman who can be pushed or corralled into what a man wants her to do."

"That's true," she said, one corner of her mouth pulling upward.

"I just needed time, Cav. And now, we have it."

If he could get his physical body to agree to that, Cav could easily go the distance with Lia. "My mother always said that good things were worth waiting for." He touched her hair. "You're a good thing in my life, Lia."

"I wish," she said, "I'd gotten to meet your mother. I think you're probably a lot like her."

He nodded and tipped his head back against the couch, satisfied just to have her warm and in his arms. "I took after her, thank God,"

Cav realized belatedly that Lia wasn't wearing a bra. He could feel the firmness of her small breasts against his chest, feel her nipples hardening, becoming points, and teasing him mercilessly. He wondered if she got rid of her bra every chance she could. A lot of women hated wearing them.

He had always enjoyed looking at woman's breasts moving freely, watching their nipples pucker behind the silky clothes they wore. It was sexy. Sensual. Fully feminine.

And it was a pleasant surprise for him to see that, behind closed doors, Lia was comfortable with her own body. Except for those scars. With time and patience, Cav hoped to ease her up and over that last hurdle between them.

"When I found out Dilara wanted to talk to me about a job offer," he told her, "I did a little SEAL investigating. I scoped out the area for nearby caves you might want to visit."

"And what did you find?"

"There's Grand Caverns, near Harrisonburg, Virginia," he said. "I checked it out on the 'net and it's not offered to the public as a spelunking cave, but it's an interesting one. I thought this coming weekend we might drive out there, maybe leave on a Saturday morning, take the cave tour and do a little hiking in the area afterward. There's a nice restaurant nearby where we could finish off the day with a nice meal, and then I'd drive us home."

In fact, Cav wanted to make a reservation at a civil war era bed-and-breakfast nearby, remain over night, love the hell out of Lia, wake up on Sunday morning, love her again, get a late breakfast, and then see where things led. The SEAL in him always planned in detail.

"Oh, I'd like that," she whispered, sitting up. "I haven't even thought about doing any caving around here. I know the Smoky Mountains have a lot of limestone caves in them, but I've just been so busy."

He moved his hand down her bare arm feeling the warm, firm velvet of her flesh beneath his fingertips. "Then let's make a day of it. We can pack a picnic lunch if you want. No spelunking, but I think you'll like looking at the two hundred shield limestone formations. They're definitely worth studying."

He saw the excitement rise up in her, and couldn't help but smile.

"That sounds perfect, Cav. I'm sure next week is going to be long and brutal for me. Dilara is hiring fast and furious, there's all the building going on around us, and every day there are new demands on us." She smiled broadly. "This Saturday getaway sounds just perfect." Silently, she crossed her fingers that Cav would take the job offer Dilara was going to speak to him about on Monday.

"Good," he murmured, his hand stilling on her shoulder. "I was thinking of asking the owners, once we check out the cave, if we might do some caving on another weekend, if they'd allow it. There are twenty miles of passages in that cave."

"I'd love to do that!"

"I thought you might," he gloated, teasing her.

Cav was surprised when she slid her hand against his unshaven jaw, leaning into him, pressing her lips against his mouth. Taken off guard, he groaned, his arms coming around her swiftly, bringing her close. Lia had a way of being spontaneous that delighted him, but she was unknowingly pushing him to his limits. Her lips were soft and pliant—searching his, her moist breath feathering across his cheek as she hungrily let him know she wanted his reaction. And she got it.

The moment her tongue tentatively touched his, a sheet of fire roared down through him. Lia was definitely more assertive than before and it made his body hum with possibility. How far did she want to take this? Was she ready to stand naked before his gaze and not retreat from him or push his hands away as they grazed her body, even touching those scars?

Cav was reveling in the shy touch of her tongue against his lower lip. This was definitely a sign of progress, revealing that Lia had decided to trust him.

As she moved her hardened nipples against his chest, Cav had to consciously stop from lifting his hand to curve around the delicious breast closest to him. He wanted to move his thumb teasingly across her nipples that were just begging to be touched. He wanted hear Lia's sounds of pleasure as he did so.

More than his physical body reacted to her shy venture with him. Cav recognized her courage, her wanting to overcome her wounds to be spontaneous and loving with him. He allowed a growl of satisfaction to rumble through his chest, letting her know how much enjoyed that small tongue of hers on his lower lip. He felt her quiver as he barely touched her tongue with his own, inviting her to go further.

And then he felt her hesitate. He knew that, for tonight, it was enough. It was more than enough. In fact, it was more than he'd dreamed could happen between them after being apart for over a week. As she eased away, her lips glistening, slightly swollen from the power of his kiss, he saw dark, stormy arousal in her half closed eyes. Her fingers were flexing against his shoulders and he could literally feel her wanting so much more.

He caught the scent of her sex and knew she was wet between her thighs from the kiss they'd just shared. Settling his hand on her hip as she sat down next to him, he rasped, "That was one helluva welcome home kiss, baby."

Lia tried to take stock of herself by the week's end. The best news was on Monday? Cav had talked to Dilara and he'd taken the job she was offering him. The surprise on his face when he entered her office later, to tell her that he'd taken the job, had made her smile with joy. Cav didn't realize that he'd be working in HER office and he'd grinned, more than happy about it. She was nervous, giddy, hopeful and crashing back into old fear on a daily basis. All week long she and Cav, had been working long, hard hours together. He never made any kind of sexual move toward her, never touched her inappropriately, or even let on that they had a budding relationship with her. She was grateful for his decorum because the construction people were constantly in sight and Lia didn't want to be the subject of gossip.

But at night after work, either Cav cooked dinner for them, or she did. Lia was finding it easy to spend every night with him, talking at length over a variety of topics. Cav was intelligent, a global-traveler, and knew much more than she did about the world in general. He never bored her and his stories ranged from heart breaking to uplifting, to just plain funny.

She could feel him opening up to her on every possible level, and she was doing the same. More than anything, when Cav walked her up to her condo after a meal and chaste kiss her goodnight, Lia was left aching, and later dreamed erotic dreams of Cav loving her, touching her.

Of course she knew he wanted to love her, and she hated herself for her sensitivity about her scars, even after all this time with Cav.

There wasn't a night that didn't go by when they didn't cuddle on the couch after dessert. Those moments were what Lia looked forward to more than anything. She loved his touch, and how Cav made her feel about herself as a person, as a woman. And she could always feel him holding back. At last, she'd begun to understand that he was allowing her to go as far as she wanted, and where she stopped, he would stop, too.

Just knowing that gave her a newfound sense of power and re-lieved her of most of her fears. She'd been with men in the past that didn't "get" nonverbal signals to stop, and when she gave a verbal reminder, it was usually the end of the relationship.

Lia knew a man would never use her again. She wanted an equal relationship between herself and the man that interested her. And more and more, she saw that the man she wanted was Cav.

She thought of his poor, abused mother. Probably, as a child, he'd seen his brutal father use his strength and violence against his mother. It had taught Cav never to treat a woman like that, and the lesson stuck, because he was always careful and respectful with her.

Lia swore she could feel Cav monitoring her, gauging her reaction, reading her body language, listening to the tone of her voice, watching her expression for clues or signals. She wished more men had that developed sense within them. It would save a lot of relationships from hitting the rocks.

Every day, she wanted to talk to him about that terrible scar across her belly. And every day, she chickened out. She was so ashamed of it. Her head told her that Cav wouldn't react at all, and would probably disregard it. But her emotions still weren't ready for that particular roller-coaster ride.

She felt like a hurt child wanting to hide it so he couldn't see it, and she knew that was childish. But it told Lia how deep the wound was. If only she could talk to Cav about it. In fact, she might just get up the nerve to speak about it without showing it to him. Just talking about it might help, and prepare him for seeing it when she felt courageous enough to stand before him naked. She hadn't prepared Manuel to see it, and when he did, the look on his face was repugnance and disgust. No, she had to talk to Cav, had to prepare him for how ugly looking it was. She didn't want him looking at her like Manuel had. She just couldn't handle that kind of rejection again.

Lia hated her crazy emotions, and wanted desperately to ignore them, but she couldn't…at least, not yet.

A soft knock on her condo door made her start. It was Cav. She picked up the small wicker basket that held the picnic lunch she'd made for them. Opening the door, she smiled up at him. Today he was wearing his typical casual outfit: body-hugging jeans that showed off his long, hard thighs and tight butt and a bright red t-shirt that played off the power of his chest. Her fingers immediately itched to slide beneath that fabric and luxuriate in the feel of his flesh against hers.

He wore a small green pack on his shoulders and there was a dark green blanket draped over his left arm. On his feet, he wore boots because they were going into a cave. A dark blue baseball cap sat on his head, and when she saw his big grin, her whole body went on red-hot alert. Lia saw that he wanted her, too, and loved the lusty look he shot her way.

"Ready for our local first adventure together?" he teased, taking the wicker basket from her hand.

"More than you could ever know," she bubbled, shutting the door and locking it. "The day is perfect!"

Cav nodded, pleased that Lia's jeans showed off those cute cheeks of hers, as well as her curved thighs. "It's a perfect day because you're in it," he told her, walking her to the elevator.

Because they were going in a cavern that was only fifty-four degrees year round, Lia wore a long-sleeved red blouse and carried a jacket in her other hand. She too, wore hiking boots.

"Do you always say the right thing?" Lia teased, entering the elevator.

Cav grinned, pushing the button that would take them down to the parking area beneath the building. "Don't hold me to that high a bar," he chuckled. "'Cause sure as hell, I'll fall off it."

He'd bought a Jeep Wrangler three days ago, just in time to take them to Grottoes, Virginia, where the caverns were located. Cav intended to take them on a lot of back roads because he knew Lia loved caving and nature, just like he did. It was yet another thing they had in common.

Soon, they were speeding westward away from the craziness of

Washington, D.C., the Jeep's tires humming on the freeway, putting plenty of distance between the city and the Blue Ridge Mountains in the distance.

He took I-66 West, heading for I-81. Without traffic, it was a two and half hour trip one way to the Grand Caverns. Saturday morning traffic at 8 A.M. was light, and he pushed the Jeep, making good time as they headed toward Strasburg, Virginia. There, they would pick up I-81 South, which would take them directly to the caverns.

It was a hundred and fifty three miles of quality time spent with the woman he was falling deeply in love with. Cav's heart lifted as he looked at Lia, the wind whipping lightly around them with the Jeep's top down, open to the turquoise, cloudless sky. It really was a perfect day for them.

Earlier in the week, thunderstorms had moved across the area. From time to time, he glanced at Lia. She had put her head back on the seat, her dark glasses on, like his own, a hint of a smile on her lips. She needed this, he realized. No one worked harder or longer hours than Lia, and already Cav could see part of his job was to gently disengage her from her duties and get her out of that office after her eight hours were finished.

She had a tendency to take work home with her, too, and he was already discouraging that practice. Because Lia was so responsible, she didn't know where to draw a line and tell herself, "That's enough for today."

They stopped in Strasburg for mocha lattes at a small stand in one of the plazas, and then hopped onto I-81 South, aiming for the Grand Caverns. At one point, Cav wanted to pull over, put the Jeep in park, and lick a spot of whipped cream off the corner of Lia's mouth. Then, he'd kiss her until she melted into him but Cav put those yearnings away for another time.

So he was pleasantly surprised when Lia placed her hand on his thigh as he drove. It was a small thing, but very significant for both of them. He yearned for such intimate gestures as much as she did.

By 11 A.M., they pulled into the parking lot of the Grand Caverns. Lia inhaled the clean, fragrant air. She saw a lot of tourists parking their cars. She smiled as she watched children jumping up and down excitedly as their parents held their hands while walking towards the huge cave complex surrounded by trees.

Cav put everything in a small locker that was bolted down in the rear of the Jeep so no one could steal it. Lia shrugged into her jacket and zipped it up. There was also a pair of gloves in one pocket. Because she'd become used to a tropical climate, her blood was thin. Fifty-four degrees was cold to her, so she dressed appropriately.

Cav came around the Jeep and slid her hand into his, leading her toward the ticket office near the caverns. "It's going to seem odd not to be pulling on our caving gear," he grinned.

Lia had a suggestion. "Maybe they'll let us cave. If they do, we can come back here another weekend and spend Saturday and part of Sunday in those twenty miles of tunnels."

He raised a brow. "You'd stay overnight?" His heart thudded. He felt her beginning to worry a bit, and suggested, "We could always get two rooms."

Instantly, her expression changed and relaxed. "I'd like that."

She gestured toward the maw of the cave. "It really looks beautiful and I'd love to see a lot of those shield formations. They can't all be located in the one-hour trip we're taking into the cave."

"True," he said. At the booth, Cav paid for their tickets and asked whether spelunking was allowed. The young woman said "Yes," and gave him a brochure for cavers. She suggested that after they read it, if they wanted to spelunk, they could make a reservation.

Lia was thrilled, and eagerly took the brochure as they walked toward the waiting line of tourists who would enter the cave shortly. She entrusted herself to Cav, who gently guided her toward the line as she devoured the brochure. When she looked up, she saw five cavers going in at another entrance point. Cav had noticed them, too.

"Can we do this next week?" she asked. "I'd love to spend the whole weekend exploring this cave system. It's alive, it's wet and it's still growing. That would be really exciting to see."

Cav could never be immune to her excitement. She was like a child in that moment and he realized how badly Lia needed to go back to that part of her life. He smiled over at her. "Sure, let's do it."

The joy that shone in her eyes made him ache with love for her.

Lia listened intently as their guide moved them through an amazing one-hour walk into the living cave system. It was cool inside, and she was glad that Cav put his arm around her as she walked next to him, enjoying his extra warmth. The woman told them that there were hundreds of Civil War soldiers' signatures scrawled into the walls of the cavern, which had played a role in the War Between the States. It was often a place to hide, to rest, or to ponder strategy.

Lia liked that the cave had such a wonderful history, and she appreciated that their guide told tourists not to touch anything in the cave, since human germs and bacteria could destroy the delicate ecology of the cave.

That was why cavers wore gloves, to protect the living beauty of the caves they were grateful to be able to explore.

All too soon, they were wandering out into the bright noon sunlight.

"Hungry?" Cav asked her as they walked back towards the ticket booth.

"Starving!" Lia agreed.

"Let's see if we can sign up for caving next week."

Lia smiled and took off her gloves, glad to be out in the warm, low-eighties temperature once more. "Fingers crossed," she said excitedly.

In a few minutes, Cav had signed them up and they'd filled out the forms. There was a long list of rules they had to follow but they were rules they already followed when caving.

Cav knew not all cavers were aware of these rules and could damage, by accident, a cave or a formation as a result. There were not only state laws to follow when caving, but federal ones at all. Caves were zealously guarded precisely because they were living, changing and beautiful formations that could be easily destroyed by ignorance.

Lia spotted a picnic table and benches near the parking lot, so they took their wicker basket and their blanket over to it. They weren't the only ones who were hungry. The area was alive with squeals and laughter of children.

Cav sat opposite Lia, munching contentedly on a beef sandwich she'd made earlier, and watching her watch the children.

He tried not to think about her carrying his baby, but Cav couldn't help himself because Lia was a natural mother. She also loved animals. He saw her watching, enchanted, as a Dalmatian played with a Golden Retriever nearby. Just to be able to sit here with her and see all the tension shed and released made him smile.

Lia wasn't a complex person; in fact, she was simple in many respects. For Cav, that was a plus. She was wonderfully adaptable, a quality many people didn't possess, and was easy to be around. Lia would never be a drama queen or a prima donna, and he asked himself again, *how did I get so damned lucky?*

After lunch, they girded up for a hike into the Smoky Mountains surrounding the area. Cav had gotten a trail book, and they'd chosen a nice, one-way, three-mile hike up to the top of a treed mountain. The Smokies resembled rounded loaves of bread, thought Cav. There were no rocky, jutting mountains thrusting up to the sky. Instead, these were old and worn down into limestone lumps covered with trees, but that didn't detract from their beauty. The "smokiness" was really the fog that lay among the mountain chain, giving it a mystical and ethereal look to the visitors lucky enough to walk through them.

Cav carried the knapsack with water, a small first aid kit, a radio and food. He urged Lia to take the lead up the damp, muddy trail between the hundreds of trees surrounding them. Cav was content to follow, and the trail they'd taken was empty, compared to a lot of shorter trails that led from the parking lot. He was glad to have the silence, broken by birds singing, or the soft movement of leaves in the breeze.

A good hiker could do twenty-minute miles, and he was pleased to see that Lia was holding to that maxim. In an hour's time, they had crested the mountain and were able to find a small clearing, where they could look out across the mountains in the afternoon sunlight.

They drank deeply from their water bottles, took photos with Lia's small digital camera, and then Cav spread their blanket on the limestone precipice to absorb the bluish haze across the loaf-like mountains.

Lia had gathered her knees up toward her body, her arms around them, blending with the beauty around them. She was utterly relaxed, and although he'd seen her relax little by little with him, she had reached a whole new level of relaxation today.

"Here," he urged, sliding away from her and patting his thigh, "come and lie down. If you use my leg as a pillow, you can just drift off." She nodded and lay down on her back, her head resting against his thigh, her eyes half closed.

"You're spoiling me rotten, Cav. You know that, don't you?" She closed her eyes, their long, thick lashes sweeping down across her cheeks. Longing hit him hard as she entrusted herself utterly to him, her hands clasped over her stomach. And then, miraculously, she fell asleep.

Cav absorbed the moment like a man who had been without water all his life. The play of breeze ruffled Lia's hair, the sunlight emphasizing the purity of her skin and how relaxed it had become as she slept. What would it be like to sleep with this woman in his arms every night? To awaken and see her just like this beside him?

Cav was building many new dreams—new because in all his life, he'd never entertained any of these thoughts. He'd come from a dysfunctional family where any feelings of love had been destroyed when he was still a child. Now, for the first time, he could understand how love could take such deep roots in a person's heart.

Lia gave him the time and space to see his life differently. Better. More hopeful. And she had become *his* hope and healer, whether she knew it or not.

Cav gazed down at Lia, and realized that on some level, Lia knew he was with her. She knew she was safe and protected with him. Cav always wanted her to feel like that with him. He would never use his strength against her. He would always use it to hold her safe, give her a world of peace and joy. With him.

He watched the breeze play among the maples, elms and oaks crowding the summit where they sat. Light and dark shadows danced as shafts of sunlight wove down through the branches. So much of his early life had been in total darkness. The SEALs had given him a way out, a way toward the light.

As he gazed at Lia's serene features, he realized on a profound soul level that she was his light and his life. She would help him get out of his self-imposed prison. Lia might have physical scars that revealed she'd spent time in her own personal prison, but he had just as many, if not more, handed down to him from the moment he'd been born.

As he sat on that precipice with Lia sleeping peacefully, Cav realized they'd taken another important step together. Gratitude flooded through him because he had never believed he was worthy of such happiness. All his life, his father had told him he was worthless, that he was no good, that he was a loser. Cav had actually believed it, until he'd gotten into the SEALs.

Those men had become a far better family for him to grow into, develop with, and realize he wasn't a worthless piece of shit, as his old man had told him over and over again. His "Sea Daddy," Chief Jacoby, had wisely guided Cav through his late teens and early twenties. He made Cav aspire to go beyond his limits, and had been responsible for Cav getting his BA from Cal Poly.

By doing so, his mentor and surrogate father had prepared him for a life beyond being a SEAL. Jacoby had told him that one day, he'd be too old and beaten up to continue at the breakneck pace the team required. One day, Cav would return to civilian life, and when he did, Jacoby said, he would need a career that he could step into, make money, and never look back.

Jacoby had pounded into his head that someday Cav would find the right woman, one he'd want to settle down with and start a family.

Cav had retorted that he'd never get married and have a family—not after having barely survived the one he'd left behind. It was then that Jacoby began inviting him to meet his wife, Rebecca, and their two boys, Sean and Paddy. Every time Jacoby could get him to his house, he did, and soon Cav began to see the difference.

In his own way, his Sea Daddy was showing, not telling, what a real, loving family consisted of. Jacoby was a tough old salt in the SEALs and he didn't take shit from anyone. Everyone respected him officers and enlisted alike. And he'd shown Cav that getting married, finding the right woman, and having a family was a dream that could come true.

Family was a positive thing, not a negative one. It didn't have to be dark and toxic. It could actually be light and joyful. Gazing at Lia, Cav cupped her cheek, leaned over, and pressed a light kiss on her smooth brow. He wanted this woman forever.

Jacoby had given him his hope back. And now, Cav was going to throw his entire heart and soul in pursuit of Lia, hoping that she wanted the very same things he wanted with her.

CHAPTER 19

July 4ᵗʰ

L IA BROUGHT A huge bowl of potato salad to Robert and Dilara Culver's home for their annual Fourth of July picnic. She was surrounded by many of the people who were building Artemis Security, and the atmosphere was festive in their backyard.

About forty people stood around holding cold beers, iced tea or other drinks, chatting amiably with one another. Lia knew most of them, nodding hello as she skipped up the steps into the huge screened-in porch. Cav moved ahead of her to open the screen door leading to the kitchen.

"There you are!" Dilara called as she stood over the sink cleaning ears of corn.

"Sorry," Lia said, "We're running late. There was an accident on the freeway while we were trying to get over here." Cav opened up the huge double refrigerator so that she could put the bowl of potato salad in it.

"Oh, dear," Dilara murmured, wiping her hands on her dark blue apron. "Anyone hurt?"

"It didn't look like it," Lia said, coming over to the sink. "The ambulances were there and the police were just trying to get traffic past the area."

"More like a stupid fender-bender," Cav put in, leaning against the granite counter, nodding hello to Dilara. "Probably some careless kid who was texting while driving."

"It's an epidemic," Dilara agreed. "I have about two dozen corn-cobs to husk, Cav. Would you like to take over? You have big, strong hands."

"Sure," he said. "Is there anything else I can do to help?"

"I'm sure Robert would like company out at the huge gas barbecues after that. He's going to start with the hot dogs and hamburgers in one barbecue, and in the other, he'll put all the veggies. When you get done here ask him what he wants to come out first."

She pointed to the fridge. "All the meat is on the top two shelves. Veggies are below."

"Got it," Cav said. "You two take off and do what women do best," he grinned, grabbing an ear of corn setting on the counter.

Dilara gave him a quick hug. "Watch it or I'll talk *you* to death, Cav."

Everyone chuckled.

"What can I do to help?" Lia asked.

"Nothing, actually. A lot of the wives are here and they've pretty much organized the chaos, so we're in full forward motion." She glanced at her delicate Rolex watch on her wrist. "In about an hour I think we'll be ready to eat. The ladies have all the picnic tables set up with linens on them. Let's go out back and sit on the porch. Do you want some iced tea? Wine?"

"Just iced tea," Lia said. "Thanks."

Dilara poured them each a glass, leaving Cav to his shucking duties. He smiled, watching the two women amble past the large windows in front of the sink. Lia looked particularly beautiful. Today she wore a capped sleeved bright red top, and white shorts that fell to just above her knees. She'd boldly worn clothes that clearly showed her scars.

Cav knew it was a huge step, and he was damned proud of her. Her hair was longer, curling softly around her face now, giving her a sensual look. Cav didn't think women realized how much of a turn-on their hair could be for men. While he understood the need for short hair in a hot climate, he still liked a woman with longer hair.

He supposed it was stamped in his DNA. His mother always wore her hair long, too.

He spotted Robert out with the construction owners who had won the bids to build Artemis. They were all power players. Cav smiled a little. Robert was damned tall, standing over everyone, which matched his General status. Even in a pair of brown Bermuda shorts, sandals and a white polo shirt, he couldn't hide his military bearing. He'd just flown in from France after a NATO exercise, and Cav was sure the man was reeling from jet lag. But if he was, it didn't show.

He liked Robert and had seen him occasionally at Artemis, checking up on the building progress of the three upper floors, as well as supervising the two-story digging going on where the basement used to be.

Cav, when he could steal a moment, was interested in the "underground bunker," as it was called. The bunker was being built with the latest materials, which would make it immune to being opened up by an overhead satellite, laser intrusion, heat seeking infrared, or any other device. All the top-secret files, computers and equipment to hold and create security, would be in those two underground floors. The bulk of the construction was going on there right now, because without it being built first, other construction couldn't move forward.

Cav's gaze moved to his left, watching Dilara and Lia sit down on the large, comfy swing at one end of the enclosed screen porch. He felt light and hopeful. Over the past month, Lia had been steadily making progress regarding her scars. He noticed what kinds of clothes she wore, and more and more often, she was exposing her arms to the public.

Cav also noticed that when new people entered her office, they would look at the scars casually, not focusing on them. Lia's warm personality was far more interesting to them. It truly was a non-issue, and he could see Lia begin to ease up about her concerns that people were staring at her.

And that was good for them both.

Cav shucked the corn quickly, placing it in two large aluminum pans sitting on the counter. The fact that Lia boldly wore shorts for the first time actually amazed him. They no longer talked about her scars or how she felt about them. Cav wasn't sure this was a positive development because he'd learned that if Lia could talk about whatever was bothering her, it no longer had the power over her. Maybe she wasn't as bothered by the scars anymore, or at least it was less upsetting than it had been.

Cav decided he wasn't going to push his agenda on her. She was coming along nicely, and far more quickly than he could believe. Inside, he knew it was the emotional support he was giving her, which pleased him that he could play that kind of "rear guard" action with Lia.

He had special plans for their next weekend, and he could hardly wait to spring it on her. He imagined how she'd look when he told her where they were going.

Finishing up, he washed and dried his hands. Cav had made some good friends among the construction crew and decided to see if Robert needed anything yet. Then, he would join the group standing beneath the large elm tree. A cold beer sure would taste good on a hot, muggy July day.

"How are you and Cav getting along?" Dilara asked Lia directly, not mincing words.

Holding the beaded glass of cold iced tea in her hands, Lia said, "Really well, actually." She wasn't sure that Dilara knew of their after-hours relationship, and decided she was referring to their work at Artemis.

"He's a very insightful young man," Dilara murmured, sipping her tea, pushing the swing a little with the toe of her white leather shoe.

"I'm amazed at his knowledge of Asia and Africa," enthused Lia. "I'm learning so much from him."

Dilara hummed a bit, then smiled. "I was referring to your private life, Lia. Not that it's my business, but I rather pride myself on knowing the people who work with me. Cav seems very devoted to you."

Squirming inwardly, Lia chose her words carefully. "He's very sensitive. I know he's a security contractor and my original judgment about him was wrong. He is so much more than that."

Cav had been right when he said Dilara was a cosmic mother hen of sorts. She truly cared for everyone and made it her business to know them on a personal level. That, in part, was why Lia wanted to work at Delos—precisely because she'd heard talk that Dilara Culver was the dream boss to work for. And the gossip had been accurate.

"You seem to enjoy his company on weekends. I hear talk from the girls at HR that you two are usually gadding about, like going caving in Virginia."

Lia smiled a little, running her fingers through the cool beads of water on the tall glass. "Yes. My father is a spelunker and he started teaching me caving when I was ten. I love it. And Cav does, too, as it turns out."

"I know nothing about caving," Dilara admitted. "And I did know Cav was interested in them. I whispered to him one time that he should take you caving while you were both in Costa Rica."

"Yes, he did." Lia smiled at her. "And he later admitted that you'd whispered that information to him about me. He said he had to learn about caves when he was a SEAL."

Dilara studied her through her thick lashes. "Well, I think you two are well matched. I knew about Cav's training as a SEAL and knew you loved spelunking, so I thought that was a natural fit for you two."

"I was, actually," Lia admitted. "It brought us together, Dilara and I'm glad you told him."

"I rather pride myself in pairing up men and women who I instinctively feel are right for one another," she admitted.

Lia chortled. "You know you're called the Royal Matchmaker behind your back, don't you?" She saw Dilara's aquamarine eyes gleam with amusement.

"Indeed I do. I tell Robert that I wear that badge with a great deal of pride." She reached out, touching Lia's knee. "And what does caving do for you? There must be some kind of positive experience you receive from it…"

Lia appreciated Dilara's insight. "A cave makes me feel safe, Dilara. I feel like I'm in Mother Earth's womb and I'm the child she's carrying. A lot of caves are alive, wet and humid. There's life in there, and you can feel it. Every cave breathes, and I can almost feel it, like our Mother Earth is breathing. I feel completely alive in a cave system and love exploring them and discovering all their secrets."

"I see. And Cav? Does he feel similarly?"

"Yes, he does love exploring the caves," Lia admitted,"

"I know you were caving while in Costa Rica. It must have helped you a lot."

Lia knew she was referring to her struggles with the attack. "Yes, it did. It's a very healing hobby for me, Dilara."

"I can see the results of it right now. To me, that's amazing."

"Maybe you'd like to go with us? We could show you how to do it."

Laughing, Dilara held up her manicured hand. "Oh, no! You've discovered the chink in my armor. I'm claustrophobic! I can't stand being in enclosed places and I could never go into a dark, wet, small place like a cave. I'd panic."

Lia's heart went out to her. "I didn't know," she murmured, reaching out to touch Dilara's arm. "Were you always that way?"

"No, dear, but when I was six years old Turkey had an earthquake.

You know Turkey has earthquakes quite often?"

"Yes."

"I was with my mother in an old mosque they wanted to repair and save. She was going to give the owners money for repairs. It was a very old building in a small town, inland and north of our home. We were down in the basement when an earthquake struck." Dilara grimaced. "We ended up being trapped there for two days before they found us and dug us out. I can remember the earthquake's roar, the feeling of ground heaving, and then everything falling in on us.

Luckily, there was an old, sturdy wooden table that my mother had the wits to drag me beneath. A huge amount of bricks and mortar fell on us but we were shielded by the table. I remember choking on the dust, and the darkness terrified me. I couldn't breathe and began to panic. My poor mother held me and told me it would be all right. But at six, I didn't believe her."

"That must have been awful," Lia sympathized. "No wonder you're afraid of small, dark places. I would be, too. Did you have any way to call for help?"

"No, we didn't. And I was dying of thirst, and cried so much that the tears stopped forming in my eyes. My mother was beside herself because I was so frightened."

"Were you hurt?"

"No. My mother had a broken arm, but she never let me know it. After they found us and dug us out, I saw how swollen and bruised her arm was. At six, you don't realize very much about other people," and she gave Lia a wry look.

"Of course not," Lia agreed. "How long did it take you to get over the shock of that, Dilara?"

"Many, many years. Originally my room at my parents' villa was very small, an inner room without windows. I remember that first night when my mother tucked me into my bed and I cried my eyes out. I said it felt like I was trapped in that mosque basement again. I refused to stay in the room, leaving my bed and went out into in the hall. There my mother found me the next morning, sleeping on the swing out on the patio. There were nice, fat cushions on it and it was during the summer, so it was very warm. I slept well out there. My parents wisely moved me to a new bedroom in another part of our villa, with huge windows and lots of light. I was very happy there, and I could sleep and not feel as if the walls were closing in on me."

"It's so amazing, Dilara. Looking at you, no one would guess you'd had such a devastating experience. You're so self-assured!"

Patting Lia's hand, she said, "We all have scars, my dear. Some are just better hidden than others."

"You're right," Lia agreed quietly. "How did you handle the feeling of being buried alive?"

"A day at a time," Dilara said. "I was traumatized, of course. The claustrophobia was subtle at first, but by the time I was twelve, I realized how imprisoned I was by it. I'd look at every building and assess it. If it seemed too small, too dark, or if I had a bad feeling about entering it, I didn't. My father finally sat me down one day and had a long talk with me. He was very loving about it, but he told me I had an invisible jail cell I carried around with me."

Her lips twitched. "He painted me a very visual picture of what was happening to me and I got it."

"What did you do, then?" Lia asked, interested for her own reasons.

"I realized the only one who could change this was me. I started challenging myself, Lia, like going into places I feared. I walked through my fear, and I must tell you, it wasn't easy. It was the hardest thing I've ever done. Sometimes, I'd cry, just standing in a small, enclosed room. It terrified me, but I'd stay because I didn't want to live in a self-made, invisible prison. I was becoming afraid of my shadow."

"That took so much courage," Lia whispered, deeply moved.

"It took me seven years to undo the psychological damage I'd received," Dilara recalled. "My parents supported me, of course. I would tell them on a given day what I'd done to move that cell door open an inch more than it was the previous day. They were wonderful parents, and always made time for me when I needed them. They knew that I was doing psychological process called *desensitization*. The more I did it, the less reactive I became to the situation. And it has worked for me for the most part."

"You're so inspiring to me," Lia admitted enviously. "You're so brave!"

Dilara raised one eyebrow. "And you're not?"

"What do you mean?"

Dilara placed her hand over Lia's. "I've watched you grow. I've seen you working hard to escape your own invisible prison."

Nodding, Lia murmured, "It's been tough, Dilara. Well…until lately."

Removing her hand, Dilara sipped her tea. "I see Cav's influence on you, dear, and it's all been good. Don't you agree?"

Lia smiled shyly. "You don't miss much, do you?" She saw Dilara's eyes sparkle with delight.

"I don't think I miss much, but you tell me, all right?"

Setting down her glass of iced tea on the wide arm of the rocker, Lia sat back and gazed out of the screened windows, looking at the guests below them.

"Cav supports me completely, Dilara. He's not obvious, and we don't talk about my scars, but we both know that I'm afraid to show the more intimate areas of my body that were scarred from the attack."

"But look at you today!" Dilara said proudly, gesturing toward her. "I've never seen you in shorts before. And you look terrific! You have no idea how much I applaud your personal courage."

"Thanks," Lia whispered, meaning it. "I was scared about coming over here today, but no one seems to notice me, or that I have scars. That's *such* a relief."

"You've taken another big step in pushing open your invisible cell door," Dilara congratulated her. "And I'll bet it feels good."

"Truly, it does, but it's a daily struggle," Lia admitted, looking down at her lap.

"Yes, but it's a worthy one. In time you'll no longer worry about these scars you carry. In my case, my claustrophobia is under control. I don't let it run my life any more. And…," she tapped Lia's arm, "When I met Robert? He didn't know about my issues. We'd taken a hike in the mountains of Turkey, going on a picnic. There was an earthquake, Lia, and where we had sat, the mountain fell around us."

"Oh," Lia whispered, "…no…"

Dilara rolled her eyes. "Poor Robert. I was sitting there clinging to him, the dust making me choke, crying and losing it. He wasn't aware of my terrible childhood experience. But you know what? He got me to settle down, and typical of being in the military, he started to try and find a way out for us. No one knew we were there. We knew no help was coming. The only way we could survive was to dig our way out. He gave me his courage, his hope and he put me to work. We had only the water and food in our knapsacks to sustain us those three days. I didn't think we'd get out alive, but we did. Robert broke through the debris, working nonstop, day and night. I did help, but he had the strength and brawn to endure when I couldn't go on physically speaking."

"What an experience," Lia whispered, shaking her head, her respect for Robert and Dilara growing even more than before. "Did you get help after you got out?"

"Oh, yes," Dilara said, smiling tenderly. "I fell in love with Robert during those three days of being in the darkness with him. He feared nothing. He was so brave and supportive. I eventually broke down and told him why I was so shaken by being buried alive and he understood. I was privy to his tender side, the man who had emotions and who cared for me. We had many other experiences before he asked me to marry him. It seemed like he drew danger to him and I finally got over it because he loved me, he protected me and he respected me as his equal. Those are all things I needed in a man to think of marrying him."

"So?" Lia said, giving her a warm look, "you said yes?"

"I did," Dilara sighed. "And I've never been sorry about it. He's my hero, Lia. He's a brave, resourceful and intelligent man. Our children have his DNA and I'm so glad they do."

"Well, they sure have yours, too," Lia laughed, patting her hand. "I've met all of them during our encrypted video sessions with them from over in Afghanistan where they're still serving. When you and Robert talk about Artemis, the building, and get their input and ideas about it, I see both of you in Tal, Matt and Alexa during those sessions. They have your composure, your kindness and compassion. Not that Robert doesn't have any, but I really think he gave them is leadership skills, their risk taking personalities."

"That's all true," Dilara said. Her lips curved ruefully and she shared a look with Lia. "But to knowingly go into a dark, small space like a cave? That's where I have to draw my line!"

"That's completely understandable," Lia said, smiling over at her.

Then, Dilara said something that Lia never expected. "You know, you might want to include Cav in conversations about your scars. I think he'd understand, don't you?"

Lia grimaced and didn't answer her directly. "He's seen all but the worst one," she explained, touching her stomach region.

Dilara reached over, giving her a quick hug around the shoulders. "That man cares a great deal for you, Lia. Surely you know that by now?"

"Yes, of course."

"When I met Robert in Turkey…"

"Yes?"

"I was at a NATO meeting in Istanbul giving a talk on the Delos charity to the top generals from fifteen countries. Robert was there." She sighed and smiled fondly. "I was twenty-two at the time, my usual confident self. He was such an impressive, attractive man, and so tall that he literally stood above every other man in that room. And he was so brazen! He asked me out to dinner that night after my talk." She laughed, remembering. "But the place he chose was a tiny basement restaurant—with no windows."

"Oh, dear," Lia murmured, giving her a pained look. "What did you do?"

"I saw how tiny it was and told him to stop. We stood outside on the sidewalk, and I told him I couldn't go in there, but not why. I was afraid he'd make fun of me or think I was a coward."

"Yes, I've experienced that with men." Lia admitted.

"But Robert was very sympathetic. He asked me to choose a restaurant that made me feel comfortable, and I did." She laughed. "Silly me! I was so enamored with this man, already falling in love with him. I didn't know it at the time, of course. But I so wanted him to like me. Before that, I'd avoided dating because I didn't want to get dragged into small, cloistered places and have to explain why I couldn't tough it out. I was quite ashamed of myself."

She became serious. "Of course, six months later when we were out hiking and we were in the earthquake, that is when he found out why I didn't want to go into that restaurant. And now, in my early forties, I know it was silly of me to feel that way. Age and time have given me a different perspective on my vulnerabilities."

"I didn't know this about you, about avoiding dates with men because of it," Lia confided. "I've been doing the same thing."

"Well," Dilara said wryly, "when I was seventeen and on my first date with a boy, he took me to a small room where a classical quartet was to play Beethoven. I couldn't go into it because it was too small. I told him I was afraid and he turned on me, called me a coward and a 'stupid girl.' He embarrassed me in front of twenty other people who were standing in line to go into that room. I ran out crying."

"That's horrible," Lia whispered, her heart breaking for her friend.

"That one encounter scarred me for years," she said, shaking her head. "I was twenty-two when I met Robert. And I was so taken by him that I said 'yes' to a date. And then, I was petrified I'd make a fool of myself again when he took me to that tiny restaurant."

"But he reacted differently," Lia said, relieved. "Although he didn't understand my reasons for not going into it, he respected me. I think I began to fall in love with him at that moment."

Dilara gave her a gentle look. "Yes, just as Cav has done with you. I strongly believe you need to come completely clean with Cav. He reminds me so much of my Robert. He has the intelligence, the compassion, the intuitive sensitivity to hear your fears, and he'll never judge you. And for people like you and me, it's the most important quality a person, whether a friend or lover—can have. I don't believe Cav has ever judged your behavior, has he?"

"No," Lia whispered. "He's acted as if the scars meant nothing to him. I honestly don't think he sees them, Dilara. He only sees the real me."

"Exactly," Dilara murmured, smiling. "Robert loved me enough to understand why I was the way I was. He didn't try to change me, but over time, because he was aware of my issue, he worked with me on it. After we married, he worked with me even more."

"Today," and she shrugged, "I honestly don't think about being claustrophobic, and Robert honors me by not taking me to tiny, enclosed places. He's aware of what my needs are and makes sure they're met. He's been my biggest cheerleader and supporter, Lia. And I believe Cav is your cheerleader, among other important things."

Lia nodded, feeling her heart swelling with love for Cav. "You have no idea how much this talk means to me, Dilara. Thank you for sharing this. I would never guess you had any problems that were similar to mine."

Laughing, Dilara said, "My dear, none of us is quite right. If our parents didn't do something to hurt us, we experience a traumatic event that wounds us. No one on this earth escapes being wounded, Lia." She tapped Lia's arm. "More important is to be compassionate toward them and try to understand their actions and reactions, knowing something bigger is behind it, pushing them."

"Cav has been horribly wounded, too," Lia confided to her quietly.

"I know," she said, giving Lia a sympathetic look. "Between you and me, one of the reasons Robert uses Cav a lot is because of who he is. We sat down one time over lunch, and Cav told me a light version of his nightmare childhood."

"He told you?"

Dilara smiled a little. "We don't see our employees in the same light that other corporations do, Lia. To us, you're all members of our extended family. I was raised in a big, noisy, loving Turkish family. I saw my uncles treat their employees like family, and observed how it bred such loyalty and respect between them. I want that same energy with the special people who run our charities. Thank goodness, we have that. So it's not unusual that Cav opened up a little bit to me. Despite his obvious pain in recalling those events, he demonstrated the inner strength and courage to overcome his personal adversity. Cav has grown because of his wounding—he's not imprisoned by it any longer. I believe Chief Jacoby, who was a very positive father figure to him in the SEALs, helped him out of that dark place within himself. Just as my parents, and later Robert, helped me out of that place within me. They helped to free me."

"And now, Cav is helping me out of my dark place," Lia whispered.

Dilara wrapped her arm around Lia's shoulders. "Who better than him? He's a wounded healer. Cav has gone through his own personal hell, so he can relate to your hell. And I know there's something very special and beautiful blossoming between the two of you."

She squeezed Lia's shoulders. "Let him help you walk into the light so you can push that invisible cell door wide open. Walk toward him with your head held high, Lia. Like my Robert, he's a kind soul beneath that hard, military exterior"

She looked closely at Lia. "So? Will you allow your heart to trust his heart? My Sufi uncles and mother would tell you that 'the heart has eyes that see through the dark.' It can lead us out of the shadows so we can honestly see where we are, and where we want to go."

Lia felt tears of relief behind her eyes as she absorbed Dilara's gentle words. She gripped the woman's other hand, holding on to her kind gaze. "Thank you for sharing this. It helps me so much, Dilara."

Dilara released Lia's hand. "Ah, I see your Cav now," and gestured towards him as he went through the screen door, heading outside with a tray of corn. "Why don't you enjoy this afternoon? You know, it is the Fourth of July, a time when your country fought for and won its freedom. In some ways, Lia, you have been fighting for five long years to win your freedom back, too. Cav is there to support you in your bid for that well deserved freedom." Her voice lowered. "And remember this, Lia. No one gets healed from their wounds without the help of others. I think in your case you've been afraid to allow someone in your life and trust them to handle your fears with love and support. But now, my intuition tells me you trust Cav, and you need to keep moving in that direction. He's the person who will help you achieve the freedom you so richly deserve."

CHAPTER 20

C AV TRIED TO contain his excitement as he drove the Jeep along one of Virginia's scenic country roads. The mid-July heat was in the 90s, and so was the humidity. The "dog days" of summer were upon them.

He glanced over at Lia, who was equally excited about the surprise he had in store for her. All week, since the Fourth of July celebration at the Culver house in Alexandria, he'd teased her about it. Now, he hoped he hadn't oversold the surprise.

The road was a twisting, winding two-lane asphalt with woods on the left and a white wooden fence and corral on the right. Virginia was horse country, pure and simple, and he'd packed them a picnic lunch for them, put the blanket in the rear seat, and they'd taken off for parts unexplored.

This area of Virginia was wooded, beautiful and rural. He could almost see Lia shake off the workweek stress as they drove. Her job at Artemis was demanding, and new employees were coming in weekly, needing to be trained. HR had hired three new women and that department was scrambling, too. That was what happened when a huge project like Artemis was being created and readied to take off.

"Did you see Dilara's memo on Friday night?" Lia wondered, tipping her head, towards Cav. "Tal Culver, their oldest daughter, is going to become CEO of Artemis."

"Yes, and I think it's a good call. She's turning in her military commission shortly, which they've been planning for quite a while."

"When Dilara came in on Friday, we had lunch together in my office," she began.

"Yes. I saw your door was closed so I figured you two were having some kind of summit meeting, he teased.

Lia snorted. "Actually, she told me that Tal was getting ready to leave the Marine Corps after being injured in that sniper op that went south on her."

"Yes, and it was a good thing Wyatt Lockwood was there to save her life when it happened. I think getting our CEO installed will be a major step so we can move ahead. Tal's got the right stuff to pull it all together. She'll be good for Artemis."

"Yes, Dilara's over the moon about Tal coming home. She and Robert worried a lot about her when she got injured. They flew into Bagram and as soon as Tal could, they flew her back on an Air Force jet to here. I wanted to go over to introduce myself to Tal, but Dilara asked to give her a few days to acclimate and I will. Matt and Alexa are still over in Afghanistan. They want their kids out of that hot mess, and I don't blame them."

Grimly, Cav agreed. "And it's going to the dogs now that the drawdown is complete and only a few thousand troops are left behind. I knew it would turn out like this."

"Me, too," she sighed. Lia looked out at the scenery, her hair picking up the breeze as he drove down the quaint country road. "This is a beautiful area, Cav. Is the secret nearby?" she asked, changing the subject. No more work talk for now, she vowed!

Lia's gray eyes were clear and sparkling. She was now getting a good eight hours sleep a night, and the tense expression she had worn when they were in Costa Rica had disappeared. All thanks to Cav's influence on her.

Cav hinted, "We're getting close. I'm just glad you wore jeans and boots."

"Well, you strongly suggested I should," she teased. "You're dressed the same way, only your polo shirt is dark blue." Lia loved looking at his lean, hard body. The dark blue baseball cap on his head gave him that black ops look. He was dangerous to her in every way, but in a good sense. And the yearning in his eyes was stronger than ever.

She felt herself moving closer and closer to having that talk with him. Dilara's decision to confide her own story had made an enormous impact on Lia, and she had thought about it often, mulling everything over and feeling her way toward the next step she knew awaited her.

Cav's excitement grew as they approached his surprise for her. He slowed the Jeep down as they approached several large pastures. Inside the fencing was every imaginable kind and color of horse. Lia instantly sat forward, straining to see these beloved animals come into view. There was no mistaking it—he saw the longing in her eyes, and knew he'd made the right call.

"Is this where we're going, Cav? Is it?" she asked eagerly.

He heard the excitement in her voice. "Yeah." He slowed the Jeep. "I found this place on the Internet," he told her, making a turn and heading toward a two-story white farmhouse with a big red barn behind it.

"Do you notice anything about these horses?" he asked as they slowly passed the first large corral.

"Oh!" she started. "Oh, my God, Cav! They look like mustangs!" She gave him a look of disbelief. "Are they?"

He grinned. "Yep. This is a mustang and burro rescue farm. The people who own it are Deb and Jack Fagone. They work with the BLM, Bureau of Land Management, and they rescue wild mustangs and burros from the West and bring them back here. They offer these horses a place to live and have a decent life. They're a charity of a different sort, but like Delos, they do good work. In their case, it's with four-leggeds that need help."

He gestured toward a group of buckskin horses with black manes, tails and lower legs standing together, their noses nearly touching one another. "They gently break and train these horses and then put them up for sale."

Gasping, her eyes huge, Lia whispered, "That's so wonderful! Goldy was part mustang. Did I ever tell you that?"

"Yes, you did mention that," he said, parking in the gravel yard in front of the white farmhouse with dark green shutters. He grinned over at her as he turned off the Jeep's engine.

She looked around the neat, clean farm and saw a black dog sitting up on the porch watching them, slapping its bushy tail against the wood. She turned toward him. "Why are we here?"

"Well," he drawled, "This is your surprise. They have trail rides into the woods. They've kept some of the mustangs as trail horses. We can rent them by the hour and go out with or without a guide."

He loved to create opportunities for the little girl in her to come out and play. And that was exactly what Cav had in mind today: play.

"I know how much you love to ride and since you've been back here to the States, you haven't had a chance to do it. As I recall, one of the families in La Fortuna used to let you ride their horse, and you'd go down jungle trails for a few hours every week."

She smiled. "You found that out, did you?"

"I'm a SEAL, remember?" He couldn't resist teasing her. As he met her smile, he saw the gratitude in her eyes. "So? Are you ready to put our lunch in a set of saddlebags, throw a leg over a good horse, and go take a ride into those woods behind the farmhouse?"

"Cav," she said, her voice suddenly strained, "This is beyond wonderful." She reached out and gripped his hand. "Thank you…"

He closed his fingers over hers, watching her blink back tears. Some day, Cav hoped that Lia would allow those tears to fall whenever they wanted. He would be there to hold her when she cried, but right now, she didn't know that. Lia squeezed his hand again, released it, and eagerly climbed out of the Jeep.

Deb Fagone met them on the porch, smiling and shaking their hands. For the next hour, she gave them a tour of the facilities. The black dog, Champ, followed them everywhere they went. Lia felt so many old memories surfacing as Deb took her through the huge, airy barn. It was over a hundred years old, but freshly painted and well cared for. She saw a number of mustang broodmares nearly ready to foal, standing in large, clean stalls on the first floor. She sighed as she inhaled the sweet scent of timothy hay. It brought back so many wonderful memories of her childhood, and of being with Goldy.

Jack Fagone was out in a smaller wooden corral as Deb led them down to the rear of the barn area. Lia saw two horses with western saddles and bridles standing with legs cocked, half asleep. She instantly liked Jack, a man of about forty-five with a big, welcoming smile as they drew up to the gate. He shook both their hands, handed Lia a trail map encased in plastic, and pointed out several trails they might take. And then he opened the gate, inviting them in.

Lia immediately zeroed in on one particular mustang—a palomino like her Goldy. Jack was actually leading him out to where she stood. Glancing to her right, where Cav stood, his hands on his hips, she whispered, "You found a palomino!"

He leaned down, placing a kiss on her hair. "Yep, I got lucky. I explained to Jack and Deb that you'd once owned a palomino and they just happened to have Sunny, here, as one of their trail horses." He became serious and touched her ruddy cheek. "I want you to be happy, Lia."

The gruffness in his voice, the thickening of emotions carried within it, made her heart open as nothing else ever had. The care burning in his eyes for her, the love she knew Cav had never spoken about to her, was there. She turned, throwing her arms around his shoulders, crushing him against her with the strength of her own love. "This means so much to me, Cav," she cried, closing her eyes, she held him as his arms slid around her waist. "Thank you…thank you!"

She reached up and kissed him.

He embraced her, kissed her cheek and when she offered her mouth, he took it gently. His gift to her was a day to be with horses again. His breath was stolen by the incredible joy her kiss conveyed against his mouth. While Cav wanted time for them to simply be with one another, he knew that wasn't today's reality, but he felt it coming.

"Hey," he grinned, "Let's go for a trail ride."

Just the clip-clop of a horse swaying rhythmically beneath Lia made her want to shout to the sky. She led on Sunny, the beautiful, gentle mustang gelding. The horse obviously knew the quiet, wide trail that wound through the hills and vales of the woodlands. Behind her, Cav was mounted on a much taller mustang called Ziggy. He was a grulla dun, a gunmetal gray color with a black mane and tail and lower legs. He even had that telltale black dorsal stripe running down the center of his back, proclaiming his Spanish heritage.

Lia knew that the Spanish had ridden their horses into America, and some of the Spanish horses, part Arabian, had escaped from where they were tied each night. It was from those escapees that mustangs had been born and ran the plains and mountains of western United States.

She knew her mustang history well because when she found out from her father that Goldy was half mustang, she'd hungrily explored their history. At one time, ten thousand years ago, a small type of horse had lived in North America, but eventually died out. When the Spanish explored the Southwest, the stallions and mares that had escaped from their owners populated the West. The horses were later caught and tamed by Native Americans.

Today, the BLM rounded up huge herds of mustangs, especially in Nevada, Wyoming and Montana, and sold them to the highest bidder. Many ended up going to factories to fill dog food cans. Other luckier ones, like the mustangs they rode, were bought and cared for. These were later sold to people who appreciated these incredible animals, whose background blended with the rich history of the West.

Most mustangs were small and Sunny was the standard fourteen hands tall. Ziggy, the grulla dun that Cav rode, was the exception, fifteen hands tall, heavily muscled and a lot more active than Sunny. Lia was glad to have quiet Sunny to ride.

According to the map she carried, there was a small stream on the other side of the wooded hill. Jack had told them there was a nice place to have a picnic near the banks of the river, where the horses could also drink. The sunlight danced between the leaves, dappling her and Sunny as the mustang gingerly moved up a slope to the top of the hill. Cav rode up to Lia with Ziggy.

"We need to ride that way," he said, pointing in the direction of the still unseen stream. He sat in a comfortable slouch on his mustang.

Lia smiled, thinking that Cav would make a great cowboy with his rugged good looks. True, he didn't have a real Stetson on his head, but he still had that outdoor look she loved so much. And she loved him for this thoughtfulness, leaning down and rubbing Sunny's dampened neck. "Every minute in the saddle just makes me happier than the last minute," she confided, giving him a tender look of thanks.

Cav's heart expanded fiercely with love for her, seeing how much the gift of riding a horse once again, brought out in Lia. "It's not far now," he'd said. They had been riding a good two hours, moving deeper and deeper into the hills thick with trees. The sun was overhead and she knew it was near noontime. Cav had placed their lunch in the large saddlebags behind Ziggy's saddle, and Lia carried the water bottles in Sunny's leather bags.

"This is really nice," he murmured, giving the place an appreciative look.

"It's a lot like where I grew up," she said, turning. "Well, not exactly like this," and she gestured to the trees. "My Dad's farm is on flat land, mostly sandy soil and there aren't many trees. A good half of Oregon is Great Basin land, dry and desert-like."

"That's interesting," Cav said. He liked the bits of information that revealed more about Lia. He had found that each weekend with her was like opening up a treasure chest—her gift of herself—to him, whether she realized it or not. And every weekend had yielded a new jewel about this woman he loved.

There was a sweetness to waiting for her to open up and trust him fully. Cav could see Lia struggling sometimes, and knew it wasn't about him, but rather about putting her trauma behind her. He warmed with the realization that his support was helping her get there sooner. And God, how he anticipated the day when Lia could entrust her broken, scarred body to him, walk into his arms, and stand proud and naked before him.

That would be the day they'd both celebrate her last day of imprisonment. The past would no longer hold her captive.

And then?

As he followed Lia and Sunny down the other side of the hill, Cav smiled to himself. Life was never easy. Some days were better than others, and his idea to bring her out to this horse rescue facility had been one of his better ideas. He'd never seen Lia so lively, so spontaneous, and smiling so often.

He was a patient man, which was a good thing. Cav wanted to give her the world, but he knew he had to pace his desire against her inner growth. He could relate to her struggle—all he had to do was look at his own background and his emergence from his own toxic past, with the help of Chief Jacoby. And Lia. Cav never forgot that she was also healing some of his deepest, oldest wounds by simply being herself around him. She was a gift to him but didn't realize it. Yet.

The weekends he'd spent with Jacoby's family had taught him more than any book could have. It was then that Cav realized that having a family could bring pleasure, not always a promise of pain and suffering.

And he wanted the same for Lia and himself. He enjoyed watching her ride Sunny. Just the way her hips swayed back and forth in that saddle made him ache to take her. He himself wasn't much of a rider, not like her, but he could appreciate her straight back and her proud shoulders drawn back in perfect riding form.

There was no question in Cav's mind that Lia loved to ride. And he loved to see her happy.

At the small, clear stream, they dismounted. Cav allowed the horses to have their fill of water. Lia helped him to remove their bridles and hang them over the saddle horns. Each mustang had a nylon halter on, and she tied the rope to a low limb beneath a spreading elm tree. She then showed Cav how to loosen their cinches so the horses would get some relief.

He smiled and took the food out of the saddlebags. Lia was always looking for ways to improve the lives of those around her—even animals.

Spreading the green wool blanket next to the stream, shaded by the branches of the tree, Cav knelt and placed the plastic boxes on it. Lia hadn't worn a hat today, so her hair was mussed, giving her a young college girl look. Her cheeks were pink, her gray eyes luminous with happiness as she knelt opposite him, handing him a bottle of water and keeping one for herself.

"Have you always been around horses?" he asked, opening up her plastic box holding a turkey and cheese sandwich.

Lia rested on her side, propped up on an elbow, and took the proffered sandwich from him. "Ever since I could remember, we had a horse. My dad also had a milk cow, Polka Dot. She was a black and white Holstein. I can remember him putting me on her back when I was very young, while he milked her. I think that's what got me into horses, eventually. You can't ride a cow," and she smiled fondly in remembrance of those times with her dad.

"You weren't scared of the cow?" Cav marveled, appreciating her long, slender legs. She had taken off her cowboy boots and socks, wriggling her toes.

"Never. Polka Dot loved me. I used to lie on her ridged back, my feet hanging over her tail and my arms stretched out toward her neck. She'd just let me lay like a blanket on her, thinking nothing of it. My dad always laughed and shook his head, saying Polka Dot must have been a horse in a previous lifetime to accept me on her back as a cow in this one. Cow's do NOT want anything on their back. Besides, they have a high, hard spine and you can't ride them at all." She munched on the sandwich, studying him. "Where you grew up, did you have animals?"

"No, although my mother loved dogs and cats," he recalled.

"Did you ever have any pets?"

"Well," he said, "I had a cat, an old yellow tom that had half an ear missing. His face was all scarred up from so many catfights. He was a stray and I found him out in the alley in back of our apartment one morning."

"How old were you?"

"Ten." Cav picked up one of the sweet pickles from another box he'd set down between them. "I found him in a dumpster I wanted to climb into."

She frowned. "You were dumpster diving?"

"Yeah," Cav admitted, shrugging. "My mom's birthday was coming up in a month and I wanted to buy her a gift. Sometimes, people threw things in dumpsters that you could pull out and go sell to a pawn shop."

She felt the pain reflected in Cav's eyes. "But you found that cat in there, instead?"

Chuckling, Cav said, "I don't know who was more surprised. The lid was up on it, and I just hopped in. I almost landed on the cat and scared the living daylights out of him. But I was just as scared because he reared up on his hind legs, hissing, spitting and clawing at my legs with his front paws."

"What did you do?" she tried to picture the confrontation between man and beast.

"I jumped out," he said, grinning. "That was one pissed off tomcat. I'd seen an old chair in the dumpster and it had a lot of nicks, was really old looking and pretty much broken down. But I thought I might be able to get some money by selling it. Where we lived, there were a number of pawnshops. I thought if I could get the chair out of there and clean it up, maybe one of the pawn guys would buy it."

"And you'd done this before?"

"Yes. It was a way for me to make a little money for things we needed. My father's drug habit took all our money. There were nights when my mother had no food for the three of us, so she wouldn't eat. She'd make me eat, instead. Said I was a growing boy and all." He frowned. "She'd go to bed hungry at least once or twice a week and I hated it, so I was always trying to find ways to make money. My old man wanted me to start selling drugs, but I refused. I knew it wasn't right. And hell, Lia, I didn't want to turn out like the bastard I hated so much."

Her heart broke listening to Cav's story. He rarely spoke about his childhood and she was hungry to know more about him, even if it was painful for him to share.

"What about the cat?" she wondered softly.

"Oh, him. Well, he was after a rat in the bottom of the dumpster. He caught it and then jumped up and out of it, and took off down the alley. I didn't have any food to give him, of course, so I climbed back into the dumpster, retrieved the old chair and cleaned it up. I learned from Charlie, a pawn shop owner, that it was a real antique." He shook his head. "He gave me a hundred dollars for that piece of junk."

"Or what you thought was junk."

"Right. But I didn't care. I had a hundred bucks in my hands."

"What did you do with it?"

"I hid it in a jar in the shack behind our apartment building. That's where the owner kept all his tools. If I'd tried to put the money in our apartment, my old man would have found it and immediately spent it on coke."

"And did you get your mom a birthday gift." She saw Cav's eyes lighten, a softening in the set of his mouth.

"Well, she'd been wanting a stand mixer. She had arthritis, and it was tough for her to stir anything for a long time. So I bought her one," he said, pride in his tone. "A bright red one. She'd always loved red."

Lia nodded, aware of how often Cav wore his favorite red t-shirt. He was a lot like his mother, and her heart burst with feeling for him. "She must have been overjoyed."

"She was. I got her a birthday cake and ice cream, too. Lucky for us, my old man had passed out from the drugs, so we had a really nice birthday there in the kitchen."

Lia's heart swelled, understanding how much Cav needed a loving family. So much had been taken from him. A huge part of her wanted to be the woman who helped him create a loving family once again. It was a dream, but she held to it, knowing that it might be possible. Cav deserved all the love she held for him. And she knew he'd be a wonderful father to any children they might be gifted with, too.

"And the cat?" Lia wondered, finishing her sandwich.

"I bought him a can of tuna fish from the change I had from that hundred dollar bill. Felt sorry for him."

"Did you see him eat it?"

Cav wiped his hands on his jeans after eating the sandwich, closing up the plastic box. "Yes. From then on, we'd see each other in that alley from time to time. I gave him the name, 'One Ear.' Over time, on some days when it wasn't safe to be in the house, I'd wander out to the alley and sit down next to the dumpster. One Ear would come out of his hiding place and jump in my lap and let me pet him. He even started singing for me, which I thought was pretty neat."

Her heart breaking, Lia could imagine Cav as that skinny, sensitive ten-year old boy. "I wish," she whispered softly, "I could take away all that hurt from your childhood, Cav."

Studying her, he shrugged. "It's made me who I am today, Lia. I know I'm far from perfect, but I like who I've become over time. Chief Jacoby was the father I wished I had—I just got him later in my life, but he came in at the right time and helped turn me around. I was a pretty angry young man when I became a SEAL. I was a loner, a fighter and had tons of anger stuffed inside me." He held up his hand. "Jacoby got the anger out of me with martial arts and Krav Maga. He taught me discipline and probably most important, patience."

"He saw the good in you, Cav. He saw your heart, the fine person that you are."

"It was a damned good thing he did, because I was a willful, wayward kid just looking to find someone to hurt. I realize now it was all that stored but misplaced anger toward my old man."

"Anyone would have those feelings with someone like him," she replied, urgency in her voice. "He abused you and your mother all the time."

Straightening, he studied her. "Thankfully, those days are gone, Lia. Jacoby taught me to look at what was good in my life, and that was my mother. Now, when I start going down that rabbit hole of hatred for my old man, I switch to her. I think about the good times we had together. The laughter we shared, and how she held me when I was hurting." He looked sad for a moment. "But she never had anyone to hold her after he'd beat the shit out of her. I didn't dare go care for her or my old man would come after me…"

Lia got up and moved over to Cav, kneeling beside him and sliding her arm around his broad, capable shoulders. She wrapped her arms around him resting her brow against his "She had you to support her, and I know how much that meant to her. You loved her and showed her your love. Do you know how important that was to her, Cav? I do."

He absorbed her words, and the soft press of her breasts against him. "Come here," he rasped, lifting her and settling her across his lap. "I want to hold you and kiss you…now."

CHAPTER 21

L IA WHISPERED CAV'S name, framing his face with her hands, leaning forward and upward, taking his mouth with all the love she held for him. She heard him groan, felt his hands grip her shoulder more firmly, holding her there, hungrily seeking her mouth. If there was ever a time to cross that great divide between her mind and heart with Cav, it was now.

As she eased away slightly, her heart beating double time, he loosened his grip on her shoulder, allowing her to lean against him. Lia reached out, tenderly touching his flushed face, feeling the intensity of his need.

"You've been so patient," she whispered unsteadily. "Thank you for giving me the time…the space, Cav. I know I've tied you in knots. I know how much you want to love me."

She allowed her hand to rest against his powerful chest, feeling the thud of his heart beneath her palm. "I'm ready now. I'm scared, but I'm ready because I'm falling in love with you…"

She saw his eyes widen with surprise, and then relief.

"I've been falling in love with you from the day I met you," he admitted hoarsely.

"Really?"

"Yes, really."

Lia laughed awkwardly, allowing her hands to rest on his chest, loving this connection with Cav, his large hands so warm and comforting to her now. "You know, looking back on it," she admitted, "The moment I saw you I was so drawn to you, Cav. It scared me to death. I'd never been attracted to a man like that. Not ever."

He released her, enclosing her hands with his own. "You've been on one hell of a journey with me, Lia. I know we haven't had a lot of quality time together. But look where we are now."

"I know," she said, holding his soft gaze. "And these last few months together have helped me so much, shown me so much about myself, and about you."

"I was hoping it would." He placed his hand over hers.

She looked down at their hands for a moment, and then began to tell him about her talk with Dilara on the porch swing. When she finished, she added, "I remember you saying how much Chief Jacoby helped you, showed you that a family could be a happy, healthy thing in your life. Dilara did the same with me, only it was about the wounds, the scars we all carry."

Silently, Cav blessed Dilara. "How did it help you, Lia?"

She took a ragged breath and whispered, "I'm ready to make love with you, Cav. I've been wanting to for the longest time, but I was so scared."

He nodded, his hands grasping hers tightly. "I kind of figured that. The more I got to know you, the more I realized you were still battling the trauma from five years ago."

She squeezed his hand to let him know how much she appreciated his patience. "But instead of pushing or crowding me, you stepped back and gave me the room I needed to figure it all out. I've never met a man like you, Cav. You gave me permission to honestly relax in your presence, to take things as they naturally unfolded between us."

He shook his head. "You're worth any kind of wait, Lia. I'm not going anywhere, and I'm fine giving you whatever it is that you need. Because…"

Because he loved her. It was there, hanging gently suspended between them. Lia felt her heart wrench. "You had so much more to overcome than I ever did, Cav. I see that now. And you're a powerful role model for me to get over this wound that's kept me from ever wanting to reach out to someone again…"

Pushing a few curled strands away from her temple, she whispered, "I want to go home with you, but I'll need your help, Cav." She touched her belly region, placing her hand over it. "My worst scar…the one that Manuel freaked out on…is right here." She felt her fear rising again anxious that he would be disgusted once he saw it.

"Then," he said evenly, his gaze steady, "I'll let you show it to me when you're ready. I know this is hard for you, Lia. And honestly, I don't care what it looks like. It's part of someone I care for, so it's all beautiful to me."

She felt tears rush to her eyes. Cav was utterly sincere, his hands warm and firm around hers. "I-I know that. I mean, my head knows it."

"I can feel you already starting to close up on me, Lia," he said quietly. "And you don't need to. You know that now. I don't pay any attention to your other scars. Does it make me angry that you were hurt like this? Hell, yes. But I'm not going to let those wounds keep me from you."

He released her hand and gently brushed his fingers between her breasts. "It's your heart that I love. And your heart is you. That's all that matters to me."

Relief sped through her and she released a rough breath. "You've told me that before. And I know you're being honest. I just have to get Manuel's reactions out of my way."

"Well," Cav said, amused, "I believe it's time he stopped standing between us. How much power are you giving this guy, Lia? Isn't what we've shared so far miles away from what you had with him? I've watched you grow, opening and trusting me more and more over time. That tells me that what we have is solid. Special. We do trust one another. I know you see that."

Managing a small half smile, she whispered, "You're right. When we get home I want to show you that scar."

She was as good as her word. When they arrived back at her apartment, Lia went into the bathroom to get a shower. When she walked out of the shower she wore a pink towel wrapped around her upper body. Her hand clenched the two ends between her breasts.

They had agreed to go to her condo after returning from the horseback ride, stopping on the way home at a diner for an early dinner.

Cav had watched Lia wrestle with her decision, ached for her, wanted to help, but knew this was a path she had to walk alone. His role was as cheerleader and supporter, giving her the confidence she desperately needed to do this.

Now, as she slowly walked toward him where he sat on the edge of the king-sized bed, still dressed, he held her eyes, pouring all his love out to her. He smiled at her bare feet, those small, delicate toes and her slender legs that remained hidden from her knees upward. The late afternoon sunlight slanted through the opened drapes, the more diaphanous, cream colored ones diffusing the light.

"You look like a beautiful goddess transported from Mount Olympus, down through a shaft of light, coming to see her mortal lover," he teased. Cav instantly saw his words had a powerful affect on Lia. She relaxed her hands, her knuckles returned to their normal pink color, and she relaxed her grip on the towel.

"That's a beautiful way to see me," she admitted, her voice almost a whisper. She came and stood hesitantly within an arm's length of him.

"Well," he murmured, lifting his hand, moving it down her moist upper arm, "you will always be that young, gorgeous goddess in my eyes and heart." He felt such chaotic emotions around Lia, felt her waffling, torn and afraid. Yet, also wanting to trust him. He suddenly had an insight. "Hey, let's make this easy on you."?" he rasped, His hand moved slowly up and down on the scar on her outer arm that was nearly three inches long where his fingers were resting.

"How?" she choked.

"Come lie on the bed and close your eyes. Let me run my hands over each of the scars that are visible, the ones you don't worry about. See how that feels to you."

Cav knew this was called "desensitizing" a person. And he'd been deliberately doing this to Lia from the beginning. When he'd first touched the left side of her face, she'd jerked away. Now, he could touch it with no reaction from her. Being able to show her how far she'd come already, he hoped, would take her the rest of the way with the last scar, now covered by the towel.

"That's a good idea," she finally breathed, nodding.

Cav moved aside, allowing her to lie on her back. He watched her keep the towel draped to hide her torso, her hand trembling. Calmly, he sat down, his hip brushing against her calf.

"Good," he soothed. "Now, close your eyes. I'm not going to do anything before I tell you what I'm going to do first. And I won't do it until you tell me it's all right, okay?"

She licked her lips nervously but managed a nod.

"Good," he soothed. "Close your eyes, baby. Just trust me."

Lia tried to be brave and to cling to his warm, hazel gaze. She saw the tenderness burning in his eyes, and also noted how relaxed he was. And that helped her relax, too.

"Okay," she whispered, "let's just get this over with."

He chuckled quietly, his hands on his thighs. "You make it sound like you're in the dentist's chair."

That got a small smile out of her. Cav knew he could tease and coax her with his voice, his humor. It had always worked in the past and he saw it working now.

Her hand stopped moving restively against her stomach and lay across her. She was still protecting that region.

"You're right. I'm closing my eyes now."

"You're so brave," he said. "And that's what is going to make this easier than you think, Lia. I'm going to lay my hand on your right arm, over your scar. Ready?"

She licked her lips and nodded. "Yes…go ahead."

Cav allowed his fingers to trail the length of the scar, watching her face. She'd closed her eyes and scrunched them shut. With each gentle stroke, he saw her face relax. For the next few minutes, he caressed each scar. And each time, Lia relaxed more.

He could feel the trust simmering between them; feel her wanting so desperately to let herself be free of the past.

Finally, he said, "I'm going to lay my hand on top of your hand that's over your stomach. Are you ready?" He saw a slight wrinkle form on her brow, but she opened her hand from the fist that it had been in, trying to relax.

"Yes," she whispered shakily. "Go ahead…"

Cav laid his hand over hers. Even now, with the towel as a barrier, he knew he was touching some parts of that scar. Feeling her tense, he whispered, "It's all right, Lia. You're safe here with me. Let the heat of my hand relax you…"

And he saw his low, gruff tone create a small miracle as she did exactly that. Cav waited, allowing all that tension dissolve. He didn't move his hand. He remained still, giving Lia time to adjust to his physical touch on that hidden scar.

"You're doing well," he encouraged her.

Lia whispered, "It's a step…"

"A good one. Now? Will you pick up my hand and gently place it against your belly with the towel in place? Can you do that for me?"

Cav watched Lia hesitate, but then she pulled her hand free of his and allowed it to rest against the towel. He loved her so damned much for that act of bravery. And he was so proud of her because he could feel how much she loved him.

"Good," he crooned. "Now, I'm going to just let my hand rest here until you're okay with it." He saw her nod, felt her trying to relax. The towel was thick and fluffy, but he knew his hand completely covered the scar over her belly region because it was so large.

Cav couldn't feel anything with the towel as a barrier. "Now," he said, "let me gently move my hand across your belly back and forth a little, just getting me familiar with being there."

"Yes," she breathed, opening her eyes. "This isn't as bad as I thought it would be," she admitted.

Smiling a little, Cav began to lightly move his hand across that portion of her, feeling the soft roundness of her belly. "In awhile, after you realize it's like all the rest of your scars, it won't bother you at all," he promised. He could see in her eyes how much she wanted to believe him.

It took another five minutes for Lia to fully relax. More and more, she trusted him and he was moving closer and closer to asking her to let him remove the towel, to actually place his hand over the scar itself. Would she allow it? Or was this is far as Lia could go?

Cav wasn't sure. He just knew he wasn't going to force her. She had to truly want him to touch her and see it.

"You're doing so well," he praised her, his voice low. He stilled his hand. "Want to go the last mile with me, Lia? Can I open up that towel and place my hand over it again?"

Cav's breath hitched because he felt her tense.

"Y-yes, go ahead," she whispered raggedly. She took her hand and placed it against her throat, as if to steel herself against her fears.

"This isn't going to be anything to write home about," he said. Instead of pulling the towel open, Cav simply slid his hand between the folds, leaving them in place. Her flesh was still moist from the shower as he skimmed her belly with his hand. There was a scar there, no question, and he lay his palm against it, allowing her to adjust to the physical contact.

"See? Not so bad, right?"

He'd tricked her by not removing the towel. He knew Lia was more jumpy about him seeing the scar than feeling it. At least, that's what his intuition told him. And if that was true, she was going to relax right now.

And she did.

"See? Not so bad. Right?" he teased her gently.

"You're right," she whispered.

"The rest is easy, baby. I can feel your scar. It feels just like the other ones. There's nothing different about this one," and he eased his hand upward, allowing his fingers to trace the long scar that curved across her belly.

Cav could tell by the puckered skin, the rougher surface of the scar that if the blade had gone just a quarter inch deeper, those bastards would have gutted her, spilled her intestines. Closing his eyes, battling rage, he continued to move his fingers up and down the scar, getting her used to his touch, desensitizing her.

Lia had come dangerously close to being killed. He knew that now. The cut on her neck that had nicked her carotid artery had damned near bled her to death. It was clear to him that Schaefer and Dominguez wanted to murder Lia after she fought to escape them, and survived their assault.

"There. Is it so bad now?" he teased. "It feels like all the rest of them, Lia. No different. There's no way I'm going to be surprised by it."

His words had a powerful effect upon her, and Cav watched as her fingers relaxed against her throat, saw her swallow several times. He saw relief in her expression and he reveled in it. The worst was over. The rest would be easy.

"I'm going to open the towel now. I don't expect to see anything that I haven't already, Lia. Do you trust me to do this, baby?"

"Yes, I trust you, Cav…"

He placed his hand over the towel. "Open your eyes." and he watched her lashes flutter, revealing her soft gray eyes to him. "I want you to watch my face, all right?" Cav knew he was asking for the ultimate gift from Lia, but she had to realize that the scar she thought was the worst wasn't. And the only way she could believe it was to watch his expression.

He felt a shift within her. Saw her gray gaze turn softer, saw the love in them as he waited for her permission. Never had Cav loved her more than in this moment, the silence thick around them. He saw her give a slight tip of her head, her gaze clinging to his.

He opened the towel, pulling it aside. He did the same with the other end of it, fully exposing her abdomen. His palm was so wide that he actually laid it on the curls of her mound. There was the scent of her sweet body rising into his nostrils, the fragrance of her sex scent that powered through his lower body, thickening his erection that pressed heavily against the zipper of his jeans.

Cav pushed all of that away, keeping her gaze as he slowly lifted his hand away, fully exposing the pinkish scar. It was almost four inches in length, just below her belly button. And he'd been right: it looked like all the rest.

Leaning over, he cupped the sides of her belly with his hands, pressing a kiss at the top of the scar, licking it and then kissing it. He heard Lia's sudden gasp, then felt her whole body tremble, and it wasn't from fear. He continued to lick and then kiss the entire length of the scar, feeling her sink into the delicious sensations his tongue and lips were creating.

Cav wanted her to realize that she was so beautiful to him. He could love what she considered the most ugly part of her body— because it was a part of her.

Gasping, she abandoned her tension, her fears, and instead released a deep cry of pleasure. When he looked up at her through his lashes, he saw Lia's head flung back, giving herself to the passions he was stirring in her.

And then, he felt her surrender utterly to him in every way. He was still dressed and she was nearly naked on the bed, writhing between his hands, those wonderful, low sounds in her throat telling Cav everything he ever wanted to know.

He moved his lips above her scar, continuing that slow line of licks and kisses up the center of her body. Her hand released the top of the towel and he felt feral pleasure as she pulled it aside, exposing her small, perfect breasts for him. Even better, those pink nipples were hard little points that invited him to lick them, and he allowed his lust to flow like molten fire through him.

Lifting his head, he looked into her half-closed eyes and said, more deeply aroused than ever before, "I need you, Lia."

"Don't stop," she whispered, lifting her hands, sliding them around his face. "Don't ever stop, Cav. I need you, too."

He captured one of her hands, kissing the palm, heard her swift intake of breath as he moved his tongue into the center of it and then kissed it afterward. He wasn't going to mention the scar unless she brought up. Gauging from the look over her smoldering gray eyes, she yearned for more of what he was sharing with her, Cav said, "I need to get undressed. Are you protected, Lia? I'm completely healthy."

"I'm just over my period by four days. And I'm clean, too."

He grimaced. "I don't have any condoms on me." He saw her give him a tender look.

"That's nice to hear. Don't worry, I'm fine without one."

So was he. "Stay where you are," he commanded gruffly, standing.

Lia lay back, enjoying watching Cav undress. His movements were always spare, his muscles lean, tight and ropy. Watching him pull the polo shirt over his head, she appreciated the dusting of dark hair across his massive chest, and how the clean lines of his collarbones exposed his broad shoulders.

But her whole body went on red-hot alert when he quickly climbed out of his boots, jeans and boxer shorts. A pleasant kind of shock, a yearning, filled her as she saw the length and hardness of his erection.

She felt her juices flowing with just the thought of him inside her, filling her, giving her excruciating pleasure. And Lia knew Cav would do all of this because he was a tender, considerate lover, unlike any she had ever known.

As he came and leaned over her, helping to remove the towel from beneath her, she felt her thighs becoming damp, imagining him filling her with his power, his masculinity, his care and love. As she shifted and got to her knees in the center of the bed, holding his narrowed green and gold gaze, she smiled up at him.

Cav came and sat on the edge of the bed. Lia slid her arms around his shoulders, drawing near, her nipples brushing his chest, making him tense. Her scent filled his flaring nostrils and he smelled her sex fully this time, his hands moving to her hips, sliding down her thighs, his fingers brushing around their curves, meeting her juices flowing down them. His erection throbbed.

Instantly, Cav exerted steely control over his body. He liked Lia's unexpected boldness, liked that she wasn't afraid to show him that she wanted him. As fearful as she had been, she was now the opposite, which delighted and relieved him. He knew Lia was a fighter at heart and she could be bold and even brazen if she was given a chance. And Cav was going to give her all the chances she wanted.

Her eyes closed, her arms tightening around him, drawing his lips closer to her breasts as he continued to slowly slide his long fingers along her inner thighs, so close to her entrance.

She quivered and he smiled. "You're so wet...so ready..." He closed his lips around a pleading nipple, suckling her slowly, deeply. She began to come apart, a little cry escaped her as she tipped her head back, her body curving into his, her fingers digging frantically into his strong shoulders.

Cav smiled and released the nipple, tasting her, breathing in her fragrance, and then, cradling her head in one of his hands and with the other, guiding her down onto the bed beside him. She lay on her back, staring up at him, her breath ragged.

"How long has it been for you?" he asked, skating his hand lightly across her hip and down her firm thigh.

"A long, long time," she gasped, arching as he began pulling her thigh a little wider, giving him access to her.

"Then," he growled, moving his lips across her parted ones, "I'm going to go slow. You tell me if it hurts, all right?" He lifted his head, his eyes fixed on her smoky gaze.

"I will...it all feels so wonderful, Cav...and I want to please you, too..."

He caressed the side of her breasts, watching her expression turn to utter pleasure. "In time," he rasped, "it will happen, baby. Right now, let me love you, introduce myself to you. We have the whole night in front of us and I intend to know your incredibly loving heart and beautiful body intimately.

CHAPTER 22

L IA DAZEDLY WONDERED why in the world she had made such a big deal about her belly scar. Cav was lying beside her, his leg across hers, gently opening her thighs and exposing her sacredness, the heat and love of his hand lingering on her torso, moving across her belly, ignited with nothing but sheer, ongoing fire, transforming into pleasure for her.

She had wanted to be a full partner with him, but he wasn't allowing her to right now, his arm beneath her neck, holding her against him. A current of pure tenderness blazed from his eyes as he swept his hand across her body, down her hips. She was drowning in pleasure, all her objections dissolving beneath his touch.

Sounds caught in her throat as she leaned closer to him, feeling his fingers touch her wetness, moving closer to her arching entry. She lay there, eyes closed, lost in the powerful heat rising between them.

Some part of her functioning brain understood how Cav felt at this moment—his fierce, undying love for her aroused as never before. She was completely open to his desire to make love to her, and to put her on the receiving end first, rather than second. He was so unlike most men she'd know, who expected to get satisfied first.

With Cav, everything was different. New. Wonderful.

And Lia surrendered to him in every way because she knew that some point, he would allow her full access to him, too. And she loved him enough to compromise because ultimately, they would both be gifted with one another.

Now, as he moved to take her mouth, he eased his fingers against that swollen, throbbing knot just inside her entrance. Her hips bucked as the extreme contraction, the fire, licked upward into her, and she cried out. His mouth curved hotly upon hers, intensifying the tightening within her, his fingers sending wave after wave of lust within her. The moment his tongue tangled with hers, a violent, almost painful release flooded her channel.

Her scream was caught and absorbed by Cav as he continued to milk her willing, opened, trusting body. Lia felt as if her entire being was coming apart as he held her tight, his captive, not allowing her anything but sizzling, deepening pleasure. Her entire world burned up and transformed. The orgasm undulated through her, sending her into a world she'd never entered before.

She nearly lost consciousness as she floated in that world, feeling her body respond to Cav's passionate ministrations. Whimpers caught in her throat as he continued to ask her body to give him more, and it did. She was hurled out into a cloud of burning heat, barely aware of anything but him, his mouth taking hers, his fingers coaxing her hungry body.

Lia had no idea of how long she floated, the ripples of gratification moving in every direction within her. Cav was giving her such intense satisfaction that as he left her wet lips, all she could do was sigh, the corners of her mouth curving upward as she lingered in this hot zone. She felt him release her, felt him kneeling between her parted thighs, and slowly opened her eyes, once more drowning in the gold and green of his gaze.

Weakly lifting her arms, she tugged him forward, wanting him to enter her. She saw the tension in his face as he grazed her entrance, the pressure moving slowly within her. He was now stroking the knot within her, on fire with wanting, needing satisfaction.

He had been right, she realized, closing her eyes. She was so tight and small. But he wasn't an ordinary man, either, and she felt him grip the covers on either side of her head, the warmth of his body hovering across hers as he continued to introduce himself into her. With every stroke, quivers of raw pleasure moved through her. Cav filled her. She knew he was monitoring her every sound and movement. Sensing the brute power under his control, she wanted that part of him, too, but her body had to be able to accommodate him. He leaned over, capturing one of her nipples, she groaned, arching upward, drawing him even deeper into herself, the fanning of the flames arcing from where he suckled her, straight down into her filling channel.

She felt a momentary burning, and he stopped to allow her body to compensate for his size, but he never stopped suckling her nipples. Lia urgently lifted her hips, taking him deeper inside her, despite the momentary discomfort. It was swiftly replaced with pleasure, and she eagerly met him, moving her hips in slow rhythm with his.

As he left one nipple, capturing the other, the scalding sensations increased and she gripped his narrow hips, driving him as far into her as he could go. Sounds of joy flowed from her as her back arched, hips fused with his, luxuriating in him in every possible way. Her heart was beating wildly in her chest, her body alive as Cav began a new, loving assault upon her, stroking in and out slowly, accustoming her awakened body, engaging it now on every level.

The pleasure increased tenfold for Lia, and she once more felt that building pressure within her. He must have sensed her needs, because he moved powerfully against her, sliding one hand beneath her hips. As soon as he angled her against him, Lia cried out, awash with another intense orgasm that swept through her, constricting around Cav. She felt the hot release of fluids coating him within her. This time, she was hurled out so swiftly into that delicious pleasure zone that she nearly fainted. Never had she felt such driving, deep satisfaction as he was presently giving her.

Lia felt Cav tense and heard him breathe deeply as he covered her with his sleek, powerful body. She could feel him trying to hold off, but she wanted to give him equal satisfaction and wrapped her legs around his hips, moving strongly against him, increasing their connection, wanting to break through his control, wanting to give back to him, wanting to love him as much as he was loving her.

And it was love, she realized, feeling him begin to tremble violently, hearing his breath change, getting shallow. His hand slipped from beneath her hip and he held her face between his hands. Then, he thrust hard inside her, holding her, growling her name. She opened her eyes, sinking into his stormy green and gold ones.

Suddenly, he gasped, tensing, his brow against hers, groaning as Lia felt his own climax flood deeply within her. She smiled faintly as he prolonged all those wonderful sensations this first time. Cav had given her so much, but most of all, he'd given her back her freedom. And if that wasn't love, what was?

Cav groaned against Lia's neck, kissing her, nuzzling her, feeling her thrumming with satisfaction. He felt so weak but he knew his full body weight was upon her. His mind wasn't working at all, but he knew he couldn't continue to crush her into the mattress.

Groaning, he slowly pulled away, but she resisted his withdrawal, her hands sliding to his shoulders, pulling him back down upon her. It felt so good being inside her tight, small body, and he breathed in her heat and the heady musky scent of their immersion into each other.

He slid his fingers into her hair, caressing her strands, rising up enough to take her mouth tenderly now. How he loved this woman. He was overcome with the intense desire to always protect her, to make her, his own, to stamp himself into her in every way. She was his universe, and he kissed her long and sweetly, feeling her smile beneath his mouth, her hips moving slowly, continuing to engage him, continuing to give him pleasure. There was nothing but unselfishness in her, something that Cav had immediately recognized. As he carefully eased off her a bit, despite her objections, he opened his eyes, studying her.

Lia's hair was mussed, her cheeks a deep pink, her gray eyes large and lustrous. Her feminine softness captured him fully as he smiled down at her. Words weren't necessary. Cav could feel his body pulsing and throbbing with fulfillment. There was no one like Lia in the world and she was his. He didn't want to dominate Lia but wanted to feel an equal kinship with her. He considered them co-owners of each other. He leaned down, kissing the shell of her ear. "I don't know how we got so damned lucky to find one another, but I'm so glad we did, baby...."

Lia slid her fingers through his short hair. Cav's face looked so different, so relaxed. "Me too," she said, her voice wispy sounding. "I never realized it could be this good, Cav. Did you?"

He shook his head, awe in his deep, gruff tone. "No, baby, I didn't." He slid his fingers through the curls sticking to the dampness of her brow, pushing them above her hairline. "But it's you, you know? Us. We're good together. I always knew we would be." He kissed the tip of her nose, watching as she grinned with delight.

"You just had to work me up and over that fear of my scar, was all," she pointed out archly.

He heard the humor in her low, smoky voice and continuing to feather his fingers across her scalp, seeing that she enjoyed it. "We all have hurdles, Lia. Every last one of us."

"You looked so whole and confident to me when I'd met you, Cav."

A sound rumbled through his chest, his grin deepening. "That's because I'd worked through some of my hurdles a little earlier than you did, was all." His voice deepened with emotion. "You need to know, Lia, that you've been healing me ever since we met. I had wounds that were still open and when I was around you, they began to heal." He kissed her mouth tenderly, easing inches from her wet lips and rasped, "You've helped me so much and I don't think you ever realized what you've been doing for me all along."

"Oh, Cav…no, I didn't realize it…"

"You do now, baby. We're slowly healing one another over time. We've entrusted ourselves to each other."

Sighing, she framed his sweaty face, lost in the happiness in his gaze. "Thank you for helping me with that last one…"

"That's what love is about—helping one another, offering a hand, and wanting to see your mate grow and be happy." Cav pressed his mouth to her brow, her cheek and then slowly captured her willing mouth beneath his.

Wanting to kiss her with all the love he held in his heart for her, Cav pushed his hips forward to show that he was here for her as long as she wanted him.

As he left her lips, he opened his eyes, holding her glistening gaze. "You've done the same for me, Lia. I wanted you to walk free, baby. To be able to be who you really are, not what had happened to you. You'll never forget that event, but now it no longer holds its former power over you. You had the courage to destroy its power. I wish you could see, from my eyes, how much you've grown since we met."

Tears leaked from the corners of her eyes, her lower lip trembling as she caressed his face, never wanting this moment to end. "You loved me enough to be patient."

"That's true," he murmured, moving his thumbs across her cheeks, removing her warm tears. Cav silently celebrated that Lia wasn't trying to stop from crying this time. He knew how sensitive and vulnerable she was, and reveled in her latest positive step. "I like you open like this," he growled against her cheek. "Never stop being yourself. I saw who you were, Lia. I fell in love with that woman. And she's incredibly beautiful, whole and perfect for me. And she always will be."

Lia was warm. Moving up through the delicious layers of sleep, almost to the edge of wakefulness, she smiled, cuddling into Cav's body wrapped around hers. The sense of love, of being fully protected, flowed through her. Joy was on its heels as she nuzzled beneath his jaw, absorbing the hard, tensile warmth of his chest, his hair tickling her nose.

Her other hand was draped across his narrow waist. Her one leg was entangled with his, drawing her as close as she could be against his hips. Feeling his erection thickening against her soft belly, she sighed, remembering the other two times that they'd awakened and made urgent, hungry love with one another. Each time it was better and better.

Lia was still floating in that cloud of absolute pleasure she hadn't know existed until Cav had taken her there with his hands, mouth and body.

Now? Now she knew what real love was. It was more than the physical. It consumed her on every level. She felt so whole right now, more than at any other time during her life. And it was because of Cav, his love for her overlaying her own for him. Her heart dwelled on them as a couple. They had both been terribly wounded. Cav had walked a much harder road than she had as far as Lia was concerned. And he'd had the inner strength and desire to break free of it and become the man who lay in her arms this morning. His courage made tears come to her closed eyes.

Cav had turned around, recognizing her own imprisonment by the past, and miraculously helped her to break free and clear of it.

Lia knew the scars would always be there to remind her of that night. But it didn't mean that the past had to keep her imprisoned. She moved her hand slowly from Cav's waist, her fingers moving up his chest, tangling into the silk of his dark hair across it.

Cav's love for her had set her free. Love had done this. She knew she had a part in this, too, but Cav had taken her that last mile, carrying her, supporting her, asking her to walk into a new life, with him. And she had.

She was almost incredulous now, looking back at her ridiculous fears about that last scar. Cav was right: it was no worse looking than the others he'd already seen and accepted, *simply because he loved her*. Shaken by how love could change someone like herself, Lia felt a special gratitude for Cav's unexpected arrival in her life.

He'd been a caring bodyguard for her while she was dealing with political dangers swirling around La Fortuna. He'd been her safe harbor emotionally when she was stretched and strung out so tightly that she thought she'd never make it. His sensitivity toward her was almost awe-inspiring.

Just seeing him as a security contractor didn't even begin to plumb his depths. Lia wanted to spend the rest of her life discovering this man and all his layers of being. She was starved to hear what he thought, how he saw things, including her, himself, and the world around them.

Perhaps because Cav had gone through so much and survived it, it had made him stronger. But it had also made him compassionate toward others like himself. Lia appreciated anew how lucky she was to have come from a loving, healthy family. She could hardly wait to take Cav home to Oregon to meet her parents. Lia knew they would instantly love him as she had done. And more than anything, she wanted to offer Cav the gift of her family. She knew her mother and father would willingly embrace him, and include him in their family immediately. They were like that.

Hearing about Cav's terrible childhood made Lia appreciate her parents so much more. They had raised her right, given her a sense of selfhood, courage and confidence. Cav stirred at her side. She stopped stroking her fingers across his chest, waiting to see his eyes barely open. Smiling into them, Lia caressed his stubble cheek. "I want to wake up like this for the rest of my life with you," she whispered. Leaning upward on her elbow, she caressed his mouth, feeling the returned heat of his kiss. Lifting his hand, he skimmed his fingers along the line of her shoulder.

"Mmmm," he growled, "I feel the same way." He lingered against her lips, seeing her smile, feeling the softness of her body against his, the way her fingers glided over his back and hips, inciting him, making him want her all over again. And his erection grew between them. Her hair was tousled, her gray eyes inviting, her wet lips parted, breathless. His love deepened even more for Lia, if that was possible. This morning she was a new woman. The change was remarkable. Magical.

"I don't want to leave this bed," she admitted, kissing his cheek, his jaw, and then the corner of his mouth as he smiled.

"Aren't you sore?" he asked, tipping his head back enough to engage her full gaze.

"Well, a little," she said, and then shrugged. "But it's a very small price to pay, believe me."

He settled on his back. "Come here," he growled, and he eased her fully over him so that their bodies were pancaked together. "There," he said, moving his hands down her strong, curved spine, ending at her sweet cheeks.

Moving his erection against her, he saw her eyes close, those sweet sounds in the back of her throat telling him everything he needed to know.

Lia sighed, feeling her body growing wet, dampening her inner thighs as he languidly moved his hips against hers, and teasing her.

"I'm so hungry for you, Cav. All of you. Again."

He framed her face, drawing her down to his mouth, caressing her lips. "Well," he murmured against them, "I don't want to disappoint the woman I love, do I?" In response, she laughed, her whole body shaking, and he pulled back, absorbing the pure joy she was releasing.

"I want you again because I love you, because I can't get enough of you, Cav. You've given me so much since we met. Now, I want to give you the same."

He nodded. "Well, then, I think we need to make this a little more official, Ms. Cassidy." and he brought her to his side. Reaching for the top drawer of the bed stand, he opened it and pulled out a box. Closing it, he coaxed her up into a sitting position next to him.

"What are you talking about?" she asked, seeing the sparkle in his eyes.

"This," Cav said, bringing a bright red velvet box between them, pushing it into her hand. "Open it, so I can see if we're sharing the same dream."

Lia frowned as he propped himself up on one elbow, watching her through half closed eyes.

Opening the box, Lia gasped, unable to process what she was seeing. Inside was an engagement and wedding ring. They were gold; a single solitaire diamond stared back at her.

"Do you like them, baby?"

The diamond was a soft pink, her favorite color. Lia was enchanted by it. She gently touched the sparkling solitaire, giving him an incredulous look. "They're gorgeous, Cav!"

"But do you like them?" he asked again, grinning at her.

"I love them!"

"I want to marry you, Lia," he told her quietly, holding her gaze. "No rush, baby, but I wanted you to know I was serious. I'm committed fully to you. I have been from the day we met."

He pointed to the rings cupped in her hands. "This proves it. You don't have to do a thing with them right now." He searched her face, his voice deepening. "They're there when you want them. I know how you feel about one-night stands, and just for the record, this isn't one."

Her heart spilled over with love. She saw the sincerity in his burning gaze, heard it, and absorbed every word of it. "Yes," Lia whispered, her voice unsteady, "I understand." She placed them on the bedstand, then turned, rose to her knees, leaned over, and enclosed Cav's shoulders with a hug—hugging him as hard as she could.

Her voice was wobbly as she whispered against his ear, "I love you so much...so much..."

Cav brought her against him, her head rested on his upper arm as he tucked her in, knowing she needed that sense of protection right now. "The last two months have been a special heaven and hell," he told her, resting his palm against her cheek. "We have the time now, baby, to really get to know one another. I don't know how you feel about this, but I'd like nothing better than for you to move into my condo with me. I want you in this bed, beside me, every night."

He moved his thumb across the warm velvet of her cheek, watching for a reaction. "What do you want? Because in the end? I'll do what you ask of me, Lia. I never want you to feel pressured by me. A relationship is about two people, not one."

"You've never pressured me, Cav. Not ever." She smiled a little. "Dilara is going to be over the moon about this!"

Snorting, Cav grinned sourly. "Yeah, she'll be saying, 'I told you so.'"

Giggling, Lia pressed her full length against his hard, lean body. "First," she said, "I want you to come home with me and meet my folks."

"I thought about that," he said, curving his hand across her shoulders, holding her gently. "Name the time. I'm sure Dilara will give us a week off."

"Yes," Lia said with a half laugh, "and in the next breath, she'll want to know when we're getting married. I know how that woman's matchmaking brain works."

His grin broadened. "I agree." Seeing her become pensive, he squeezed her shoulders. "What are you thinking about?"

She sank into the warmth of his gaze. "That I'd like to marry you before Artemis Security is fully operational because once it is, our lives are going to be crazy. It's going to take a good year to get all the wrinkles ironed out of the company and moving smoothly."

"No disagreement there. They're looking at next June for it to go live."

"Yes." She chewed on her lower lip, thinking. "There's so much for us to get ready for, both at home and at work."

"Uh, oh," he muttered, "You're going into worry-wart mode," and he kissed the tip of her nose, amusement dancing in his eyes.

Grudgingly, Lia nodded. "What would you think of a March wedding next year, Cav?"

"Baby, you just name the date and I'll be there." He caressed her cheek. "I want you and your Mom, and of course, Dilara, to plan this. I'll be there to support anything you want. Just don't ask me to get involved in the planning, okay?"

A small smile flitted across her face. "All you want to do is show up at the altar. Is that it, big boy?"

Chuckling, Cav said, "Yep. I want you to have the wedding you've always dreamed of, Lia, nothing less. Why should I put my ideas about the wedding in there? I'll be waiting for you at the end of that walk down the aisle."

"Men!" she muttered, shaking her head, stifling another laugh. "I know Dilara will want to be involved in the planning stage, and so will my mom."

Cav grinned. "I'll bet your father is just like me. He'll want nothing to do with it except to pay the bills."

"You're probably right," she conceded, still smiling. "How about if you choose the flowers?"

"Baby," he growled, kissing her brow, "I want you happy, so I want you to choose the flowers that mean the most to you."

"But don't you have a favorite flower?"

"The one in my arms right now," he said gruffly, sliding his hand down her spine. "And I love the way you smell."

"You're hopeless, Jordan."

"Thank you. I am. Now, can we segue to us? To the fact I can smell your sex scent? That's its driving me crazy? And I need to do something about it or else?"

His erection was hard as warm steel against her belly, pressing insistently against her. "Promise me one thing, Cav?"

"Anything. Everything, sweet baby."

She nearly swooned as he took her mouth, cherishing her, letting her know how much he really loved her.

Letting him know just how good a kisser he was, Lia surrendered to him again and again. When he finally left her mouth, her lower body was throbbing like a fire that had to be put out.

She saw him give her a boyish look and her heart flew open. "Promise me," she said huskily, sliding her hand over his stubble cheek, "that we can have at least two children when the time's right?"

His face crumpled with emotion, and tears filled his eyes for a moment. And then, they were gone. But his voice was rough with feeling when he answered,

"I want as many or as few children as you want, Lia. Each one will be special, with two very loving parents who want to do the best job they can of raising them right."

"I'm going to be thirty soon," she offered. "I don't want to wait very long, Cav."

Shrugging, he said, "You just name the time and place"

Laughing, she threw her arms around him in a deep, fierce hug. "Oh, I love you so much!" she whispered against his ear. "Those kids will be so spoiled, I can hardly wait to get started!"

THE END

Don't Miss Lindsay McKenna's
next DELOS series novel.
Tangled Pursuit
Coming to you in November 2015!

Only from Lindsay McKenna and Blue Turtle Publishing
Available wherever you buy books and eBooks!

Excerpt:

Tangled Pursuit, Book 2, Delos Series

C HIEF WYATT LOCKWOOD kept his gaze averted but was still able to find Captain Talia Culver, who stood restively in the chow line. She was with her brother, Matt, and her sister, Alexa. He knew Matt well because they'd worked together on a number of black ops missions over the years. Alexa was an unknown simply because she was an Air Force pilot and he was a ground-pounder.

As he hungrily scooped up his second helping of six eggs, along with a tray piled high with bacon and toast, he smiled to himself. His "animals," the other SEALs in his platoon, had their heads down, concentrating on wolfing down as much protein their empty stomachs could hold.

But he had other fish to fry. Namely, Tal. Damn, she was an Amazon-warrior knockout. Of course, he'd never tell her that. She'd get royally pissed off, turn on her heel, and leave him in a huff without another word. She was like that, quick to give him an icy glare. She didn't have the time of day for him, which her body language had told him again and again—for three years, in fact.

He watched Tal and her sister, noting that Tal was taller than most women, although Alexa was only two inches shorter than her. Tal had a lean body that he found himself fantasizing about on far too many nights. Despite her height, she couldn't have hidden her femininity if she tried.

Granted, out here in the badlands, women didn't wear makeup or perfume—especially a sniper like Tal. The scent would carry on the wind, straight to the Taliban. They'd follow it and discover her hiding place. He couldn't even think about what might happen after that.

Turning to his breakfast, he shoveled more eggs into his mouth, delighting in the line of sight he had on the woman he wanted in his bed—one way or another.

Wyatt had always danced away from serious, long-term relationships. Hell, he'd seen too many SEAL marriages fail horribly. A 90 percent divorce rate didn't offer him the odds he'd need to even consider the idea, which was why he kept his hookups light and short-term.

He often told himself that he was doing women a favor by walking away in the morning. To lead a woman on by making her think there was hope for a serious relationship would be a dark falsehood. SEALs who were in love, he thought, had to lie to themselves about their odds of keeping a marriage together, given their brutal rotation cycle and the fact that they were often away from home for six months or more at a time. He wouldn't put himself or a woman he wanted to love through that kind of minefield. Wyatt was always upfront with a woman who interested him—that it was for a night of sex, and that was it. If she agreed, they both walked away satisfied and happy the next morning.

Wyatt drank his coffee, watching Tal smile at Matt. He'd actually gotten to know Matt very well because SEALs and CAG/Delta Force often worked together on many overlapping HVT missions.

Because he liked the guy a lot, it only added to Tal's appeal. After all, someone with as great a guy as Matt for a brother had to be pretty special herself. As the years rolled by, Wyatt counted Matt like a younger brother to him. They worked together often. The Delta Force sergeant was reliable, loyal, and guarded everyone's back. That counted in Wyatt's world. Plus, he liked Matt's easygoing nature, which was a lot like his own. He often teased Matt that he was his twin but they'd been separated at birth and sent to a different family. Matt laughed and agreed.

Finishing off his eggs, Wyatt turned to the strawberry jam he'd dropped onto his aluminum tray. There was enough there to kill a horse, but Wyatt knew from experience that protein and sugar were two of a SEAL's best friends when either going on an op or just coming off one.

Wyatt had been out for twelve exhausting days on a long direct-action mission, or DA, with seven other team members. They had all dropped at least ten pounds in weight, but now they were going to wolf down enough food to make up for it.

He watched an animated Tal tease her brother and sister and grinned as he saw her issue a rare smile in their direction. He liked her smile. She had an oval face, high cheekbones, and a strong, stubborn jawline. Yeah, she was stubborn, all right. Why wouldn't she come down off that icy cliff she always sat on and at least be civil toward him?

Even with her long, black hair in a ponytail, she was all woman. Wyatt knew she pulled at least two sniper ops a month, even though she was in charge of her sniper unit here at Bagram. Tal wasn't an officer who sat behind a desk; she needed to be out in the field with her people.

That was another thing he liked about her. And sometimes, he'd gotten lucky and run into Tal and her spotter, Jay Caldwell, out in the Hindu Kush. While Jay was cordial, Tal always seemed pissed off at him because his team was in *her* territory. He was running through her area, creating a disturbance, she said, messing up her hide, where she was camouflaged and couldn't be seen by the enemy. Hell, there was nothing to disturb except rocks, brush, and those fucking goatherds.

She would sit in a chosen hide for days, even weeks, if necessary, with her .300 Win-Mag trained on that Af-Pak border, waiting for her HVT to show up. Yeah, she had patience to burn all right. Wyatt just wished she'd lose some of it where he was concerned.

Didn't the woman ever get horny? Hungry for sex? God knew he did! But then, she was a woman, and her hormones were different from a man's, although he did know plenty of women who liked having sex. Too bad Tal wasn't more like them.

Wyatt had once heard Matt hint that there were two main reasons Tal wasn't interested in him. First, he was enlisted and she was an officer. The UCMJ rules were very clear that it was taboo for men and women in those categories to get together. Of course, Wyatt never worried about that. SEALs had a hell of a reputation for breaking rules in the military and living to tell about it.

In fact, he knew plenty of officers and enlisted here on this base who would eagerly fraternize with one another. The key, of course, was keeping it hidden from a superior officer or individuals who might want to make trouble for the couple. If an officer was caught fraternizing with an enlisted, his or her career could go to hell pretty damn fast.

Maybe he could convince Tal Culver that he'd personally guarantee that no one on this base would *ever* find them out. He'd say whatever he had to in order to get her into bed. Then again, he'd have to get her to talk to him first, so the chances were slim to none that he'd have to bother with guarantees!

The other reason Matt had given him was cause for serious concern. He'd told Wyatt that Tal had lost the man she loved, a Marine sniper, six years ago. The couple had been deeply in love, Matt confided.

Wyatt had wanted to continue their conversation and was frustrated that he'd have to wait to learn more—if Matt was in the mood then to continue his confidences. Maybe she was still grieving. Wyatt had never been in love, so he didn't understand someone having to work through years of grief.

The strangest thing was, he had a feeling—call it intuition—that deep down, Tal actually respected him. That was the thing about being a SEAL, working for years under life-and-death conditions. A SEAL's intuition was so developed, it often flew off the charts. He'd seen intuition save a man's life, and Wyatt's psychic ability was damn near in the paranormal range. His platoon knew about his gift and always deferred to him on a DA when he told them to stop, that there was a Taliban ambush ahead of them. And he was never wrong.

He watched Tal lead the way from the chow line to the opposite end of the hall from where he and his team sat, and smiled. Yeah, she knew exactly where he was sitting and was going to avoid him bigtime. Pushing the emptied tray away from him, he picked up his mug of coffee and finished it off. God, how he'd missed good, strong espresso. Six months without a sip of it had been starting to stress him out.

Wyatt watched Tal move between the tables. His body responded as he silently observed her. She had one of the nicest-shaped asses he'd ever seen on a woman. He could tell by the way she walked, the way her loose-fitting Marine outfit flowed over her hips, that she would be exciting to explore. His hands itched. *Damn.* He had it bad for his ice queen.

Yet, when Wyatt did manage to snag her attention and get a few words in before she'd turn on her heel, he detected genuine interest in her eyes. That gave him hope; he suspected she was attracted to him but would face a firing squad before admitting it.

Which was why he continued to pursue her. Sooner or later, he was going to wear that wild filly down.

Rising from the table, he told his men he'd see them back at HQ. Sauntering down one of the polished aisles, a drop holster on each thigh, his Ka-Bar strapped to his right calf, Wyatt ignored the curious looks from the civilians and soldiers. A SEAL stood out precisely because of what he wore.

He'd shucked down to his SEAL day uniform of a desert blouse and cammies, leaving his Kevlar vest and rifle back in his locker at HQ. Now he wished he'd at least showered, trimmed up his beard, and made himself look halfway presentable before flying into Tal's face again.

On the other hand, her brother, Matt, looked just as dirty and grungy as he did, and she clearly wasn't repelled by his close proximity. Maybe, Wyatt hoped, with her family here, she'd at least be polite and let him try to charm her.

Tal's neck prickled with warning. Oh, damn! Her back was toward most of the chow hall, and she could see out the two windows on either side of them. Matt had said he'd bite the bullet and sit with his back to the window, a huge no-no in the black ops world, but he'd done it because Tal was there and she could see any threat or attack from the Taliban that might come their way. And Bagram had been hit many times before with mortars and hit squads who managed to get under the wire to do damage. It paid to remain constantly alert.

Alexa sat next to Matt, her fraternal twin, not caring too much one way or another where she sat. After all, she was an A-10 Warthog driver, flying in one of the most protected cockpits in the world. The Air Force didn't have to work on the ground with the troops, Tal thought. Her red-haired combat-pilot sister, who radiated a dazzling, bright energy, never saw life and death up close, just through the sights and computers on board her Warthog. This was a huge difference between the air and ground war. Alexa used the Gatling gun on the nose of her A-10 and dropped serious ordinance on the enemy, often at very close range and well within reach of enemy gunfire. The A-10 pilots like Alexa were highly respected by the ground troops because of their ability to swoop down low level, well within range of enemy bullets, and attack the enemy, pushing them back to save their lives. A-10 drivers, regardless of gender, among the troops were regarded to have the biggest sets of balls in the Air Force because every time they flew, there was a helluva good chance they could get killed protecting those on the ground.

Tal reflexively rubbed the back of her neck, a warning bell going off. This wasn't something she ignored, so she twisted to look over her shoulder. Her mouth turned downward as she met the friendly gray gaze of Wyatt Lockwood. Damn it to hell!

Tal jerked around, scowling darkly, her lips tight. Matt, aware of the immediate change in her attitude, looked beyond her to find out what had generated this response. Then he grinned.

"Hey, Gunslinger!" he called, rising from his seat, thrusting his hand across the table toward Wyatt. "Good to see you, bro."

Wyatt stopped about two feet away from Tal, who stared down at the food on her tray, deliberately ignoring him. He gripped Matt's outstretched hand. "Hey, Culver. I thought I'd come over and say hello since I was in the area. Who's this pretty little redhead sitting beside you?"

Tal snorted derisively. Wyatt's soft, easygoing Texas drawl always got to her. She wanted to tell him to leave, but she knew he and Matt had been like brothers for many years. Alexa lifted her head and beamed up at the SEAL. Tal squirmed. Lockwood was too close to her! She could literally feel the male heat rolling off him.

"This is my twin sister, Captain Alexa Culver," Matt said, gesturing toward her. "She just flew in with her A-10 and we met by accident here in the chow line. Alexa, this is Chief Wyatt Lockwood, a SEAL and a good friend of mine."

Alexa stood and offered her hand. "Hey, nice to meet you, Chief Lockwood."

Wyatt nodded and smiled. "Believe me, the pleasure is all mine." He grinned back and then released her hand as she sat down.

Matt said, "Hey, why not join us? Sit down, bro. I need to catch up with you."

Wyatt leaned over just enough to catch Tal's disgruntled stare in his direction. "Ma'am? Do you mind?" He gestured toward the empty chair about a foot and a half away from her.

Tal gritted her teeth and glared at Matt, who gave her a confused look. "Sit down if you want," she growled at him, cutting into her breakfast steak. Of all things! She *knew* Wyatt would somehow find her! He was a damned SEAL and they had that all-terrain radar.

She saw Alexa give her a questioning look because of her sour reaction to Wyatt. Her sister knew nothing about Lockwood's three-year campaign to woo her into his bed, and she sure wasn't about to tell her right now. Not with this Texas cowboy sitting down next to her.

"I'm a little worse for wear," Wyatt drawled, gesturing to his dusty uniform.

"Aren't we all?" Matt said with a grin, sitting down. "How are you, Wyatt? What's going on over in SEALdom?"

Wyatt took a coffeepot and a clean cup from the center of the table and poured himself some. "Been up in the Hindu Kush, Af-Pak border area. Doing a little HVT huntin'."

"Did you get the guy, Chief?" Alexa asked between bites of her scrambled eggs.

"Yes, ma'am, we did, although it took six days longer than we'd planned." He shrugged. "We'd estimated six days for the DA, and it turned out to be twelve. Ran out of MREs at day six and bought a goat off a Shinwari farmer so we could run and gun on meat."

"Wow," Alexa murmured, giving him an impressed look. "You SEALs rock."

"We think so," Wyatt agreed smugly with a nod and grin in her direction. He heard Tal Culver choke and press her hand against her chest. When Wyatt gently patted her on the back like a mother might a child, she gave him a "get your hands off me" look that even a SEAL had to respect. He quickly lifted his hand away, wrapping it around his mug of coffee in front of him.

The Books of Delos

Title: *Last Chance* (FREE Prequel)
Publish Date: July 15, 2015
Learn more at:
delos.lindsaymckenna.com/last-chance/

Title: *Nowhere to Hide*
Publish Date: October 13, 2015
Learn more at:
delos.lindsaymckenna.com/nowhere-to-hide

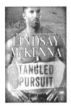

Title: *Tangled Pursuit*
Publish Date: November 11, 2015
Learn more at:
delos.lindsaymckenna.com/tangled-pursuit

Title: *Forged in Fire*
Publish Date: December 3, 2015
Learn more at:
delos.lindsaymckenna.com/forged-in-fire

Title: *Broken Dreams*
Publish Date: January 2, 2016
Learn more at:
delos.lindsaymckenna.com/broken-dreams

Everything Delos!

Newsletter

Please sign up for my free quarterly newsletter on the front page of my official Lindsay McKenna website at lindsaymckenna.com. The newsletter will have exclusive information about my books, publishing schedule, giveaways, exclusive cover peeks, and more.

Download FREE Novella *Last Chance*!

Last Chance is the prologue to *Nowhere to Hide*! It is available on most publishing platforms or you can download it from my Lindsay McKenna bookstore at lindsaymckenna.selz.com. *Last Chance* is in eBook format only.

Delos Series Website

Be sure to drop by the website dedicated to the Delos series at delos.lindsaymckenna.com. There will be new articles on characters, publishing schedule and information about each book written by Lindsay.

Quote Books

I love how the Internet has evolved. I had great fun create "quote books with text" which reminded me of an old fashioned comic book…lots of great color photos and a little text, which forms a "book" that tells you, the reader, a story. Let me know if you like these quote books because I think it's a great way to add extra enjoyment with this series! Just go to my Delos Series website delos.lindsaymckenna.com, which features the books in the series.

The individual downloadable quote books are located on the corresponding book pages. Please share with your reader friends!

Follow the history of Delos:

The video quote book will lead you through the history of how and why Delos was formed. You can also download the quote book as a PDF.

The Culver Family History
The history of the Culver Family, featuring Robert and Dilara Culver, and their children, Tal, Matt and Alexa will be available as a downloadable video or PDF quote book.

Nowhere to Hide, Book 1, Delos Series, October 13, 2015
This quote book will lead you through Lia Cassidy's challenges in Costa Rica and hunky Cav Jordan, ex-SEAL. Download the book and enjoy more of the story.
FREE sample chapter of *Nowhere to Hide*, Book 1:
https://lindsaymckenna.selz.com/item/nowhere-to-hide-sample

Tangled Pursuit, Book 2, Delos Series, November 11, 2015
This quote book will introduce you to Tal Culver and her Texas badass SEAL warrior who doesn't take "no" for an answer.
FREE sample chapter of *Tangled Pursuit*, Book 2:
https://lindsaymckenna.selz.com/item/tangled-pursuit-sample

Forged in Fire, Book 3, Delos Series, December 3, 2015
This quote book will introduce you to Army Sergeant Matt Culver, Delta Force operator and Dr. Dara McKinley.
FREE sample chapter of *Forged in Fire*, Book 3:
https://lindsaymckenna.selz.com/item/forged-in-fire-sample

Broken Dreams, Book 4, Delos Series, January 2, 2016
This quote book will introduce you to Captain Alexa Culver and Marine Sergeant Gage Hunter, sniper, USMC.
FREE sample chapter of *Broken Dreams*, Book 4:
https://lindsaymckenna.selz.com/item/broken-dreams-sample